Praise for
LIZZIE BORDEN
and ELIZABETH ENGSTROM

TOR BOOKS BY ELIZABETH ENGSTROM

Black Ambrosia
When Darkness Loves Us

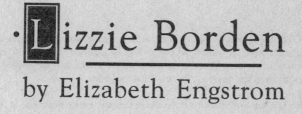

·Lizzie Borden
by Elizabeth Engstrom

TOR ®

A Tom Doherty Associates Book
New York

LIZZIE BORDEN

Cover art by Paul Stinson
Design by Judy Dannecker

A Tor Book
Published by Tom Doherty Associates, Inc.
175 Fifth Avenue
New York, N.Y. 10010

Tor ® is a registered trademark of Tom Doherty Associates, Inc.

ISBN: 0-812-50591-3
Library of Congress Catalog Card Number: 90-48777

First edition: January 1991
First mass market printing: August 1992

Printed in the United States of America

0 9 8 7 6 5 4 3 2 1

For Melissa Ann Singer and Anna Magee

FLOOR PLAN OF THE BORDEN HOUSE

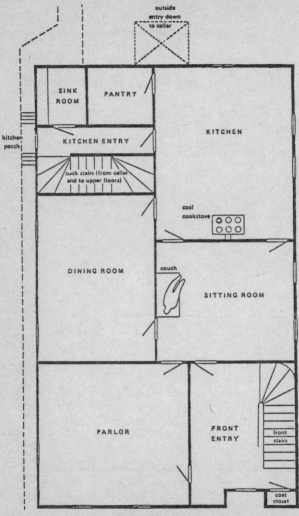

outside
entry down
to cellar

SINK
ROOM

PANTRY

KITCHEN

kitchen
porch

KITCHEN ENTRY

back stairs (from cellar
and to upper floors)

coal
cookstove

DINING ROOM

couch

SITTING ROOM

PARLOR

FRONT
ENTRY

front
stairs

coal
closet

First Floor

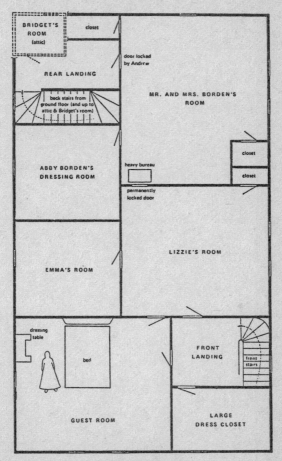

Second Floor

Adapted from: E. Porter, *Fall River Tragedy* (1893); V. Lincoln, *A Private Disgrace* (1967); And A. de Mille, *Lizzie Borden: A Dance of Death* (1968).

There is an astonishingly tiny universe of knowledge about Lizzie Borden, her friends and family. Most of what is known comes directly from trial transcripts and newspaper articles, both of which are filled with conflicting information.

This is a work of fiction, written within the framework of an actual incident. As such, personalities and character traits have been assigned to those who played a part in the great Borden mystery. Some of these are not flattering, and I apologize in advance to any descendants of those with whom I have taken liberties.

My purpose is not to offend; it is to justify.

Elizabeth Engstrom
Eugene, Oregon

Prologue, April 1865

"Come over here, Lizzie. Sit beside me. That's my girl. Your worm still on the hook?"

Little Lizzie Borden, age five, sat down on the stream bank and lifted her fishing stick to show the pale worm to her father.

"Good girl. Put it back down there now, and we'll wait for a big trout to come and eat it."

Slowly, feeling sorry for the worm, Lizzie lowered her stick. Her papa had whittled the stick for her the day before up at the farmhouse. Tied onto the end of the stick was a length of black fishing line, and tied onto the end of the line was a hook. Stuck on the hook was a worm, a big one they'd dug out of the stream bank. But then it was happy, fat and red, and now it was kind of skinny, shriveled and white. Lizzie didn't think too much of fishing.

"Isn't this peaceful?"

She looked up at her father. Then she looked downstream for sight of Emma. Emma was squatting at the edge of the water, looking intently into its depths. She'd been like that for what seemed like hours. Lizzie was always amazed at the way Emma could be absolutely still for the longest time. Waiting was something Emma could do very well. Lizzie had no patience at all. But then Emma was fifteen. Emma knew everything, and Lizzie was sure that when she turned fifteen she would be able to wait, too.

The country was silent, or so it seemed at first, but then Lizzie heard the stream running, she heard the flutter of the

2

reed that was caught in the water, she heard birds clucking and chirping and a sudden flutter of wings, she heard the underlying hum of all the insects as they went about their business.

Maybe Emma wasn't waiting after all, she thought. Maybe she was listening.

It was odd to be away from home, out in the country, all the way out at the farm. It was odd to have Papa home all day long, but that's what they called a vacation. Lizzie loved the farm, though. She loved being out here with Emma and with Papa. Mother was back at the farmhouse baking wonderful pies. Lizzie had helped pick the bunches of rhubarb with their gigantic green leaves. She wiped the dirt off one of the stalks and took a bite. It tasted good, it was the right kind of sour, but it made her mouth wrinkle up and go dry. It would be better in a pie with lots of sugar. Then, Mother said, when they came back with their mess of fish to fry up she'd be cooling sweet rhubarb pies on the windowsill. Lizzie grabbed her fishing stick and was the first one ready to go. She wanted to get back home to those pies.

She looked down at her shoes. They were new, a pretty brownish red leather, but she was sure she'd get them dirty here, and vacation or not, Mother would be cranky about it. She lifted up her fishing stick again to look at the worm.

"You have to leave the worm in the water, Lizzie. The fish won't bite it if it keeps flying out of the water like that."

"He's cold."

"He's not cold. He's a worm. Put him back."

She let the worm go back down into the water. She leaned over and watched him disappear into the green.

"Isn't this is nice," he said, and leaned up against a rock. "The spring is my favorite time of year. The sun is hot and the air is cool. Everything's green and fresh. . . ." He put his arm around her. "And I've got my best girl right here by my side."

3

Lizzie leaned into his side, putting her head against his chest.

He stroked her hair. She closed her eyes.

"We have a nice mother, don't we?"

Lizzie nodded. Her eyes felt sleepy.

"Yes," he said, smoothing her fine blond hair from her forehead. "We have a nice mother now, and Emma is old enough to take care of herself as well as you, and things are back to being normal."

He reached down and took off his shoes, then his socks. His toes were white and hairy, and his toenails were long and cracked. Kind of yellow. He wiggled them.

"This is the kind of day that you should try to memorize, Lizzie," he said. "Look around you and see everything. Focus on everything. The way the water runs so shiny and fast in the middle of the stream, yet swirls slowly near the bank. The way the reeds grow in the shallows here. The color of the new leaves, the dampness of the earth. The clouds . . . This is the kind of day that you put in your heart and you remember during those times when life isn't quite so good, when life turns hard and mean, you pull out this streambed and you and me under the clouds . . ."

Lizzie looked around. Then she put her head back against him, hoping he'd start to talk again.

"I have wonderful dreams for you, Lizzie. Wonderful dreams. Do you want to hear?"

Lizzie nodded. She thought she saw a fish come up and take a gulp of air on the other side of the bank. But her eyelids were getting heavier and heavier in the warm sunshine. She'd mention it to him later.

"You'll be beautiful when you grow up. Your blond hair will be long and luxuriant. You will live in a big house on the hill with a nice view, and have many, many friends. Dozens of friends. Famous friends."

Lizzie could feel him talk more than she could hear him.

4

Her ear rested on the side of his chest and she felt the vibrations of his deep voice.

"I'm going to make us rich, Lizzie, very rich, very, very rich, and you will have your pick of thousands of eligible young men who would come courting. But you hold out for the very best. You'll have a substantial dowry, and you should have the very best husband. The very best."

Lizzie dreamed about the little rag doll that Emma had made for her.

"Lizzie, are you asleep?"

"Hmm?"

"Lizzie, I have to know. When you are so rich and popular, and I am such an old, old man, will you still love me?"

"Of course, Papa," she muttered, her voice thick.

"You will?"

Lizzie looked up at him and she couldn't tell if he was joking with her or not. He had a queer expression on his face, as if *he* didn't know if he was joking or not. She nodded, then settled her head against him to hear his vibrations some more.

"That's good, Lizzie," he said. "That's very, very good."

Lizzie wanted to look at her worm again, but as she brought the stick up, something grabbed it from down below and began to pull on it.

"Papa!" She was wide awake in an instant, holding onto the stick with both hands. "Papa!"

He laughed. "It's a fish, Lizzie! You've caught a fish! Hold on tight and bring him up. Have you got him? Do you need help?"

Lizzie put her bottom lip between her teeth and held onto that stick as tight as she could. She dug her heels into the soft mossy grass at the edge of the bank and pulled up on the stick. Something silver flashed in the water below her.

Then her father's hands were on her waist and he helped

her to stand up. "Okay now," he said. "Easy. Just bring your stick up and swing the fish right over here onto the bank."

When she was steady, he let her go and stepped back.

She swung the fish—a big one!—onto the bank and began to giggle as it flipped and flopped, its pink-striped speckled sides flashing and throwing off raindrops in the sun.

My fish, Lizzie thought. My beautiful fish.

"Look at my fish, Papa. I caught a fish, Papa. Emma, come look!" she said, but Emma was already standing there, tall and gangly, staring down at her fish.

"You certainly did, Lizzie. A beauty, too." Then he picked up a rock and slammed it down on the fish's head.

"Papa, no!"

"It doesn't hurt, Lizzie. It's just a fish. We have to kill it."

Again he smashed the rock onto the fish's head. Again. And again. He just kept doing it, over and over again, and when he finally stopped, beads of sweat stood out on his forehead, and where the fish's head had been was a red, pulpy mass.

"There." He stood up and threw the rock into the stream. "Good catch, Lizzie. Let's take this home and have Mother fry it up for supper."

The fish had lost its shine, the day had lost its magic and even Lizzie's new shoes weren't so nice anymore, she noticed as they walked back to the farmhouse. Her father carried the fish by the tail because she wouldn't touch it; it had been so beautiful and full of life just a moment before, he could have let it just die, it could have just *died,* or it could have flopped back into the water, that would have been all right, too, anything, *anything* but caving its head in with a sharp rock.

And Emma smiled.

Lizzie came to the dinner table that night, but she

wouldn't sit next to her father and she wouldn't look at the fish.

She held on to her little fishing stick, though, and vowed to remember this day just like her papa had told her to.

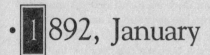

1892, January

izzie heard the front door open and close. A moment later, the draft of frigid air swept up the stairs and under her bedroom door. She gently refolded the letter from Beatrice and slipped it between the pages of the book she'd been trying to read.

Father is home.

She set the book down, smoothed her hair and skirt, then opened the bedroom door, closed it, locked it behind her and gently descended the stairs.

There was a package on the hall table. A book-sized package, wrapped in brown paper and string, with stickers and stamps and official-looking ink all over it, and Lizzie knew it was for her before she could see to whom it was addressed. It was the book Beatrice had promised to send from England. Heart pounding, she stepped down into the hallway in an orderly manner, ignored the package and went directly to the sitting room.

"Hello, Father."

"Lizzie. There's a package for you. I left it on the hall table."

"Thank you. Tea?"

"Please."

She left him to the reading of his mail, excitement gurgling in her stomach as she jangled down the ashes in the wood stove and put in a few more pieces of wood. Then she filled the kettle with cold water from the faucet and set it on the stove to boil.

Lizzie cut three of the little cakes Emma had made that morning, put two on a plate and ate the third while waiting for the kettle to heat. Then she poured two cups of tea and took the tray to the sitting room.

She set the tray on the coffee table and sat down next to Andrew Borden on the sofa. "Anything interesting?"

"No, not really," he said, and threw the open envelopes onto the tray next to the cakes.

Then he looked at her. "How about you?"

"Emma baked. I did some laundry."

Andrew Borden took a bite of cake and sipped his tea. "Not much taste to these, is there?"

"Wait until summer, Father, when there will be fresh fruit."

"Yes," he said. Then he sat back against the sofa and sighed. "I've got troubles at the mill," he said. "Employee troubles. Financial troubles. Bad troubles. And more problems at the bank."

"I'm sorry." Lizzie sipped her tea and thought about the book on the hall table. She'd heard this talk from her father before. Every day.

"Things are supposed to get easier as you get older, Lizzie, but they don't. They don't. They get much harder. Much harder. I work hard, and I try to be fair, but things just keep getting harder and harder."

"You're tired, Father. Here, let me take off your boots."

Lizzie untied his boots, slipped them off, rubbed his feet for a moment, then said, "Would you like me to read to you for a while? Maybe a little rest would do you good."

Andrew nodded. "You're a good girl, Lizzie. I don't know what I would ever do without you."

Lizzie knew the routine by heart. They did this same dance every day until she wanted to scream. Where is his bloody wife? She is the one who should be comforting this old man, she should be rubbing his feet and reading to him. "What shall we read today?"

"Anything. You choose."

She stood up and got the book they'd been reading daily for the last month. The bookmark was toward the end. "How about this one that we read yesterday?"

"Fine, fine."

"Remember where we were?" Is this what it's like to have a child? A brain-damaged child, perhaps, one that will never grow up?

"I think so."

Lizzie settled herself on the couch again, book in lap. She thought again of the brown-wrapped book on the table and resisted the urge to throw this tome at her father and go get her new book, hold it tightly to her breast and run up the stairs to rip it open in the privacy of her room.

"Let's see. . . . Here we are at chapter seventeen."

"Lizzie?"

"Hmm?"

"Don't ever leave me. I could never survive without you, you know."

"You have enough things to worry about, Father," Lizzie said. "Don't worry about that. It isn't likely that I'll leave you."

"When you were in Europe, you know, it was a terrible time for me. I thought you were never coming back."

This was new. He'd never mentioned her trip abroad, not once, not even when she wanted to tell him about it. She'd been gone only six weeks with some friends from church, but he hadn't wanted to hear a word about it. He was just frantically relieved that she was home. It made her want to kick that fat old cow of a stepmother. Did she do nothing for the man?

"But I did come back, didn't I, Father? And I'm here now. So don't worry. Try to relax."

Lizzie cleared her voice and began to read. Within moments, her father was asleep. When he began to snore quietly, she covered him with a lap robe and took the tea tray back into the kitchen. She wrapped the uneaten cakes in a napkin, got her book from the hall table and went quietly up the stairs.

She sat in her rocking chair, package in her lap, her mind still on her father, sleeping on the sitting-room sofa. Many times, once he had begun to snore and she had closed the book, she had studied his face, looked at the lines deepening in his brow, his cheeks, and wondered about her recollection of a younger, vibrant man who showed outward affection, who had time and energy to spend on his family, a man she had thought was as handsome as any god.

Time is cruel, she thought. Time and age have turned him into something else, something totally different from the way he used to be. He used to be such a . . . such a *father*. And now he was old, miserly, bitter. A wretch.

And whose fault was it?

Time. Cruel, cruel time.

Lizzie felt the familiar sadness when she thought of her aging father.

But those thoughts are for days when time lingers, she thought. Not for today. She looked around her room, at the dingy wallpaper that had been there since they moved into the house twenty-seven years earlier and had probably been there since the house was built. It had some little flowers on it, but she couldn't determine their color. She looked at the washstand, basin still filled with soapy gray water from her morning washing. There was one single bed with a chamber pot beneath, a small round rug in the center of the floor, a four-drawer dresser and the rocking chair she sat in. Two photographs hung on the walls, pictures of buildings Lizzie had never seen. The room was austere, just like all the other rooms in the house. Beatrice saved her from this room. A letter from Beatrice made her forget everything else. For a while.

She looked again at the package she held in her lap. She studied the handwriting, almost as familiar as her own. She had met Beatrice in Europe, a brief meeting, but sometimes lasting friendships are forged in just that manner. Swiftly, surely, and forever. Their letters began tentatively and soon grew intimate. They discussed matters of life Lizzie could never discuss with another human being on earth. Lizzie told Beatrice all about her family: her hardened and embittered father; her fat slug of a stepmother, who was all but useless; and her jealous, suspicious sister Emma, who had nothing better to do than poke her nose into things that were not her concern.

Lizzie and Beatrice met on the ferry from Britain to France. Beatrice was fashionably dressed, all in peach from her hat to her shoes. Lizzie felt dowdy in her travelling blacks, and watched this lovely young woman take in the sights, have a cup of tea and be on an excursion by herself while totally self-possessed. Lizzie envied that quality.

And apparently, her envious stares did not go unnoticed. Lizzie sat at the end of a row of chairs with her travelling companions, their suitcases and packages littering the floor at their feet. Lizzie rubbed her temples, tired already of Sandra, Rebecca and Winnie. They moved and acted like consummate Americans, weird and ugly tourists to be taken for all their money and treated with no respect. They embarrassed Lizzie.

She hoped a headache wasn't coming on. She didn't want these three women to spoil her one and only opportunity for some real travel in her life.

And then she felt a presence at her side, a peachy presence, and Lizzie looked up into the world's deepest brown eyes, and the woman asked Lizzie to join her for a refreshment in the salon.

14

Lizzie had flushed a deep crimson, she still felt the blush when she remembered. The woman must have seen or sensed her staring. She looked at the litter at her feet as if it didn't belong to her and her group and accepted the invitation. Even as she did so, she wondered at herself. She felt so terribly inadequate and was quite puzzled that a woman such as this would spend a moment of her time with an American such as was travelling in that foursome.

"My name is Beatrice Windon," the woman said, pronouncing it Be-AT-tress.

"I'm Lizzie Borden," Lizzie managed to say, as they were settling themselves at a table.

"Oh. American."

"Yes."

"Travelling with that group of women?"

"Yes. We're a church group."

"Wonderful. You'll see many cathedrals and things on the Continent."

"I'm sure."

Lizzie ordered a cup of tea from the steward and Beatrice ordered a fruit juice; they waited in uncomfortable silence until the drinks were placed before them.

"British?" Lizzie finally asked, although it was a stupid question and she well knew the answer.

"Oh yes. I'm on my way to Paris to do some business for my father. He's fallen ill, and is unable to travel."

"I'm sorry."

"Yes. It happened quite suddenly, but he's now out of danger. So until he is able to resume, I shall run his little errands for him."

"So exciting, to just dash off to Paris."

"It was at first, but it becomes tedious, nonetheless." Beatrice sipped her tea. "Where in America are you from?"

"Fall River. In Massachusetts. It's a little tiny town, in quite a little state on the eastern coast."

"And what do you do there?"

"Do?"

"Yes. Are you married? Have you children? Do you teach, perhaps?"

"No, no, no." Lizzie's familiar discomfort rose to the surface. Lizzie didn't do anything. She was not educated and not equipped to do anything. Everybody else she knew did something, but Lizzie did nothing. Everybody thought she should be married. Everybody but she, Papa, of course, and Emma. "I live at home. I look after my father."

"Well, that's something we have in common, isn't it? Is he widowed?"

"He was . . . that is, my mother died when I was very young, but now he has another wife, quite a worthless one, I might add." Lizzie surprised herself. This was the type of gossip that came from other people's mouths, not from hers.

Beatrice leaned close. "I have a worthless stepmother as well. There's nothing more distressing, is there?"

"No. Do you live at home with them?"

"No, no, I have a flat in the city."

"London?" Lizzie's imagination fired up.

Beatrice smiled. "Yes, London. My parents live well out in the country." Beatrice had large, full lips and Lizzie found her eyes irresistibly drawn to them. Certain sounds were almost lisped, and it was so very becoming. . . . "Do you read?" Beatrice asked.

"Avidly. And you?"

"Yes. And I hunt."

"Do you? I fish."

"I love to fish. What will you see while you're in Europe?"

Lizzie rummaged in her bag for her itinerary and brochures, notes that she had taken. The papers came out looking like a terrible mess, a big wad of untidiness. She looked up at Beatrice, with her peach smile and her peach dress, trussed up tightly at the bodice, and she felt foolish and inept.

"Oh," Lizzie said, "Just probably the usual . . ."

"Do let's see," Beatrice said. "You look like a true traveller."

Lizzie smiled. She'd love to be a true traveller. For the next hour, they went over all her notes and checked the itinerary, and Lizzie took more notes while Beatrice told her all the best places to eat, to visit, to see and to smell. "Europe is best seen, smelled, tasted and felt. Remember this, Lizzie. You must be yourself and make use of all your faculties on this trip. Let nothing escape. And that will continue when you return to America."

What an odd thing to say, Lizzie thought, yet this woman, undoubtedly in her middle to late thirties, had something Lizzie did not. Lizzie was happy to take advice— any advice—from a woman such as this.

Then Beatrice took her pen and wrote out an address in Surrey. "Send me postcards, Lizzie. I would so love to hear of your trip. You can only see Europe for the first time once, you know. Tell me everything."

And when the ferry landed, they hugged.

Lizzie sent her a postcard every day, and when she got home there was a letter waiting from Beatrice. Before she unpacked, she wrote back, telling of her return trip, and every day since then, Lizzie had written portions of a letter to Beatrice, her best and only friend in the world, so she could share every minute detail of her life with someone who cared. She considered it her living diary. She mailed her musings off to Beatrice once a week, but it often took more than a month to receive an answer to a question, as the mail service to Britain was so slow. Sometimes she worried about what Beatrice did with all her letters: Did she keep them, someday to be discovered and used against her, or did she destroy each one after it was answered?

She saved every letter from Beatrice, and when she read them, each word had the flush of those succulent peach-painted lips and that soft lisp with a British accent.

Beatrice was a godsend.

And now she'd sent a book. That book.

Lizzie had had a particularly bad time the previous summer. She was plagued with the sick headaches that were so severe they made her vomit. They came upon her suddenly, frequently, with no apparent cause, and no apparent remedy. It was a torturous time, and relief didn't come until fall, when the weather turned somewhat cooler.

Beatrice had written, "My dear Lizbeth, I am afraid for you. Three weeks have gone by without a letter (most unusual), and I am afraid something terrible has happened. Please . . ."

And Lizzie had written back a humble letter filled with graphic descriptions of the headaches, their history, their symptoms and things she'd tried, hoping to alleviate them. To her surprise, a letter came right back. Beatrice had a book, she said, a book that had changed her life. "Would you mind if I presumed to send you a copy? A gift, of course. Following the program outlined in this book has allowed me to make so many changes in my living habits, I am afraid I would be quite helpless and a sheepish person if I had never come across the principles . . ."

While Lizzie could never imagine Beatrice helpless or sheepish, she was excited about the idea that there might be yet another method to try that would rid her of the wretched headache curse.

And now the book had come. Lizzie held the book next to her. If only she could be rid of her headaches. If only she could wear peach. If only she could have a figure like

Beatrice's. If only she could be as self-assured and self-contained. If only she had good, wise advice to give to others. If only she could have a flat in the city. . . .

She untied the string.

Three brisk knocks sounded on her bedroom door. Emma opened it without a word from Lizzie. In her hand she held a white sheet of paper. Emma's mouth was a firm line and there were lines between her eyebrows.

"Have you seen this?"

"Seen what, Emma?"

"This letter from Father's attorney."

"No, of course not. Is it addressed to you?"

"No, it was on the tea tray. I was cleaning it up and wanted to throw out the trash, but I thought I ought to go through it first."

"Is Father still sleeping?"

"Yes." Emma stepped in and closed the bedroom door behind her. Emma, Lizzie's older sister, was forty-two years old. She stood tall and thin, and wore the same kind of dark, heavy clothes their father chose. She wore her brown hair pulled back so tightly it seemed to stretch her face, trying to tame the wiry graying hairs that always sprung loose. Emma had the deep brown eyes of their father; otherwise she was the very picture of their mother, with a long, thin face, a thin nose, eyes close together, shoulders sloped. Sarah Borden, Lizzie and Emma's mother, as Fall River remembered her, had been lively enough, and pleasant enough that people looked beyond her basic unattractiveness. Emma was not. And to compound matters, the years had not been kind to her.

"Father is deeding the farm in Swansea over to *her*."

"No, that can't be."

"Here." Emma thrust the sheet of paper at Lizzie. "Read for yourself."

Lizzie scanned the page. Emma was right. The new deed was being drawn up. "But that's our farm. That's *mother's* farm."

"So it is. *And* a large portion of our inheritance." Emma looked smug. Furious. Dangerous.

"What are we to do?" Lizzie was flabbergasted. For anyone but Emma and her to own that property was unthinkable. They had spent summers at that farm when they were children, and while it had now been rented to tenants for twenty years or more, it still evoked strong childhood memories. Lizzie frequently daydreamed of going back to the farm to live, where life was peaceful and rhubarb pies cooled on the windowsill.

"I don't know what *you* are going to do, my dear, but I won't stand for this. Not for a moment. That horrendous woman has the poor man so flummoxed he doesn't know which way is up. She and her poor relations. This is somebody's terrible idea and I intend to put a stop to it this instant."

"What will you do?"

"Think, girl, what will happen if I do nothing. That cow will have us as penniless as her kin when Father dies, and I won't stand for it." Emma snatched the letter from Lizzie's lap and twirled on her heel. She slammed the bedroom door so hard the walls shook.

Lizzie listened as Emma stomped down the stairs and began to argue with their father.

Lizzie held the package, still unopened, string dangling, to her breast, and rocked back and forth, listening to the sound of angry voices, her stomach knotted so tightly she was afraid to move. Within a few moments, a little wavy spot appeared in the center of her vision. She closed her eyes, but the spot remained. Lizzie sighed, and a tear escaped the corner of one eye. A headache approached. The spot enlarged and became a ring as the center cleared. A ring of what looked like heat waves. The ring became larger and larger.

"No, no, please no," she said, and put her palms to her temples, but the ring remained. It got larger and larger, and soon was out beyond her vision.

And the headache began.

The sound of her father's footsteps up the back stairs as he went up to his room echoed in Lizzie's head. Somewhere, she realized that that meant he had had enough of Emma, which wasn't unusual, and that he was going upstairs to finish his nap. She heard his sigh in the next room. It was as loud as an elephant's trumpet. She heard his change jangle as he removed it from his pocket and placed it in a little bowl on his dresser. It sounded like tools clanging into a chest. Then the bedsprings creaked as he lay down, and Lizzie saw him in her mind's eye, a tired, worn-out old man who didn't know how to deal with life anymore.

She felt like running out and putting her head into the snow. She thought if she did, the snow would sizzle and melt in the heat of the headache.

She could understand Emma's feelings—after all, they had a right to that money, more right than their stepmother had, yet it was truly Father's money, wasn't it, and even though he'd promised it to them . . . it was his to do with as he pleased.

No, Emma had no call to argue with him the way she did. She found any excuse, any excuse at all to keep the emotional pot boiling in the house. She sometimes had no shame, that woman, and while Lizzie loved her with a fierce devotion, there were times when she not only did not understand Emma, she did not like her. Not at all.

This was one of those times.

Lizzie rocked back and forth in her chair. She heard Emma downstairs talking to Bridget, the maid, their voices thundering, echoing in her migraine, and then the kitchen door opened and closed. A chill ran up Lizzie's legs. The winter outside was a raw one.

Emma's cooking sounds began. Lizzie shivered.

Lizzie wanted to go into her father's room and comfort him, she wanted to yell at him, she wanted to ask him why, gently and tenderly, and hope for a rational, reasonable answer.

She wanted to go downstairs and throw something at Emma, she wanted to sit at the kitchen table and sympathize with her, plan retaliation toward their father for his actions.

She wanted to leave this house, move to a new town, where no one would know she was even remotely related to Emma and Andrew Borden, adopt a new identity and begin a new life. Teaching, perhaps. Wearing peach.

The lure of the freedom was delicious, but she had lived in this house for twenty-six of her thirty-one years and would grow old in it, probably. Her family was too important, and anyway, women did not just run off, leave their elderly parents and strike out on their own.

Besides, she had no money. And—so it would appear— if Abby Borden had her way, she would never have money. No money of her own, at least. She and Emma would forever be dependent upon the graces of their stepmother and her family.

Lizzie rocked, empathizing with Emma's fury, yet unable to fabricate fury of her own. There had been too many years of understanding, too many years of mediating, too many years of loving the man who held her hostage. It was easier to ignore. It was easier to have no opinion.

It was easier to be crippled by a headache.

In her mind's eye, she saw her father lying on his bed in the next room, hands folded over his stomach. She saw a horrible old man whose claws grasped money and held it to his soul as if it would be the saving of his species. She saw a pitiful old man whose meanness tried to mask his terror of growing old alone. She saw an embarrassment. She saw the patriarch of her family as a whining wretch, incapable of showing leadership and love to a family, yet oh-so-capable of running a financial empire. Lizzie could no longer be proud of the Borden family as headed by Andrew Borden.

Lizzie rocked, holding onto the book, which no longer felt exciting. She rocked and rocked, thinking about the house and how it had a hold on her.

She rocked and her head pounded until she was afraid she would fall onto the floor. And then she undressed, got into bed and held the book close.

The past receded, the family receded, wants, desires, inadequacies and all other thoughts were beaten down, pound after pound. Eventually, there was nothing but the pain, the awful, humiliating, all-encompassing, equalizing pain.

Lizzie delved into it, horrified by it, discouraged by it, yet freed because of it.

● ● ●

The next morning, feeling shaky and fragile, Lizzie avoided quick moves and bright lights. She lay awake in her bed for a long time before rising. She gently lowered herself onto the metal slops bucket and listened to voices in the kitchen. There were happy sounds, even a trill of laughter from Emma. Joyful sounds were such rare occurrences in the Borden household, Lizzie was intrigued. She cleaned herself, noticed with dismay that her menses had begun during the night and messed her nightgown, laid a cloth over the soiled pot and slid it back under the bed. She would empty the slops later. She donned robe and slippers and slowly, careful-ly, descended the stairs.

"Lizzie, you lazy thing. Aren't you ready yet?"

"Ready?"

"Our appointment at the dressmaker's. It's in a half hour."

"A half hour!" Lizzie jumped, then put a hand to her fragile head. "Why didn't you tell me?"

"I did tell you, I most certainly did. I told you when I made the appointment, and I reminded you last week. You've just had your head in the clouds, that's all. You need to learn to pay attention, child!"

Lizzie glared at Emma. She had not told Lizzie of the appointment. Going to pick out fabrics for spring dresses was one of the nicest things they did during the long winter. She would have remembered it. She would never have forgotten.

But Emma wanted to keep her off balance. Emma, Lizzie noticed, was dressed smartly, ready for a fitting with the best of the townswomen, while Lizzie . . . Her hair was dirty, she hadn't cleaned and pressed her town dress. . . . She felt her face go hot. "I'm not going," she said.

"Not going? Lizzie, dear, you *must*. Your spring wardrobe. Your summer dresses."

"I'm not fit. I need to bathe."

"Go, then, quickly, and bathe. We have time."

"My hair . . ." Lizzie had forgotten about being angry in a whirlwind of thinking how to be presentable enough to go for her fitting. Her mind was barely able to function after a night of racking pain, and she felt ill equipped to spar with Emma this morning. But that didn't change the fact that Mrs. Longworth wouldn't have another appointment available for months.

"Dash your hair. It's fine."

Lizzie looked at her older sister. It wasn't fine, and Emma knew it. Emma took every advantage to look, act and be superior.

"You never told me," Lizzie said as she took a bowl to the sink, filled it with cool water and warmed it with water from

the kettle. "Remind me to ask for some fabric scra₋
we're there."

Instead of taking it upstairs, where she normally bathed, Lizzie took it down cellar where she could bathe in privacy and then discard the water, which would be bloody with her menses, without embarrassing any other member of her family.

"I'm sure Mrs. Longworth saves them for you by now." Emma's voice followed her down the stairs. "You could buy yourself a yard or two of cotton at the store, you know."

Lizzie set the basin on the stand, then ran back up the stairs as fast as her brittle head would allow, through the kitchen and the sitting room, and up the stairs to her room, where she fetched clean underwear. She shook out her only presentable dress and brought them all downstairs and on into the cellar. Then she had to stop for a moment, hand on the clammy cellar wall, while the darkness cleared from her vision.

She undressed, throwing her soiled housedress into the corner, putting her menstrual rag into a bucket filled with a dozen others soaking in ice-crusted water under the sink. Then, dancing in the cold, Lizzie took a sponge, filled it with warm water from the bowl, soaped it and rubbed it all over her ample body. It was freezing cold in the cellar. The worn piece of wood that covered the dirt floor rumbled as she danced. Goose pimples rose all over her skin and her nipples shrank down to hard little nuts.

"Quickly, quickly," she breathed. She squeezed the soap out of the sponge and rinsed herself off, then briskly rubbed a scratchy towel around her skin. Then she donned a freshly laundered pad, pinned it to her own homemade belt—this one pink cotton with little red flowers, courtesy of Mrs. Longworth's scraps—got into her long underwear, her slip and petticoat, then pulled the dress over her head.

Then she squeezed out the sponge, rinsed the bowl,

...down and ran upstairs, barefoot, buttoning

...ness, Lizzie," Emma said.

...down there."

...catch your death in your bare feet."

...in Europe we had bathrooms. Every floor had its own water closet and bath. Every floor."

"I know, I know," Emma said. "Every house in this neighborhood does, too. And gas! We're the only house not hooked up."

Lizzie noted the time. She still had ten minutes before they had to leave. She went upstairs, unpinning her hair, powdered a touch of cornstarch along her hairline and brushed out her long hair; it flew with static electricity. She twisted it, knotted it up, pinned it and checked the results in the mirror. Her glorious light-brown hair with its reddish highlights was not shiny and silky as it would be if she had just washed it; instead, it was cornstarch-dull, but at least it did not look oily.

She pinched her cheeks to bring up a little color, smoothed out her dress, donned stockings and her new button shoes, and she was ready. Not as ready as she would have liked to be, but ready nevertheless.

She walked down the stairs, opened the closet and took out the seal cape her father had given her on her thirtieth birthday, one of only two extravagances she'd ever known him to bestow, put the cape around her shoulders, picked up her bag and her gloves and walked back into the kitchen.

"I'm ready now, Emma."

Emma looked her up and down. Lizzie stood still for her appraisal, waiting for the deprecating word, but none came.

"Let's be gone, then," Emma said, and began to give orders to the maid.

They walked from the pinched little house on Second

Street to the dressmaker's, four blocks through the biting January winter. They walked in silence, Lizzie trying on different shades of peach in her mind, still miffed with Emma for taking most of the pleasure out of her semi-annual fitting. Next time, she thought, I'll make an appointment myself and go alone. It would be ever so much more fun. But they had always gone together, and no matter what Lizzie thought of Emma and her jealous ways, Emma did have superb taste. "How many dresses are we allowed?" Last year, Father put Emma in charge of the household budget, something that had only momentarily placated Emma's lust for control.

"We can each have three housedresses, one church dress and two town dresses."

"One church dress? That's hardly enough. I have enough ugly housedresses. I'll trade them in for another church dress."

"One church dress costs more than three housedresses, Lizzie, you must know that."

"So? I can't possibly go through the whole spring and summer with only one more church dress. The pastor's wife snickers over my wardrobe as it is."

"Lizzie!"

"Well, she does."

"All right. Two church dresses for you, then, if you must, but it will mean a month of decent meat."

"I don't care."

"See if you care when Father gets mutton instead of pork."

● ● ●

Mrs. Longworth had laid out the most fascinating array of colored fabrics in her salon. In every possible color and color combination, there were cottons, woolens, flannels, silks, linens, in solids, plaids, stripes and flowers. There were brocades and tapestries and beaded fabrics. There were laces and nets, eyelets and chintz. It was a feast for the eyes, and Lizzie wanted to gather them all up in her arms and whirl around the room.

"Good morning, Mrs. Longworth," Emma said.

"Emma. Lizzie. Excuse me for a moment while I tidy up. I've just fitted a bride and three bridesmaids."

Lizzie went to the pastels and began fingering some peach-colored calico. Emma, she noticed, went directly to the darker colors.

"Lizzie, come look at these fabrics. This green would accentuate your eyes."

"I think something pastel this spring, Emma," Lizzie said. "Like this peachy one, for example."

Emma curled her lip in distaste. "It clashes with your hair, with your eyes and with your complexion. It would make you look dead."

Lizzie picked up the bolt, unrolled a yard and held it in front of her face in the mirror. It did, she had to agree, make her look greenish. Lizzie's mousy brown hair and pale-green eyes needed the blues and greens, Emma was right. And the darker colors were more slimming. Beatrice had dark-brown hair, snapping brown eyes, and dark brows. She also wore makeup to accentuate her looks, whereas Father would allow no "paint" on any member of his household. No, peach was definitely a color for Beatrice, but not for Lizzie.

She put the bolt back and picked up a sunshiny yellow.

"No," Emma said, without even looking. "Come look at this blue. This cornflower color would look lovely."

Everything in Lizzie's closet was blue. She took the bolt from Emma and held it up. It was nice. It was very nice. But it was blue.

A familiar feeling began to come over Lizzie. She remembered now, about these fittings. It was the same every year, twice a year. She was bowled over by the shouts of the fabrics, but Emma chose the same colors, patterns and styles for her over and over and over again.

The feeling grew as Mrs. Longworth took her measurements and wrote them in her black ledger. Each number was larger than the one she had written down last year, and Mrs. Longworth mentioned that with each measurement. Emma clucked with every inch.

By the time they got to choosing the styles, there was no fun left for Lizzie. Emma chose all her fabrics and her styles, and they were just the same as she'd always had.

When they left the dressmaker, Lizzie was downcast.

"I don't know why you're such a brat," Emma said. "Those dresses will be very smart on you."

"Blue, green and lavender," Lizzie said. "No pinks, no yellows, nothing bright and cheerful."

"It's what you look best in," Emma said.

"Says you."

"Do you want to go back?"

For a moment, Lizzie considered it. But, just before they were finished, Mrs. Kelly and her daughters had come in for their fittings, and the shop would now be filled with emerald greens and bright yellows with eyelet and lace, and with feminine giggles. The redheads had all the luck when it came to wearing vibrant colors. Not so Lizzie Borden.

"No," she said.

"Then be grateful. You got two church dresses, you know."

"Both blue."

"Both expensive. They will last for years if you take care. And, of course, if you watch your weight."

Lizzie felt like a child. She felt as if she'd never break out of the icy igloo that having four parents had built around her. She was never allowed an opinion, she was never allowed her own taste, she was never allowed to express herself in any manner, if it were the least bit unconventional.

"I'm going to stop by the dry-goods store and buy some yellow and pink cottons," she said to Emma. "At least I can stitch myself a couple of dusters."

Emma nodded her approval.

She would sew them, Lizzie knew, but she had neither the patience nor the talent for needlework that Emma and their stepmother had. Abby Borden created masterpieces at the sewing machine, and Emma did intricate work by hand. Lizzie did adequate work, but it was rustic, and the result usually ill-fitting.

The sisters parted ways in town, Emma going to stop by the post office before heading back home, Lizzie going to the dry-goods store for her little calico symbol of rebellion.

That evening, when the two quiet knocks came at her door, Lizzie went down to take up her supper before Andrew and Abby were called to the table. Supper consisted of crusty bread spread with salted lard, and a bowl of stewed cabbage. Lizzie wondered if the household budget had really expired this early in the month or if Emma had made such a meager meal in order to spite Father. She ladled her bowlful and took it up to her room. She was glad she'd pilfered the cakes from yesterday's tea, because she had no appetite for the meal.

As always, she was glad to have slipped in and out of the kitchen without meeting anyone else; as far as she knew, Father was in his room, Bridget in hers, and Abby was out.

She dipped her spoon into the stew and blew across it to cool. It didn't taste bad, but Emma's culinary expertise had clearly fallen by the wayside for this meal.

Then her bedroom door opened and Emma came in, her eyes downcast.

"Emma. What is it?"

"I am at my wits' end with that old man, Lizzie."

"Emma, he's our father." She looked at the door that separated her bedroom from his. "And he might hear you."

Emma lowered her voice. "You may call him Father if you like. To me he's a miserly, mean old man. And I don't care at all if he hears me. He's heard it all before."

Lizzie set her bowl of stew aside.

"I'm going to leave."

"Emma, no."

"I cook for him, I clean for him, and he cannot even speak to me with a civil tone. The household budget makes allowance only for swill. We are ordered to wear a very few dresses, and those made of inexpensive fabric. We are never allowed to entertain. In fact, we have no friends, Lizzie."

"That's not true, Emma. . . ."

"It might as well be. I'm going to ask the wretched old man for my inheritance, and I will leave."

"Leave!" Lizzie was stunned. "Where will you go?"

"We have cousins. Mother has many relatives in Fairhaven. I can be in touch with them. Surely there are opportunities for a woman of my talents."

"Oh, I've no doubt about that, Emma, but whatever shall I do here without you?"

"You could come with me"—she took a deep breath— "if only you didn't have to be a nursemaid to him."

"Oh, no, no. I could never leave Father like that. I couldn't go . . . to another town, I don't think. Please don't make me choose between you, Emma."

"Why? That might force his lovely wife to start washing his underwear and drying his pots and pans. She might have to start *earning* her inheritance." Emma's face began to show that tight redness again. "That farm belonged to our mother, you know, Lizzie. He has no right to deed it to that woman."

Lizzie knew there would be no talking to her sister in this state. "You talked with him again, didn't you? Why didn't you just let it rest for a while, Emma?"

"I got nowhere."

"Let him think about what you've said for a couple of days. Maybe what you said will make him consider what he's about to do. Maybe he'll change his mind."

"Maybe."

They both heard the front door open and close. Emma sat on the edge of Lizzie's bed, looking at her hands in her lap, while Abby Borden's heavy footsteps stopped at the coat closet, continued through the dining room to the kitchen, stopped at the stove, then clomped up the back stairs to her bedroom. They both heard the door to their parents' bedroom open. Lizzie had pushed her dressing table up against the connecting door, but sounds were clearly audible.

"I can't stand to listen to the existence of that woman," Emma said, and walked through to her own room, leaving Lizzie to sit with her cold cabbage stew and sour stomach.

She set the food on the floor by her door, unlaced her shoes and took them off. Then she lay on her bed and brought a quilt up over her. She knew that her dress would wrinkle and that someone was sure to comment on it, but for the moment, she didn't care, she didn't care, she didn't care. She settled herself comfortably, unclenched her fists and tried to think of happy thoughts. She tried to think of some happy memories, but they somehow eluded her. She tried to remember her mother's face, but all she knew was one photograph of a young woman, a young Emma really, and a description of her personality from her father. She tried to remember games she and Emma used to play when they were little, but it seemed as though there never were games in this house; it seemed there never were children in this house.

So Lizzie went to the only place she knew that never let her down. She went to a place filled with warmth and beauty and solace.

In the midst of turmoil around her, Lizzie closed her mind, closed her eyes and went fishing.

mma finished wiping down the kitchen counters and hung the soiled dishrag over the sink in the little washroom off the kitchen. Her stomach still burned from the confrontation with her father. Her unreasonable father. Her *elderly,* unreasonable father. Then she unlocked the kitchen door and threw the basin of dishwater into the snow. The dining-room clock chimed the half hour; Emma assumed it was eight-thirty. Her father and his wife had gone to bed an hour before, as had Bridget, the maid. Lizzie had never come down after dinner.

She fit a fresh candle into a candlestick, lit it and blew out the lanterns in the kitchen.

Why was it, she wondered, that she so cherished time alone in this house during the day, yet at night she longed for company? Emma walked through the empty dining room, places carefully set for breakfast by Bridget before she retired for the night. The candle she carried threw exaggerated shadows on the walls as she walked. They weren't satisfactory company at all.

She checked the front door to make sure it was tightly locked. For over two years—ever since the threats against Andrew Borden by his ill-treated employees began—security at the Borden house had been tight. Extra tight. Obnoxious. Every room in the house had its own key, and every personal room was always locked, whether it was occupied or not. The front door had three locks, the back door two, each of the bedrooms one.

What was there to steal, anyway? Abby Borden kept a few dollars and a few pieces of jewelry on hand, but there was nothing of value, nothing even of sentimental value, in this house.

Except, perhaps, the suspicion. The locking and unlocking of doors had created an air of suspicion about the house. Whenever Emma left her bedroom and locked it with a key, she always tried the knob one more time, to make sure it was locked. To make sure no one could get in. No one. And even though she *knew* that nothing was kept in any of the other rooms—to which she could have access if she wanted—just knowing that the other rooms were locked made her wonder what they were hiding. Emma had her secrets—oh yes, she had her secrets all right—but they were not in her room and they could not be found by prying eyes.

Even so, the thought of some stranger in her bedroom, next to her bed, looking around and having thoughts, or making comments, touching things or passing judgment on the state of affairs in her bedroom, made her sick to her stomach. It made her skin crawl.

The locking of doors had started with the threat from a former mill employee. Andrew Borden was not a kind man, and his manner of doing business was profit-motivated. As a result, those people who made his businesses actually run were frequently ground under the heel of his enterprising zeal.

And Andrew took the threat to heart. He would never let his family be left to the mercy of those inadequate souls who could not even cut the mustard at the mill.

Emma wandered into the sitting room. There should be storytelling going on in this room, she thought. A fire in the grate, gaslights in every corner and a spirited game of chess, or hearts, or some music or something. Something should be happening in this house at night, but there was nothing. There had been nothing since Mother died.

The gaiety died when Mother died, Emma thought. This house died, this family died when Mother died. And now the whole household goes to bed when the sun goes down, because there is no gaslight in this house and Father begrudges the expense for lamp oil and candles. "Go to sleep and save the candles," she had heard him say on more than one occasion.

Emma set the candle on the end table in the sitting room, then pulled the little drawer all the way out, trying to keep it from rattling, and set the drawer in her lap. She sat for a moment, listening. If anyone heard her rattling in the drawers, they would be down in a minute. If there was anything this family shared besides aloofness, that was its nosiness.

The photograph was still where she had first put it thirty years ago, in the little space behind the drawer. Emma reached in and pulled it out. A photograph of their mother. So young, so thin. The people of Fall River always said Emma took after her mama, and so it was, she saw again. She was her mother's daughter. They had the same cheekbones, the same fine nose, the same arched eyebrows and close-set eyes in a narrow face. They had the same medium-brown hair. But Sarah Borden had light-colored eyes—blue, her father said he thought he remembered them to be—while Emma shared his deep brown eyes.

Mama was so young. The photograph Emma held in her hand was the last one, taken just before she died. Mother would have been about thirty—about Lizzie's current age. . . .

Even though they told Emma that she was the one who had found her mother dead, Emma could not remember it, and she still could not remember the details of Sarah's death. Nor could she bring herself to ask Father.

Emma ran her finger over the photograph of her mother's face as if to feel the delicate skin. "I know there's a reason you died, Mother," she whispered. "It's taken me a long time to understand, but now I think I do." She gently kissed the photo and thought of taking it upstairs to her room, where she could keep it, either hidden or on display, and then decided to put it back behind the drawer again. It gave her pleasure to see Abby Borden sitting next to the end table, using it, with Mother secreted safely inside. Abby had destroyed everything in the house that remained of Sarah Borden, her predecessor in Andrew's bed. Everything except a locket that Lizzie had, and this photograph that would forever remain next to that wretched woman without her ever knowing it.

"I understand, Mother," Emma whispered again. "And I've raised Lizzie well. I know you'd agree. I know you'd be happy." She touched the paper face, touched the picture to her cheek, then tucked it back into the hole in the end table and reinserted the drawer.

Since Emma had changed bedrooms with Lizzie, the only way she could enter her own bedroom in this odd little house was to walk through Lizzie's. As a result, she always carried two keys in her pocket: a key to Lizzie's perennially locked door, and a key to her own. It was a nuisance, and she had the smaller room now, but at least her bedroom shared a wall with Abby Borden's dressing room rather than with the parents' bedroom. Lizzie now had that honor.

Emma carefully unlocked Lizzie's bedroom door, hoping not to wake her parents, not minding if Lizzie wanted to sit up and talk for a while.

She saw Lizzie lying on her bed, fully dressed, half covered with her quilt. Lizzie opened her eyes.

"Did I wake you?" Emma asked.

"I guess so," Lizzie said, rubbing her face. "I didn't intend to sleep."

"My goodness, child, you're fully dressed."

"I just lay down for a moment this afternoon after the

fitting, and then again after dinner. I imagine I needed the rest. What time is it?"

"About nine, I should think."

"The house is quiet."

Emma nodded, then sat in the rocking chair at Lizzie's bedside.

Lizzie plumped up her pillow and set it next to the wall, then hiked herself up the bed to a sitting position. Something crinkled in her bed.

"What's this?" She reached under the quilt and fumbled with her skirts. Then she pulled out a piece of string and a brown-paper-wrapped parcel. "Oh. The book. I forgot all about it."

"What book is that?"

"It's a book that Beatrice sent to me."

"Well, open it. Let's have a look."

"Maybe later."

"Why later? Aren't you curious? You rip open every letter you get from her the very moment the postman puts it in the box."

"I know, but . . ."

"Oh. It's *personal*." Emma couldn't help her sarcasm.

"Yes, in fact."

"Well. I never knew we had secrets."

"We don't have secrets, Emma. I just want to have a chance to look it over first, that's all."

"Hmm. Your relationship with that woman is odd and I daresay a little dangerous, perhaps sick, Lizzie. I should be very careful, if I were you."

Lizzie looked at her with wide-open eyes. "You know nothing about her. You have no idea. . . . You have *no* idea. . . ."

"Yes. Well. Nor am I interested. Mark my words, though, child." Emma rose. "Shall I light your lantern?"

"No. I'll do it."

"Suit yourself," Emma said, and unlocked her own bedroom door. Sometimes Lizzie could be so defensive. So confounding. Emma worried that she was so gullible. What on earth could this woman want from Lizzie, this woman from England? Something no good, that was for sure.

Emma undressed quickly, hanging up all her clothes, then donned her winter nightgown, leggings and cap, and knelt on the hard floor to say her evening prayer. She even included her father.

Duties done, she slipped between the cold sheets and blew out the candle, seeing the shaft of muted light under her door as it escaped from Lizzie's room.

The girl could do so much with her life, Emma thought. If only she'd try. She has so much potential. She has so many gifts. Her youth, her looks, her closeness to Father, her friends at church . . . it's all so *wasted* on her. Emma clenched her fists. Why *her*? What has *she* done to be the lucky one, while I wither, growing old in the house of my childhood, with a traitorous father and his . . . his . . .

A moan escaped her lips, and she clapped both hands over her mouth before she made more noise. Her face felt hot and her hands shook.

It was the same every night. Every night she went to bed and ranted and railed at the devastating blows life had given her, while her beautiful, clever younger sister got all the attention.

"I try to be selfless, Lord," she whispered, then knuckled her lower lip hard until she got herself under control.

Then she turned on her side, away from the long slice of light that said that Lizzie even had friends in England, and she curled her knees to her bony chest and eventually fell asleep.

•   •   •

In the morning, Emma woke to the sounds of roosters in the neighborhood. It was still dark outside, but she heard sounds in the kitchen and imagined that the cookstove was hot and its warmth had filled the whole kitchen. Emma's room was freezing. She arose, carefully used the chamber pot without touching it to her bottom, and dressed quickly in black leggings, long underwear and a maroon wool dress with a high collar. She made her bed and set the chamber pot next to the door. It would be bad for Maggie if she had to empty frozen slops. She brushed her hair, pinned it up, carried the covered pot out into Lizzie's room and locked her bedroom door behind her. She barely gave Lizzie a glance, knowing the girl would still be sound asleep. No one would know, save Lizzie herself, what time she turned out the lantern. She probably would not be ready for breakfast until noon, lazy brat.

She felt the warmth from the kitchen as soon as she reached the landing. Then she descended the stairs and turned into the dining room.

Bridget Sullivan, the little redheaded Irish maid, was lighting the lanterns in the dining room. She was disheveled, as if she hadn't quite put herself together yet. Emma could see her stepmother, Abby, thumping her two hundred pounds around the kitchen. Emma walked into the warm glow of the kitchen and set her pot of slops in the utility room.

"Good morning," Abby said.

"Why are you up so early?"

"Babies due this morning."

"How do you know that, did a message come?"

"No, but Mrs. Churchill said she thought Sophie Warren was in labor last night, so I'll make up a casserole now and take it over. She's supposed to have twins, you know. Runs in her family."

"So for that you got up before dawn?"

"It'll be a busy day. Is Lizzie awake?"

"No. Nor is she likely to be for a time yet. It's freezing cold upstairs."

"I know." Abby opened the oven and checked on the cakes.

"Didn't anybody make a fire in the furnace last night?"

Abby turned and looked directly into Emma's eyes. "Did you?"

"No." Emma hated it when the little pig woman looked at her like that.

"Well, I reckon nobody else did, either. Don't complain unless you do your share around here, Emma."

"I do my share, Abby. I do more than my share. I do more than my share *and* your share."

Emma poured a cup of coffee and stood in the middle of the kitchen, looking out the black window. Actually, what she saw was the reflection of her stepmother, concentration on her round, lined face, as she sliced vegetables and mixed them all together in a casserole dish. Abby had barely more gray hair than Emma did, a point that bothered Emma terribly. Abby's hair was long and brown, shot through with a silver that would look beautiful on a woman of smaller stature, and done up in a bun at the back of her neck. She had a wide nose and large, fleshy lips, two facial features totally foreign to Borden blood.

Abby turned abruptly and bumped into Emma. "Emma," she said in frustration. "Please. I'm busy in here."

Emma took her coffee and sat at the table in the dining room.

"Oatmeal, Miss Emma?" the maid asked.

"Thank you, no, Maggie."

"Bridget."

"What?"

"My name is Bridget, Miss Emma."

"Well, of course it is."

"You keep calling me Maggie. Maggie was your other maid. She left here two years ago, Miss Emma. My name is Bridget."

Emma looked at the girl's face. She was deeply freckled, with curly red hair and dark-green eyes. Typical Irish. And she had the temper and the brat attitude to go with it. She seemed impatient as well this morning. "Well, *Bridget,* then, no thank you. Toast, perhaps. And then be a good girl and make a fire in the furnace."

Bridget brought two slices of toast, the dish of butter and a jar of plum jam. Emma ate the toast dry.

Abby brought her breakfast in and set her place across from Emma. She had a bowl of oatmeal, two pieces of toast with butter and jam, and a plate of fatty fried bacon.

They ate in silence, avoiding each other's eyes.

Then Abby cleared her throat, looked at the tablecloth and said, "Your father has many pressures upon him."

"They are of his own making," Emma said, looking straight up at Abby, wishing she would raise her eyes.

"Be that as it may, he tries only to make a fine home for us."

"For you."

"You are an ungrateful girl."

"I am not a girl. I am a grown woman, and so is Lizzie. We have a right to say what goes on in this house and how the family finances are handled."

"You have no such right. The money is your father's to do with as he wishes."

"To do with as *you* wish."

"These conversations have cost him sleep."

"Oh. That's a terrible shame."

"Emma . . ." Emma put down her toast and regarded her stepmother. "I'm sixty-seven years old. Your father is sixty-nine. We won't live too much longer. I just wanted a little something to leave to my baby sister, Sarah. She's just married again and trying to make a go of things. You and Lizzie, you'll have everything."

"He's already given her a house in town."

"And he gave you and Lizzie just compensation. Besides, that house is much too small for Sarah and her family to live in."

Emma snorted. "Just compensation! He deeded us a pile of sticks filled with unruly tenants. If she doesn't like the house, she should sell it and buy a larger place."

"It isn't that easy, Emma."

"Then why doesn't he leave it to her in his will?"

"She needs a place to live now, Emma. He just thought this would be a better way—"

"Well, it's not." Emma felt her face flush again; she was in danger of losing control. "That property was our mother's. He can deed some other property to your stupid half sister. He can give her some bank shares. But that property, that *particular* property is the most valuable of them all, and it has the most sentimental value to Lizzie and me."

"I'll speak with him about it again."

Emma threw her toast onto her plate. "I'm sure you will." She threw her napkin on top of the toast, pushed away from the table and left the room.

She walked up the stairs quietly, the rage burning brightly within her. She unlocked Lizzie's bedroom door, hands pale and trembling in the pre-dawn light. She stumbled against Lizzie's chair and then dropped the key to her own bedroom on the floor. Tears began to blur her vision and she got down on her knees to find the key, furious at the prospect that she might cry, furious even more that she couldn't get into her bedroom to seethe in privacy.

She moved and heard the key slide across the wooden floor.

"Emma?" Lizzie's sleepy voice. "Emma?"

"Shut up," Emma said; then her fingers found the key

and she stood up, but she couldn't fit it into the lock. Her fingers trembled and it was dark and Lizzie was listening and her fury, her helplessness, her *impotence* were in a rage beyond thought.

"Emma?"

"Shut up, shut up, *shut up*!" Then the key fit into the lock and she turned it and opened the door. She took a deep breath. "I'm leaving here *today*, Lizzie," she said, and then entered her room, shut and locked the door behind her.

I'm leaving here today, she thought, as she clenched her fists and crossed her arms over her chest. I'm leaving here today. She paced back and forth from her bed to her closet. Her suitcase was in the closet, she had only to get it down and pack it full of her clothes, but she didn't trust herself at the moment. If she loosened her hands from their grips upon themselves, they might do something. So she paced, her face on fire, the muscles in her legs stiff and tense, her back straight, her jaw so tight it ached. I'm leaving here today, she thought.

A soft knock came to her door.

"What?"

"Emma," Lizzie said, "please let me in."

"Go away."

"I won't. Now open the door and talk to me."

Emma pressed her fingers to her eyes, pressed them hard until she saw yellow spots and it began to hurt. Then she opened the door.

Lizzie came in, her hair up in curling rags, nightgown wrinkled and smelling of sleep.

"What has happened?"

"Lizzie, there's nothing . . . I can't do . . ." She made a sweeping gesture toward their parents' bedroom. "He . . . oh God!" The tears threatened again. Her breaths came in sobs.

"Sit down and tell me."

Emma sat on the edge of her chair. The sobs began to abate. She took a deep breath, fetched a handkerchief from her pocket and ran it across her face and lips, then twisted it in her lap. "I'm going to New Bedford for a couple of days."

"No, Emma. Please don't. Please."

Emma felt better as soon as she said it. "I'll be all right, Lizzie. I'll stay with friends." Emma nodded. She would see friends, that was for sure.

"For how long?"

"A week." As long as it takes, she thought.

"Please don't. The last time you said one week, you stayed away three. And were half dead when you finally did return."

"Stop it. None of that is your concern. I hate it here. I'm going there for a breath of fresh air." Emma found she couldn't meet Lizzie's eyes. Lizzie knew who her "friends" were in New Bedford. Lizzie was the only one who knew, and Lizzie didn't approve.

"I'll come with you."

"You won't. Now leave me alone. I have to pack."

"I worry so, Emma."

"I'm a grown woman. There's a train at nine. Now good-bye."

"If I got down on my knees—"

"Leave me, Lizzie."

Lizzie stood looking at her for a long moment. Emma felt she should say something, do something, but she sat on the chair and avoided Lizzie's eyes. She felt alone, so alone. She wanted to say Yes, Lizzie, save me from having to go to New Bedford, but she didn't. She sat there, hands on her lap, eyes on her hands, and finally Lizzie left, closing Emma's door quietly behind her.

Emma lifted down the suitcase. Suddenly, the rage drained away, and in its place was anticipation. It had been a long time since she'd been to New Bedford. It was time, surely it was time. She took the money envelope from her bedstand drawer and counted it. Forty-three dollars was all she had managed to save from her weekly allowance of four dollars. Well, it would have to do.

She left with only a nod to Lizzie, who was still in her room, walked to the station in the early morning light and sat in the unheated waiting room. The train arrived at eight-fifty precisely; at nine o'clock it jerked and they were on their way to New Bedford.

The anticipation Emma felt in her freedom was sporadically deposed by the hatred that welled up inside her. The smell of a man's pipe touched it off. So did the cut of a matron's expensive wool coat. A fat woman jiggled down the aisle and Emma raged within again, trying in vain to calm herself. There were only two thoughts that had an effect on her rage. One was that she would never have to marry, and so she had this freedom, as meager and as simple as it was, to leave home, alone, for a week; and the other thought was of what lay at the end of this short train trip to New Bedford: peace.

In less than an hour, she arrived.

Emma hailed a cab; it took her to the Capitol Inn, a small hotel on Madison Street, one that she frequented whenever she came to New Bedford. She checked in under the name of Lucy Billings, with the cabby carrying her baggage, and she left the usual instructions with the clerk and made sure he wrote them down. She was under no circumstances to be disturbed until the night before she was to check out. There would be no maid service, there would be no messages relayed, there would be no giving out of her hotel room number to anyone for any reason. She sealed this promise with a most generous two-dollar tip. Then she went to her room.

The bellboy opened the draperies, but Emma hustled him out with ten cents in his palm. She was filled with excitement at the prospect of an entire week here in New Bedford, with no Abby Borden, no Andrew Borden, no Lizzie Borden, no church, no neighbors, no Maggie—or Bridget, or whatever the maid's name was—no pressures, no expectations of her or her behavior, no nothing.

She took off her travelling hat and sat on the bed. She checked her watch. Almost eleven o'clock. She left the room, pocketing her key, and searched the halls until she found a little Irish chambermaid. Emma gave the girl money and instructions, then went back to her room to unpack and to pace, awaiting the arrival of the week's cache of rum.

ff and on all day, Lizzie thought about Emma.

Emma had demons. There was just no other way to explain her behavior. The Borden household was not without its pressures, and its members certainly had their quirks, but Emma . . .

Emma went to New Bedford at least once a year, usually twice, and had done so ever since Lizzie could remember. She went without parental approval, without chaperone. She never asked permission and her parents never stopped her. She took all the money she'd saved from the allowance Father gave her, and went. There was never a letter from anyone in New Bedford, and Emma never spoke of anyone there, so Lizzie knew she had no friends there. Once, while nursing Emma after one of her trips, Lizzie came upon a receipt for a room at the Capitol Inn, so Lizzie knew where Emma stayed in New Bedford, and it wasn't with any friends. She never let Emma know she'd found the receipt. She just felt better knowing she could find Emma should the need ever arise.

There was no trouble guessing what Emma did when she was alone in the hotel room. Lizzie shivered to think of it. Her sister. Her flesh and blood. Her surrogate mother. Emma, the woman who raised her, the woman she had always looked to for guidance and inspiration. Emma.

Emma drank. She drank, and whenever she drank she also got into trouble.

Emma always came home from New Bedford sick, bruised, in pain and reeking of alcohol.

47

Lizzie marveled at her older sister. She couldn't imagine going off alone the way Emma did. She always tried to picture it in her mind. Where would she go to find liquor? True, it was a commonplace enough item, yet ladies didn't frequent saloons and taverns. Was it purchased in a regular store? And what did Emma do, once she had her bottle? Where would she go? Would she carry it around in a paper bag, to sit in her hotel room and guzzle? Did she use a glass, or did she swig straight from the bottle? Did she wake up in the morning, wash her face, brush her teeth and begin again, or did she moan and roll over, search blindly for the neck of her bottle and continue, never really beginning, never really ending? Was it her companions who bruised her so? What would happen if somebody got overly rough with Emma? What if someday she just didn't come home?

Lizzie had no idea what really went on in New Bedford, and it was the activities she conjured up in her imagination that worried her so much. Lizzie joined the Women's Christian Temperance Union when she realized what Emma was doing. She hoped legislation would be a way of averting her sister's seemingly inevitable downfall. Lizzie went to the meetings, Emma at the forefront of her mind, and she prayed for Emma's soul.

At dinner, Andrew Borden drew his white eyebrows together when Lizzie told him that Emma had gone to New Bedford to visit friends.

"Again?" he asked, his voice thunderous and disapproving.

Lizzie nodded, her eyes on her plate.

"Who does she know in New Bedford?"

"I don't know, Father."

"It seems that Emma gets upset about the least little thing and then goes running off to New Bedford to do whatever it is she does up there that lays her up at home for a week afterward. I don't like it, Lizzie, I don't like it one bit. One of these days she's going to do something to bring shame on the Borden name. And I won't stand for that. Do you hear me?"

"Yes, Father."

"Be sure you tell her that."

"Yes, Father."

"Drat the girl!" Andrew threw his napkin onto the table. "Does she think she has no responsibilities here at home? Does she think she can just up and leave us to assume her duties?"

Lizzie remained silent.

"Is she airing family laundry?"

"I don't think so, Father."

"Be sure you tell her, Lizzie."

"I will, Father."

There was a long silence at the table. Then, just as Lizzie finished and readied her dishes to take into the kitchen, Andrew Borden spoke again. "And what have you been doing all morning?"

Lizzie sat back in her chair. "Reading."

"Reading what?"

"I received a letter and a book from Beatrice. In England. Remember the package you brought from the post office?"

"Oh. A book. Is it worthwhile? Will it teach you anything practical?"

"I think very much so, Father, only I've just begun, so I can't tell too much about it yet."

"This is a good friend of yours, this Beatrice?"

"Be-AT-rice, Father. Yes, she's a wonderful friend. We carry on quite a lively correspondence."

"I should imagine. I can't think what you women do, day in and day out, to keep yourselves occupied. I should go mad without the challenges of the business world. And Lord knows, you don't do too much around this house, the lot of you. I can never find a cleanly pressed handkerchief to save my soul."

"I'm sorry, Father, I'll try to get some pressing done this afternoon."

When it was clear that her father had had his say about the state of the household, Lizzie cleared the table, did up the dishes in a hurry and ran back to her room. She could barely wait to get back to the book Beatrice had sent. Such a book! It was better than anything she could ever have imagined.

And Beatrice had inscribed it, just inside the cover.

"To my darling Lizbeth, so all your heartfelt desires may come true. Affectionately, Beatrice."

"Affectionately, Beatrice." How Lizzie wished to send something to someone signed "Affectionately, Lizbeth."

Lizbeth.

Beatrice knew that her name was Lizzie, that she'd been born Lizzie Andrew Borden, but in one of her first letters, she'd written, "My dear Lizbeth, I know that is not your true name, but it is ever so much more romantic, don't you think? Lizzie brings to mind a whole different style of woman than you, so if you don't mind, I shall keep you in my heart as Lizbeth, and it is on that ground that we shall meet via our letters."

Lizzie had fallen in love with the name immediately. Not "Elizabeth," a name so popular it was almost vulgar. Not "Lizzie," which, Beatrice was too kind to say, sounded like a barmaid, chambermaid or whore. No. "Lizbeth." Different. Daring. Wonderful. If only she could be a Lizbeth in true life, and not a Lizzie.

She sprawled on her bed, her room a rumpled mess. Lizzie always allowed herself the luxury of a messy room when Emma was in New Bedford. No one would enter her room for any reason, and so there was no reason to keep it neat. It was great freedom to throw clothes on the floor and pick them up not for the sake of neatness, but for practicality, and Lizzie would only pick them up when she wanted to. A small, distinct pleasure.

She unlaced her shoes, let them drop quietly onto the floor and picked up the book. Beatrice's letter fell out from under the front cover, to lie on Lizzie's chest. She ran her hand over the dark cloth cover of the book and set it aside. She picked up the letter and began to read:

My Dear Lizbeth:

There are many people in this world who are content to let life do with them as it will. There are few who set their sights on particular goals and never rest until the goals are accomplished. Those who do can be divided into two groups: 1. Those who strive for personal and selfish gain; and 2. Those who strive for the betterment of their fellows.

I send you this book, my darling, because I believe I know you well enough to know you have the interests of your family and your community at heart. You are a soft, sensitive, lovely woman, and with the proper training, there are no limits to the things you can accomplish.

The program outlined in this book is a simple one. If you follow the rules exactly, I guarantee that you will discover powers deep within yourself that you never knew existed. You will begin to take charge of the direction of your life and cease to be swept about by the winds of change blown by others. Let your winds do the sweeping.

But one word of caution. This is a serious work. Approach it with respect.

And may the moon and the stars be yours.

Affectionately, Beatrice.

• • •

Lizzie refolded the letter and laid it on her chest. Then she picked up the book again. She couldn't tell in the light whether it was maroon or black in color. It was a very slim volume, as slim as any volume of poetry ought to be. It felt nice to the touch. It was new. It smelled new.

On the title page was written *PATHWAYS*. There was no author, no date of publication, no publisher. The second page had two short paragraphs:

> You hold this book as the result of a friend's love and regard for you. It outlines a program of growth which demands rigorous self-discipline. It will take more than your passing interest to follow the exercises outlined, but if your desire is strong enough and your sincerity pure, you will succeed.
>
> Do not read ahead. Practice each lesson daily. Do not advance to the next lesson until you have mastered the first, by doing it daily, without exception, for an uninterrupted period of thirty days. Begin to master your life by practicing each lesson in the same place at the same time every day.

Lizzie read those paragraphs over and over again. She tried to squeeze another ounce of meaning out of them, but couldn't. She wanted to open the book and begin to read, to read it straight through, and she wondered why they advised against that.

They. Who were these Pathways people?

Would the program frighten her? Would it intimidate her? Would she think it a waste of time? Would she think it too easy? She puzzled over these questions, trying to glean some knowledge about the author or authors of the book without actually reading it. She studied the cover, the binding, the quality of the paper.

But with dinner over and a long span of time on her hands in which to do nothing but iron some handkerchiefs for her father and worry over Emma, Lizzie turned the page.

It was time to begin.

fter dinner, Abby Borden made sure that Maggie would be in charge of preparing supper; then she retired to her bedroom and picked up her hand sewing. The long afternoon loomed empty before her. Andrew was sure to come up in a moment, quizzing her about Emma's departure. She felt sick to her stomach, a familiar sickness, a regular sickness, considering her dealings with Emma and Lizzie.

If only the twins had been born this morning, she thought, there would have been a little brightness in this dreary January day. Abby loved a good birthing. Especially twins. When twins came, there was twice the joy. Birthings were terribly exciting, filled with midwives, parents, grandparents, neighborly ladies and other children, cousins and ruckus. And Abby always fed the whole lot. It made her feel good; it made her feel useful; it gave her a chance to do something constructive in the community.

And she had been looking forward to it so much. But no, Mrs. Churchill had been mistaken; Mrs. Warren was not in labor at all. Just a touch of indigestion. Dr. Harding thought it would be at least another two weeks. So Abby left a casserole that Mrs. Warren couldn't eat and took home a disappointment for company.

Abby slipped the needle in and out of the fabric; she was making Andrew a new silk shirt, and no sewing machine could detail the collar and cuffs the way she could.

Growing older makes life complicated, she thought. One

day you're saving for your old age and the next day you're dividing up everything you've saved among all the relatives biting and scratching for a piece of it.

She wished Andrew would retire. He no longer needed to work for the money—it was for mental stimulation that he continued to keep his irons in all the fires. Abby would have liked to do a little travelling, but that didn't interest Andrew at all. He was a homebody. At least he'd reduced his obligations at the office: Some days when he came home at noon for dinner he just stayed at home. Other times he came home, ate a bite and then went back until four or so.

Abby was grateful to have a husband in good health. She could live with a lot if she didn't have to nurse a sick husband for years.

She glanced at the clock, anticipating him. He'd gone out after dinner for a pipe, gone to stand on the landing of the back stairs in the cold, tamping his ashes out into a black pile that would continue to grow until spring.

She heard his heavy step on the back stairs.

Her muscles tensed.

He unlocked the bedroom door and came in, closing and locking it behind him.

"Have a little lie-down?"

"Yes," he said, "I think I will." He slipped off his shoes and suit coat and lay on the freshly made bed. Abby rose and covered him with the wedding-ring quilt she'd made for their wedding bed. "Did you speak with Emma this morning, Abby?"

"She came down to breakfast while I was making a casserole for Mrs. Warren."

"How was her mind?"

"She was agitated, I think, Mr. Borden. She spoke again of the property you've generously decided to give my Sarah."

"That damned property."

"I told her I'd speak to you about it. Perhaps . . ." Abby

suddenly felt on shaky ground. She looked down at her needle.

"Perhaps what, woman?"

"Perhaps another piece of property would be more palatable."

"But we decided on that property because of its location. Sarah needs more than a roof over her head."

"I know. I just hate . . ."

"*Finish* your sentences."

"I hate to see you persecuted because of your generosity."

Andrew Borden sighed and seemed to sink deeper into the mattress. "Perhaps she'll move to New Bedford."

Abby snickered, careful to make only the tiniest of sounds, sounds she could explain away if she were called upon to answer for them. Emma would never move out: She would fear that the Borden household could not run according to her way of doing things without her assistance. Without her direction. Without her meddling.

Abby kept stitching, her stomach easing up a bit, and soon Andrew was snoring.

If Emma knew all the facets of Andrew's will, she would have a fit. The thought of Andrew dying before her was abhorrent to Abby, but she would *love* to see the look on Emma's face as the attorney presented Andrew's last will and testament at a reading. Emma would discover that the bulk of his estate, of course, was divided between her and Lizzie; but a generous third—a *generous* third—was left to Abby for her old age. And Abby, of course, would leave her estate, including any assets obtained from Andrew's, to her heirs, namely Sarah, her half sister. And there were others—people significant in Andrew's success—to whom he meant to leave some money.

But Emma thought that everything Andrew had worked for all those years somehow belonged to her and her sister. As if they had ever done anything to deserve his generosity.

As Emma saw it, she and Lizzie should inherit everything should Andrew die before Abby, and Abby ought to be put out of the house instantly, penniless. After raising both girls. After putting up with them through their teenage years, through their young maidenhoods, through their coming of age, and even now, for Emma at least, through their middle ages. Even so, Emma would leave Abby without a cent. Oh yes, Abby knew Emma's mind. And it was not a pretty sight.

When she was finished with the shirt, she roused Andrew. He hrumphed himself awake, then dressed and left for the office. Abby followed him downstairs, stoked the fire and put the flats on the wood stove to heat; one good pressing and his new shirt would be fit to wear.

While she waited for the iron to heat up, she snacked on the cookies Emma had made the day before. She enjoyed the silence of the Borden house; well, she enjoyed the *empty* silence of the Borden house. Usually the house was filled with people and it was still silent, but that was more of a cold silence than an empty one. She didn't care for the cold silence. It made her edgy. It made her frantic, sometimes, to fill it, but she didn't know how.

"I wonder where that Maggie has got to," she said to the wood stove, and just then, the maid came around the corner, broom and dustpan in hand.

"Maggie?"

"Yes?" The Irish girl rolled her eyes at the insistent use of her predecessor's name. She was through trying to correct this odd family; if they hadn't gotten it in two years, they never would.

"What have you been up to?"

"I swept the stoop, ma'am, keeping the snow from turning to ice. I was going to warm up a bit in here and then get to dusting the sitting room."

"Oh. All right. Have you seen Lizzie?"

"She's in her room, the last I knew, ma'am. I freshened the sheets in the spare bedroom and heard her rocker."

"Fine." Abby spat on the irons. They sizzled. She set the ironing board up in the dining room and commenced to iron the silk shirt. It came about beautifully. Probably the finest silk shirt she'd ever made.

She ironed and thought about Lizzie. There had been a rift in the family several years ago—again over money—again over property—again over the girls' inheritance—and again over Abby's relatives and their share of it—and ever since that time Lizzie had called her Mrs. Borden. It was not so much that Emma did it; Emma had been fourteen when Abby married Andrew, and Emma had always called her Abby. But Lizzie had been just four years old when Abby entered the family, and had called her Mother. There was no other word like "Mother" to the ears of a spinster, and to have that so cruelly taken away in her latter years was a heartache Abby couldn't quite abide. And for that, she would never forgive Emma.

Abby met Andrew when she was thirty-seven years old and a spinster. She, had, of course, given up all manner of hope of raising a little girl, and then along came Andrew Borden, staid, staunch, rich (as rumor had it), and with two daughters, one still a baby. He took her walking after church one day, and the next Sunday he picked her up for church in his buggy, both girls dressed up in their Sunday best, and they rode to church like a family. Abby was thrilled. For once, hope that she would have a family blossomed in her heart. She would be able to raise a little girl—two, actually. That day, Andrew invited her to be his wife. He needed a mother for the girls, he said, and he would make a proper husband, and promised to be a good provider.

Abby was overwhelmed with the idea of having a family of her own, and she agreed before he was finished speaking.

They were wed the next day, and she came to live in the Borden house.

He made no false promises to her—he never lied—and if she had it all to do over again, she would probably jump at the opportunity, just the way she had. Only . . . only she might have looked a little bit closer at that fourteen-year-old Emma before she agreed to take her position by Andrew's side.

She thought of Lizzie up in her room, and wondered if there was something she could say to her. She could walk up the stairs, knock on Lizzie's bedroom door and say something, she could say something soft and gentle, or something clever—except that Abby was not a very clever person, not nearly as clever as Lizzie, and they both knew it—she could say something that would touch Lizzie's heart and leave it healed.

But there wasn't anything. There wasn't anything she could say.

She'd been over this and over this—a million times in the past few years, trying to reach back to the daughter she had raised. The daughter who thought her older sister had raised her. The daughter who mistakenly believed that blood was thicker than water.

Oh, Lizzie, Abby Borden thought. I want to come up to your room and play.

But she finished her ironing instead, and left the board up for Maggie to put away. She filled a plate with cookies and took them and the shirt up the back stairs to her room.

Abby pulled the shirt to and fro on a hanger, until it lay just right. Then she hung it on the closet door, ready for Andrew to wear in the morning. And tomorrow when he put it on, he'd never notice that it was new, or that it was handmade. Abby shook her head. Andrew was preoccupied, as always.

Then she straightened the bed.

Maybe Emma *will* move to New Bedford, Abby thought. It was a wonderful idea. Even more wonderful, it was Andrew's suggestion. She wondered if giving Emma money would really encourage her to go. The breath caught in her throat. Then the three of us can be a family again—it's not too late for Lizzie and me. We've shared too many memories for there to be an irreparable chasm between us.

Abby sat on the freshly tidied bed and felt tears coming on. I wish Emma would never come back, she thought, and began to nibble a cookie. I hope she stays at least a month this time, she thought, finishing that cookie and starting another. And when she comes back, perhaps she'll be sick to her death.

When the last cookie had been eaten and the crumbs brushed from her bosom, Abby went back down to the kitchen for more. She loaded up the plate again, leaving five behind. She looked at the plate and remembered happier times, when she and Lizzie might have shared a plate of cookies and a session with Lizzie's paper dolls. Oh, how Lizzie loved to play pretend with those dolls!

Maybe this is just the thing, Abby thought. She arranged the cookies nicely on the plate. She'd just knock on Lizzie's door and say, "Lizzie? I've brought you a cookie." Lizzie's enthusiasm for paper dolls had of course faded, but she loved her cookies just the same now as she did then. Perhaps the two of them could get in some good chatting, some girl talk over a plate of cookies.

I wonder. Should I bring a tray with tea as well?

No. Don't make it look too contrived. Make it look casual. Make it look like a spur-of-the-moment decision. This plate of cookies reminded me of you and paper dolls, Lizzie, and I wanted to bring it up to you.

Emma never played with paper dolls. Emma mooned

over her dead mother and spoke of death, destruction and hate. Always had, even to this day.

Carrying the plate, Abby went through the dining room to the front hall and looked up the stairs toward Lizzie's room. She would just go knock on Lizzie's door and offer her a cookie.

Slowly, she started up the stairs, but at the top she looked at the door so firmly closed; Abby knew it was locked. Lizzie would have to be interrupted from whatever she was doing —reading the book from her English friend, probably—and they would share a cookie and have nothing to say to each other. Or perhaps Lizzie wouldn't even open the door all the way. She would probably open it only four or five inches, just enough to see who it was and what was wanted. Then a hand would snake out of the open doorway, take a cookie, she would mutter a thank-you, *she would call me Mrs. Borden,* and she would close the door again. And lock it.

No, Abby thought, perhaps the time is past for that kind of gesture. Perhaps Lizzie will come back to me when she is a little older.

Abby passed by Lizzie's door and went directly into the guest bedroom, where Maggie had swept and dusted and freshened up.

A pattern for a new housedress was cut out and lying atop the sewing machine. Abby put the plate of cookies on the bed, took one off the top, and sat at the sewing machine.

She looked at the fabric, a heavy corded cotton; it would make a fine town dress. Too bad it would be as large as a tent. She ate another cookie and sighed. Then she opened the sewing machine, threaded it with the proper color of thread, ate another cookie and began to pin the pieces of the dress together.

If only Mrs. Warren had had those twins this morning, she thought.

• • •

When Andrew came home from work, his brow was furrowed and his temper short. Maggie fixed a nice supper of boiled meat and potatoes, then fixed herself a plate and retired to her room. Abby and Andrew ate in silence in the dining room.

"Seen Lizzie?"

Abby shook her head and helped herself to another portion of potatoes. They had just gotten a bowl of fresh sweet butter from the tenant at the farm, and it was wonderful on the boiled spuds. "I had hoped she'd come down for supper, but . . ."

"Did you call her?"

"No. Maggie did, I'm sure."

"She usually comes down when I come home from work."

"I know she does, Mr. Borden. Perhaps I should check on her. Perhaps she's ill."

Andrew nodded, then loaded his fork up again. Abby knew her potatoes would be cold by the time she returned. She smashed the butter down into them, then excused herself.

No one had set a fire in the sitting room, no one had even lighted the lamps. Abby got the matches from the mantel and lighted first the lamps, then a candle, which she carried up the dark stairs.

"Lizzie?" she called, halfway up.

There was no answer.

"Lizzie? Supper is on the table. Maggie has made one of your favorites."

Still no answer. Abby puffed the rest of the way up the stairs, then knocked on Lizzie's door.

"Lizzie, dear, do come down for some supper."

Then the door opened, and Lizzie stood there, looking slightly glassy-eyed in the light of the candle Abby held.

"Lizzie? Are you ill?"

Lizzie smiled warmly at Abby. "Not at all, Mother. Not at all." Then she looked around the hall. "Supper? Oh, I missed my afternoon with Father. I'm sorry. Tell him I'll be right down."

"You haven't been ill?"

"No, I'm fine. I've been, uh, reading." She rubbed her face and then brushed at the skirt of her dress. "Let me freshen up a bit and I'll be down."

"I'll keep a portion warm for you."

"Thank you." Lizzie pulled the bedroom door shut and Abby heard her lock it.

Abby turned around toward the stairs. She felt as if she'd been told some absolutely fantastic, unbelievable news. She felt like blinking and shaking her head in disbelief.

While Lizzie had always been a nice girl, a courteous girl, a conscientious and polite girl, there was a new dimension here that had been missing for quite some time. There was a warmth that hadn't been present—not since she was a child. There had been concern in her eyes. Lizzie had known she'd missed her afternoon "session" with her father, and had been apologetic. That was uncharacteristic in these latter days.

And she'd called Abby Mother. Mother. Again. At last. Mother.

Yes, Abby thought. We must do something to keep Emma away. When Emma is gone, everything is right.

Abby fairly floated down the stairs. "She'll be right down," she said to her husband, and touched his neck affectionately as she passed behind him. She pretended not to notice that he swiped at her hand as if the touch were from a troublesome fly.

Abby fixed a plate of food for Lizzie, then put it in the bun warmer on the cookstove. By the time she'd come back from the kitchen, Lizzie rounded the corner, smiling at her father.

"So," Andrew said. "Decided to finally come join the living, eh?"

"I'm sorry, Father. I was reading. I became quite engrossed."

"Oh? So engrossed you forget to eat? So engrossed you forget your family?"

"I'm sorry."

Abby fetched the warmed plate and set it before Lizzie. Lizzie whispered a thank-you and began to eat as if she hadn't eaten in days.

Abby's own plate had chilled. Half-melted butter had congealed on the potato, and it didn't look at all as it had before she left to coax the girl from her room. She added salt and ate it anyway.

Andrew cleared his throat and set his fork upon his plate, tines down, with a sound that commanded attention. Abby's potato stuck in her throat. She looked at him out of the corner of her eye, dread coursing through her. He was going to spoil whatever it was that had just begun to happen. Should she speak? Dare she?

"Lizzie, I've been thinking."

Dear God, Abby thought.

Lizzie looked up from her plate, chewing slowly, thoughtfully. She took a long drink from her water, then dabbed at the corners of her mouth and waited patiently for her father to collect his thoughts.

"I think I'll give Emma the money she wants so badly, and ask her to see if she can't live with her friends there in New Bedford."

The thrill that ran up Abby's spine at her husband's words stopped dead when she saw the expression on Lizzie's face.

Andrew cleared his throat. "Or. Well. She'd be a wealthy woman by any standards. She could buy her own house there, or here in town, for that matter."

The expression on Lizzie's face was unreadable. There was shock there, and disbelief, but something more, something Abby couldn't identify, and it seemed to disturb Andrew as much as or more than it did her.

Lizzie's fork, forgotten in her hand, slowly lowered itself to the plate with a light *ting*.

"She's become disruptive to the family, Lizzie," Andrew said.

Lizzie was silent, her eyes still on her father's face.

"She's a grown woman, Lizzie. She should have a life of her own, in a home of her own."

Lizzie set the fork down. Abby swallowed. Her eyes darted back and forth between her stepdaughter and her husband. She silently prayed, Dear God, not something new to rend this family, please, not something new.

"I would go with her," Lizzie said quietly.

Andrew let out a sigh. "Lizzie, don't say that. Don't lets make any firm decisions about this. It was an idea, a suggestion. I say we all sleep on it tonight and then discuss it again in the morning."

"Nothing will be different in the morning, Father," Lizzie spoke in full voice. "If Emma is to leave the house, then of course I must go with her. I, too, am a grown woman, and if you think she should be on her own, then I should also."

"But the three of us," Andrew pointed his fork at Abby, "get on so well together. And it would be *better* for us, given the chance."

"There are things you don't understand, Father," Lizzie said.

"Tell me." Abby heard a wistfulness in his voice, and she knew he had lost the battle. He would never, ever let Lizzie leave his side. Never. Ever.

"She's my sister."

"So?"

"She raised me, practically." Lizzie did not look up to see the knife twist in Abby's heart.

"You may think that, child, but—"

"I'm not a child, and I do think that. I also think . . ." Lizzie put her napkin to her face.

"Go on, Lizzie."

"I also think that Emma cannot get on by herself. I think she would die. And I owe her too much to let that happen."

"That's foolish talk, girl."

"You may think that," Lizzie retorted with a small smile.

Abby wanted so much to jump in and pour out her heart. She wanted to tell Lizzie how much she loved her, how she had always loved her wonderful green-eyed little girl, and how hard it had been for her all these years, deferring always to Emma and Emma's ways. Abby wanted to come around the table and clutch Lizzie to her and say, "Please, Lizzie, make an old man and an old woman happy in their last years. Please." But the words were not there. This was a discussion between Andrew and Lizzie, and while it affected her entire life, she was not to have a say.

Pictures came to Abby's mind. Pictures of Lizzie following Emma around like a puppy. Pictures of Lizzie copying everything Emma did. Pictures of a little girl idolizing her older sister, and an older sister who took advantage of that position. Emma had been jealous of the plump baby Lizzie since the day she was born, Abby was sure. Emma treated Lizzie poorly, always telling her she had no worth, and Lizzie believed every word. Abby would spend all day with Lizzie, talking to her, making her laugh, being friends and playmates, and as soon as the front door opened with Emma home from school, gaiety vanished in the household and Lizzie was once again Emma's.

Lizzie and her father were close, but there would be nothing to break the tie that held Lizzie to Emma.

"Just think about it overnight."

"As you wish, Father. Excuse me." Lizzie folded her napkin and arose. The icy exterior had returned. For some reason it had melted during the day, this frost that had covered Lizzie for the past few years, and now it was back, horrible and cold, yet . . . yet . . . Abby hated to admit it to herself, but the coldness was familiar. It was safe. It was comfortable.

She looked at her husband and the look on his face touched her soul. Such a good man. Such a good man. She hated to see his heart break over his daughters. Again. She touched Andrew's arm and he moved it away from her.

 arch

ndrew Borden looked into the mirror and carefully combed what sparse white hair the Lord had seen fit to save for his declining years. He checked his shave with a hand that trembled and then straightened his bow tie. He didn't care much for mirrors; mirrors had a way of attracting one's scrutiny, and the more one gazed upon oneself, the more attention one paid to one's appearance. Vanity was employment for the foolish, he had always believed, and so there were only the necessary mirrors in his house; hand mirrors in each bedroom and a small one downstairs, on the wall in the foyer. Especially women, he thought. Give a houseful of women a houseful of mirrors, and there will be trouble. Serious trouble.

He finished his inspection, placed the mirror facedown upon Abby's dressing table and laid his towel over the bowl filled with cold soapy water and gray whisker-shavings. The warm smell of fresh biscuits baking wafted up from the kitchen. He knew there would be gravy left over from the evening meal to enjoy with them.

He patted down his pockets. He had the rent bills, his keys, his wallet, his money clip. He left the bedroom and locked the door behind him.

It was Saturday. Andrew liked Saturdays. They were a change of pace. They bore the fruit of his labors. On Saturdays, Andrew Borden collected his rents. It was usually one of his favorite tasks. Sometimes one of the tenants could not pay, and eviction made not such a pleasant day, but he hadn't had to evict a tenant for some time.

The thought of his pockets filled with money as he came home today brightened his outlook. Almost everyone paid in cash. He'd probably even come home with a treat or two from one or another of the farms. Some fresh butter—how Abby loved that freshly churned sweet butter—or maybe some milk or eggs. The very thought of his pockets full of money and his hands full of fresh food for his wife sparked his appetite. He went downstairs ready to enjoy a full meal.

He was right. Fresh biscuits were in the warming oven. He took two, cut them open and laid them on his plate, then ladled warm gravy from the pot over them. He took his plate to the dining room, where Abby and Emma were breakfasting. Abby poured him a cup of tea.

"Good morning."

"Morning, Father."

Andrew tucked his napkin into the neck of his shirt and spread it out over his front. He cut the biscuits into deliberate squares with his knife and fork, then sipped his tea and took a bite of biscuit and gravy. It was wonderful.

"Father?"

Andrew looked up at Emma. Her eyes were on her plate. Not a good sign.

"Do you think we could put in with some remodeling this year?"

"Remodeling? The house is comfortable. It has heat."

"I know. The wood furnace was a wise investment. No, I mean some other things that might make the house a little more comfortable. Like hot water in the kitchen. And perhaps a bath and W.C. upstairs."

Andrew felt his temperature rise. "We've been over this before, Emma."

"I know. How well I know. I thought I would ask you one more time." Emma set her fork down. "I thought that perhaps you had given it some consideration and come to a *sane* conclusion for once."

Andrew heard Abby gasp. He felt his face getting red and hot. "You may be excused."

Emma threw her napkin on the table and stomped from the room. Andrew pinched and pulled the skin on his forehead.

"I'm sorry, Mr. Borden," Abby said. "I don't know why she does that at your breakfast."

"I don't know either." Andrew took a deep breath and looked squarely at his wife. "Are you inconvenienced? Would hot water from a faucet and a bath upstairs be terribly different?"

"It would be nice, I grant you that, but . . ."

"But?"

"Well, I know how business is, Mr. Borden. Money is tight, as you say, and there are other things best done first."

"That's right, Abby. If I thought for a moment that it would make a difference, a substantial difference, or even a modest difference, I would have the plumbing installed today. But we have lived thus for twenty-seven years, and I am quite accustomed."

"Emma sees the neighbors . . ."

"Dash the neighbors! I know all about the neighbors. Emma and Lizzie care too much about appearances. They ought to concentrate instead on what goes on in their minds, not what happens in their bathrooms." He looked down at the gravy cooling on his plate. It had lost all its appeal. "I must go collect rents. My tenants expect me before noon. Good day."

He set his napkin beside his plate, donned his suit coat, his overcoat and his tall black hat, picked up his umbrella, although the day looked perfectly clear, and walked out into a perfect spring morning.

72

He turned and looked at his house. It was not the pretentious home that his daughters would prefer. It was not built in the prestigious neighborhood on the Hill. It was a small house, an unusually narrow house, no more than twenty or so feet wide as it fronted on Second Street. And it was indeed an odd shape, as he noticed again, what with the maid's bedroom he had added as a third story only on its very back. When he bought the house, it had been a two-family dwelling. They had put in a couple of doorways in order to connect some of the rooms and that had been the end of it. As a result, the layout was unusual, with the rooms strung along like beads; getting to one meant going through the others. His and Abby's room was only accessible from the back stairs off the kitchen, as was the maid's tiny cubicle, just above their room. The girls' rooms and the guest room were gotten to from the front stairs off the sitting room and parlor.

Yes, it was an odd little house, pinched a bit, he supposed, but it was serviceable, and he was in no mood to move to a new house at this stage in his life. Nor was he about to have the house torn up so pipes could be wandering about.

And so, dismissing his decision as being right, Andrew sniffed the air. He smelled the campfire scent of the cookstoves busy heating kitchens in the neighborhood. He smelled loamy earth awakening from the winter. He smelled the horses on the streets, their leathers freshly waxed and proud. The world seemed new, and Andrew felt like striding importantly down the street. All the dim unsettledness of the household was left behind, and it only came to mind when he caught a whiff of his overcoat, permeated as it was with the scent of the Borden home. And even then, the familial troubles seemed vague. Unreal.

At the corner in town, he stopped and pulled out his package of rent bills. He shuffled through them, knowing all the while which one was first. He always traveled the same route. He began his Saturday in town and finished it at the farm in Swansea. Whenever he added a new property to his portfolio, he would sit and plan the rerouting of his rent-collecting to include the new tenants. His method was efficient; he didn't want any unexpected inconveniences to mar the pleasure he got from his Saturdays.

He turned left down Main Street and passed the First Congregational Church. He'd be walking down this way again tomorrow morning, with his wife, if she felt up to it. Lately, Abby had taken to preferring to stay at home of a Sunday morning. But Andrew would be there with her or without her, and he would sit in the Borden pew with his two daughters. Lizzie taught Sunday school, and would have to be there an hour before the worship service, so she didn't join him on his Sunday walk to town. Perhaps Emma would. Perhaps Emma would take kindly to a Sunday stroll through town and perhaps the Lord would smile down on Emma and remove some of the bitterness that ruled her life.

Andrew collected all three rents due in town. Every tenant was home; every tenant expected his visit; every tenant had cash in the right amount ready and waiting for him. Feeling flush with the successes of his life, he walked around to the livery stable to borrow the carriage belonging to the bank so he could collect his money in the outlying areas.

The stable boy had the horse dressed and ready. Andrew climbed up into the seat and flicked the reins, turning the rig down the street and out of town.

Fall River was a small town, but even so, it had its ethnic sub-areas. There were areas filled with Poles, the Irish had their little town-within-a-town, the Italians had a neighborhood; Andrew rode through them all, keeping his eyes straight ahead, keeping his nostrils from breathing too deeply the odors of their nationalities. Andrew preferred town. He knew town. He owned some of town and was comfortable there. That was where he had raised his family, and where he would stay until the day he died.

The farm properties were very nice, and if Andrew ever gave a thought to retiring, he imagined being on the farm alongside the creek where he used to take the family for leisurely weekend vacations and where he took the girls fishing when they were younger. But Andrew and his family belonged in town.

Remembering those earlier times, those carefree times made him eager to drive out to the country. He snapped the reins and clucked the mare into a little more speed.

The buggy he was driving was not a particularly comfortable one; the springs squeaked and the leather seat was cracked and poorly patched in two places. But the bank was making money and as long as Andrew Borden had a say in its financial affairs—that is, its expenditures—the buggy was perfectly suitable as it was.

They trotted out of town onto a poorer road, one quite muddy with the spring thaw, and badly rutted. Andrew slowed the horse and found the change in countryside refreshing.

The fields were greening after being snow-covered for months. The air was fresh; there were even some newborn lambs curled up and sleeping as their mothers grazed beside them. The buggy carried Andrew over a clattering bridge that covered a swollen stream, muddied with runoff from the melt. He pulled his overcoat a little tighter around him. And he wished he'd brought Lizzie along for company.

Lizzie used to go with him when she was just a little thing. She used to sit jostling alongside him on this very same seat leather and talking a blue streak, asking questions about everything they saw, everyone they passed. A warm knot pressed against his breastbone as he thought of Lizzie. She was, without a doubt, the most precious thing that had ever happened in his life.

He worried about her, mostly about those dratted headaches she got that made her so sick. They were the same headaches her mother used to get. Sarah, Lizzie's mother, had had headaches so bad she would fall unconscious to the floor. Andrew remembered Emma running to him the first time it happened; she must have been three or so, and she was shrieking and shrieking that her mama was dead, she was *dead,* she was DEAD! and Andrew found her lying unconscious on the kitchen floor. He carried her to their bedroom, and within a half hour she was awake, her headache gone. In its place, of course, was a large purple knot where she had hit her head as she fell. Dr. Bowen came right over when Andrew ran to fetch him, and he prescribed a sedative, which Sarah wouldn't take.

Dr. Bowen saw Sarah for many problems. Sarah had those headaches, and she had terrible tantrums, fits of rage so bizarre that Andrew used to take Emma and leave the house. He never knew if the house would still be there when they returned. He feared for the safety of his daughter when he was off at work all day, but nothing she did seemed to trigger her mother's spells. That always happened when he was around to rescue Emma and get her out of range. Sarah had a mighty throwing arm and she threw everything she could get her hands on. And her face screwed up into a mockery of humanity and turned purple-red. She would rage, using foul language and all, stomping and kicking, biting and scratching when he got too close to her, and he would grab up Emma and run for a neighbor's house.

When the storm was over, Sarah would cry for hours, sometimes days, apologizing over and over. She didn't know what had gotten into her, she said, and her remorse was indeed pitiful. Her face would be swollen from crying, her eyes red, lost in the puffy tissue around them. Andrew couldn't bear to see her in such misery, but she would not be consoled.

When Emma was five years old, Sarah gave birth to Alice, who screamed from the moment she came into the world. Alice screamed so loudly and so long that the whole household was set on edge. She would not stop screaming in order to eat, and Sarah grew gaunt and hollow watching her baby daughter starving to death. On the third night, when Sarah had fallen unconscious from exhaustion, with Andrew by her side, the baby died.

Sarah's "spells" grew ever more vicious after that.

These spells put Andrew in a terrible frame of mind. He became frantic for a cure. Dr. Bowen could do nothing. He found no reason for the rages, and though he tried prescribing this and that, Andrew knew that Sarah took none of the medication.

Sarah had told him there would be no more children, but when she was well, she was so beautiful to his eyes, and playful, and . . .

Four years after the infant Alice Borden died, Sarah found herself again with child. Fear took over her life. For entire days at a time, she would sit, immobilized by the possibility that the life she felt moving within her would scream until its death. Andrew would walk Emma to her school, and Sarah would be sitting on the sofa when he left. When he returned, she would be sitting in the same place, and she would not even know that he had been gone. Emma learned to care for herself.

Fear for the baby's life almost consumed Sarah. He had to remind her to eat. Emma was entirely ignored. Andrew prayed for a healthy son, one he could name after himself, one who would grow up strong to be a man for his mother when Andrew grew older.

And a girl was born. Sarah snapped back to life when the

greedy little mouth suckled so efficiently, and she was lost in rapture, cooing to the fat, pink little creature.

This would be their last child. Andrew would not have his son. He named her Andrew anyway. Lizzie Andrew Borden.

For a while, Sarah's health improved. Ten-year-old Emma began to receive attention again, as her help was needed in the house. The baby Lizzie grew pudgy and healthy, and Sarah doted on her.

And then, about the time Baby Lizzie began to walk, the spells returned. Again, Andrew was snatching up the children and taking them out of harm's way.

Andrew's hopes for a normal, happy home life vanished, and he mourned those shattered dreams every day. But he loved Sarah more than he thought anybody could ever love another human being. So he lived with her rages. And her headaches. And the fainting spells that accompanied them and seemed to be more than just fainting spells. She would be fine one moment, a graceful hand to her temple, her eyes just a little bit off center from the headache pain, trying to manage her household just the same, and the next moment she would be slumped in her chair or lying on the floor, absolutely unconscious. Not in a swoon, but as if she were dead.

And then she did die. She'd fixed him a fine breakfast, seen him off to work and twelve-year-old Emma off to school, and was feeding baby Lizzie in her high chair when he left. When Emma came home from school, Lizzie was still in her high chair and Sarah was dead on the dining-room floor.

Emma calmly walked down the street to where Dr. Bowen lived and had his medical practice, brought him home with her and tended to the baby while Dr. Bowen attended Sarah. When Andrew, summoned, came home, Emma handed him the baby and then went to pieces.

Like her mother, Emma did what had to be done in a crisis. And like her mother, Emma raged. Andrew had long ago given up on changing Emma's behavior. A stronger will he had never seen in his life. He had even ceased to worry over her. She would go off, fueled by the fever of resentment, and be gone for weeks at a time. Then, when she returned, she would take to her bed for equally long, recovering from whatever damage her rages had done to her. Emma was a strong one, all right. She seemed able to handle herself. And if one day she ran off and never came back . . . well . . . that would be all right, too. It wasn't that Andrew didn't love Emma, for he did. But she had abraded that love until it was lusterless and shabby.

Emma never got over the death of her mother. It was during Emma's formative years that Sarah Borden put her through the worst tests of all, and then died when Emma was at the most sensitive age of twelve. No wonder the poor girl had grown to be a humorless woman. Emma blamed Andrew for Sarah's death. She made that very clear from the first moment. He didn't take good enough care of Sarah, or he made her work too hard, or he didn't hire a nanny for Lizzie though he knew that his wife was prone to those terrible headaches.

And Andrew wasn't so sure he didn't agree.

As a result, Andrew and Emma always appeared to be viewing the family—and life itself—from opposite angles. They seemed to be fighting even when there was nothing to fight about. They seemed opposed on every matter. Whether they were or not, Andrew always felt as if they were.

Emma blamed him and Andrew blamed himself. Upon that one issue they did agree. Upon that one issue and no other.

Sometimes it was very hard for Andrew to look at his family. Theirs was not a picture he cared to have on his desk. He did not brag about his wife and children the way other men did. He did not flaunt them about town. He used to, but those were younger, freer times. Life had taken Andrew's grief for a picture-perfect family and twisted it tightly around him.

Andrew pulled the buggy up in front of the first farmhouse, scattering a half dozen scraggly chickens. These tenants were not to Andrew's liking, being so private and personal about their affairs. Both husband and wife worked in the mill, and they left their children with Irish people during the day. He set the brake, found their rent bill in his pocket and got down from the buggy with weary legs.

They took care of the building and grounds, but the whole area smelled like the goats he heard in the back. The smell grew stronger as he walked toward the house.

The woman opened the door. "Mr. Borden," she said, smiling with bad teeth.

"I've come for the rent," he said, and handed the white bill toward her.

She shushed her children and slipped out the doorway to stand in the sunshine with him. She was disheveled and dumpy.

"Mr. Borden, my Howard took to his sick bed last Wednesday and didn't pick up his pay envelope on Friday. He's better now, and will be a-going to work on Monday. Can he drop the rent 'round your office then?"

Andrew thought of the husband that belonged to this woman standing in his bank office, smelling of goat and Lord knew what else.

"I collect the rents on Saturday, madam."

"Yes, I know, Mr. Borden, we been rentin' from you now for two years, and we always had the rent on your Saturdays. But this time, well, Howard just got so sick, and you know they wouldn't let *me* pick up his pay envelope . . ."

"I will confiscate his last paycheck, take the rent plus a

surcharge for my trouble, and he can pick up the balance of his pay."

"Surcharge?"

"Yes. It costs me time and money to come out here every Saturday. If you're not going to have the rent for me, then I must charge you for my time."

"How much, do you think? We barely make ends meet. . . ."

"One dollar."

The woman's hand fluttered to her throat. "A dollar? Mr. Borden, that would feed us for a week, what with raising our own goat milk and hogs and all."

"Then you should have your rent here on time."

The woman looked at the porch. Andrew felt ill at ease. It was these people who made him ill at ease. He didn't like their kind, not at all, and as soon as he could get them off his property, he would likely rent to a higher class of folk.

"Mr. Borden," the woman said, "would you please take some goat cheese to the missus?"

"If you fetch it in a hurry," he said.

She did, and he walked, itching, back to the buggy. He knew that she hoped the paltry gift of goat cheese would help ease the penalty. Well, maybe it would and maybe it wouldn't.

He climbed back into the seat, his ill-temper making the horse fidget. He took off the brake and snapped the reins. He knew the woman still stood on the porch, but he gave her no backward glance.

Now if Lizzie were here, he thought, she would say something gay, and the ride to the next farmhouse would be pleasant on this spring morning. Instead, he knew that he would grumble to himself the rest of the way, running through his mind things he should have said to his tenant, preparing what to say to the next tenants if they should try the same story with him.

He missed Lizzie on these rides, but he could understand her refusal to join him. Shame turned the spring day dark for Andrew as he thought about his sweet Lizzie and the terrible things he did to her on these trips.

It started years ago, when Andrew worked as an undertaker. He was frequently called to the outlying areas to confer with families, retrieve corpses and collect money. More often than not, these rides were less than joyous, so he would take Lizzie with him to elevate the atmosphere. It was his job to view the dead bodies of these people, and those who died from sickness or accident didn't bother him. It was the ones who died old who haunted all his moments. He feared for himself when age began to take its toll.

Lizzie would chatter all the way out and, little girl as she was, usually slept the whole way back, completely tuckered out from the fresh air and sunshine. She always brought along a blanket, and she would sleep curled on the seat next to him when she was little, with her head on his lap when she got a little older, and then in the backseat as she got too old to do that.

And when she was asleep, he began to talk to her. He told her things he would never tell another soul, never. He talked to her in a way that was quite surprising to himself; and every time he took off for the country, his angel of a little girl with him, he would promise himself not to talk to her in "that way" anymore.

But he seemed to have no control over the strange behavior that erupted during those moments.

They would jog along, the filly making a nice little trot over unused roads in the backcountry. Lizzie would be asleep next to him, her reddish-gold hair shining and blowing in the wind. He would reach down and put a work-hardened hand on her head and the very idea of her being his daughter would stun him.

He began to make promises to her. He promised her money, gold, health, happiness, a husband who would adore her, a house on the Hill, servants who knew how to serve, wealth and glory. He told her about the workings of business and the workings of life—as Andrew Borden saw them, not always a pretty picture. He told her of his life as a young man, of his family and the struggle he had to make a financial gain in Fall River.

And the more he talked, the more he realized that he struggled so hard for *her*. For her sake and for no other reason. He worked himself harder than he had any right to ask of an employee. He was amassing his fortune for her. Just for her. His purpose for being was to provide for his daughter, *this* daughter, and as the realization took place over several weeks, he realized also what would happen were he ever to make good on all his promises.

She would move away. She would move away and marry some man unworthy of her beauty, unworthy of her talents, unworthy of her affections and attentions. She would take everything he had given her—his *life,* for the love of God—and she would dismiss him just as the new generation dismissed the corpses of the old people he hauled.

From the time he understood the depth of deception that would take place were his unselfish, loving gifts received, Andrew Borden tried to hold his tongue and found that he could not.

And his running monologue toward his sleeping daughter grew more bizarre, even to his own ears.

Worse, he occasionally wondered if she was really asleep, or if she just pretended because she knew he would begin to bare his soul to her somnolent form as soon as he saw evidence she could no longer hear him.

He began innocently enough, talking of her future, and ended up talking of his future. He would describe to her, in lurid detail, every inch of his failing flesh. He would talk of incontinence and bedsores. He would ask her over and over again, the rawness of the question salt to his wound, if she would still love him, still care for him, still bring him tea and read to him when he was not fit for company other than that of the grave worms. He would imagine himself wrinkled beyond compare, old, old, a hundred years and more, drooling, blind, palsied, and he would describe the breakfast-table scene, for example, once Lizzie had carried him down to the table. He would go on and on about how she had to feed him and how irritable and mean he would be. He drew such scenes in great detail, always at the end wondering, agonizing, if she would continue to stand by him.

He wanted to know if there would be a line, further than which she would not go in her love for him. He had to know that boundary of Lizzie's affections, for he wished to die before crossing it.

But she was always asleep, and never answered those questions. As a result, they burned within him, brighter and brighter as each week went by.

And because he could never voice those terrible, detailed worries to her face, he resented the fact that he was so emotionally dependent upon her approval.

And he began to shame her in public.

This was the crux of the matter, as far as Lizzie was concerned. She would no longer accompany him on his Saturdays, because surely at one time or another, he would insult her or speak falsely about her to someone of Fall River or its environs, and Lizzie would never hear an apology.

He hated himself every time he did it; but how could he ever explain to her that she was the one who made him do it? She was the one. She was the entire reason for his existence. She drove him to conduct business that was sometimes unethical for collection of the dollar. She drove him to mutter to her sleeping form. She drove him to marry that Abby woman because he knew she needed a female besides poor, disturbed Emma to help bring her up. She was the one who made him tightfisted with the money, his money, *her* money, so she would never be able to fulfill all those disloyalties he was sure she harbored in her heart.

And, in fact, hadn't he proved it? He gave her money for a trip abroad, then begged her not to go. Did she listen to him? Not for a second. She made arrangements and was gone for six weeks. Six weeks during which he thought he would expire from worry and frustration. Six weeks without the light of his life plunged him into a dark depression so severe he wasn't sure he would ever come out to see the light of day again.

And then when she returned, his world righted itself and the family went on as a whole once more. It was as if nothing had changed. And nothing had, really, except that now Lizzie corresponded, a little too enthusiastically for his peace of mind, with a friend from Britain. That couldn't be too bad a thing, as long as he made sure she had no money to visit there.

His dependence on her shamed him. And for that, he shamed her among her peers.

And that made her angry. Angry enough to change churches! To change churches, after he bought the Borden pew at the First Congregational!

But Andrew couldn't blame her. She was angry at him, and with just cause. He hated to see her angry, but anger was all right. The girl had fire, and that was one of the wondrous things about her. She had fire in the midst of a houseful of ice.

Andrew sighed. There were many things in life that he could do nothing about. He snapped the reins. But his tenants and their rents were not among them.

He looked down at the package of goat cheese as it rode alongside him on the buggy seat. Those people made a fine cheese. I imagine that would fetch two bits at market today, he thought. I'll stop there on my way home. No sense in letting it go to waste.

I t didn't take Lizzie long to realize that if she were going to do the exercises in the book Beatrice had sent, she would need some privacy. She never knew when Emma would come barging through, and she needed to concentrate, particularly when she started on the second exercise in the book.

So, as soon as the weather turned warm, Lizzie packed up candles, candlesticks, book and a few other personalizations, and took them to the hayloft in the barn.

The barn was an old stable, but Andrew had gotten rid of the lone horse over two years ago. Since then it had been used for practically nothing—a little storage space, but nothing really. Lizzie enjoyed the barn. When she was young, she used to love to go upstairs into the loft and look down upon the horse, smelling his richness. Even after he was no longer there, she still liked to go up and lie in the dusty hay and read of a long summer afternoon.

And she needed a place of her own. A private place to be, to read, to study. It was central to the exercises in the book. The barn was perfect.

Emma had been in the kitchen getting started on the evening meal the day Lizzie began to move her study to the barn.

"Where are you going with those candles?"

"To the barn."

"The barn? What on earth for?"

"I like to go out there and read, you know, and sometimes I can't read when the sun goes behind the tree in the afternoon."

"You'll set the whole place on fire."

"No, I don't think so."

"Sounds like a stupid idea to me," Emma said. "Young women just don't read in the barn. They read in the sitting room."

Lizzie unlatched the screen door and walked out into the fresh spring air. It was a beautiful day. The pear trees were filled with blossoms. The neighbors were all out working in their yards. Lizzie took a deep breath and smiled.

The barn door swung open with its customary creak and Lizzie made a mental note to oil the hinges so she could come and go from her place without the entire neighborhood knowing it.

There was a small tack room on the left and a workbench area on the right. Father had sold all the tack, but the smell of oiled leather remained in the small room. The workshop area was filled to overflowing with piles of magazines, broken machines that her father fully intended to have mended someday—when he found someone who didn't want to charge him an arm and a leg to do it—a small pile of kindling that had lasted through the winter and boxes and crates of miscellaneous junk. Two empty horse stalls were next, their damp dirt floors smelling musty. They needed some fresh straw. The barn would smell hot and dusty as the summer wore on, but for now, Lizzie thought about putting some fresh straw in the stalls to freshen up the air and get rid of the moldy stench of a wet winter just passed.

She put the candles and candlesticks in a pocket of her duster, then climbed the ladder to the hayloft.

There were two piles of hay at the top, both brown and dusty. Lizzie had long thought about forking them down and using them as winter cover on the garden, but the garden was fairly overgrown anyway, sorely neglected, and the hay was where she lay to read. She thought of cleaning it all up, bringing table and chairs, maybe even a cot or sleeping mat of some sort.

She set the candlesticks on the windowsill, then flopped down into the hay. She'd have to buy a new mirror, and then hide it, for surely Emma would come up to investigate, to ascertain that Lizzie wasn't doing something Emma didn't approve of up in the loft.

The room needed a table of some sort, something to set the mirror and candles upon.

Lizzie jumped up, climbed down the ladder, emptied a produce crate of its load of mildewed magazines, tamped the dust out of it, then threw it up to the loft and climbed back up after it.

The box was perfect. Lizzie plumped the haystack up a bit to provide a backrest, set the box down and put the candles on top of it. She had an old silk scarf that would lend an air of elegance to the setting. Up she jumped again, and climbed down the ladder.

This reminded her of a "fort" she'd made as a little girl. It was out at the farm in Swansea. It was a secret place of her own. There was an old willow tree that had been storm-damaged and it leaned over all to one side. The curtains of willow leaves provided a wonderful green translucent screen, which let in plenty of light and no other eyes. Lizzie stole a scissors from the kitchen and very carefully cut the green trailing fingers out of the center, apologizing to the tree the whole way. Then she brought a pillow and her favorite picture book, a doll and some cookies. And whiled away a long summer day.

She heard Emma call her and it made her giggle behind her hand, even as her heart pounded, wondering if Emma would give her a spank for being naughty. She *was* being naughty, hiding from her sister, hiding from her mother, and she knew it, but that little green room in the middle of the tree was just a treasure. She couldn't bear to leave it, she couldn't bear to have Emma find it, she knew it had to be hers, though probably hers only for just that day.

So she put her head on her pillow and played with the baby doll and ate cookies while she listened to Emma and her mother call and call and call.

That night she was sent to bed without supper, but Lizzie didn't mind. She didn't get a spank, she got a hug and a lecture from Mother instead. Emma told her that she had better things to do, so the next time Lizzie wanted to disappear for the day to just bloody well tell someone so Abby didn't make Emma run around hollering for her all day long.

Lizzie had forgotten all about that day. She wondered if the pillow and the doll were still in the midst of that tree. She wondered if another child had found that wonderful, peaceful paradise within that living, fragrant room. She'd ask Father if she could accompany him the next time he went out to the farm. She'd like to look for that old tree and see. She'd like to go out to the farm and spend some time in the quiet. Fishing. She'd like to go fishing.

She wondered if this was the way Beatrice felt the first day she rented her first flat in the city, and had a home of her own.

In her room, Lizzie got that silk scarf she'd envisioned, a needlepoint pillow and her hand mirror. She'd get another mirror the next time she went to town, but for now she was anxious to do her exercises again in her new space, to see if things were different.

Abby was busy with Maggie doing the spring cleaning, so nobody noticed, really, when Lizzie left by the back door. Even so, she stopped at the barn door to make sure she was going in unseen.

I'll have to get a latch for the door, she thought, so it can be locked from the inside. Then she climbed up the ladder, which always made her feel like a man, and began to rearrange.

When everything was in its place up at the hayloft, it looked like a shrine. Lizzie stepped back to the edge of the loft and surveyed her new room. It did look like a shrine. Like an altar, with *Pathways,* the Beatrice book, lying on the center of the overturned crate like a bible.

The book. The marvelous book. Even though it admonished her not to, Lizzie had read a few of the later exercises. All harmless. All, in fact, seemed a little bit ridiculous, just like the one she just performed with the candles and the mirror, but she had faith that Beatrice would not steer her wrong.

Each exercise was to be done for a full thirty days, so she was still only on the second exercise. Her letters to Beatrice were full of questions: Who wrote this book? Why? Who publishes it? How is it distributed? Can I buy copies? Why is it so mysterious? What will the end result be?

And Beatrice, cool, with her written British accent so clear in Lizzie's head, told her to mind her lessons and more understanding would eventually come. But cool as she might seem regarding Lizzie's strict adherence to the rules governing the lessons, she was overwhelmingly pleased that Lizzie was such an ardent student.

The first exercise was nothing more than two paragraphs to be read aloud three times a day for thirty days.

Within each individual reside many others. Your personality is made up of an infinite number of facets, continually turning and twinkling in the ever-present Light of Life. When we take control of our lives, we design the patterns of light. We line up the personality facets to accomplish that which we were born to do.

I now claim that which is divinely mine. I claim absolute control over each fragment of my personality, to be strengthened through purposeful, conscious unity. I now will that the Divine Power which motors the Universe now deed me the control over my own destiny. I now claim that I, and no other, am the architect of my future. I now command my rightful, unique place in the order of all material. So it is, so shall it be.

It was written with Lizzie in mind, she was sure. She'd never read anything like it before. It reminded her that she was responsible for her own emotions, attitudes and future. It mentioned God, and it seemed to suggest a spiritual way of life, both of which Lizzie approved. And when Lizzie read the passage aloud, especially the "I now claim" part, her heart pounded, and it felt to her as if it really *meant* something. She hoped it wasn't wishful thinking.

The second exercise was even stranger. She was to light two candles, and place one on either side of a mirror. Then she was to sit in the dark and view her face in the mirror for no less than one-half hour. Every day for thirty days.

At first, she could not do it. Her face turned gargoyle within three minutes, and her eyes, always pale, seemed to dissolve and fade away, leaving only empty sockets through which she could see unpleasant things floating about.

It was a week before she could spend fifteen full minutes at the task, and another week before a half hour passed and she could still view herself without nausea.

It could have been the setting—the darkness, the mystery surrounding the exercises in the book—it could have been the shadows the candlelight threw upon her face, or it could have been that she was fresh from the "within each individual reside many others" exercise, but the face that Lizzie saw in the mirror was not her own. It was close, it was very close, but it seemed to be just slightly foreign. It was almost her, but not quite.

92

Regardless, she started counting her thirty days from the day she first spent thirty minutes. Beatrice complimented Lizzie on her thoroughness. "Cheating on the exercises will not harm you, Lizbeth," she said, "but it could invalidate some of the work you're doing. Invest this time in yourself. Do it right and reap the full benefits." And in the meantime, to fill the other twenty-three and a half hours in every day, Beatrice suggested some books Lizzie could read, most of them on business. "Business is just busy-ness, Lizbeth," she said. "Life is about getting on with other people. And the more you practice, the better you get at it. But before you can practice successfully, you must have a fine image of yourself. The exercises will give you personal power. The books on business will tell you how to act with others. Be sure of yourself. Be bold. Be adventurous." And then she'd sign off with the inevitable "Affectionately, Beatrice."

Lizzie would hug those letters to herself, knowing that the next time she met Beatrice, she would not be a fumbling fool. She would be well practiced, bold, adventurous and self-assured.

Yes. Soon she would be ready to be a fit friend for Beatrice. But would she ever be ready for her father?

Lizzie lay back against the hay and thought about her father. He was becoming increasingly odd. A function of age, surely, Lizzie thought, as he'd always been quite eccentric; but of late he had become most abusive.

In church two Sundays ago, for example, he told the organist that Lizzie couldn't carry a tune even if it had two handles. Then he went on to explain that the laundry basket had two handles and she didn't seem to be able to carry it, either. Lizzie and old Mrs. Watkins listened in horrified silence as he expounded further on Lizzie's laziness. Lizzie finally turned and walked away.

Andrew caught up with her several paces down the church walk, catching up her arm in his hard little fingers.

Lizzie pulled away from him.

"Don't you dare walk away from me like that. You embarrassed me."

"*I* embarrassed *you*? Father, how could you say those things to Mrs. Watkins—especially since they weren't at all true. I can sing, you know I can sing. And your laundry doesn't go wanting, either." Lizzie felt herself near tears and that infuriated her.

Her father looked at her with astonishment. "It was said in jest, Lizzie."

"No, it wasn't, Father," she said, her breath coming in gulps. "It was said in meanness." Lizzie stalked away from him, fuming. She was conscious of him walking about two paces behind her, silent, all the way home.

She fumbled about while trying to unlock the front door, and when she couldn't fit the key in the lock because of the tears of rage and hurt that befuddled her, Andrew calmly took her keys, unlocked the front door, turned the knob and pushed it open. Angry though she was—angry too about her failure to control her emotion—when her father came and performed the simple task she seemed unable to do for herself, she felt small and cared-for. A surge of unbidden and unwelcome affection warmed her. But she took her keys from him without looking at him, and went upstairs to her room and locked the door behind her.

Emma was in her room, Lizzie could hear her rocking chair, and she hoped that Emma would stay there. She was in no mood to talk about family matters, or the sermon or Sunday School or anything else.

She flopped on her bed, fists clenched, wondering why he did such things—he always treated her poorly in public—and her gaze landed on the book from Beatrice.

She felt an immediate change in attitude. Instantly, the anger and frustration melted and she wondered how she could have handled the situation better. How could she have been more bold, more adventurous, more in control?

She could have laughed at his "jesting," and made light of it.

She could have turned to him calmly and gently, told him and Mrs. Watson both that those things were not true and asked him to explain himself.

Either one of those things would have been a far superior reaction than stomping off and crying. Either one of those things would have been far more adult. She would have been in control. She could have been self-assured.

The rocking stopped in Emma's room and Lizzie held her breath. Oh God, don't let her come in here.

But the key turned in the lock and Emma's door opened.

"How was church?"

"Fine." Lizzie hoped if she kept to monosyllabic answers, Emma would take the hint and go away.

"I'm going down for a bite. Can I bring you something?"

"No."

"I think there's a piece of pie left."

"That would be nice, thank you."

"Is everything all right, Lizzie?"

"Yes," she said, but the anger returned in full force. Her fists clenched, and Emma noticed before she could relax them.

"You had a tiff with Father again?"

"He *insulted* me in front of Mrs. Watkins."

"Mrs. Watkins?"

"The organist at church."

"Oh, pooh."

"Yes, I know, it doesn't mean much in front of the organist, but why does he do that? He always does that. He *always* does that in front of other people."

Emma sat on the edge of Lizzie's bed, the last thing

Lizzie wanted. She wanted to puzzle this out in her own way—in Beatrice's way—in her own time. She wanted to be forgiving instead of complaining, but old habits died hard. She didn't want Emma to be interfering, confusing her with her twisted ideas of Father's behavior.

"If I were you," Emma said, "I would tell him that unless he can behave himself like a gentleman, he can bloody well find himself another escort. And then I would change churches."

Lizzie was speechless. She just stared at Emma. Emma patted her leg, got up and slipped out the door.

Change churches. Find a new start. A new pastor. A new Sunday school class.

All things new again. All things new. Beginning a new life, *starting down a new Pathway. I now command my unique and rightful place in the order of all things material.* It was a wonderful idea.

Lizzie had immediately changed churches. Last Sunday morning she had turned right when her father turned left, and had gone to the Central Congregational Church. To her delight, it was populated with people who lived on the Hill, exactly the new type of friends Lizzie was interested in making. And she immediately took a Sunday school class of Oriental children and joined the Christian Endeavor Society.

For the sad person Emma had turned out to be, now and then she had a good idea.

But there was nothing at all good about her ideas in New Bedford.

When Emma came limping home from her January trip, her face darkly veiled, she took to her bed for two weeks. Lizzie brought her meals up, but Emma would hide her face with the covers.

Only when the bruises began to pale and turn yellowish did Emma, starved for company, allow Lizzie to see her.

She had taken quite a beating. Her lip was split, her eye

was blackened, and there was a big bruise high on one cheekbone. She moved about in bed with severe discomfort, so Lizzie knew that the damage was not limited to her face. How could she? How *could* she?

And the worst thing, Lizzie knew, was that within another six to eight months, Emma would return to New Bedford for like treatment. It made Lizzie sick to her stomach.

But every time she tried to talk to Emma about it, Emma turned her head. It was something that was not to be discussed.

And in the two weeks during which Emma was bedridden, neither Andrew nor Abby had come to visit her in her room. Not once.

Not that Emma would have seen them; but not once did either of them make an effort, and Lizzie knew that Emma would have enjoyed refusing them admittance.

So Lizzie had changed churches, and knowing that her father had to explain the change to everyone in Fall River gave her a naughty little glee. It was a welcome respite from the guilt that always resided within her. She could never live up to the person he needed her to be.

Beatrice never had to live up to unreasonable expectations like that, did she? No. That was one of the most attractive things about Beatrice. She never strived for anyone else's approval. Lizzie felt boxed in most of the time, scrabbling for the approval of those who would never grant it.

She wanted her father to be proud of her, but clearly she had failed him in every way. He ridiculed her and humiliated her in front of others. He never missed an opportunity to shame her, especially in front of her friends and those people who counted in the community. But this was nothing new. Andrew had been saying terrible things about her, in front of her, since she was a little girl.

And she went out of her way to be a good daughter. She tried to keep peace in the family—not an easy task. She took off his boots every day when he came home for a rest. She rubbed his feet. She brought his tea. She read to him every day. She looked presentable and kept a good house.

And there were certain things that let her know, in spite of his actions, that he did love her, that he did approve of her. One was the trip he bought for her to go abroad with her church friends. That was an extravagant expense for him. He'd never done anything like that for Emma. Or Abby, for that matter.

Another reason she thought he really did love her was the way he fawned over her during their afternoon "visiting." He always mentioned something about growing old, and he always needed to extract her promise never to leave him. But that kind of need was different from approval for herself as a woman, as a person, as a contributing member of the family in particular and society in general. No, that he *needed* her, Lizzie had no doubt. But whether he *liked* her was another matter entirely.

And then there was the ring. If there was one single thread of proof that Andrew Borden loved his daughter, it was that he wore her high school ring on his pinky finger.

She had never been a scholar, and had not finished high school, but when all her classmates were buying their class rings, Lizzie saved her allowance and purchased hers along with the rest of them. She wore it proudly on the ring finger of her right hand. It was gold, with a yellow stone, and it had her initials on the inside.

Some months after Lizzie got the ring, a boy walked her home from school. That night, Emma told Lizzie that she would do better to be at home where an eye could be kept on things that were important, rather than frittering time away on silly social matters and the kind of schooling that taught people nothing but nonsense. Emma forbade Lizzie to see the boy again and withdrew her from school.

Lizzie didn't put up much of a fight about it—she wasn't very good at school, and it was true, much of the lessons were nonsense. She was not at all interested in the boy, but she found Emma's reaction to be quite amusing.

The next day, Lizzie was home when her father came home at noon. Lizzie, bored and missing her classmates on her first day of leisure, made him a fine meal and served him in the sitting room. She took off his boots and rubbed his feet. She waited on him and fluttered around him like a little bird.

When he finished eating, Andrew folded his napkin and set it on the tray next to his plate.

"That was very good."

Lizzie beamed.

"Come sit next to me, my dear." Lizzie snuggled up to him, and he put his long arm around her shoulder. "Have you decided against school, then?"

Lizzie nodded.

"It's just as well," he said. "There are better things. Education causes more trouble than it cures. You stay home here and let Emma and Abby teach you how to be a good woman, a good wife, a good housekeeper. Those are skills that will do you more good in the long run."

Lizzie nodded against his chest.

"I love you, Lizzie. You are the most beautiful thing that has ever come into my life."

Overcome with affection for this man who so rarely spoke of love and beauty, Lizzie slipped the gold ring from her finger and put it on his. It only fit his pinky. But there she left it, and she never saw him without it again.

Surely he valued her, surely he approved of the woman she had become. Otherwise, he would put the ring in the drawer, or conveniently lose it, or something—wouldn't he? Of course he would.

But though he loved her, Andrew would never approve of Lizzie, because Lizzie was not a boy. Andrew wanted a son so badly he named her Lizzie Andrew Borden in disappointment, for he knew that she would be his last child. He would have no son to pass the family business to, he would have no son to teach the ropes of wealth accumulation. He would have no son, and he would have no grandson, and he was bitter and resentful.

Try as she might, Lizzie would never gain her father's approval. She was guilty of far too many infractions.

Emma had never approved of Lizzie, and never would. Emma had her ideas of how Lizzie should behave at all times. Emma had *standards,* and Lizzie would never rise to meet them. They were far beyond her. Emma had been charged by their dead mother with Lizzie's upbringing, and she had taken that task so totally to heart that it had left her mirthless, ruthless and disapproving at every turn. Emma didn't have a hard heart, but her heart had cooled over years of life's disappointments.

Lizzie had neither the taste, nor the good manners, nor the good breeding that Emma thought she ought to have, nor did Lizzie have the inclination to gain the same. Lizzie loved Emma, was devoted to her, but Emma wanted a small model of their mother in Lizzie, and Lizzie clearly had little in common with their mother. And even if she had, Emma had enlarged their mother's memory to goddess proportions, so Lizzie could never match her expectations. And Lizzie, in fact, had little enough in common with Emma.

Abby Borden would never see the family resemblance to a Durfee or a Gray in Lizzie's face. Lizzie knew how terrible it must be to have to raise another woman's children, never to be able to see one's likeness in the face of a child. Abby was thirty-seven years old when she met and married Andrew

Borden, a last-minute move that saved her from the curse of spinsterhood. She was too old to begin raising another woman's children at that age; she resented Lizzie. She tried only to have Andrew's attentions *and Andrew's money,* and other than that, she paid little attention to Emma and Lizzie. She was busier with her duties as midwife's assistant, and with her young half sister, who was more like a daughter to her than the Borden girls.

Sarah Whitehead, Abby's half sister, was a year younger than Lizzie, but had made some poor choices in life; and Abby seemed to take on Sarah's life as a puzzle that must be solved once and for all. For all the good that did. Sarah continued to get herself in the family way, something that Abby had never done, something that exasperated her no end. It secretly delighted Lizzie, and openly delighted Emma. Emma gloated over every little wrong turn in poor Sarah's life.

Abby had her own interests and they did not include Lizzie.

Lizzie had only herself to please. She would claim her rightful place in the order of the Universe. She need please no one else but herself and Beatrice, for Beatrice had no preconceived expectations.

Bold, adventurous, self-assured. From now on, Lizzie would do as she pleased and hang the lot of them.

Lizzie looked out the barn window. It was a beautiful spring day. Yes. The weather had turned, and while it was still cool enough to wear a coat in the barn, soon it would be summer, and she could while the entire day away in the loft.

She wet the wicks of the candles to be sure they were out. Emma would like nothing better than for Lizzie to set fire to the barn, so she could say "I told you so" about candles in the hayloft.

Lizzie took the candles, candlesticks, scarf and book, and hid them all under the corner of the haystack.

Father would be home soon from collecting his rents, and he would have picked up the mail in town. Perhaps he would bring home a letter from Beatrice.

And then the good idea came to her. The great idea.

Why not do the second exercise three times a day like the first? And why not keep doing the first along with the second, just adding the new lessons as she went, until she was finally performing all of the lessons three times a day?

It was a wonderful idea, she agreed—and besides, what else had she to do besides iron Father's handkerchiefs?—and she sat down, uncovered her ritual implements, lit the candles, and opened the book.

aggie? Where has that Lizzie got to?"

Bridget Sullivan stopped dusting the top of the china cabinet and looked down on Emma from the top of the ladder. She wiped her forehead with the back of her hand. "I don't know, Miss. Outside, I think."

"Don't give me that exasperated look, if you please. You have plenty of work to do, so I suggest you get on with it."

Emma spun on her heel and went back to the kitchen. She looked out the window at the barn. Yes, Lizzie was undoubtedly inside. Emma was overcome with curiosity about what Lizzie could possibly be doing in there, but she hadn't asked. A million times the question had poised itself on the end of her tongue and she'd always bitten it off. She wanted Lizzie to offer the information without being asked. She wanted Lizzie to confide in her. She wanted so badly for Lizzie to be her friend that she would rather die of curiosity than have to dig the information from her little sister. At least that *had* been her attitude.

But it had gone on long enough now. Things were missing from the house, and Emma knew that Lizzie had taken them out to the barn. Lizzie seemed to be slowly moving out of the house, piece by piece—only instead of moving to someplace respectable, she had taken up residence in the barn. At least she still slept in the house, but Emma had begun to wonder about Lizzie's mind.

As she stood there, hands on the counter, looking out at the barn, she heard her father's key in the lock and the front door opened. He was back from collecting rents. Emma closed her eyes and took a deep breath. Things had gone on long enough, she thought. Best apprise Father.

Emma walked into the sitting room, where her father was going through the mail.

"Hello, Emma. There's a letter here for Lizzie."

"Father." Emma took the letter. It was from that woman in Britain. "Father, have you noticed that Lizzie is acting rather peculiar lately?"

"Hmm? No. Why?"

"She spends all her time in the barn."

"Making herself a study, she told me."

"Oh?"

"Yes. Cleaning up the place, adding a few touches, said she needed a private place to read and study. I told her I thought it was fine idea."

"Oh." Emma had more to say on the subject, but she heard Lizzie come in the kitchen door. She appeared in the sitting room doorway, flush-faced and smiling.

"Hello, Father."

"Lizzie," he said, opening another letter. Emma handed Lizzie the letter from Beatrice and left the room. She had no stomach for what the two of them did together every afternoon. Lizzie rubbing the old man's smelly feet, then reading to him and listening to his moans and groans of old age. It was revolting. It was terrible. It was unnatural.

Emma went back to the kitchen, got down the big mixing bowl and a cake of yeast. Might as well bake some bread. She stoked the fire in the wood stove and went to work.

There was more to Lizzie's oddness of late than her propensity for spending days in the barn. She seemed always to be smiling. She had stopped going to church with Father, had joined another church, which had scandalized the town, not to mention Father, and had begun teaching a Sunday school class for Chinese children, of all things. Chinese children! Where on earth did she get such an idea? Emma hadn't even known that the Chinese people could be Christians.

She heard the maid moving furniture and the ladder around in the dining room, and knew she was getting ready to clean the chandelier. That would take some time. She heard Lizzie's voice droning on in a cadence that could only mean she was reading.

Emma had time.

She untied the apron from her waist and slipped out the back door. She would see what Lizzie had been up to in the barn—something shameful, she supposed. Why else would Lizzie keep it so tightly to herself?

But the barn was locked. An old hasp and padlock that Emma remembered seeing in one of the old cartons of junk inside had been resurrected, reassembled and secured to the barn door. Emma gave the lock a shake, but it held fast. She would have given the door a kick, too, but she didn't take the time. She walked quickly back to the kitchen, where Lizzie held the screen door open for her.

At first, Emma was ashamed that she had tried to spy on Lizzie, but the smirk on her sister's face was too much to bear. "Why is the barn locked?" she demanded.

"It's no longer the barn," Lizzie said. "It's now my study. And I need my privacy."

"Privacy! Hmph." Emma shouldered her way past Lizzie and returned to her bread-baking.

"Why, what did you want out there?"

"Nothing. I just wanted to see what you'd been doing out there."

"Why didn't you ask?"

"Because you've been so obnoxiously secretive about the whole thing."

"So you waited until you thought you could spy and not get caught. Not very nice, Emma."

Emma slowly turned, willing the flush to leave her face. "I'd been hoping you'd tell me, Lizzie, but since you hadn't, I thought I ought to take a look for myself. A barn is not a proper place for a young lady to spend her days. You should be practicing your needlework. Or . . . or a thousand other chores that could be done around this house."

"Anything but keep secrets from you, right, Emma?"

"Don't get smart with me."

"You have *all* forgotten that I am an adult."

"Yes, Lizzie, I guess we have. You so rarely act like one."

"And your behavior qualifies you as a *lady?*" Lizzie's pale eyes, usually calm and peaceful, now smoked.

"I don't care to discuss it further," Emma said, her heart pounding. This was definitely new behavior for Lizzie, and Emma didn't like it. She didn't like it one bit. She turned from Lizzie and put her floured hands back into the dough.

"Well, *I* care to discuss it," Lizzie said, her arms crossed in front of her chest. She leaned up against the counter so Emma could not avoid her.

"All right, Lizzie," Emma sighed, giving up. "What is it?"

"You accuse me of secrecy, when all I want is privacy. I want to tell you that all I'm doing is fixing myself a place of my own where I can read and study undisturbed."

"What are you studying? That book from that woman?"

"Beatrice is her name. Yes. That's one of the things."

"Well, I'm sorry if my presence upsets you so. I had no idea that you needed to be so far away from me."

"It's not that," Lizzie said. "It's not *you,* although you *are* always in and out of my room."

Emma felt tears build up inside her. Nothing ever goes the way one wants it to, she thought. She shook her floured hands into the bowl, then pushed past Lizzie into the washroom, where she rinsed them in bone-achingly frigid well water. The blast of cold helped her get a firm grip on her emotions. She never wanted Lizzie to see her cry. Never. "Perhaps it would suit you if I moved." She turned and faced Lizzie again, in control.

Lizzie's face began to melt. "No, Emma, that's not what I mean, you're misunderstanding me. It's not at all what I want. You're fine. Coming in and out of my room is fine. I just want to have a place in the barn where I can go to read. Really. It's nothing about you. Nothing." Lizzie began to tremble and Emma heard the catch in her throat.

A close call, Emma thought.

"Well, all right, then, Lizzie, but I do wish you wouldn't keep it locked. Sometimes one needs to get in and out of the barn."

"Yes, Emma," Lizzie said and, head down, she walked through the dining room. Emma heard her walk quietly and slowly up the stairs to her room.

Emma found that she was trembling. Yes indeed, a change had come over Lizzie Borden. Never before would she have acted in such a manner. Imagine!

There's trouble brewing here, Emma thought. And the last thing I need in this life is trouble from Lizzie.

She went back to her bread. She could understand Lizzie's wish for privacy, a longing for a place of her own. It would be nice to have a place where she could do as she wished, without prying eyes or judgmental voices following her from room to room.

Perhaps the barn could be converted. Perhaps the old stalls could be torn down to make two studies, one upstairs for Lizzie, one downstairs for me. I could decorate it as I wished, even pounding nails into the walls to hang photographs. I could come and go as I pleased with no one knowing where I was at any particular time.

But that was the problem. Emma was needed at home, and the need in the house pulled her like taffy. She couldn't even go to the store without the tether that bound her to this house pulling tighter. This household needed her. Without her, any number of dreadful things might happen. Father would most assuredly give all his money to that Abby woman and she, knowing her financial future was set, would without doubt deed it all over to her worthless kin.

Father needed watching, too, so he did not bring scandal down upon the family. He, who was so worried about his good name being sullied about town, had the roving eye of a randy seaman. Many a time, Emma had escorted her father away from a situation he was only too eager to fall into. Why, one time, when at a church social, Andrew had been introduced to a nice-looking woman, a cousin or some other relation of one of the congregation. Andrew had stood talking with her for a short while, until the woman excused herself, and then he began to follow her around. The woman was clearly uncomfortable about it, and Emma had to step in and take Andrew's arm and escort him home before the woman began to shriek. Emma was sure it was innocent attraction on his part, but sometimes he had no common sense about him at all.

And Lizzie! If Emma wasn't there to keep close tabs on Lizzie, she might get married, or do some equally disastrous thing.

No, this house needed Emma to hold it all together. And what made her situation so miserable, was that none of them knew this, and none of them appreciated all the sacrifices she had made in their names.

Yes, Emma thought. A home of my own in the country where I could keep some laying hens and a milk goat would do me just fine. But it is not in my destiny. I must stay here and keep watch over the family.

For if I don't, who will?

I only wish Lizzie would understand. I only wish Lizzie *could* understand. But she can't. She won't. She couldn't possibly understand the kind of commitment a promise to one's dead mother means.

Emma turned the kneaded dough into a bowl liberally greased with bacon fat. She spread her towel over the top of it and set it on the shelf next to the woodstove. Then she washed her hands.

Father was still asleep on the sofa. Abby was some-where . . . out with Sarah, her twit of a half sister, no doubt. Maggie was still working on the chandelier. Emma walked through the dining room and up the front stairs. For the first time, she thought she ought to knock before opening Lizzie's door. But that was silly, and it was a precedent she didn't care to set.

She took the key from her apron pocket and opened the bedroom door. Lizzie was in her rocking chair, letter in her lap, staring out into space.

"Lizzie," Emma said. "I almost forgot to tell you. Kathryn Peters has invited you over for supper tonight. Six o'clock. I told her that you would be there, and that if you could not make it you would send a message."

Lizzie still stared into space.

"Lizzie?"

Slowly, her eyes focused on Emma.

"Lizzie, did you hear me?"

Lizzie cleared her voice. "What?"

"You're expected at Kathryn Peters' for supper tonight. Six o'clock. Are you all right?"

Lizzie looked down at the letter in her lap. "Kathryn Peters?"

109

Emma walked over to her, touched her shoulder. Lizzie quickly folded the letter and slipped it back into the envelope. "Are you all right?"

"Yes, of course. I'm fine. Six o'clock at Kathryn's. Fine. Thank you." Lizzie stared off again.

Emma unlocked her bedroom door, went in and locked the door behind her again.

Lizzie was definitely not herself lately.

Lizzie stared at the envelope in her hands. Her mind had gone numb. She couldn't concentrate on the news, she couldn't begin to fathom the ramifications, she knew only that she had to *do* something, and she had no idea what.

Stop it, she told herself, and began to rock. The familiar noise her rockers made as they chewed over the same worn spot on the wooden floor settled her nerves. Then she heard Emma's rocker, and how fast Emma rocked, and a small smile came to her lips. Emma *worked* her rocking chair.

She stood up, stretched, threw the traitorous envelope on the bed and moved around the room, waving her arms. Motion. Movement. Something had to be done here, and the first thing to do was to move around, clear her mind, and begin to formulate a plan of action.

She couldn't imagine what kind of plan she could make. The news was so startling. She was dumbfounded. Thrilled. Terrified.

She flopped down on her bed, grimacing at the sound it made. Father and Emma both had admonished her for falling like a ton of bricks onto her bed. But she heard nothing from Emma's room about it, and Father was surely still asleep. She picked up the lavender envelope and smelled it. It smelled of Britain. She opened the flap and removed the letter.

My dearest Lizbeth,
I have the most wonderful news. Father has recov-

111

ered his health enough to resume his business in most of Europe. That is good news in itself, but the better news is that his affairs have travelled as far as America, and I shall be coming over to handle things for him, as he will not be able to undergo a journey of that magnitude, at least for a couple of years. Imagine! We shall be sitting together talking and resuming our friendship on a more personal note very soon now.

I have booked passage, and will tend to Father's business in New York City and Philadelphia. When that is finished, I shall come to your town, Fall River, and spend a few days, if that is agreeable to you. I'll post a letter to let you know exactly when I shall be arriving, but I imagine it will be sometime in late July.

I can hardly wait, I am so excited. I must close now, for there are many things to be done all at once, and I am behind in my preparations. I will write a longer letter soon, and continue our discussion of the varied topics we both seem to find fascinating.

Affectionately,
Beatrice

The wording hadn't changed at the second reading, or the third. Or the fourth. Beatrice was coming to Fall River. In July! That gave Lizzie as little as three months, perhaps four, to prepare.

Goodness!

In three months, Lizzie had to lose weight, fashion a new wardrobe, do *something* with the house, with the family, catch up on her studies, read all the business books Beatrice had suggested. . . . There were too many things to be done, too many things to be done. Too many! She wasn't ready. She couldn't possibly be ready.

Hold onto yourself a moment, she thought. Beatrice loved you two years ago. She will love you now. As you are.

Lizzie's heart calmed for a moment.

But *I* don't love me as I am. Not yet. And Beatrice cannot possibly respect me when I am as slothful as a garden slug. I must make progress. I must make appreciable headway prior to July, or Beatrice will not look kindly upon me anymore; her friendship is at stake here, and I cannot afford to fail.

Lizzie squeezed her eyes tight and rubbed her fists into the sockets. "Lord, please, help make me ready!"

She sat up suddenly and pulled all the pins out of her hair. She fluffed it out with her fingers, feeling the heavy silkiness of it.

"All right, Lizbeth Borden," she said, smiling to the ends of her auburn hair. "Here's the challenge: In every way, in every thought and every deed, be the person you want Beatrice to see. *Every* thought. *Every* deed. Beginning now. Bold. Adventurous. Self-assured. Claim control of your life and *live* it. *Be* it."

So saying, Lizzie found her heart calmed, the sweat dried on the palms of her hands.

I can be ready for her by July, she thought. I will just have to work harder than I thought I would. I shall be bold, adventurous and self-assured. And I shall begin now. Tonight. At Kathryn Peters'.

She slipped the letter back into its envelope and took it to the desk. The side drawer was filled with Beatrice's letters, tied up in bundles with peach-colored ribbons purchased at the dry-goods store. Lizzie added the newest letter on the top, then closed the drawer.

She smiled. I must be bold, adventurous and self-assured about Beatrice's arrival, she thought.

And she found that she looked forward to seeing Beatrice again.

She went to the closet and threw open the door. What shall I wear to Kathryn's tonight? she wondered. Something different. But it was all the same. The same clothes in the same closet. Lizzie closed her eyes against them.

But the dark-blue shirtwaist and black skirt always flattered her figure. They were silk, and well made. She would look nice, at least in her own mind, and it was only Lizzie now that Lizzie had to please, right? Right.

She grabbed her bathrobe, then flew down cellar to her bath.

Kathryn Peters, at thirty-one years old, was just a little younger than Lizzie. Kathryn had been a classmate and friend, but she had a more outgoing nature than Lizzie, had been far more popular, and had gone on to study nursing after school. She had traveled widely and was considered as much a pillar of the small Fall River community as a spinster lady could be.

Lizzie had always enjoyed Kathryn's company. They were both members of the WCTU and they had worked on various committees together. Lizzie thought of Kathryn's shining teeth and dainty hands as she soaped the musky smell from her body.

Kathryn stood about five feet tall and could not have weighed more than one hundred pounds, all told. She fancied laces and dainty handkerchiefs, tiny hats with delicate veils, shoes so small they would fit in Lizzie's hand; and she had a small trilling giggle that leapt up the scale and charmed everyone within earshot.

Everyone in Fall River, at one time or another, wondered why Kathryn had never married. Surely she was not without her suitors, but she never seemed to take any of them seriously, and had never kept steady company with a single one.

Kathryn's mother had died when Kathryn was small, another thing she had in common with Lizzie, but then her father had died while Kathryn was away at school. She came home to manage the affairs, which did not turn out to be a substantial task, and just never returned to school. She traveled often, managed the affairs of her dead parents with admirable aggression and lived on the income her investments afforded her.

Lizzie liked Kathryn. They seemed to enjoy each other, yet there was ever present a slight tinge of wariness in their companionship, as though neither truly trusted the other.

Nevertheless, Kathryn was very good at games and, in addition, perhaps other guests had been invited. Lizzie was looking forward to the evening.

Bold, adventurous and self-assured, she thought, as she rinsed and toweled dry with the first sun-dried towel since last autumn. I wonder how Kathryn will like my new approach to life?

• • •

Kathryn answered the door dressed in a stunning wine-colored gown trimmed in black lace. A white cameo gleamed at her throat; her hair was done up with a twist and it shone in the gaslight. She even had a touch of lipstick on, Lizzie noticed, and some rouge.

Lizzie hugged her hostess, and the evening's first feeling of inadequacy came over her. If there was one thing about Kathryn that truly intimidated Lizzie, it was Kathryn's diminutive stature. Tiny, she was, almost like a fairy. Lizzie felt like a moose next to her.

Kathryn kissed her lightly on the lips, then chattered away gaily as she took Lizzie's cape and hat; the two women went into Kathryn's correctly appointed sitting room. Lizzie glanced into the dining room on her way past, and saw the table set for two. Wonderful. An intimate evening.

They shared a cup of tea and talked first about the good work the WCTU was accomplishing, then gossiped politely about some of the members. Lizzie became more and more relaxed. When Kathryn left the room to check on the progress of dinner, Lizzie had the profound realization that Kathryn had invited her to her home for no other reason than that she enjoyed Lizzie's company. There was no committee work to be done, there was not a dinner party with an odd number of guests, there was no other reason. Kathryn had invited Lizzie because she wanted to share a dinner with her.

Lizzie blushed in spite of herself and sipped her tea.

Kathryn returned and they talked of art, a subject about which Lizzie was as ignorant as Kathryn was well-versed. They talked Fall River politics for a moment, then general Fall River news and personalities, and then it was time for dinner.

Kathryn had roasted two squabs and served them with an orange sauce, small freshly-dug carrots that she'd overwintered right in the ground, and a portion of goat cheese that she'd purchased last Saturday at the market. This spawned a discussion of cooking, another thing in which Kathryn was accomplished and Lizzie not.

But the holes in Lizzie's training did not confuse her this night with holes in her personality. Kathryn's life had taken different directions, and had led her down different paths. Lizzie did not feel more or less fortunate (except in looks and body) for once. She just felt different, and for the first time, instead of dwelling on her own insufficiencies, she reveled in Kathryn's accomplishments and queried enthusiastically about her life.

After dinner (Lizzie ate her entire bird down to the bones; Kathryn barely ate half a breast), Kathryn gave Lizzie a thorough tour of her kitchen, and then her artworks, which spread about the house. Lizzie had long admired the art that hung on Kathryn's walls, but as she'd only been at the house during a meeting, she'd never had opportunity to view each one in its glory. Each painting, sketch and drawing had a little story about where it came from, the artist, and how and where Kathryn had acquired it. Lizzie was totally charmed with this little, tiny, beautiful woman and her enthusiasm.

Eventually, the tour landed them back in the sitting room, where Kathryn sat on the settee next to Lizzie.

They talked about Europe and compared notes on what they had seen in common; and as Kathryn poured a fresh cup of tea, her hand touched Lizzie's, and it stayed there.

Lizzie was surprised at how warm it was, how soft and warm, and without thinking, she took Kathryn's tiny hand in both of hers. Emma's hands were harsh and bony, Abby's hands were fat and bloated, Father's hands were horny and hairy. This little perfectly manicured hand was warm and gentle. Tender. Lizzie turned it over to look at the palm, ran a finger down the center of it, and when she looked up, Kathryn had a most peculiar look in her eyes.

The expression on Kathryn's face reminded Lizzie of days long ago when she would sit in the window seat at the farm and look out the window, dreaming of things to be when she finally became an adult. She longed to be a housewife with a dozen children. She longed to have a protector, a provider, one she could kiss and hug, one she could sleep next to on a cold night. She longed to make her own decisions and not be driven instead by a ruthless older sister, she longed . . .

That was the expression in Kathryn's eyes. Longing.

Lizzie flushed and looked again at the tiny hand she held in her own.

"Lizzie?" Kathryn spoke so softly that even in the silent room, Lizzie was not sure that she had heard. She was suddenly shy, and almost afraid. Her heart pounded louder than Kathryn's tiny word. Eventually, she looked up into that beautiful face, and Kathryn's lips were gently parted, and she moved closer and closer, until Lizzie could smell her hair as well as see right through it, and she could smell the closeness of Kathryn, freshly bathed and powdered. She could smell Kathryn's breath, warm, scented with tea and cinnamon, and then Kathryn's lips were on her own, soft, so soft.

Then she was gone, and Lizzie found her eyes closed, so she opened them, and saw Kathryn, who was flushed and laughing, both of them embarrassed, and the small hand slid out from between Lizzie's and helped the other hand hold the trembling teacup.

But that wasn't right. It wasn't something to be laughed at. It was something to be explored. Once was not enough. Lizzie had to taste that again, she had to know that feeling, that sensation that had burst upon her senses and then fled before she really knew what had happened.

She moved closer to Kathryn on the settee, feeling like an elephant trying to capture a mink. But Kathryn was all too ready to be captured, and their kiss this time was lingering and sensitive.

Lizzie's mind reeled. She could feel her pulse in her panties. She wanted to get closer to Kathryn, closer and closer still, until they were of one body.

With a hand that seemed to have a mind of its own, she pulled the pins from Kathryn's hair and fluffed it as it fell around her face.

She broke off the kiss and stared into the other woman's eyes, eyes that held love and desire. Lizzie had never seen that before in anyone's eyes and it was hypnotic. It was intoxicating. She felt overheated. She felt foolish for wearing such cold-weather clothes on such a balmy spring evening.

"You are so beautiful," Kathryn breathed, and Lizzie was sure she had heard wrong.

Again she neared Kathryn, brushing her nose along Kathryn's cheek, taking in her perfume, but their positions were not right, they were both uncomfortable on the settee, and Kathryn kissed Lizzie lightly on the lips, then stood,

118

holding her hand, and guided her through the house to the bedroom at the back.

And there, she proceeded to tenderly undress Lizzie, and then bed her, showing her the fascinating ways one woman can love another.

• • •

"Of course, discretion is all," Kathryn said quietly.

Lizzie, snuggled down in the soft, soft covers of Kathryn's bed, nodded. She couldn't take her eyes off the extraordinary profile. What Kathryn had just done to her, with her, for her, was the most amazing act of love Lizzie could ever even imagine. It was far beyond her imagination. In fact, she still couldn't believe it had happened.

The clock in the dining room chimed eleven.

"Eleven o'clock, Lizzie," Kathryn said, still staring straight ahead. Then she turned to look at her and their noses touched. "As much as I'd like you to stay, I think you'd best be going now."

Lizzie knew it was true, and reluctantly and shyly arose and dressed. She dared not meet Kathryn's eyes as she donned clothes that were wrinkled, inappropriate and too tight, knowing that Kathryn watched every move. Then she was dressed, and without knowing what to say, she just looked at Kathryn, and smiled.

Kathryn seemed old, somehow. She smiled back at Lizzie, but it was a wan smile, a tired smile. "'Bye," Lizzie said.

"'Bye."

Lizzie left by the front door and walked through the chill toward home. The night air felt fresh and wonderful. It tingled her skin with an icy touch.

A shocking wave of unreality stopped Lizzie in the middle of the road in front of the Anderson house. It couldn't have happened, she thought. It hadn't been real. It was something she had dreamed, some terrible sinful dream. It could never have happened that she and Kathryn Peters had just . . . No, never. She walked on. In the cold air of reality, what they had just experienced together seemed as foreign and as distant as her trip to Europe, or Beatrice coming. . . .

But Beatrice *is* coming, she thought, and anxiety began to pull on her.

Then she turned the corner onto Second Street, and the overwhelming brown feeling fell on her shoulders. Emma. Father. Abby. This house. This house.

She opened the front door with her key, locked all three locks once she was inside, blew out the lamp and took a candle with her up to her room.

Inside her room, her dingy, dark, boring little cell, Lizzie undressed, throwing her rumpled clothes in a pile on the floor.

She slipped under the covers and tried to believe that what had happened with Kathryn had truly happened.

It was unmistakable. Her scent was still in Lizzie's nostrils; neither the cold of the night nor the moldy stench of this house could mask that wonderful smell. The taste of her was still on Lizzie's tongue. The touch of her was still on Lizzie's skin. The memory of her rippling shudders at Lizzie's touch would never be forgotten.

Lizzie began to plan when she could see Kathryn again. Soon. Very soon. Lizzie could never bring her here, of course, but she had to see her again, soon. Very soon. Tuesday, in fact, Lizzie thought with a leap in her heart. There was a WCTU meeting on Tuesday.

●　●　●

The town hall was packed with Women's Christian Temperance Union members. Lizzie knew all the ladies present, of course—she had been a member in good standing for several years—but she felt not at all like socializing. She kept looking about for the one person she came to see. She wandered incessantly, superficially greeting other members, not friends, just acquaintances, not stopping long enough to get involved in anyone's conversation.

And then, as soon as Mrs. Tuttle had struck the lectern with her president's gavel, Lizzie saw Kathryn come in the room, lit from within with the love of life, and she laughed and chatted and made her way to a seat in the back. She looked wonderful. Lizzie felt her face flush as she watched. She wanted to sit next to her, she wanted to touch her, she wanted to see that Kathryn still liked her, admired her, *loved* her, and she needed to see that look in Kathryn's eyes.

But she was stuck. She was already at a seat in the center of the hall, and it would be a bother, and a noticeable one, to return to Kathryn's section. She would have to wait for the break.

The Reverend Buck said the opening prayer, and Mrs. Tuttle called the meeting to order. Lizzie found it hard to concentrate. She felt Kathryn's presence behind her. She wanted to turn to look to see who Kathryn was sitting next to, who she was talking to. She wanted to know what they were saying, she wanted to know what Kathryn did after Lizzie left the night before, she wanted to know what Kathryn was planning to do tonight after the meeting.

Lizzie remembered the touch of Kathryn's small fingers as they smoothed the hair from the back of Lizzie's neck, and goose pimples rose up on her arms. She smoothed them down with a shiver.

Lizzie had waited anxiously since Saturday night for this meeting. She got nothing accomplished at home. She sat around and thought about Kathryn and thought about doing her Pathways exercises. She actually got them all done, but got little out of it. She hoped she was receiving the benefit of them anyway. She could do little but think of Kathryn and her mysterious, wonderful touches in the dark. Lizzie could still taste her kiss. Lizzie could still smell her breasts.

She fidgeted through the meeting, wondering if it would ever end. Finally, she could bear it no more and stood up, made her way between the rows of benches and walked to the back of the hall. Kathryn smiled benignly at her, not giving her a second glance. Lizzie's face flushed a deep crimson, and she made her way quickly, head down, to the W.C.

She stayed in there until the break. She felt as if a knife had twisted in her stomach. Kathryn didn't even give her a personal smile. It was as if Kathryn didn't even know her. She heard the noises of voices approaching, so she patted at her hair and clothes and put on a brave face. She would seek Kathryn out one more time and see if there was perhaps a chance they could talk. Lizzie could not believe that Kathryn didn't want her. She could not imagine that Kathryn didn't feel exactly the same way she herself did. After the way they had loved each other. The way they had trusted each other.

Lizzie felt weak at the thought of it.

She pushed out through the approaching throng of women, and saw Kathryn in the hall foyer. Kathryn excused herself from talking with Margaret Reid and came over to Lizzie.

Lizzie felt immobilized by her presence. She felt her blasted face heat up again, felt her tongue tied as firmly as it had ever been.

"Lizzie!" Kathryn came and reached up for Lizzie's face, kissing her lightly on the cheek. "Nine o'clock," she whispered in Lizzie's ear. Then she stepped back and said, "How are you?"

Lizzie caught on quickly. "Fine. You look wonderful, Kathryn."

"Thank you." Then Kathryn saw someone else, and flitted away.

Lizzie had always envied that ability to flit at a social gathering, and her spirits soared at the thought that what she first assumed was a snub was in reality nothing more than mere discretion.

And discretion was all, just as Kathryn had said.

Nine o'clock! Lizzie tore her eyes away from her lover, reluctantly, and wondered how she would ever pass the time until she was able to hold Kathryn again.

She made small talk here and there among the crowd, then slipped out the door just before the meeting was reconvened. She walked around the town in the rapidly growing dusk, then finally went home, agitated and restless. She went directly to her room, where she freshened up, changed her clothes and paced.

At eight-thirty, the minute hand began to crawl ever more slowly. Finally it was eight-forty-five, and Lizzie left the house, walking briskly through town toward Kathryn's.

By the time she arrived, her breath was coming hard from the exertion and again she vowed to take a little more fresh air and exercise, so as to be a little more appealing to Kathryn and a little less fleshy.

She knocked on the door, and it opened almost immediately.

"Come in quickly," Kathryn said. "Did anyone see you come?"

"No," Lizzie said, and then Kathryn's mouth was upon hers, and her hands were inside her clothing. It was not gentle, it was not loving, but Lizzie felt the overwhelming need as much as Kathryn did. She returned the hard embrace, the brutal kisses, and her knees failed her. They tumbled to the ground together, groping, tasting, ripping, their passions too great to be withstood any longer.

Lizzie was quite overwhelmed. It was everything she had dreamed of, and more. They rolled along the floor, biting and pulling at each other's clothes until they were down to their drawers. Kathryn jumped up and grabbed Lizzie by the hand; they ran to the bedroom, where a candle had been lit and the bed turned down, and climbed beneath the cool covers. The break in momentum seemed to settle them both down, although Lizzie's breath still came hard and fast. When Kathryn slipped into bed next to her, Lizzie saw the longing again on her face. She drank in that look. It was something she never wanted to forget.

Later, as they lay in Kathryn's spacious bed, in her large, well-appointed bedroom, Kathryn said, "I shall pretend not to know you well, you know."

Lizzie nodded, wondering at the feeling of this house. This house was really little larger than her own, and there was certainly no more furniture. But the air was spacious. There was tranquillity in this house; it could be felt in the wallpaper, in the carpeting, in the chandeliers.

The wallpaper, carpeting and chandeliers at the Borden house were dingy somehow, close and suffocating.

Kathryn's house was cool and gracious. Lizzie's house was stale and cramped.

Lizzie felt that she could even walk naked through Kathryn's house, but the thought of even *being* naked in her own home made her feel shame.

"If I were wealthy," Kathryn said, "I'd buy a sailing ship and go to Africa."

"But you *are* wealthy."

Kathryn laughed at the ceiling. "I am comfortable, Lizzie. I am not wealthy. No. I would sell this terrible house and sail for the Dark Continent and find a man to hunt elephants with. And I would drink rye whiskey and smoke cigars. Seduce native girls."

Lizzie turned in astonishment and looked at Kathryn's profile. It suddenly occurred to her that she didn't know Kathryn very well at all . . . there need be no pretending involved.

124

"What about you?"

"I'd buy a larger house, here in Fall River. On the Hill. I'd have dinner parties. I'd train to New York regularly to the theater. And I'd give a large share to the WCTU."

"The WCTU?"

"Yes, of course."

"You really believe liquor is evil?"

"I don't think liquor is evil; I think that people under the influence of liquor do evil things."

"I think liquor is lovely."

"But you're on the committee . . ."

"Oh, Lizzie. It's just a social organization."

Lizzie was stunned. "It's not!"

Kathryn still had not turned her head to look at Lizzie. She kept her eyes fixed firmly on the ceiling.

"Are you telling me that you don't believe in the work the WCTU is doing?"

"Oh, I suppose I must. I mean, the way liquor is available today, I'm sure I can't quite argue with the WCTU."

"But you've been a member for years."

"I know. That means nothing. Have you ever taken a drink, Lizzie?"

"Never."

"Would you like one?"

"No! And I'd like it if we never discussed it again."

"Well. I should think you would be in the mood to try some new and different things. I mean"—Kathryn turned and looked at Lizzie's breast, then touched her nipple. It instantly shrank—"you seemed to take to certain other things that were new and different." Kathryn looked up at Lizzie. "They *were* new and different, weren't they?"

"Oh yes," Lizzie breathed, her fire rekindling.

"Good. Then let us have a brandy."

"No," Lizzie said, and pulled the covers up to her chin.

"Why, Lizzie, what is it about a little drink?"

"It's no good, Kathryn. It makes people do things . . . terrible things."

"Suit yourself," Kathryn said, then climbed out of bed naked, picked a shirt from a hook in her closet, and walked out of the room.

Suddenly, Lizzie felt like a stranger. She didn't know if she'd offended Kathryn, she didn't know if Kathryn was coming back to bed, she didn't know if Kathryn would even like her after her comments on alcohol. It was clear that Kathryn found no harm in moderate imbibing; perhaps Lizzie was taking the WCTU issue too much to heart.

She slipped out of bed, took a robe that was far too small for her and walked into the living room.

Kathryn was looking at a magazine, a brandy in her hand.

"I'll have one too, if you don't mind," Lizzie said.

"Would you?" Kathryn raised an eyebrow.

"I think so."

"Well, good for you, Lizzie. The bottle is in the kitchen. Snifters are in the china cabinet."

Lizzie took a delicate glass from the china cabinet and poured a dollop of brandy into the bottom of it. Something had been lost with Kathryn during the course of this conversation, and she wasn't sure what, nor was she sure if she could fix it. She only knew that she was eager to fix it, desperately eager.

"Kathryn?"

"Hmm?"

"Will you care for me if this drinking goes badly?"

Kathryn laughed. "You have barely enough in that glass to wet your tongue, Lizzie. I have already had three times that much, and do I look like a raving lunatic to you?"

"No, of course not," Lizzie said, and smelled the liquor. It smelled rich and dark, sweet and bold. Bold. Bold, adventurous and self-assured. Lizzie wet her lip with it, then licked it off. It tasted just the way it smelled. She sipped a tiny bit, then saw that Kathryn was studying her with a critical look on her face. She took a larger swallow and felt the warmth slide down her throat and spread out in her stomach. "That's rather nice," she said.

Kathryn laughed. "Oh, Lizzie," she said. "We have much work to do on you."

· May

ou should have seen her, Lizzie." Emma's insides were burning as she paced back and forth in Lizzie's tiny bedroom. "She was as phony as a two-dollar bill. 'Oooh, Oooh.'" Emma tried to mimic Abby in a high-pitched whine. "'All my money is missing. All my jew-ells.' I don't think I need to tell *you* who orchestrated that little robbery. *Or* who she's going to pin it on."

"Emma," Lizzie said, "you can't possibly think that Abby is going to blame you?"

Emma looked at Lizzie, sitting calmly in her rocking chair. Sometimes the girl could be so thickheaded. "That's exactly what I *do* think, Lizzie. They're trying to make life unbearable for me here. They think that sooner or later I'll leave, and then they'll be able to do as they damned well please around here with no thought to anybody's troubles but their own. Well," she said, growing ever more agitated by the moment, "they won't have it their way. They won't." Emma stopped pacing and stood quietly next to Lizzie's door. She could remember only Abby's eyes, filled with accusation when Emma went up the stairs to her bedroom to find out what had upset her so much. Accusing eyes. Accusing eyes.

Emma felt Lizzie's hand on her wrist. Lizzie pulled her hand away from her mouth and Emma saw blood on her knuckles.

"Your mouth is bleeding, Emma," Lizzie said. "You were

rubbing your lips again with your knuckles. Come. Sit over here. You've got to learn how to calm down."

"Calm down?" The concept was ludicrous. "Calm down? Lizzie, they're likely to have me arrested."

"It could as easily have been me, Emma, or Maggie. Lord knows she didn't have much worth stealing."

"That's the point." Emma blotted her bleeding lips with a cloth Lizzie handed her. Her knuckles were cut as well. "Who would want her ratty things? Not me. Not you. I'm sure Maggie has dusted her cheap jewelry every day for two years and has so far resisted temptation. Why would she suddenly take a shine to tarnished rhinestones?"

"How much money did she say was taken?"

"I think ten dollars."

"Ten dollars! That's quite a sum to be leaving about."

"Her emergency money, to hear her tell it. She says it was in her dresser drawer. Hidden. Said the thief had to have looked through her drawers to find it. But nothing looked ransacked to me. Everything looked normal. And only certain pieces of jewelry were missing, too. It's not like the thief took the entire jewelry box."

"I wonder . . ."

"Wonder! Wonder? I don't wonder, Lizzie, and I am astonished that you would. Abby probably threw away that ugly old jewelry and gave the ten to her stupid half sister. And I am going to take all the blame." Emma felt like squeezing something. She squeezed and twisted that cloth that Lizzie gave her until it hurt her hands. She wanted to rip and tear, but she couldn't rip that cloth, and besides, squeezing, hurting, killing something living, something small and furry would be far more satisfying.

"Have you looked in your room?"

"My room?"

"Yes, Emma—if Abby is trying to blame you for the

burglary, then perhaps she put the missing items in your room."

Emma jumped up and went into her room. She looked in each drawer, under the bed, in the closet. There was no evidence that anyone had been in her room. She went back to Lizzie's. "You'd better search your room as well, Lizzie." Lizzie began to open her drawers and root about in them. "Although, you know, I don't believe either Abby or Father has a key to our rooms."

"Oh, I'm sure Father has. Leastways, Maggie does."

"Maggie. I believe we should talk to Maggie. I'll do it."

Emma went down the stairs and found Bridget stirring and seasoning the stew for supper.

"Maggie!"

"My name is Bridget, if you please, Miss Emma."

"Yes, of course. Did Mrs. Borden talk to you about her missing jewelry and money?"

"Yes, she did."

"Did she accuse you?"

Bridget's eyes grew large. "No, of course not, miss. Why . . . of course not."

"Did she let on who she suspected?"

"It were a robbery, miss. It were a burglary."

"So someone from the outside?"

"Must have been."

"The doors were locked. You and I were home."

"I . . ." Emma saw understanding cross the maid's face. "I dunno, miss." She turned back to her stirring.

"Have you seen Mr. Borden?"

"He isn't home yet."

"And Mrs. Borden?"

"She's out at present."

Emma turned on her heel and stomped through the dining room. She could hear the rockers on Lizzie's chair. She went up the stairs and into Lizzie's room. "Well," she said. "She didn't accuse Maggie. And now she's gone out. I don't imagine she'll be back until after Father gets home. He'll come home and she'll come home right after him, take him aside, tell him all, accuse me and then sit in her corner sniveling to herself while he has the dirty work of proving his daughter innocent."

"I think you're taking this a bit too far, Emma," Lizzie said.

Emma fixed Lizzie with a stare. "Mark my words," she said, then walked into her bedroom and closed the door. And she began to pace. She would hear Father at the door. She would run down to talk to him before Abby had a chance.

No, that would be falling down to Abby's level of politics. No, let Father come to her with his accusation. She would meet him face to face. She would deny it all and there would be no proof, especially since Abby herself was the culprit.

Emma's lips began to hurt and she stopped pacing and looked at her hands. There was blood again on her knuckles. A bad habit, she thought. I must stop doing that.

Within the half hour, the front door opened. Emma jumped up from where she was sitting stonily in her chair. She opened the door to Lizzie's room and exchanged a glance with Lizzie. "Don't lie on your bed with your clothes on, Lizzie," she said automatically, then opened Lizzie's door and went out, without closing the door behind her. She descended the staircase and found Andrew Borden in the sitting room, shuffling through the mail.

"Father," Emma said.

"Hello, Emma."

"Father, have you spoken with Abby?"

"Not since this morning. Why?"

"It seems she's had a few things missing from her bedroom."

"Missing? Misplaced?"

"Stolen."

"Stolen? Stolen! Has she informed the police?"

"I think not, Father. I think she has a notion that I burgled the jewelry and some money."

"You? Well, that's nonsense. Surely she was upset at the time . . ."

Emma looked him straight in the eye.

"I'll speak with her. Is she home?"

They both heard the screen door in the kitchen slam. They heard Abby's voice as she spoke with the maid. Emma's face began a slow burn. She felt the flush come up from somewhere in her chest and burn its way up her throat to her cheeks. The tips of her ears felt on fire.

"Abby?" Andrew's voice was lower with concern.

Abby came into the room, taking off the sweater she had worn to town. "Hello."

"Abby, Emma tells me you've been missing some items."

"Yes, Mr. Borden. In fact, some pieces of jewelry were missing from my jewelry box this morning. And the ten dollars I keep on hand for emergency purposes."

"When was the last time you looked at that money?"

"Oh, mustn't have been but a week or so, I saw that it was in its place. And the jewelry, well, I wore the necklace yesterday."

"Have you a thought about it?"

"No sir, I haven't a clue. Emma and Bridget were home all day yesterday, and the bedroom door was kept locked as always."

"Have you spoken with Maggie and Lizzie?"

"With the maid, Bridget, yes sir. With Lizzie, no. She was not yet up when I left the house."

Andrew turned to Emma. "Is Lizzie here?"

"Here, Father." Lizzie rounded the corner. Emma knew she'd been standing on the stairs listening.

"Lizzie, do you know of some items missing from your mother's dresser drawer and jewelry case?"

"No, Father. Not except what Emma has told me."

"You were here all day yesterday? You didn't go out at all?"

"I was here."

"And you saw nothing, heard nothing that would lead you to believe that there was another person in the house?"

Lizzie shook her head, then looked at Emma. Emma looked away.

"And the maid was here all day? And Emma?"

"Emma was in and out, Father."

Andrew looked at his wife. "We should fetch the police, Abby. If there's been a robbery, then it ought to be reported. Perhaps the police . . . But how the deuce was it done? The bedroom door is always locked. The front door is triple locked, the kitchen screen is always latched. Could someone come in through the outside cellar door?"

"Padlocked," Lizzie said.

"Yes. Hmm." Andrew rubbed his chin, then fingered the pipe in his pocket. He was anxious for a smoke. "Perhaps after supper," he said, "perhaps we'll go for the police." And he went out and lit his pipe on the back porch.

Abby went up to her room.

"See, Emma? Nobody is accusing you."

"She is," Emma said. "She is."

Lizzie gave an exasperated sigh and flounced out of the room. A moment later, Emma heard the kitchen screen slam again as Lizzie either went to the barn, or went outside to sit with her father as he enjoyed his pipe. Either way, Emma was left alone to stew. She picked up the newspaper that her father had brought, and sat on the settee in the sitting room. Her eyes scanned the print, but she read nothing. She listened to the sounds about her.

Maggie was baking biscuits to accompany the evening

meal. Abby had retired to her bedroom to rest, probably, after her excursion to town.

A few minutes later, the screen slammed again, and Emma heard Andrew tell Maggie to fetch the police. She replied something that Emma could not hear, then the door slammed again. Emma jumped up and went to the kitchen.

"Here, Emma," Andrew said. "Maggie needs someone to watch the biscuits so they don't burn."

"You sent her for the police?"

"Of course. A robbery's been committed."

"They'll accuse me, Father."

"Why you?"

"Because *she*'ll tell them that I was the one who did it."

"Emma, I think you're going a little bit too far here."

"I know who did it, Father. She did. Abby did. She threw her old jewels away and gave the tenner to her stupid Sarah and now she wants to blame it on me."

"I think I've heard enough, Emma."

His loyalty to that fat woman infuriated Emma. Her hysteria reached a new pitch. "She wants me out of here, Father, can't you see that? Can't you see what she's doing to this family?"

Andrew frowned.

"Maybe I *should* move. Maybe that would just make everybody happy. Maybe I should just move out and leave you all to your own wicked devices. Nobody appreciates the things I do around this house anyway. Maybe I should just die."

"Maybe we should go sit down for a spell, Emma." Andrew took Emma's elbow. She ripped away from his touch.

"Don't touch me! You're on her side. You're *all* on her side!" Tears choked her and she hefted her skirts and ran for her bedroom.

Lizzie hadn't locked her bedroom door, and Emma's was still standing open. Emma ran through, slamming both doors behind her, and threw herself onto her bed. She could hear the springs creak beneath her as she heaved and sobbed. It was true, she thought. Father never once tried to correct her. Her thinking was perfectly accurate. The hurt seared like a hot poker.

Why doesn't anyone ever follow me, to try to console me? Nobody cares. Nobody cares.

Her wailing masked the sounds of her father's heavy footsteps on the front stairs. He walked through Lizzie's bedroom and laid a soft knock on Emma's door. "Emma?"

Emma jumped when she heard him. He rarely came to her bedroom; in fact, she couldn't remember the last time she had seen him in here. She swiped at the tears on her face and the moisture running from her nose.

"Emma, something has happened. Please come downstairs."

Something has happened? Emma remembered hearing the kitchen door slam twice. Once, she assumed, was Maggie, returning from her excursion to notify the police of the robbery. And the other . . . the policeman. Lizzie. Her head hurt.

She stood up, shook out her clothes, patted her hair, splashed her face in the basin of cool water, and went downstairs.

The family was in the dining room. Andrew sat at his place at the head of the table . . . in fact everyone was in their eating seat, even the maid, yet there was no food on the table. The stew smelled lovely, and so did the biscuits, but there was no food on the table.

In front of Lizzie was a dirty, rusted meat tin. And inside it were some dollar bills and Abby's missing jewelry.

Emma slipped into the room and sat at her seat.

Andrew cleared his throat.

"Now that we're all present, Lizzie, suppose you tell us about this."

"I found it in the barn," Lizzie said simply.

"Where in the barn?"

"In the storage area. Sitting on top of a box. Out in the open. I noticed it first thing as I walked in."

"And has the barn been locked?"

"No, sir, not since Emma asked me to leave it open."

Emma gasped. It was as if Lizzie had stabbed her.

"Do you know anything of this matter, Lizzie?"

Lizzie took a long time in answering. Emma saw a curious look cross her face. Her brow wrinkled and her eyes lost focus for a moment, an odd response to quite a straightforward question, Emma thought, but then it was quite an odd situation. "No, sir, I do not."

"Maggie?"

"No, sir. I know nothing."

"Emma?"

"I've already told you, Father."

"A simple yes or no will suffice, Emma."

"No, Father. I know nothing of the matter." She looked at Abby, who failed to meet her gaze. "Nothing," she spat at the woman's downcast eyes.

"Abby?"

"I can't imagine how they got to the barn, Mr. Borden. It's as if . . ."

"As if what? Finish your sentence."

"Well," she said, "if someone had wanted the money and the jewelry, they would have taken them away. This is . . . this is more like someone just took them for the . . ."

"Sport," Andrew finished.

Abby nodded, her eyes again on the hands in her lap.

Tension mounted. It was clearly Andrew's turn to speak, and yet he gave no sign of knowing what to say.

Then a knock came at the front door.

"Oh my," Abby said. "The police."

Everybody stood up and went to the front door. Andrew opened it and greeted the uniformed officer.

"Thank you for coming," he said, "but I'm afraid there's been a mistake. The money and jewelry have been recovered; it seems as though this was a simple case of misplacement."

"I see," said the officer, and took out his little notebook and began to write.

"So thank you anyway." Andrew seemed nervous. "I'm sorry you've had to make a trip out here for nothing."

"Nothing to worry about, Mr. Borden. Good day."

Andrew closed the door, but not before he saw Mrs. Churchill, the nosy next-door neighbor, looking over her fence. He turned and faced his family. He cleared his throat.

"An incident like this need never happen again," he said. "And we need never speak of this one, either. Understood?"

Everyone nodded.

"Dinner will be served in ten minutes," Bridget said, and everyone dispersed to their private corners of the house.

izzie went back down for supper, out of curiosity more than anything else. She was so sick of Emma and the whole family drama, but this stealing of Abby's property was really strange. Even for Emma.

So she went back down for supper, in hopes of thinking of something besides the pain she felt as her heart was breaking. The pain over Kathryn's behavior toward her was so great when she was alone that at times she couldn't tell where the pain ended and she began.

The tin with Abby's found property had been removed from the table. Slowly, the family members gathered and had their meal together, an uncommon occurrence. Perhaps we are brought together at this time because we are such an odd family, Lizzie thought. Other families come together as a matter of course, and split apart over petty inconsistencies and discourtesies. Our family comes together only when one or another of us is under grave suspicion. Grave suspicion and heartache.

The meal progressed in silence. No one besides Lizzie had much of an appetite. Lizzie threw bread in her mouth as fast as she could swallow. She spread it heavily with salted butter and had extra portions of meat. Somehow she hoped that the hollow that Kathryn had opened in her stomach could be filled with food. She knew that all eyes were upon her. Abby began to eat a little after watching her, but Emma and her father ate almost nothing.

After supper, Lizzie lolled about a bit in the kitchen,

wanting nothing in particular. She didn't want to be in her room, she didn't want to talk with anyone, she didn't want to eat any more, she didn't want anything, except Kathryn. And Kathryn, it appeared, didn't want her anymore. Every time she thought it, she wanted to scream. Finally, when Emma shooed her out of the way for the third time, she went out to the barn. She opened the barn door and breathed deeply of its familiar smell. She looked at the piles of junk, looked at the box where the tin of booty had been found. Why on earth would someone do something so strange? It could only have been Emma. It could *only* have been Emma. Lizzie felt mildly guilty for thinking that, but Emma really was the only one who could be responsible for such a bizarre act.

Lizzie climbed the ladder to the loft. She crossed over and looked out the dusty window. From this vantage point she could see the side of the house and Second Street beyond. I'll have to bring a little box up here so I can sit and look out this window, she thought. It was a nice view, and a private one. Someone might see her looking wistfully out her bedroom window at the street below, but no one would catch her gazing out the window of the hayloft. Lizzie felt quite invisible.

She turned back to her study area, pulled *Pathways* from its hiding place under some hay, dusted it off and set it on the little table. Then she took her seat between the table and the haystack and contemplated the ritual she was about to undertake.

Lesson three was a meditation "to empower each of the individual selves which make up one's personality. We take them each in turn in order to know them, understand them, trust them, then enlist them in our endeavors. Only in this way can we align them purposefully toward our goals." And then there was a list of "selves." Lizzie was to take each in turn, spend as much time with each one as she felt she

141

needed in order to convince it that it should not work at cross-purposes in her life. The list included the Angry Self, the Greedy Self, the Jealous Self, the Slothful Self, the Prideful Self, the Lustful Self, the Gluttonous Self, the Higher Self, the Healthful Self and the Whole Self.

She had tried to visualize the Angry Self, but hadn't had much luck. Sometimes she imagined she saw that face in the mirror, that distorted picture she saw when she did the exercise with the candles, the face with the vacant eyes. But it seemed to swim in and out of focus, and she could never enlist her Angry Self in conversation the way she supposed she was to do.

She opened the book to the first lesson, but the book was heavy and her heart heavier. She didn't have much enthusiasm for her studies. She felt leaden, cast aside.

But she tried. As always, she began by thinking about Beatrice and her impending arrival. The thought of it always made Lizzie's heart beat a little faster, there was so much to accomplish between now and then, and the days just kept flying by and Lizzie just could not see enough progress to feel good about herself. She felt squeezed, and that was what kept her coming to the hayloft three times a day to do her lessons and her reading and wonder why she kept eating like a hog when she *knew* she had to take some pounds off before Beatrice arrived. And oh God, how she had just eaten! She felt as tight as a tick.

Even Kathryn had made a comment. Lizzie had gotten used to Emma's snide remarks—Emma, who was always as thin as a rail, and looked hooked because of it, was always making remarks about Lizzie's heftiness—but then Kathryn said something of the same just two nights ago.

Lizzie had sat up in Kathryn's bed and asked her if she had something to eat in the house. Some sort of a snack. Their lovemaking always left Lizzie ravenous. Usually, she would go home and paw through the pantry, but this time she thought it might be fun to see what Kathryn, the gourmet cook, had on hand for snacks.

"I can tell you have quite a sweet tooth, Lizzie," Kathryn said. "No, we don't eat between meals here."

Lizzie had flushed deeply and felt quite odd for the rest of the evening. And had gone home and eaten far more than she ever had, and far more than she should. And she ate extra portions the next day as well, knowing all the while that she shouldn't, she really shouldn't. She *really* shouldn't.

And then it happened the very next night, last night. She wandered about the house listlessly, feeling blue and bored for no particular reason, and decided that what she needed was an evening with a good friend. She wanted to see Kathryn, not to bed Kathryn necessarily, but to spend some time with a good friend. She was sick to death of Emma and her whining.

So she went over to Kathryn's house and Kathryn answered the door in the same burgundy-colored dress she'd worn on Lizzie's first dinner there. "Not *tonight,* Lizzie," she said, and Lizzie heard the sound of company in Kathryn's front room. She looked at Kathryn's face, not understanding, and Kathryn rolled her eyes and said, "I have company, Lizzie," and then she shut the door.

Lizzie stood there, stunned. And then she had stepped over the flower bed that bordered the walk and looked in the front room window. Kathryn had returned to her guest, Cynthia Miller.

Cynthia Miller!

Lizzie could not believe her eyes, but Kathryn was definitely sitting too close to Cynthia for it to be a casual evening together.

Lizzie felt dirty. Used. Cheated. Abandoned.

She went home and ate everything she could find. Then she went down cellar and scrubbed every inch of her body. Then, upstairs, she took all the clothes she had ever worn to

Kathryn's and put them in the laundry. They were soiled. She was soiled, and no amount of scrubbing could wash away the sins of the flesh she had committed at the behest of that woman.

Lizzie lay back against the haystack. She should be starting her lessons, but her mind was on Kathryn now, and she couldn't quite let her go.

She should have seen it coming. Kathryn had gotten less tender and loving as the weeks went on. Could it possibly have been only two months ago, when they first began keeping such close company? Only two months since Kathryn had been so attentive? She had come to ignore Lizzie for long stretches of time, always keeping Lizzie off balance. Lizzie had never been in control of the relationship, not from the start, and Kathryn's power over her was a powerful distraction. A distraction during a time when she needed no distractions. She had work to do. She had lots of work to do on herself. Lizzie knew it, Emma knew it, Beatrice knew it, and Kathryn knew it. Kathryn, in fact, never let her forget it.

Kathryn had become quick to find Lizzie's faults. She had become snippy at times, and snubbed Lizzie when in public. Lizzie knew that Kathryn must keep up appearances, but there were times when a friendly, affectionate smile in public would not be construed as more than that, a friendly smile. But Kathryn seemed to use "discretion" as an excuse to ignore Lizzie, give her uppity looks, look at her and then giggle with the other women . . . and Lizzie hadn't cared for that at all.

There was a place within Lizzie that knew Kathryn wasn't a very nice person. That place inside Lizzie wished she had broken it off with Kathryn first. It would have been so much easier.

But the rest of Lizzie screamed in pain. Where on earth would she ever find another lover, someone who knew

Lizzie's secret places even better than Lizzie knew them? How could she *ever* find another lover?

She never would. She would never again feel the softness of lips on her own. She would never feel that shuddering urgency. She would never stroke another tender breast. She would never feel another's hands deeply tangled in her hair, or awake to find a leg thrown over her own.

Lizzie caught herself up, sat straight and rubbed her face. No, she thought. That will never happen again. I was misled. It was sinful. It will never happen again.

She opened the book to the first lesson and began to read aloud, but the picture that came to her mind was that of Kathryn Peters, someone who took advantage of her, someone who didn't return the affection Lizzie endowed, someone who was secretive and dishonest (a drinker!), someone who was just not . . . quite . . . right.

Lizzie sat back, the lesson forgotten. I'm acting like a lovesick teenager, she thought, with little patience. What exactly did I want from this affair? What did I expect? Respectability? Marriage?

Something in her heart turned over as she realized that now she would never marry. How could she, after being so intimate with another woman? She was a freak. She would never have children. She would never move out of this house, not until Andrew died, and probably not until Andrew and Abby both died. She would never move in with another woman, she would never have such an affair with another woman—she would never have a man suitor that she could take seriously, not after . . . not after Kathryn.

Kathryn made it very clear to her the kind of lovers men made. They were rough and insensitive—not so very unlike Kathryn herself at times—and selfish. Kathryn talked a lot about how men bedded women, which always put Lizzie off. It seemed as though Kathryn had had a lot of men in her travels. And while Lizzie had never been very interested in men, they had always seemed a last-resort means of getting out of the Borden house and out from under the oppressive eye of the family.

And now that could never be.

The loss of her dreams flattened Lizzie to the haystack. She gazed up at the cobwebs in the rafters and felt her heart beating, felt her pulse at the top of her head.

I'm no longer respectable in any sense of the word, she thought. Worse, I could be a terrible embarrassment to the family—and where would I be without them?

Her gaze settled on the blue sky out the window, then drifted down toward the little table and the *Pathways* book.

Beatrice made the world the way she wanted it to be. All I need to do is follow instructions. All I need to do is what I'm told to do. She picked up the book and hugged it to her, tears of frustration and heartsickness leaking out the corners of her eyes.

I don't think I'm capable, she thought. I don't think I *can* lose weight, become bolder, more adventurous, more self-assured. I am not bold. I am not adventurous, I am not self-assured. I am not in control of my life. Can this really turn me into something I long to be, but am not?

She opened the book at random and ran her finger down the broad lines of type. A little circle of heat waves blurred her vision right in the center.

Lizzie felt all the wind go out of her sails. A headache was coming on. She sat there, immobilized by her impotence. She knew she should get up and get down the ladder, into the house, and into the dark, cool bedroom before she was unable to do those things. She had perhaps ten minutes to prepare for the pain, because once the pain came, there was only the pain, the all-consuming pain. The pain and the vomiting and more pain.

Instead, she sat there, lying back into the haystack, feeling the crinkle of the dusty hay beneath her, feeling the little pieces of it poke her, feeling the soft cover of the book, watching the little swirly parts of the headache precursor.

And then she remembered taking the jewelry from Abby's dresser. And the money from the drawer.

She sat up, her breath caught in her chest. No, no, it was impossible, it was wrong, how could she . . . *why* would she . . .

She quickly hid the book under the corner of the haystack, pushed the table up against the wall underneath the window. She climbed as rapidly as she dared, her sight unsteady, down the ladder. Then she stepped gingerly across the junk-strewn floor to the barn door.

All the while she remembered. She could see herself, her hand as it took the bedroom key from the mantel, as she walked up the back stairs and opened the bedroom door. She saw herself pick up the jewelry and go directly to the drawer that held Abby's emergency fund. Lizzie had seen her take money from that envelope a thousand times when she was a little girl. It was no secret, that envelope. She took it all, tightly clenched in her fist, and she went to the barn.

Lizzie could remember it all, she could see it all, but as the circle of wavy lines receded past her vision, the pounding pain began to fade in. She stopped in the kitchen and put both hands up to her forehead. "Please stop," she whined. "Please."

But the migraine was relentless, and it increased a thousandfold in intensity. Weak-kneed, Lizzie made it to the stairs, then very gently, she climbed the stairs, her hands on both walls of the stairwell for balance.

She fumbled at the lock on her door, entered, pulled the blind and the curtains, slipped out of her clothes, put the chamber pot in a handy place in case she needed it quickly, brought the towel from the washbasin over, and slipped, wearing only her drawers, between the cool sheets.

The headache seemed to subside for a moment while she

moved with purpose. She got into bed, and had time for only one more thought. How strange that she could remember—barely remember—taking the jewelry and the money, but she could *not* remember why.

S ometimes Andrew Borden wished his whole damned family would just go away and leave him alone. This was one of those times. Usually, he prayed for peace under his roof—"the peace of the Lord," as he liked to put it. He prayed for the peace of the Lord to be within Emma, Abby and Lizzie. He would have liked nothing better than to come home from work, have Lizzie rub his feet and read to him, then sleep, awaken to a well-cooked and palatable meal, then relax with fine humor with his family. But his prayers hadn't been answered for some twenty-five years now, and the only prayer left to him was that they would just all go away and leave him alone. Sometimes he even included Lizzie in that prayer.

But this prayer was not likely to be answered, either. And in addition, there was no peace of the Lord in Andrew, either. Too many other matters pressed on his mind these days.

The mill had not been as profitable as it should have been in the past three quarters. Costs were up, income was barely holding, and it was up to Andrew to effect a management change. That was to be a time-consuming job, finding replacement personnel, especially if he had to handle the reins himself while he found the new managers.

Lizzie was acting queer again, spending all her days in the barn and all her nights out somewhere with God only knew who. When questioned, Lizzie professed quite convincing innocence. Kathryn Peters, she said, always volunteered her

149

home for WCTU committee work. That's where Lizzie could be found most nights, she said, and Andrew had no call to disbelieve her. But now she went out almost every night. Andrew didn't approve of outside interests that required someone's attention every night. There were family matters that needed attention. The home. The home came first.

But Andrew had learned that his daughters were headstrong and had almost outgrown caring about his dissatisfactions. He learned to save his criticism for important issues. They knew very well where he stood on family propriety, and he had to trust in their judgment, even though none of them had ever shown him very good judgment in any matter whatsoever.

Like Lizzie and this barn business. It was downright peculiar. He'd been out there to Lizzie's hayloft study, and seen nothing out of bounds, but just because the eye doesn't see something doesn't mean that there isn't trouble under the surface.

He was still trying to find the time of a Sunday morning to fake explanations to all the parishioners who asked about Lizzie's sudden change of churches. That was a slap in the face to all Bordens, but she didn't seem to give it a second thought. They all dressed in their Sunday clothes, left the house at the same time, but Lizzie turned right on Second Street, and Andrew and Emma and Abby (when she had a mind to go) turned left. It infuriated him every week, that she would go *down*town, to worship with the Polish and the Italians and those uppity Hill people, instead of *up*town, with the Anglos as was proper for a Borden. And to teach the Chinese! Heathens!

He just didn't have the time to think about it all. He didn't have time for the guilt, either. It was his badgering that made Lizzie change churches. He knew that as well as he knew his own name, but he didn't know what he could do about it. There didn't seem to be anything he *could* do. It made him more than furious. It hurt him. It gave him chest pains.

And then fancy Emma stealing Abby's jewelry and her ten dollars. That was just so strange as to set Andrew's head spinning. Being in business the way he was, he was used to personality conflicts among employees, used to backbiting, petty jealousies and even violent outbreaks. But this stealing of the jewelry and money and putting it into an old, rusty meat tin and leaving it in the barn was just too bloody strange. It verged on the incomprehensible.

Emma did it, of course Emma had done it, she protested too loudly not to have done it.

And Andrew was in the middle of it all again, for Abby had his ear on the pillow at night and she talked far into the night about the girls. He was beginning to believe that he was indeed too old to deal with such pettiness, and if Lizzie had to go with Emma in order to get Emma out of the house, then perhaps that would be the best idea of all.

But his heart clenched as he thought it.

And then, *and then* there was the Widow Crawford.

Every time he thought of her petite form, her tiny little nose, her reddish hair graying at the sides, her upturned face with the sparkle in the eye and the ready smile for him, all thoughts of his family fled, and he felt a stirring within. She was a delightful woman, very respectable, with two big strapping sons, both off to college. She worked for the law firm that handled the bank's work, and Andrew found that he frequented the law firm personally as a courier just to bask in her very special smile.

From the very beginning, he seethed with plans for a tryst, almost every waking moment. He thought of suggesting that they meet for lunch, and then his day would be confused, the daydreams of the two of them gazing into each other's eyes, of discreet electrifying touches of their finger-tips at just the right moments, conflicting with the business decisions at hand.

But the daydream would only go so far. People would see them together in public, and as they had no common interest, other than each other, it would not be proper for a married man to be seen with a widow lady.

So then he thought of calling on her at her home one night, just knocking on the door. She would answer the door wearing a chaste, yet playful smile, and he would enter her chamber of pleasures and be kept a willing prisoner there for a week.

But he would never go to her home without an invitation, and she was far too proper to issue one.

He could invite her away. He could be inconvenienced, and ask that she meet him with important papers. They could meet for coffee in a public place, and as he looked over the papers in a law-firm folio, no one could possibly suspect anything but business was being carried out.

But his office was only blocks from hers, and both firms employed couriers.

Try as he might, Andrew Borden could find no way to approach this woman of his dreams, except by frequenting her place of employment, which he did at every opportunity.

And when he did show up, she brightened. He could see it.

And then the miracle happened.

Two days after the affair of Abby's missing property, Andrew stopped by the law office to sign some papers, and Mrs. Crawford halted his heart with a tiny, soft hand on his wrist.

"Mr. Borden?"

His mouth went dry. He looked into those sparkling eyes that appeared as if they had never taken anything seriously.

"Please excuse me for being so bold, but I am quite beside myself. I am truly at my wits' end."

"What is it?"

"My brother's family needs me to tend the children for the weekend—they live out south—and I haven't a way to get there. I wonder if I could press upon your kindness to see if you could loan me a rig and a driver. I should be very happy to pay."

Andrew's heart flew. "Of course," he said. "When would you be wanting to go?"

"Friday after work. It's only about an hour's drive. My sister-in-law has been ill, you see, and they need to travel to a doctor in New Bedford, and I'm the only kin . . ."

"What time shall I pick you up?"

"Oh, Mr. Borden, I couldn't possibly intrude on your generosity this way. Surely you must have a driver . . ."

"I would be honored, Mrs. Crawford. In fact, I have business out that way on Saturday. I'll just move it to Friday and be done with it."

"I would be ever so grateful," she said, and it looked to Andrew as if she meant it.

Andrew finished his business in the law office with a trembling hand. Then he said good-bye and left, chiding himself all the way back to the bank for acting like a foolish schoolboy.

And the buckboard had torn leather on the seat, too. Perhaps it could be fixed before Friday.

Suddenly, problems of the household vanished. Andrew lived for Friday. He only prayed that a runaway carriage would not strike him down, not when he was about to embark upon the hour-long excursion that would bring him true joy at last.

He had married Abby as a convenience for both of them, but neither one was very interested in nocturnal bedtime activities. At first, Andrew could not forget the soft feel of

Sarah's skin beneath him, and the glimpses he caught of fat Abby in her dressing gown put him right off. They had pretended a couple of times, Andrew always careful to spend his seed into the sheets and not his wife. He had no use for more children. But after those first halting tries, Andrew could tell that Abby was not impressed with the physical side of marriage, and he was not very interested in her as a partner, so they slept side by side every night and never again discussed it.

But never had he forgotten the feel of Sarah Borden, her smooth, cool white flesh under his fingers, her long lines, unintimidated, her abandon in their bedroom.

And now, for the first time, old sparks were rekindled when he looked into the joy-loving eyes of the Widow Crawford, and it was almost more than Andrew could hope for, but he did indeed hope that she would raise her skirts for him, at least once.

At least once. And perhaps on Friday.

On Friday, Andrew was up before dawn. He carefully bathed, shaved and donned fresh clothes. He viewed himself critically in the mirror, wondering if any woman anywhere could ever find him attractive. It was doubtful. He milled about in the kitchen until Abby got up, and then he was short with her and irritated by her behavior. He mentioned that he would be home late, perhaps very late, and then he left for the office.

But work came hard. Concentration was impossible. At ten o'clock, he went to the stable to inspect the new leather. The boy had done a fine job. The springs were freshly greased, the tack oiled, and he made sure the boy would shine up the horse in fine fashion before he came round to take the rig at five o'clock sharp.

Five o'clock! It seemed that five o'clock would never arrive.

154

But arrive it did, and Andrew helped the Widow Crawford up onto the seat next to him; he snapped the reins, feeling young and reckless, and they were on their way out of town.

At first, he was loath to say anything, feeling that perhaps his pleasure, his eagerness, would show through and put her off. But once out of town, she opened up and began chatting away. She pulled a shawl from her valise, and moved over a little closer to him when she resettled in her seat, and they talked of Fall River and common acquaintances.

Andrew found out she knew and liked Lizzie very much. Lizzie had just joined Mrs. Crawford's—Enid's—church, and was becoming a well-respected member of the congregation very rapidly.

Andrew made a mental note to visit that church someday.

As the conversation carried on, this way and that, Enid found reason to touch him, his arm, his knee, his wrist, and each time she did, a thrill ran up his spine and shuddered at the base of his skull. He could never get enough of this woman, he knew for certain.

And then she, bold as brass, suggested they pull off on a little side road so they could get out and stretch their legs.

Andrew pulled the horse up short and guided him into a small meadow. He jumped down, ran around and helped her down, and she lingered just a tad in his arms before looking down and moving away. Andrew secured the buckboard and uncoupled the horse's reins so he could eat while they walked.

They walked a ways, the shadows of spring falling long and cool over the emerald-green grass, little white and yellow wildflowers everywhere. And then Enid spread her shawl on the grass and sat upon it. "Sit with me for a while, won't you, Andrew?" Then she looked down, and said, "May I call you Andrew?"

Andrew almost fell on her, he sat down so quickly. She moved toward him, and put her hand on his cheek. Then she lifted his hand and placed it on her breast.

"You're a very compelling man, Andrew," she breathed.

"Miss Enid," he said, and then his voice failed him, for she was moving toward him in a different way, and there was no doubt at all about her purpose.

He took her, and almost without pause, took her again. He felt like a little stallion. Never, not even with Sarah, not even when he was young, had the experience been so wild for him. The smells of the meadow mixed with the scent of her perfume; the rustle of her skirts as they shifted beneath him (she wore no underwear at all!) the heat of his passion on his back, but the cool of the evening on his buttocks. And she moved beneath him like an untamed thing, quite out of control. He had never imagined someone could make sounds like that—so animal, so wonderful!

And when he was finished, and had rearranged himself, she sat up and smoothed her hair and said, "My, my."

He averted his eyes while she borrowed his hankie, then he helped her up and shook out her shawl. Then he helped her back into the buggy, suddenly shy and quite embarrassed about his—their—behavior.

They rode on for a little while, and then she spoke. "Mr. Borden?"

He noticed that "Andrew" had gone by the wayside.

"Yes, Mrs. Crawford?"

"My two boys are in college up in Boston, you know."

"Yes, so I understand."

"They're doing very well."

"You must be proud."

"I am, I am, but you know, Mr. Borden, college is terribly expensive."

Anger shot through Andrew and his face flushed. He wanted to dump her right here on the side of the road. But he looked over, and it was the same sweet face he had admired for so long, and their coupling had been so intense, so severe, so indescribably *sweet* . . . "Yes?"

"I thought perhaps you could loan me a little money for their tuition." She looked up at him and smiled. Bold as brass, that little woman.

"How much would you be wanting?"

"Oh, not much at all, Mr. Borden, not much at all. You see, I make a fair wage at the law firm, and there is still money left from their father, but . . . say one hundred dollars? Perhaps I could get it from you *next* Friday?"

And then Andrew understood. She would meet with him next Friday for one hundred dollars. And the next. And the next. But one *hundred* dollars! He maintained his entire household on half that much for a whole month! He looked over at her, sitting there, so attractive. *So* attractive. She could have chosen any man at all, yet she chose him. There was no harm in helping a nice widow lady put her sons through college. "I'd be delighted to help the boys, Mrs. Crawford. What are their names again?"

"Chester and Charles. Thank you ever so much, Mr. Borden," she said, and she laid a hand very lightly upon his knee.

Andrew felt himself stir again at her touch, and he looked across at her profile. She was smiling, the tiniest little smile. He could barely wait for next Friday.

And as regularly as clockwork, Andrew Borden took Mrs. Crawford for a ride on Friday afternoons. He discovered that little else mattered in his life. Mrs. Crawford, Lizzie and little else.

bby awoke to hear only the pounding of her heart in her ears. Paralyzed with an unnamed fear, she opened her eyes barely a slit. She saw the outlines of the furniture in her room, vaguely illuminated by the small amount of moonlight that drifted through the lace curtains. She listened.

Hearing nothing but the silence of the sleeping house, she moved, gently at first, so that if an intruder were to see her, he would merely think she was turning in her sleep. She turned over, stretched, then opened her eyes once again. Nothing. There was nothing there.

Nothing but a feeling, a feeling of dread, of doom, of menace. Abby tried to calm herself. There was nothing.

Gradually, her heartbeat returned to normal, but sleep had flown. Abby looked at the clock on Andrew's nightstand. Two-forty.

She heard a horse clop down the street. The milkman.

The feeling of dread had been ever present in the past month or so. Andrew had a mistress, she could tell, and she seemed to have him quite bound up. She was afraid of losing him as a husband, she was afraid of losing him as provider, she was afraid that the good Borden name would be scandalized by he who professed to worry so much about the integrity of the same name.

He met her on Friday evenings, only on Fridays, and every Friday.

Andrew seemed oblivious of all the goings-on at the

house. He came and went, ate, slept, read, spoke as if he were in some sort of dream state. His most common phrase was "That's fine," and he said that automatically, without even hearing what the girls or she said to him.

It worried Abby mightily.

But it did more than worry Abby, it left her to run the household by herself, and her power as head of the household was nil as far as the girls went, and very little as far as the maid. It was a frustrating situation, all right, and the pantry and icebox were Abby's only solace.

Then a shadow moved across the wall. The room was dark, but there was a place that was darker than dark, and it moved.

Abby's heart hammered. There *is* someone in here. It's the someone who took my jewelry, come back to rob us again. He's here to kill us all, some business acquaintance of Andrew's, no doubt. She tried to be still, not to give away to the person or persons that she was awake and aware of his presence, but her heart beat so fast that she could not breathe. She opened her mouth and took in small breaths, trying desperately to look asleep.

But then there were no sounds, and surely she would be able to hear an intruder's step or breath, but there was nothing. Abby squinted her eyes up tight and rolled over onto her side, facing her husband. She pulled the covers up over her head. I'll just let them be, she decided. If they want to rob me, that's fine, they won't be the first. If they want to kill me as I lie in my bed, well then, that's fine, too. I just pray they make it quick.

But no hand came to touch her, and she heard the sound of no intruder. She said a little prayer, even though she only half believed, and then her mind wandered again to her husband's neglect of the fatherly chores in the house and her heart began to pump again, only this time in anger.

I'm too old to live in a house where everybody hates me,

159

she thought. Emma hates me, Lizzie sides with Emma, and Andrew has a lover. If he wants to take a lover, that's fine with me, but why should I have to put up with that *and* those girls as well?

Just then, Abby heard Lizzie's bedsprings creak, and the sound of the chamber pot scraping across the floor. She waited for the sounds of vomiting, but they didn't come.

Abby relaxed. Her heart went out to poor Lizzie with those blasted headaches. She had tried everything, but there was nothing to be done for them, nothing but a quiet, dark room and sometimes a cool cloth for the forehead. Poor Lizzie. She suffered so. Since her teens, she'd been plagued with those terrible headaches, headaches that made her vomit all day and half the night.

Abby could be angry at Lizzie, but she could never hate her, not the way she sometimes hated Emma for the foolish way Emma acted. And a grown woman at that! Emma was a fool, a greedy, money-hungry fool, whose penchant for rages made her highly undesirable as an acquaintance, never mind a stepdaughter!

But Lizzie, sweet Lizzie.

Abby listened as the bedpan was pushed under the bed again. It wasn't a headache for Lizzie tonight. Thank the gods for that. She'd had quite a group of them lately. Maybe four or five in the past two weeks. Every time, Abby had wanted to do something for Lizzie—she used to buy toys with the household money for Lizzie when she was sick. Even when she was a young woman, just beginning this terrible life with headaches, Abby always found a few pennies to spend on a treat for Lizzie.

But now, there was nothing to be done when the headaches struck, nothing but to tiptoe around the house, reminding Emma and Bridget, *always* reminding Bridget, to keep the noise level down so Lizzie could rest. And Abby never brought a toy nor a treat. Abby's mothering instincts had begun to fade in the shadow of the abuse she'd been receiving from Emma. And Lizzie, by association.

Abby settled back into her bed, the fear of the dark shadows gone, the anger at Andrew gone, the worry over Lizzie having another headache gone. All that was left was that creeping feeling of doom.

It had been intensifying lately, that feeling. That terrible feeling that something was about to happen. The present status could not remain so for very much longer; everyone seemed to be strung just a little bit too tight. And when people are just a little too close, just a little too crowded, well, things begin to happen.

Like jewelry and money disappearing and reappearing in the barn.

A shiver ran through Abby. It was such a violation, that little robbery. It was such a slap in the face by some member of this household. On that day she almost gave the ultimatum to Andrew: We move or they move. But the tensions had eased some after that, and of course, there had been no repeat offense, nor had Abby any reason to think there would be. The point, whatever it was, had apparently been made.

And yet, the thought of the robbery was somehow inseparable from this feeling of dread that she had, this moving black shadow that was just a little darker than the dark, when nothing was there. The robbery was an omen, she thought, of terrible things to come, and if she were a real wife, and a real mother, she would *insist* that Andrew take her out of this house and save them all from themselves.

But she was not a real wife, and Andrew knew that, and she was not a real mother, and both Emma and Lizzie knew that.

So she would make do, as she always had, spending her time with Sarah and her many troubles, and the occasional birthing that came along in her little circle of acquaintances, and she would hope that when the end came, whatever it might be, it would be swift and sure, silent and without warning.

hen Lizzie woke up, Emma was already in trouble. Emma was headed for New Bedford.

The day began as normal, with Emma fighting life so hard it reduced her to stringy tendons and a cruel mouth. Emma fought with her clothes, her bureau drawers, her father, her stepmother, her breakfast, the maid.

Lizzie watched it all, listening, knowing that Emma was about to lose control. She knew the signs; after all these years, Lizzie knew the signs.

So when Emma threw her silverware on the floor, kicked at it until it skittled out of reach, and then ran upstairs—all this provoked by something innocuous that their father had said—Lizzie knew that New Bedford was not far away.

And sure enough, Emma appeared in the dining-room doorway in less than a half hour, wearing her traveling hat and carrying her valise.

Abby continued with her breakfast, Andrew read the morning paper. Neither one of them seemed to care that Emma was off to further her destruction at the hands of unknowns. Lizzie alone flew to Emma's side, her heart breaking in the midst of her pain over Kathryn. She felt as if she were drowning in emotional vapors.

But Emma would not be persuaded to stay. "I need some fresh air," she said, "some fresh scenery. I shan't be but a couple of weeks, Lizzie," and she shook off Lizzie's begging and went out the front door.

Lizzie's heart died. One of these days, Emma would be

unable to crawl back home to lick her wounds. One of these days, Emma would tangle with someone a little too rough, and be unable to crawl back home, ever.

The familiar box of worry closed around Lizzie, and she knew that it would not open until Emma came home. She knew that she was bound now to be thinking of Emma and praying for Emma day after day after day, leaving little room for study or housework or reading or preparing for Beatrice's visit or anything else. Where there had been mourning for Kathryn, there now was worry for Emma.

Lizzie watched Emma walk down the street, her back as straight as their father's, the little black plume on her hat bouncing with each step. Emma always timed it for that nine o'clock train to New Bedford.

Lizzie thought if she had any gumption at all, she'd run and pack herself a bag and follow Emma. Then she could find out where Emma went, and keep an eye on her so that she didn't get into too much trouble.

Next time, she thought with a pang of guilt. There is too much to do right now. I cannot afford to take two or three weeks baby-sitting Emma while she drinks herself half to death in New Bedford. After Beatrice's visit, when everything settles back down to normal, then I shall accompany Emma on one of her excursions and see that she takes care.

But Lizzie knew that that day would never come. She had to invent that lie, like thousands before it, to plug up the guilt before it flooded her.

She wandered back to the dining room and sat in her place. Her breakfast was cold, but she ate the soggy biscuits in cold gravy anyway.

"So Emma has gone to New Bedford again, has she?"

Lizzie looked at her father and nodded.

"Don't know what gets into that girl," he said. "Seems like she just looks for an excuse to go. Who does she visit there, again?"

"I don't know, Father."

"Well, I hope she doesn't come home sick this time. I was afraid she'd put the whole household in their beds the last time."

Lizzie chewed slowly, wondering how she could hate her father so much for his lack of feeling toward her sister, and for so many other things, yet love him so desperately and want to please him so thoroughly. She should tell him the truth about Emma, but that would accomplish nothing. Unfortunately, that would accomplish nothing. She kept on eating. Abby remained silent.

After breakfast, Lizzie went back upstairs to her room, undressed and slipped back into bed. She lay there, feeling slightly ashamed of her laziness, but the load of ironing, and the lessons, and the mending just weren't her cup of tea today. She fingered the worn lace on the edge of the pillowslips and idly wondered why Abby didn't have all the pillowslips in the house replaced with fresh ones. Surely there was enough money to sleep on decent linen!

Then she looked toward Emma's bedroom door. The days were long past when Lizzie used to go into Emma's bedroom and try on her clothes and get into her things, but for once, Lizzie was mildly curious about Emma's room. Were there things in there that Emma hid? Was there alcohol? Did Emma drink here at home? Lizzie turned over on her back. No, of course not. If Emma drank at home, they would smell it on her and she would have no need to go to New Bedford.

New Bedford. It was strange to Lizzie that Emma would have secrets from her much the way she had her Kathryn secret to hide from Emma. Emma would have a seizure if she knew the pleasures that Lizzie and Kathryn enjoyed in each other's arms. But then Emma enjoyed some pleasures of her own, didn't she? Some pleasures of some sort at the Capitol Hotel in New Bedford.

Pleasures Lizzie *used* to enjoy in Kathryn's arms. She flopped over onto her stomach and punched her fists up under the pillow. We should have a cat, she thought. It would be nice to have a cat to sleep on the bed, a cat to purr and cuddle with. . . . When I have my own home, I will have a cat.

And then the idea that came was so perfect, so logical, it startled her. *Why not now?* I could move into my own house, and it could be near enough that I could keep an eye on Emma. I don't have to have a house on the Hill—not yet anyway, there are some fine houses here in town, houses of which Father would approve, and he could either give me the money for one or invest in one on his own.

That would be so much different than if Father just gave Emma her inheritance money and told her to get out. Father had been wanting to do that for months now, perhaps years. If I had a house that was large enough for Emma and I, perhaps I could induce her to move in with me.

Lizzie jumped out of bed, her heart pounding in excitement for the first time in weeks. She had an idea, a wonderful idea, and Father was sure to go along.

She dressed carefully, did her hair up just right, smoothed down her eyebrows, made her bed—she wanted to be adult and serene around him, and didn't know if she could with her bed unmade—and then she sat for a moment, composing herself and quietly asking the God of all her selves to help her. Then she slowly descended the stairs.

Andrew was at the desk in the sitting room, going over some ledgers.

"Father?"

"Lizzie."

"Father, may we talk for a moment?"

"Certainly." Andrew finished jotting a note, then put his pen down and turned in his chair.

Lizzie sat on the edge of the sofa. It would be so much

easier if he were sitting next to me, she thought. "Do you remember some time ago—last winter—the last time Emma went to New Bedford, in fact—when you talked about giving Emma her money and having her move out?"

Andrew looked at his shoes. "Yes."

"Well, I have another idea."

Andrew's eyebrows went up.

"Come sit next to me." She patted the seat. He sat next to her. She took his hand in hers.

"If you gave me the money, I could buy a small house—"

"Never."

"Wait, you didn't let me finish."

Andrew withdrew his hand from hers. "Very well," he said. "Finish."

"I can barely speak when you have that attitude, Father."

"Don't you be talking about my attitude, Lizzie."

This was not going right. Lizzie took a deep breath. "Father? Let's start over again. I have an idea, and I'd like you to hear it." She placed her hand over his, but he didn't move a muscle. Be bold, be adventurous, but most of all, be self-assured, Lizzie, she thought. "I was thinking of another investment property for you. Another little house, here in town. A modest house. I could move in there and encourage Emma to join me. I could be close enough to keep an eye on her in case she decided to stay here, or I could even move back in here, for that matter. But, Father, I believe she would come. That would leave you and Mother here in peace, and I could watch out for Emma during her more trying times. We'd take care of each other."

Andrew was silent. Lizzie took that as a good sign.

"We could live very cheaply, Father. The house and a small allowance is all we would need . . ." She twisted her high school ring, which was still firmly on his little finger. Then she looked up into his face and saw his eyes were red and watery. Why was he crying? What made him cry? She

167

was struck quite speechless, and then tears came to her own eyes.

Whatever it was, they both let go of each other's hands in embarrassment, and they both rose at the same time, and Lizzie headed for the front stairs while Andrew went toward the rear stairs. Not another word was said.

In her room, Lizzie wondered why she'd bothered to make the bed. All she wanted to do was to get in it and cry herself to sleep. She flopped down on top of the bedspread, closed her eyes and was suddenly a little girl again, safe, with a dark-haired father and a lanky big sister, on the banks of a fresh stream, with her little fishing stick in the water.

It was midafternoon when she arose, hunger motivating her. She poured tepid water from the pitcher into the bowl and splashed her face. At least she hadn't bawled, that would have made her eyes intolerably puffy for a day and a half. She dried her face and checked her looks in the mirror. As she straightened the bed, a soft knock came at her bedroom door.

"Miss Lizzie?" It was the maid.

Lizzie walked to the door, unlocked it, then returned to the mirror. "Come in, Maggie."

Bridget entered and handed Lizzie a folded piece of white paper.

"What's this?"

"A note from a lady. She stopped by and I told her you were sleeping."

Heart leaping, Lizzie unfolded the note. "Lizzie— Dinner? Six. Kathryn." She felt a flush come to her face, felt the smile grow into a grin. Then she noticed the young maid was still standing before her.

"Not bad news, I take it, miss?"

"No, it's good—well, it's a dinner invitation," Lizzie said, trying to regain control of her composure. "Thank you."

168

"Quite all right, miss," Bridget said lightly, then turned on her heel, red curls bouncing behind her as she tripped delicately down the stairs.

The dread of family embarrassment again fell upon Lizzie. What if that wench, that flippant little Irish girl, knew, or even suspected Lizzie's involvement with Kathryn? That would give her power. That would give her terrible power.

Lizzie sat in her rocking chair and thought about that, her heart thumping, knowing she would see Kathryn again tonight. For dinner! That meant a positive, intimate experience. . . . Lizzie had avoided meetings and anywhere she thought she might run into Kathryn because she was afraid that Kathryn would spit upon her once and for all, and Lizzie could never live through that.

And now, dinner!

And that Maggie thing most likely knows too much. That insipid little housemaid could bring the wrath of Fall River down upon the Bordens. She could ruin Father's reputation, she could ruin Lizzie's standing in the community and in church. She could do much to throw the entire family into scandal—especially since she knew, or at least suspected, the nature of Emma's "illnesses" upon her return from New Bedford.

Lizzie would talk to Father about giving the girl a raise in pay. That might seal her fidelity.

Lizzie went down to the kitchen and began rooting around for something to eat. Her stomach was filled with jittery butterflies, thinking of dining with Kathryn. There were things between them that should be discussed.

She took a loaf of bread from the pantry and sliced off two thick slices.

What kind of things should be discussed?

She spread salted butter heavily on both slices, then covered that with Abby's plum preserves.

The things that upset you, Lizzie, she told herself, and the bread stuck in her throat.

She poured a large glass of fresh milk and washed down the bread.

Yes, she thought. Those things must be discussed.

She looked out the window at the barn. Her lessons awaited her, Beatrice's arrival demanded her attention, but there was no concentrating on them. This day would have to be devoted to two things: Approaching Andrew on a raise for Maggie, and talking things over with Kathryn.

Neither one provided much comfort, so Lizzie hunted around until she found the plate of cookies Abby had stashed in the tea tin, and set them before her.

* * *

Lizzie rubbed Andrew's feet as was her custom, and then she asked him to give Maggie a raise in pay. He started, and looked at her peculiarly, but he did not say no. Lizzie smiled at him while she made him comfortable, then read to him until he was asleep for his afternoon nap. Then she dashed upstairs to clean up and make ready for the coming evening.

* * *

Lizzie was so excited to see Kathryn that even though she noticed the fancy carriage outside Kathryn's house, it didn't register that Kathryn might have others for dinner besides her.

Kathryn answered the door wearing a beautiful pale-green chiffon. After the door was closed, she kissed Lizzie gently on the lips, and then danced out of the way as Lizzie leaned into the kiss, wanting it to last longer, more, taste deeper. Kathryn laughed and teased, and led Lizzie into the living room, where two men rose to meet her.

Lizzie flushed crimson and looked with questioning eyes

at Kathryn, but Kathryn only twinkled at her and introduced the gentlemen. From Boston. Scott Carrothers and Matthew Green. They were both wearing fine suits, and it was then that Lizzie upbraided herself for not noticing that the carriage was *directly* in front of Kathryn's house, exactly where it should be if the owners were inside.

She mumbled her greetings to them, then rushed to help Kathryn in the kitchen.

"Men?" was all that came out of her mouth.

"You'll love them, Lizzie," Kathryn said. "They're like us." And then she swept back into the living room, carrying a tray of small glasses filled with sherry.

The bearded man, Scott his name was, stood and held his glass aloft. "A toast," he said, and they all took their glasses. "To love and life and fine company."

"Hear, hear," the other man said, the small man, and the three of them drained half their glasses, but Lizzie barely put hers to her lips. She still was not certain if she approved of anyone drinking anything at all, much less members of the WCTU.

The evening progressed, Lizzie on the sidelines. She was caught up in the love of life that drove her three companions for the evening, and yet she wondered if any of the neighbors would see that two unmarried ladies were accompanied by two unmarried men, unchaperoned. That would bring a terrible scandal upon the Borden name. She also wondered what Kathryn meant when she said that the men were "just like us." No matter how she put herself and Kathryn side by side with these two jocular and entertaining men, she could see no similarities.

They tried with unmuffled earnestness to include Lizzie in their gaiety, yet they were careful to tread lightly enough not to embarrass her or put her off. She was impressed with their sensitivity. Kathryn seemed to be bold, almost brazen, in her laughter with these men, and it seemed to Lizzie that they must be old friends indeed. In fact much of their humor revolved around old times together.

Kathryn served wine in the parlor and then a fabulous feast that seemed to require less than little time in the kitchen and in serving it. Lizzie, beginning to be dazzled by the intelligent rapport between the men and Kathryn, was astonished at how easily Kathryn tossed off this little dinner party. There was no tension; her absences from the room to tend to culinary matters were rarely excused and almost entirely unnoticed. And she served a fine pheasant, with roasted potatoes and early lima beans swimming in butter.

The Borden household had never, ever seen such a table.

And there was brandy afterward. Lizzie had sipped wine throughout the meal, but had not attributed her warm and growing affection for her dinner companions to the wine. After Kathryn had swept through the dining room and cleared the dishes, the men invited Lizzie back to the sitting room for a brandy. And she accepted.

"Have you ever been to Boston, Lizzie?"

"Infrequently," she said, taking a sip and loving the deep flavor.

"You must come up for the weekend. You and Kathryn. We would show you such a wonderful time. Have you been to the theater?"

"No."

"Well, my dear, we have theaters—granted, they're not like New York, but still they're professional and very, very good—and sometimes we are even invited to attend the cast parties afterwards, aren't we, Scott?"

"Yes, indeed, Lizzie," Scott said, relaxing against the back of the sofa. "In fact, you and Kathryn should come to Boston and we'll go to New York, the four of us, and see some real theater!"

Lizzie flushed. What an exciting idea, to spend a weekend

with Kathryn in New York City! But then wouldn't Father be scandalized, especially if word should ever get back to him that they were accompanied—unchaperoned—by a pair of gentlemen.

"Ooh, Scott," Matthew said, "we could stay at the Carlton. Remember the first time we stayed at the Carlton?"

"Indeed," Scott said, and a look passed between them that mystified Lizzie. And then Scott put his hand on Matthew's knee and squeezed it, and Lizzie understood *exactly* what Kathryn meant, and she thought for a moment she would lose her dinner right here in the sitting room.

Her face flushed, she stood, and unsteadily set her glass of brandy on the side table. Then she hurried to the kitchen, where Kathryn was stacking up the soiled dishes.

"Kathryn," Lizzie breathed. "Those men are . . ."

"Are what, darling?"

Good breeding failed Lizzie. She knew of no names for what she wanted to say.

"In love with each other? Yes, they are. Scott and Matthew have been lovers for over five years now. They met and fell in love in college."

Five years. Lizzie thought of herself in another five years. She would be thirty-seven years old, and still chasing after rainbows. She would never be any closer to having the kind of money or independence she so desperately wanted. The walls of the kitchen began to close in on her.

And then the other thought occurred to her. What do men do to each other when they're lovers? Whatever it was, it sounded terribly distasteful, especially if they were as rough and as selfish as Kathryn had always maintained. But just enough sherry, wine and brandy made Lizzie a little giddy, and she didn't know if she would laugh at her thought or perhaps be sick because of it.

But Kathryn hustled her back into the sitting room, and there they sat and talked, Lizzie mostly silent, watching the two men, the thought of their hands on each other's naked bodies quite sickening. And soon they rose, said their thank-yous, kissed both Kathryn and Lizzie lightly on the cheek, and then they were gone.

Kathryn collapsed on the sofa. "Pour me a sherry, will you, Lizzie? That's a good girl."

Lizzie poured one for each of them, then sat next to Kathryn. They both sipped their wine.

"Aren't they rocking good sports?"

"I guess so."

Kathryn sat up and looked Lizzie in the face. "You guess so—didn't you enjoy their company?"

"I did," Lizzie said, "but they made me a bit uncomfortable, I guess."

"Uncomfortable how?"

"Well, we were unchaperoned—"

Kathryn let out a hoot. "A lady could never be safer than with those two, Lizzie."

Lizzie's face burned. "And that, too, made me a feel a little strange."

"Why? They're like us."

Lizzie didn't care for the comparison at all. People like that were a certain way, and Kathryn wasn't that way, and neither was she. But she couldn't quite put her finger on what way that was, so she didn't mention it.

Kathryn turned Lizzie's head with a gentle finger and kissed her lightly on the lips. "The night is yet early. . . ."

And Lizzie rose and pulled Kathryn along with her. Then they ran for the bedroom, disrobing and giggling like a couple of high school girls until they were again in each other's hot and passionate embrace, and Lizzie felt as if she'd come home. Home at last.

Later, Lizzie told Kathryn what the men had said about their going to join them in Boston or in New York, and

Kathryn had screamed in laughter. "What a fabulous idea," she said. "Being out on the town with those two men would be a terrible lot of fun. We certainly *must* do that sometime, Lizzie. Perhaps after the heat of the summer has passed."

Lizzie agreed. After the heat of the summer, she would go to the theater with these three odd people. Sometime after Beatrice had come and gone, after she had lost enough weight so that her gowns would fit her again, after her father had lost his mind and let her go to New York unchaperoned with Kathryn and two men.

And she lay entwined with Kathryn, thinking it was time she got home, and she wondered if Scott and Matthew were at that very moment making their strange brand of love, or lying abed with their legs entwined, talking about Lizzie and Kathryn.

"Lizzie?"

"Hmmm?"

"I had a dream about you."

"Oh?"

"I dreamed you had split into two people. In my dream, you were here with me, but somehow you were pacing back and forth in your house. It occurred to me that when you are here, you are either wishing you were home or worried that you ought to be home, that our activities here will be found out about your family."

"I feel sometimes—"

"Let me finish. And also in this dream, while you were with me here, like this, and you were also at home, you were in two places at your house, as well. You were in your bedroom upstairs, sleeping, but you were also pacing the floor, walking into the others' rooms and pacing back and forth by their beds."

"I've been worried about Emma."

Kathryn was silent.

"And Cynthia Miller," Lizzie added.

Kathryn said nothing, just reached over and squeezed Lizzie's hand.

It was clear that there would be no comfort or reassurance forthcoming from Kathryn.

And it was not until Lizzie was at home, in bed, reliving the events of the evening, that she remembered, ever so vaguely, that at times she *was* at home in bed . . . *and* pacing the floor at the foot of her father's bed at the same time.

June

Emma lay in bed, her head pounding, her body aching. She slowly, painfully turned on her side and saw the breakfast tray that Lizzie had brought, still on the bedstand. The thought of food nauseated her, yet she knew she should eat. She needed the strength. She needed lots of strength just to heal.

With a thin, trembling hand, Emma grasped the side of the mattress and pulled herself into something like a sitting position. Then she reached out and took a cold piece of toast that had been spread with jam. It looked awful. She took a bite, then another. It tasted as sour as her breath. She put the toast back, swallowed with difficulty, then slid back beneath the covers.

Her arms looked stringy and pale, and a large, round bruise puffed on one shoulder.

She was afraid to look into a mirror.

She'd been home from New Bedford for a week, and still she was hardly able to move. Since undressing with Lizzie's help and getting into bed, she hadn't been up yet, except to urinate some dark, foul-smelling stuff into the slops pail. Her hair felt greasy and her scalp itched. Her teeth were furred and the bleached and sun-dried sheets rasped her sensitive skin.

"I'll never go back there," she said softly to herself. "This was the worst. This time I mean it. I'll never go back." And yet, deep in her heart, she knew that she was as likely to stop herself, once she was riding high on the fury that was her mother's legacy, as she was likely to stop a slow-moving freight train. The lunacy was beyond her control.

She always went to New Bedford with agitated anticipation. She began to drink alone in her room and then she would suddenly "wake up" and find herself in some tavern or other, some loud, boisterous woman's voice coming from her lips. Sometimes she would "come awake" back in her hotel room, and sometimes she would awaken again in someone else's hotel room or house, and sometimes she would awaken and there would be many people around her. And each time she would have no knowledge of where she was, nor memory of how she got there. But a little more liquor seemed to soothe the stomach-clenching fear of being out of control. And it wouldn't be long before she awakened again somewhere else, in some further state of disrepair.

But somehow, it always came back to the same thing. Somehow, she always found someone to beat her. Always.

Maybe a trip to New Bedford wasn't really a trip to New Bedford without being beaten silly, she thought with a wry grin that hurt her head. Or, more likely, the trip wasn't over until she could barely walk, what with being sick half to death from a two- or three-week binge, not to mention the physical damage done to her by person or persons unknown.

This time was the worst by far. She'd awakened in her hotel room, dried blood smeared on her sheets and pillowcases. She'd dressed somehow, covering her face with her darkest veil. She called down to the front desk and the bellman had helped her down and into a cab. Then the cabbie had helped her onto the train, where she was afraid she would fall senseless and miss her stop. Another cabbie brought her home and half carried her up the walk, until Lizzie could help her up the stairs and into bed. She hated all that help, but there was no way she could have made it on her own. She would have fallen. She would have died.

At least this time she wasn't bleeding, except from a few

scrapes on her face, knees and hip. There had been times when she had bled, not her monthly bleeding, but from the same place. One time in particular it had gone on and on and on, for more than a month. She knew without being told that permanent damage had happened inside.

Perhaps that's why she never ended up in trouble, because surely during those times, men had . . .

She knew they had. At first she had been able to pretend that it hadn't happened, but as time went on, the evidence was all around her that men, faceless men, had taken advantage of her in her inebriated state. And yet, she could not remember it. She could not remember a single instance. Apparently, it only happened when she was "gone away from herself," as she referred to those vacant periods, those lapses in her memory during her drinking.

At first, her face burned with the thought of her behavior during times she could not be aware of, those times when she had no control over herself. But as time went on and lack of control over the trips to New Bedford increased, the fact that she was continually sexually molested by blurry-faced men in dark rooms was lost in the overflow of the horror of it all.

And occasionally, when she was at home afterward, secure if not welcome, safe if not protected, and warm if not loved, she would try to remember those times, and now and then a face would ripple up from the dark, or a gesture, a word, a sensation, a thrust against her hips, and she would almost remember, and she would almost smile.

The first two days at home all she did was sleep and drink the juice Lizzie brought to her. The next two or three days she lay there, staring at the stains on the ceiling, at the uneven application of wallpaper, and felt the bedsores ripen on her elbows and heels. She begged Lizzie to ask Maggie not to bleach and starch the sheets so heavily, but Lizzie was absent-minded about things, and when Maggie came and changed the sheets, their rawness scraped Emma's sores anew.

Emma tried to ignore the sores, so she thought about her life. And then she began to think about the family.

Something odd was happening in the family.

After so many years in the same home with the same people, one became so finely tuned to a place that any breath of newness reverberated soundly.

And there was newness all around.

None of it good.

Emma wished she were well enough to be up and about, sniffing out changes, seeing what affected her and how much, but the most she could do from her bed was to talk to Lizzie when she brought a meal tray, emptied slops or just sat by her bedside for a while.

She could discern little from Lizzie, although Emma had a feeling that Lizzie was the epicenter of it all.

Days and nights blurred for Emma; she slept so often during the day and was awake so often during the night that the two were completely interchangeable in her mind. During the day, the stiff blinds and heavy curtains were drawn against the sun that hurt her eyes and her head; during the night she lit a stub of a candle that flickered and waved against the walls, creating monstrous shadows, and she would lie there and think strange thoughts.

And sometimes there was another presence pacing in her room. She couldn't see it, but she could feel it. Something paced in her room at night. Something troubled. At times it seemed as if she could almost see it, just a shadow upon a shadow. Sometimes it seemed to pass right through the wall into Abby's dressing room. Emma could feel its absence. And then she could feel its presence, again, when it returned.

She didn't mention it to Lizzie, because in the daytime, it seemed like a ludicrous notion, and when she thought about it, which was not often, she more likely feared that it was the work of a brain damaged by excesses.

But at night, when it began again, there was no doubting its existence, and Emma longed to call out, to touch it, to give it peace and rest.

But she had no peace and had never rested herself, so what made her think she could offer solace to another troubled soul?

So at night the shadow paced the floor and Emma's mind paced in place.

●　●　●

Reentry into the family was always a considerable chore for Emma. She felt like a stranger. She felt almost as if, during the six weeks she was absent from the household—three in New Bedford, three in bed—her opening in the family had healed closed.

She felt reluctant to approach her father; she felt unworthy. She found she could not meet his gaze. She kept her eyes lowered, not because she was ashamed, necessarily, although she would be if her father knew where she'd been and what she'd been doing, but rather because she felt like an outsider again, and had no voice in the family affairs. She felt she had to first gain reentry to the family and then reclaim her station.

She could not speak to Abby for a long time after each trip to New Bedford. Abby did make her feel shame. As difficult as Abby was, as bewildering and dangerous as she was to Emma and Lizzie's welfare, Abby did many of the things that Emma secretly longed to do. She longed to be the mistress of a well-run house. She longed to hold her head up as a matronly pillar of the community, having reared her share of the world's next generation, and be on to one's own interests. Next to Abby, Emma felt such burning, torturous shame that she could not look her in the face for a long time after returning from one of her sojourns.

Emma had few interests outside the family. There were some cousins in Fairhaven whom she had always got on with, but Lizzie was the social butterfly in the family, not Emma. Emma had no patience for small talk and insignificant nonsense.

Lizzie made Emma believe that Emma's presence in the household meant nothing. Lizzie acted as if Emma had never been gone, and while she oohed and aahed and squeezed her hand and spoke words of sympathy to Emma while she was healing, life went on at the Borden household with nary a ripple of discomfort or neglect because Emma had been absent for six weeks.

The first family supper together was always uncomfortable as well. Emma always felt as though she ought to make application to come down. And then, once seated, Emma was always anticipating the question. The question that would have her face her father and choose to either tell him the terrible truth about herself or else look him squarely in the deep brown eyes and lie. Every time it was the same; Emma pushed food around her plate until the meal was over, the question almost visible in everyone's minds, but never spoken.

If it wasn't spoken at the first supper together, it wouldn't ever be spoken—at least not until the next time. And there would never be a next time, Emma had vowed.

●　●　●

Friday morning, Emma ferretted out the first "newness" in the house. She had come down for breakfast and found Abby with her nose in her plate, shoveling food in as fast as she could, and her father dressed slick and preening. It was as clear as the dawn. Andrew had a lover. That explained why his mind had been absent from the house.

A lover. For a moment, Emma's world rocked. What if he ran off with her? What if he took his assets and left? What if *she* took him for substantially more than he carried in his wallet?

Emma closed her eyes. There was the Borden name, she thought. He will not sully the Borden name. She breathed a little easier, and regarded Abby. It was clear that Abby knew; she was putting on weight as fast as she possibly could. Her mind was on the icebox, of that there was no doubt at all. Abby's world was crumbling, and she was finding solace in the bread box.

And while Andrew's mind was on his snippet, he would pay no attention whatsoever to the family. He would still have his afternoon sessions with Lizzie, and his naps, but besides that, he would either be at work or else lost in some sort of daydream. Emma looked at her father and felt empathy for him, which surprised her. It's a shame that the man never really found true love, she thought, at least not one that lasted. He may have loved their mother, but he had murdered her as sure as he was now murdering Abby with his wenching and his faithlessness.

So the household was without parental constraints.

That left Lizzie and Maggie.

Maggie, that simple-minded Irish twit, most likely used her unsupervised time to chat over the fence with the neighbor's maid, another Irish. She always was a lazy brat, and for sure, Emma noticed, the windows hadn't been washed in a month of Sundays. Well, that nonsense would end, and it would end right now! Someone had to take the reins of this family, and the way Lizzie had been these past few weeks, it was surely not to be her.

Lizzie.

Lizzie rarely showed her face at the breakfast table, being prone to bedding late and rising around noon. In fact, more often than not, Emma had heard Lizzie coming in the house very late every evening, and of course no one else had noticed, because they were all so busy, buried deeply within their own activities.

Well, midnight was way too late for a young woman to be coming home. Unescorted, yet.

The breath caught in Emma's throat. It could be that she's been going out with a *man*. Oh Lord, that would never do. No, that would never do. All this time Emma had assumed that Lizzie was out for some church reason or WCTU meetings or committee work of some sort—that had always been something Lizzie was prone to, poor dear, but to be coming home so consistently late . . .

Emma laid her fork on her plate and folded her hands in her lap. Her heart beat so hard she thought for sure her parents could hear it—if only they paid attention to something other than themselves.

Andrew kept smoothing his hair down—what a fool! And Abby helped herself to a huge third portion of fried potatoes and gravy.

I will sit here quietly until Lizzie comes down, she thought. And then I will get to the bottom of this.

But the more she thought about it, the more she could not sit still.

She excused herself from the table, took her plate into the kitchen. Bridget had just come down from her room, her face still puffy with sleep. She poured herself a cup of coffee and took a muffin from the warming oven.

"The windows must be washed today, Maggie," Emma said. "I'd like all the windows washed on the first floor today. You can do the second floor tomorrow."

The maid's eyes opened wide. The house was small, but there were many windows. To do all of the windows on the ground floor in one day was unthinkable. But Emma's mouth held its firm line and the maid dropped her eyes. "Yes, Miss Emma," she said, then took her breakfast into the dining room to eat.

Emma paced back and forth in the kitchen. She must stop Lizzie from seeing this man. She must stop it. She must *stop* it.

Her fists balled into knots, Emma looked toward the ceiling. "I swear, Mother, she will not marry. She will not end up like you and that poor wretched Abby. No man will do that to Lizzie. Or to me. I promise. I promise upon your grave. I promise upon your memory—"

Andrew walked through the door, and stopped, looking queerly at Emma.

"Emma."

"Father."

"Were you speaking?"

"No. Well, no. I was wondering about Lizzie. Hasn't she been coming in awfully late these past few nights?"

"Don't know, Emma. I know she's gone most every evening, but I hear there's committee meetings over at Kathryn Peters'. I don't know what time she comes in."

"Is today a special day of some kind, Father?" Emma could not help herself.

"No, no, why do you ask?"

"Well, you're all dandied up, is all. Looks like you'll be stepping out."

Fury flashed into Andrew's eyes. "Hush yourself, girl. Don't be letting your mother hear you talk like that. Shame on you. No. Be off with you. Do some laundry today." And he made little sweeping motions at her with his hands, and then went up the back stairs to his bedroom.

Confirmed. Andrew had a lover. Emma let him brush her off like that because she had a mind full of things other than Andrew.

Lizzie was the item to be dealt with this day.

186

Emma walked back through the dining room, head held high, pretending not to notice the scowl that crossed Bridget's face. We must certainly look for a new maid, she thought. Abby, she noticed, was still eating, although she had slowed down some. The flesh of her jowls jiggled as she chewed.

Emma walked up the front stairs and opened Lizzie's bedroom door. The curtains were drawn. Emma whipped them wide open.

Lizzie blinked and squinted in the light. "Emma! I'm sleeping."

"No, Lizzie, we need to have a talk."

"Later."

"Now."

"Emmm-ma," Lizzie whined.

"Sit up here, girl, and let me have a look at you." Emma sat in Lizzie's rocker and leaned over into Lizzie's face.

"Get away, Emma," Lizzie pushed at her sister, then sat up in bed and rubbed her face.

"You're gaining weight again,"

"Shut up, Emma."

"And you're all puffy. Are you seeing a man, Lizzie?"

Lizzie's eyes opened wide, but Emma could see that the element of surprise had served her well. Lizzie was innocent. She was seeing no man. "No, Emma, I'm not seeing a man. Is that what this is about?"

"You're keeping mighty funny hours for a lady, especially a Borden lady, Lizzie. I need to make sure that you're not doing something to disgrace the name." Emma said the words, but in her heart she hoped Lizzie would not be the one to point out the fact that she, Emma, had just arisen from bed where she had lain in disgrace for the past three weeks.

"I do not disgrace the Borden name, Emma. I study. I work. I go to meetings. I teach Sunday School. I'm busy,

Emma, doing the things I always do, plus some. Now can I go back to sleep, please?"

"Absolutely not. It's time for you to be up. This house has gone to rack and ruin since I've been gone and it's time somebody put it right again. There's a houseful of laundry and mending and ironing. Maggie will begin with the windows on the first floor this morning, and there is just a whole spring cleaning that was never quite accomplished. Up, lazy thing. Get up."

Lizzie groaned and pulled the covers over her head, but Emma knew that she would be up presently. Emma went into her own room and closed the door. The stress of the morning had been quite a strain on her health. She was not up to her usual energy level yet; it would take a while. She took off her shoes and lay gently on the bed. Just a quick rest, and then she would be up and about, cracking the whip on the lazy waifs who lived in this house. It was time someone gave a little direction around here.

izzie lay in bed on her thirty-second birthday until noon, with nothing to look forward to except a Christian Endeavor Society meeting at seven o'clock. Other people had birthday parties—some quite elaborate, some modest and meaningful—but nobody in the Borden family had ever celebrated the anniversary of Lizzie's birth.

When she finally went downstairs, dressed in clothes that smelled like yesterday and the day before, she found that Abby had made a cake with fresh goat milk and duck eggs that Andrew had brought back from the farm. No mention was made of a birthday.

The cake must have been meant for her, because as soon as Lizzie admired it, Abby cut it and began to eat a large slice. Lizzie had no appetite for it, so she just watched Abby waddling about in the kitchen, eating the cake and stuffing bits of this and that into her mouth. Lizzie suddenly saw herself in another thirty years.

Thirty-two years old. A spinster lady. What a terrible label! Useless in the eyes of the public, wretched and evil in the eyes of God, having relations with another woman. And there was shame, too, a shame that Kathryn had given her.

But Lizzie tried not to think about that. It burned too brightly, it stung too harshly.

The worst sin in Lizzie's life was that she was so weak. Not bold, not adventurous, not self-assured. Not slim, not pretty. Not independent. Not all those things she dreamed for, worked so hard for, and which eluded her so completely.

189

Yes, *Pathways* was right. She had myriad selves, all of them inadequate to the simple task of life.

Lizzie came down the stairs late on her thirty-second birthday because she had not slept well. She hadn't slept well for months. She'd been restless. She dreamed that her Angry Self paced all night, then she'd wake and be exhausted, as if she had actually *been* pacing all night.

And along with the sleeplessness, Lizzie's attention was continually drawn away from the barn. Even when she was in her loft, ready to do her exercises, her concentration seemed to have permanently fled. She did them anyway, hoping that somehow she would continue to grow in spite of her lack of concentration. But she got little from them, and couldn't wait to be finished. As soon as she was, she put her things away and then lay back in the hay and dreamed of owning her own home in town. She dreamed of inviting Kathryn over for the evening. She dreamed of doing as she pleased, when she pleased, with whom she pleased. She dreamed of decorating the house to her own taste, and not to dreary old Emma's taste. She dreamed of wearing peach, even if it was not her best color. She dreamed of posting a letter to Beatrice and inviting her to come stay for as long as she wished. She dreamed of eventually returning to Britain to stay for an extended visit with Beatrice in her flat.

She longed to share these dreams with Kathryn, but Kathryn again had become increasingly distant, snippy, almost rude.

But Lizzie finally broached the subject anyway.

Kathryn's response shocked her. "Oh, Lizzie, your father will never allow that."

"He will," Lizzie said. "He will, eventually."

"You've lost your mind, girl. He has you firmly under his thumb, and you do exactly what he wills. You will never be free of him, Lizzie, not until he and that silly wife of his are dead."

190

"You're wrong, Kathryn."

Kathryn turned to Lizzie and fixed her with a fishy stare. "Am I?"

"Listen, Kathryn, you don't know about my relationship with—"

"It's late."

That was Kathryn's dismissal. Lizzie was to dress and go home so Kathryn could have a nightcap alone and then go to sleep. The ritual had always irked Lizzie, had always made her feel like an underling, like a servant, brought to this house to satisfy only one certain need, and then cast aside until the next time the mistress beckoned. "I think you ought to know something about Father and me before you make such rash statements—"

"You bore me, Lizzie, you and your uppity Borden sentiments. It's time you went home."

Lizzie was struck dumb. Slowly, she slid to the edge of the bed and sat up. She began to dress, knowing she should say something, *anything,* but words were out of her grasp.

"I shan't be home for the next two weeks, Lizzie," Kathryn said casually.

"Oh?" Lizzie choked out. One more word and she would begin to cry.

"Scott and Matthew have invited us to Boston."

Lizzie's hopes rose. "Us?"

"Well," Kathryn said, "Cynthia Miller and I."

Cynthia Miller! The tears surged back where they came from, chased by a bolt of anger. "And you'll be there for two weeks?"

"Perhaps longer. Listen, Lizzie, I believe this little affair between us has run its course, don't you agree? I feel like traveling a bit, so when we come back from Boston, I might just go abroad for a time. Perhaps I'll call when I return."

"Fine," Lizzie said, the anger giving her a dangerous

calm. She finished dressing and left the house without another word.

Now the shame burned. Now the shame burned so brightly Lizzie felt brazenly illuminated in the soft summer evening.

She felt as if her shame, her sins, her shortcomings were highly visible to everyone in Fall River. Surely the newspapers would be filled with the news in the morning.

She had failed the Borden name, that was a sure thing, and even if there was no public outcry—Kathryn was, after all, most discreet—Lizzie would smolder with shame and the stench of it would be with her soul forever.

She went directly home, her feet somehow carrying her one step at a time toward the goal of her darkened bedroom. She carried herself poorly, hunched over, head down, shoes occasionally scraping the pavement.

She should have seen it coming. *She should have seen it coming!* This was the second time Kathryn just tossed her off to one side. The first time hurt so badly, hurt *so badly,* why did Lizzie imagine that the second time would hurt less?

She unlocked the front door, slipped in, locked it behind her. It was early, and there were lamps in the sitting room and in the kitchen; she didn't want to talk to anyone. She made her way up the stairs with leaden feet, unlocked the bedroom door and fell upon the bed without even removing her sweater.

She was beyond tears. She wanted to release the awful pain, but there were no tears. There were no racking sobs, those terrible-wonderful things that washed the world and made it fresh. There was no forgiveness here, not from her emotions, not from her body. There would never be forgiveness.

She thought about *Pathways* in the barn. She was unworthy of it. She was too stupid.

Automatically, she began to whisper the first lesson into

her pillow. "Within each individual reside many others." The words choked her. They were beautiful words. They were filled with hope and loveliness and power. And Lizzie had none of those things. She *was* none of those things. And not even her other selves could save her.

She thought about taking her own life, but then she knew who would find her; the one person for whom she needed to live: Emma. Instead, she just gripped her balled-up sheets in her hands and squeezed them until the cords stood out on her arms, in her neck, until perspiration beaded up on her forehead and dripped down into her hair.

Eventually, she slept. And paced.

• • •

Lizzie watched Abby wolf down cake until she couldn't take it anymore.

She slammed out the screen door and made for the barn.

She locked the big door behind her. She breathed deeply of the friendly smell and climbed quickly to the loft, uncovered *Pathways* and lay back in the familiar hay. This was a place where she could sit and think and not be disturbed by anything.

Except her thoughts. And this day her thoughts were most disturbing.

She went through her first lesson, reading the paragraph aloud. Then she lit the candles and set up the mirror and watched her face change.

And then she called forth her Angry Self.

It surged forward like a tidal wave, enveloping Lizzie, suffocating her. Her anger roared toward Emma, skinny, mean Emma. Emma, who had held her hostage all these years, Emma who held in the palm of her hawklike hand the key to Lizzie's self-consuming guilt. Emma, cursed Emma, who always looked down her nose at Lizzie, who always wanted more than Lizzie could give. Blasted Emma who stood in the way of Lizzie's future, who barred Lizzie from ever having any happiness. Damn Emma! Damn Emma!

The tide flowed and then ebbed, changed directions, and the wave washed over the head of Abby. Abby, the damned. Abby, the one who always looked at Lizzie as if Lizzie owed her something. Abby, who always wanted more from Lizzie than Lizzie was able to give. Abby, who wanted Lizzie to be her child, when Lizzie couldn't, she *couldn't*, she belonged to a tyrannical older sister and a dead mother and it wasn't her fault, but Abby just could never forgive her for that. Abby, who held her father's ear at night and filled him with traitorous ideas about Emma and Lizzie, Abby, who paired Emma with Lizzie and never saw them as two individuals, Abby who resented her husband's daughters from the moment she came into the family, Abby who never had children of her own, who tortured the household, who ate until she was a monster, whose unhappiness filled the house to overflowing.

When the wave washed back, nothing was left of Abby but pitiful bones and gelatinous mounds of lard.

And then it struck down Andrew. Andrew. Andrew, who ignored Lizzie beyond endurance, and only paid attention when it suited him to refuse her most heartfelt desires. Andrew, who didn't care at all for Emma—a man who hated his daughter!—and in so doing, chained his other daughter to her woeful older sister forever. Andrew, who cared not for his current wife, who felt nothing, *nothing* for the dead wife who bore him three children, one dead in infancy. Andrew, who worked from early until late and squeezed a nickel until it chirped. Andrew, who would never let the Borden girls claim their rightful social place by allowing any fresh air or fresh faces into the still, musky house. Andrew, who would never part with a dollar unless his life depended upon it, who made the girls bathe with a cloth and a bucket in the cellar, whose only toilet was a hole, hidden, dirty, in the cellar, who would never allow decent plumbing or a hookup to the gas line. Andrew, who would probably die of poisoned mutton that had been on the table six days in a row rather than buy enough fresh meat to feed his family. Andrew, damn you, damn you, damn you, Father!

Sweat poured off Lizzie's face and stray whisps of hair stuck to her. The tidal wave was over, wasn't it?

No, not quite. The power and fury were gone for the moment, but in their wake floated pieces of corpses. There was Mother, her thin face so like Emma's, yet with a softness that made her so beautiful. She floated with some of the others, her grave having been disturbed by the storm. I hate you, Mother, Lizzie's mind screamed. You could have made the difference in my life, but you left. You left me all alone with Emma and Abby and Father, and for that I will *never* forgive you.

Kathryn floated there as well, but Lizzie just gave her dead face a shove with her mental foot and she floated out beyond the horizon. There were classmates in there, a couple of boys, and Lizzie looked at them all with wrath and scorn.

And then the anger began to well again, and it took on more specific forms. She could see herself hitting Emma, smashing her in the face, she could see herself coming up behind Abby and cracking her hard on the head. She could see her father, lying on the sofa so coolly asleep and she could see herself pouncing upon him and ripping his eyes out.

And Lizzie's hand was up under her skirt and her fingers were rubbing and pulling hard at herself, not soft and tender the way that Kathryn had done, not at all.

She groaned and rolled over on her side.

Then she jumped up, shook out her dress and stood at the edge of the loft. I shall dive off, she thought clearly, and then did it.

Time slowed. She saw the dust motes in the slanting ray of light that came in through the dirty window. She saw the piles of trash by the door. She saw the empty stalls, she saw where she would land, headfirst, and break her neck on the newly raked dirt. She smelled that dirt as she approached it, her last thought—

Lizzie gasped and sat up. She was still in the hayloft. Had that been a dream? No, there was no way she could have dreamed that. She inched over to the side of the loft to see if her body was down there, dead on the floor. No. Nothing.

Perspiration trickled down where tears had just been.

My God, she thought, my God.

She wiped the perspiration from her head. She felt the soreness where she had pounded herself so roughly, and shame brought a flush to her cheeks.

And then another flush of shame rose to her cheeks as she thought of stealing Abby's jewelry and money. It was the same kind of thing. She could have sworn she was in the barn at the time, and yet the evidence showed . . .

And this sneaking into Abby and Andrew's bedroom at night. And Emma's. Lizzie dreamed of pacing back and forth, back and forth, and somehow, the dreams were so real, so accurate. . . . In normal dreams, things always happened, there were people who talked and acted, there were different, strange places, there were triple levels of meanings and innuendos that only meant something for a moment or two upon awakening, but not this, no, not this, this was just endless pacing, back and forth, back and forth, worried pacing, the weight of the world upon her shoulders.

And when she awoke, she was exhausted, and even the muscles in her legs were cramped as if she actually *had* been pacing, but she knew *she* hadn't really been, it had been something else.

Something else.

Something else stole Abby's jewelry. Something else paced at night as Lizzie slept. Something else just dove headfirst off the loft. Something else, something else, something else.

What?

Something in me? Something of me? Me? Another self?

What if I could tame that other thing, make it work for me. What if I could have that "something else" all the time?

Wouldn't that be tricky?

And wouldn't Beatrice be impressed?

ndrew Borden found a quiet moment at home, when everyone else was busy, to sit at his desk in the sitting room and contemplate a major decision. He looked again at the paper in his hands.

If he were to change his will at this time . . . He set the paper back on the desktop, facedown, and folded his hands on top of it. If he were to change his will at this time . . . Well, there was no other way but to keep all knowledge of it strictly away from Abby, Emma and Lizzie. If any of them were to find out, there would be hell to pay, and that was no exaggeration.

And yet, there was this burning desire to make some strong move, to do something lasting, something reasonably permanent for the Widow Crawford and her sons.

She was using him, that had been clear from the beginning. He was no fool. But she did save every Friday afternoon for him. She did it for her sons, for her boys, for her family, and, Andrew had begun to believe, she also did it for Andrew. And for herself.

Their Friday afternoons had become something extraordinary. Their trysts had become so special, so looked forward to, that even he was moved by their intensity. And intensity of that nature cannot be had by one person alone. It must be shared. There was intensity of lust, there was intensity of secrecy, there was that naughtiness that accompanied the forbidden.

And she made him laugh. She made him laugh with

abandon, something that hadn't happened to him since he was young and first in love with Sarah.

Life had made an old man out of Andrew Borden, and Mrs. Crawford was reversing that. He was young again in her presence, and for that he was eternally grateful. He was grateful to the tune of something substantial in his will.

He unfolded his hands and took up the paper of instructions to his attorney. There were several problems with this. The first problem was that his attorney was Mrs. Crawford's employer, and eyebrows would be raised. Andrew couldn't be sure of confidentiality if he used the same Fall River lawyer who had drafted his original will. And confidentiality was mandatory. That was a solvable problem, but it was not the only problem.

There was also Abby, Lizzie and Emma. Didn't the money belong to them?

Not necessarily. If the money belonged to anyone, it belonged to Lizzie, who loved him and cared for him. Abby deserved something for her faithful service through the years, but all he felt for her was the fondness one would have for a loyal servant of thirty years. And Emma! Well, Emma deserved little more than her current four dollars a week, just enough to keep her mean every month for the rest of her life. Emma was a cantankerous sort, and Andrew owed her little.

But what would they say if they found out about the will before he died? Would they make life hell for him? And what on earth would they do to Mrs. Crawford?

What would they do to Mrs. Crawford even if they didn't find out until after he died? Would they contest the will and make a public spectacle of his affair?

And then again, there was no reason to assume that Mrs. Crawford would continue their liaison until Andrew died. It could just be that when the boys graduated, she would put him off with a wave of her dainty hand and that would be the end of it.

He couldn't bear to think of the end of it. No, he thought, she enjoyed his company too much. She would not do that.

What were his alternatives? He could deed an asset to Mrs. Crawford without her knowing it, and merely put the deed in an envelope addressed to her. Any attorney would post it upon his death.

Another would be to rewrite the will, as he felt so strongly moved to do, and damn the results. Let the women have a catfight over the stupid money; he would have no further use for it.

Another would be to make a generous gift to Mrs. Crawford now, while he was alive and they both could enjoy the moment.

This was a good idea. He drummed his fingers on the desk for a moment, then unlocked the side drawer and drew out a copy of his most recent financial statement. He checked over his real estate holdings to see if there was a property suitable for her—one on which she could collect rents to help with the college payments of her sons, and that she could sell when they were finished with their educations.

But a rental property is such a bother. She would have to collect the rent from the pikers, and sometimes they were difficult enough for him to deal with, never mind having a woman try to make them pay up.

Mrs. Crawford's feisty face came up before his memory, and he had no doubt that she could handle a recalcitrant tenant. But perhaps that was not the best way. One more burden—and a tenantless property was indeed a burden, especially at tax time—was not what the fine woman needed. No.

Andrew folded up the new instructions, put them into the envelope with his old will, refiled them and locked the desk drawer. He would go round to the attorney's office tomorrow and get the original. Mr. Pratt wouldn't like that very much, but he could send his will and the changes over to another attorney in Fairhaven, where nobody knew Mrs. Crawford, and that might be the best way all around. At least it would give him more time to think on it. And perhaps he could even confide in this new attorney, and receive some good legal advice. For free, of course.

But there was another issue that Andrew would not be able to dodge much longer. Lizzie wanted her own house. She had mentioned it once, and she would mention it again soon.

His first thought was to absolutely forbid it; unmarried women just did not live by themselves, not when they had family. And Lizzie's idea of "modest" would probably not stay that way, once she began to decorate and furnish this little nest of her own. Andrew could see his investment dollars winging away on the breeze.

But not having Emma underfoot was an idea that merited further consideration. And Abby would enjoy the peace. Abby would be able to be the mistress of this house at last, and Andrew felt as if he owed her that. It would be good for Abby to have the household to herself. She could instruct the maid—perhaps without the girls, there would be no need for a maid!—she could take care of the menus and the meals herself; there would be far less laundry to do, and the house would be free of the godawful tension that reverberated through its rafters.

Yet it is probably the tension that keeps this house standing, Andrew thought.

But on the down side, the girls and their involvement in family affairs that were really none of their business, provided a diversion for Abby, so that she probably noticed not at all about his Fridays. And those Fridays were so precious to him. . . . If she were mistress of the house, surely she would ask after his whereabouts of a Friday evening, and he would have to lie to her. That would not be good.

A decision must be made on this issue, he thought. Lizzie will be wanting an answer.

Friday nights were so precious. . . .

The only answer he could give her now would be no. He needed Lizzie around. He needed Emma. So until something happened to change his priorities, for now they would continue to live under his roof. Emma would have to go visit her friends from time to time, and Lizzie would just have to wait.

He sighed. Telling Lizzie this would not be easy.

He saw her moving about in the kitchen. Might as well get it over with.

He stood from his hardbacked chair at the desk and slowly straightened up. His seventy-four years were just beginning to catch up to him. Sometimes this fact made him very cranky, and sometimes it just made him sad. He took a couple of faltering steps, then walked into the kitchen.

"Lizzie?" There was no answer. "Lizzie?" He opened the screen door and stepped out onto the porch, automatically reaching for the pipe in his pocket. He leaned against the post and lit the pipe. "Lizzie, are you there?" Still no answer. He stepped down off the porch and looked around the house. There was no one there. He sat on the steps. It was going to be a hot summer, he thought, yes indeed, it was going to be a hot summer.

Just then, the barn door opened and Lizzie stepped out. "Did you call me, Father?"

"Come sit with me a spell, Lizzie."

Lizzie walked toward him, but stopped and examined a branch of the pear tree. "I've never seen so many baby pears, have you?"

Andrew regarded the tree. "Never," he said. "We'll have a fine harvest in a couple of months."

Lizzie sat next to him on the step. Andrew puffed on his pipe.

"Been thinking about fishing, Lizzie," Andrew said.

"Me too."

"Been thinking we ought to go one of these days. It's been a long time."

"A long time."

"Too long."

They sat in silence for a while, Andrew puffing great clouds that were borne away on the early summer breeze.

"I'm going to tell you no on buying the house, Lizzie." He found he could not look her in the eyes.

Lizzie slumped.

"Let me tell you why."

"It doesn't matter." Lizzie stood up.

"It *does* matter. Sit down."

"I've got things to do, Father."

"Lizzie, please. It isn't right for two unmarried ladies to be living by themselves, not when they have family. It isn't right. It wouldn't look right for the Borden name."

"I'm miserable, Father, Emma's miserable, Abby's miserable, you're miserable. But the Borden name is right. The Borden name has always got to be right."

"Yes, it does. Misery passes, Lizzie, but scandal never does."

"Plenty of women live alone."

"Not when they have family."

"Yes, they do."

"Bordens don't. You'll have plenty of life, both of you, when Abby and I are dead. Then you can do as you please."

Lizzie just walked back to the barn without a backward glance.

Andrew's Fridays were secure for the time being, but at what price? He felt as if he had lost something else, something perhaps even more precious. He tapped the ashes out onto the step and put the pipe back into his pocket. It was time for his nap.

hen the sun slanted in the barn loft window, Lizzie knew she had to leave and make ready for the church meeting. She was probably already late.

She hated to leave the barn, but she had to. The church's Christian Endeavor Society, a fancy name for the church council, met at seven o'clock, and she had to make her report. Her committee was "Bringing the Message to the Orientals," and since she was the only one doing anything about it by teaching a Sunday school class to the little brats, she had to attend.

She'd much rather stay in the barn.

She was still overwhelmed by the experience of having dived off the loft. Having dived off the loft and yet not. And then after the little talk with Andrew, it had happened again.

She carefully hid all the things she'd taken to the loft, then climbed down the ladder. She shook the hay from her clothes, patted down her hair, and then opened the door into the yard.

It was indeed late. She quickly crossed over the yard and knocked on the screen door. Maggie let her in.

Lizzie grabbed two muffins from the steaming stack that had been laid out for supper and trotted through the sitting room and up the stairs.

Andrew had turned down her request for a life of independence. It infuriated her that he used that same worn-out old excuse of maiden ladies living alone. And the

Borden name! Bah! The real reason he didn't want Emma and her to leave had more to do with Abby. He didn't seem to care much for that hippopotamus, and no wonder. If she and Emma left, well, then, that would leave the two of them and the Borden name. Scant comfort for an old man's seventies.

When he'd told her that, her first reaction was resignation. She'd known he would respond that way; she hoped against hope that it would be otherwise, but she knew that his ultimate answer would be no. Kathryn knew it, too. And this was what made Lizzie the unhappiest. Kathryn knew it, too.

After their talk, she'd gone back to the barn, where her anger again began to burn. She started kicking hay and kicking at the wall, and suddenly she could see herself walking in town, with long, purposeful strides. She stared at the loft corner, unpainted planks nailed together and covered with dust and cobwebs, but while she could see them, she could also see herself walking in town. She wore the same clothes: the white shirtwaist with the blue patterned silk skirt, her hair was done up the same, but this was no daydream, this was something else, for she could see out this Lizzie's eyes.

And other people could see her! People on the street nodded as she strode past.

The barn wall looked flat and dull, as if she were seeing it through a thin dark film. The street in town seemed extraordinarily bright, as if suffused with a little of the sparkling heatwaves she saw when a headache approached. She walked down Main Street, then turned onto Third, where she stopped. She looked quickly around her, noticed that no one was looking, and then all of her was back in the hayloft, staring at that same corner. The vision was over. The *something else* had come back.

As before, a cold sweat covered her brow, her breathing

was heavy and rapid, and she sat down and leaned against the haystack.

Lizzie was absolutely dumbfounded. She didn't know what to make of it at all. She could not control it. And she wondered: Could it speak? Could it move things around? Was it just an apparition? Did other people really see it as well, or was it a hallucination? Did this happen to anyone else? Why had she never heard of anything like this before?

Lizzie ate a muffin on her way up the stairs. The day felt so strange, as if she had just been living through a very vivid dream. She could hardly believe that those things had really happened. She rinsed her face in the washbowl in her room, tidied her hair a bit and changed her clothes. She didn't want to go to a church meeting at all, *at all,* she wanted to stay home and ponder what on earth could have caused her to be so odd, *so* odd.

But she was duty bound to go. She locked her bedroom door behind her, flew down the stairs. "Going to church," she said to nobody as she unlocked the three front-door locks and stepped into the warm evening.

It was still daylight as Lizzie strode toward the church. If Emma had been with her, she would have said, "Take more care, Lizzie, you're beginning to walk like a cowboy." And then Lizzie would have given her a look and Emma would have said, "It isn't ladylike."

Ladylike. Bah. Sometimes one just had to walk hard. Loosely. Feel the muscles. Something Emma never did. There were a lot of things Emma never did.

Lizzie strode hard and looked forward to the meeting, because as soon as it was over, she could leave again. She only joined this Christian Endeavor Society because changing churches created such a scandal that she thought Andrew ought to have something to say in explanation. So she joined the council and offered to work on a committee to reach out to all the newly transplanted Orientals—Chinese, mostly—

who had come to Fall River to work in the mills and in the laundries.

And then she got saddled with the stupid Sunday school class. But it was all right. The children were strange, but they also had their good points.

Lizzie slipped in the side door of the big church and went right to the meeting room, just off the side of the main chapel. The meeting was already in session. Good. She came late; she could leave early. There was only one vacant seat at the long table; she sat down as unobtrusively as possible.

The pastor was in the middle of a discussion on the summer activities for the church youth group. Good, Lizzie thought. My report can't be far behind.

She looked around the table. In every organization, there was a central core of people who did all the work. Lizzie looked at each face. Give or take a couple of people, she would bet that ten years ago, this table had the same people around it and still would ten years hence. There was a certain appeal to that sort of commitment. But Lizzie didn't have it. Not to this church, anyway. Perhaps that was something that came with time. She was only thirty-two. Most of the faces around this table were in their late fifties and early sixties. Some, though, were her age. She avoided those. They might want to get chummy, and she had no time for chums.

The pastor called on the woman sitting next to her. She stood, then addressed the council in a clear voice. She gave the names of all those who had agreed to grace the altar with flowers for the next six weeks. She also reported the roster of which men had agreed to take care of the churchyard and cemetery for the coming month.

Lizzie listened to her. She was calm, self-assured and clear. She was prepared. That was something that Lizzie never was. In fact, she was never any of those things. The woman sat down, turned and smiled at Lizzie.

She was beautiful. She was petite, like Kathryn. She had a

large, soft mouth and twinkling blue eyes. The skin at the corners of her eyes wrinkled up beautifully when she smiled, and her skin was lightly bronzed from the sun. Such a refreshing change from all those who kept their bonnets on for fear of freckles. Freckles abounded on this woman's face, and her teeth were even and white.

Gray shot through the reddish-brown hair, which was cut short and brushed back from her face. She was absolutely breathtaking. And unconventional in many ways. Lizzie liked that. Lizzie was intrigued.

She heard the pastor call her name, and the woman next to her reached over and gave her hand a little squeeze. Lizzie's heart pounded in her chest. Her mouth went dry. She stood, and felt her knees tremble and her breath come hard, as if she had been running. She wasn't sure she could make her voice speak clearly at all.

But she did. She made her report, and didn't leave anything out. She told that plans were already under way for a celebration of Chinese New Year next year, and that more Oriental social events were coming forth in the fall. She reported on the progress of teaching about Jesus to the youngsters, and the help the mill was giving her in encouraging the Orientals to come to church on Sunday. She didn't mention that she'd had to beg her father to make a bulletin and have it translated. He thought all Chinese were heathens, and godless to boot. He thought her ministry was a colossal waste of time and had no problem expressing himself to her. But he did it anyway, and the turnout was getting better all the time.

There were now Bible-study groups for them, and once they were *in* the church, then they could become integrated into the church community.

It was an adequate report. She sat down again, breathless. The woman next to her turned again and smiled, then gave her attention across Lizzie to the man on the other side of her, who then stood and began to speak. But Lizzie could not take her eyes off the woman.

There was no wedding ring on her finger. She looked to be in her early forties—perhaps Emma's age, but what a difference! This woman was vibrant. This woman was healthy. And she had kindness written in each of those tanned wrinkles.

Nothing at all like Kathryn . . . yet . . . yet she exuded *something* akin to Kathryn. There was that same sensuousness in her touch, there was that smile.

Could she possibly be like me? Like Kathryn? Would there be the slightest possibility that this woman could know the same kind of loneliness?

Lizzie knew she was staring, but she could not stop herself. She could not take her eyes off the possibility of another woman in her life, a source of tenderness, of joy, of togetherness. Someone to share her life with.

The woman shifted her gaze and looked directly into Lizzie's eyes.

Immediately, Lizzie flushed and looked away. But not before she thought she perhaps had an answer. The woman did not look offended at Lizzie's steady gaze, she merely met her eyes.

Lizzie put both hands in her lap and struggled to take even breaths and to remove the color from her face. By the time she had done so, the man had finished speaking and another woman was talking about the Fourth of July picnic. Lizzie took one deep breath and then brought her eyes up to rest on the person who was speaking. She fought to keep from sliding around to look at the wonderful lady in the seat next to her.

She remembered her plan of escaping the meeting early, but now that seemed impossible. She couldn't draw more attention to herself. Besides that, she might have the opportunity to meet this sparkling woman, she might have the opportunity to be touched again, by accident, perchance. She might find that the woman was interested in a friendly chat over a cup of tea—if not tonight, well, then, sometime.

If she didn't walk away from Lizzie with a backhanded comment about someone uncouth enough to stare.

Lizzie's mind turned back to the woman's appearance. Was her hair really short? No respectable woman wore short hair. Those who did were either white trash, ill kempt or loose. Yet this woman carried it off. Without meaning to, Lizzie turned and looked at her again. Yes, her hair was short. Wavy and brushed away from her face. She was beautiful. And suddenly her face was very familiar. As if Lizzie'd seen her hundreds of times. As if they were old friends, but Lizzie just could not remember her name.

Lizzie called upon her Self of Fear. Help me through this, she prayed. I must be bold, adventurous and self-assured. I must speak with her after the meeting.

The meeting ground on, with Lizzie's stomach in such an uproar she knew she would have to take some cod-liver oil when she went home, to soothe the agitation. She waited, her mind filled with the scent—real or imagined—of the vision next to her. She was constantly out of breath, trying to imagine her first line of introduction when the meeting ended. There was no way she was going to leave this hall without at least discovering this woman's name. Oh, how her stomach hurt, and oh how strange life suddenly turned out to be.

Then the committee reports were finished, there was no new business to be discussed, the minister said a blessing and the meeting was adjourned.

Lizzie suddenly froze in her seat, distracted and panicky.

Then there was a touch on her shoulder. She whipped around to see the woman next to her standing, with one finger on Lizzie's shoulder. She smiled down at Lizzie, tapped her once on the shoulder, and then walked away.

Lizzie almost turned her chair over in her hurry to catch up with her, but by the time she collected herself, the woman was walking slowly with the minister, deep in conversation. Lizzie went over to Alice Russell, who was picking up the leftover cookies.

"Alice."

"Hello, Lizzie. Say, you're doing such wonderful work with the Orientals. We've needed someone to do that type of ministry for a long time. Bless your heart for taking it on. It must be terribly time-consuming. I know just the secretarial dut—"

"Alice, who was the woman sitting next to me?"

"Next to you? Hmmm." Alice tapped at her head. "I can't seem to recall—"

"Short hair. Graying. Her face had been in the sun."

"Oh, Enid Crawford. You must mean Enid Crawford."

"Enid Crawford," Lizzie whispered.

"She's very active in the church. Has been since long before her marriage. She was a Fall River girl, you know, parents died just after she married Charles—"

"She's married?" Lizzie struggled to keep her voice even. She took cups and swept cookie crumbs to act casual.

"Oh, her husband died a few years back. Has two sons in college up in Boston. Wonderful woman, Enid. Quite an inspiration, the way she works so hard to put those boys through school. They're both going to be lawyers, she says."

Enid Crawford. Lizzie was sure she'd never heard that name before. But she would never forget it.

She looked around. Enid was gone. Alice was still prattling on about how expensive it is to rear children, never mind college, and Lizzie just let her continue talking and wandered off. She shook hands with the minister and then went out into the soft summer night.

Enid Crawford. Enid Crawford. Enid Crawford.

I must have her, Lizzie thought.

 uly

I swear this is the hottest I've ever been," Sarah White-head said as she poured a glass of cool tea for Abby Borden. "Can you imagine how hot it is, Abby?"

Abby mopped her forehead with her handkerchief—freshly ironed this morning and now damp and gray from the sweltering humidity and her own perspiration. Abby picked up the tea and drank it right down. "Pour me a little more, child."

Sarah dutifully refilled the glass. Abby sipped at it, then wiped her face again. She didn't tolerate the heat well at all. Never had. Sometimes it felt as if her heart were swelling in all this heat, and she worried—walking on around town the way she did—that one of these hot days it would just up and burst and she would fall dead on the walk.

"Yes, indeed, if you think it's hot now, Abby, you just wait until August! You know it's always hotter in August, and it's just been getting hotter and hotter all month long."

Just the talk of it brought more perspiration out on Abby's face.

"Sebastian calls these dog days, isn't that funny? I mean what could that possibly mean? Dogs don't like this heat any better'n the rest of us, now, do they? He also says that this is the weather where people go crazy. He's a policeman, you know, or at least he used to be, and so he would know. He says that when the heat gets bad, it turns the world into a steam cooker and people start popping their seams. Isn't that a funny thing to say?"

Abby felt a little dizzy. She set her tea on the coffee table and tried to catch her breath. She mopped at her face again.

"You look a little peaked, Abby. Let me get you a little something."

Sarah left the room and Abby leaned back against the sofa. Her breaths were coming in short—like panting, she thought. Maybe that's why these hot days are called dog days. They make people pant. But the humor was lost in the discomfort. She would have liked to share that with Sarah, it was the kind of thing that would make her little sister laugh and laugh, and her light little laughs were joyful and the sole reason Abby visited her so often. There was so little laughter at the Borden house. Sarah had her manifold troubles, and still she laughed.

Sarah returned from the kitchen with a generous slice of lemon meringue pie on a plate. "It's cold, Abby, I kept it in the icebox. Sebastian ate almost the whole thing last night, but I kept a slice out for you, because I know it's one of your favorites."

"You're a dear," Abby said, but made no move to take the pie. She needed to lie back on the sofa and rest for a while.

Sarah set the pie on the table, then sat down and picked up her knitting.

"Sebastian can't understand how I can knit in this heat. He's always looking at me and telling me I'm crazy for holding this heavy afghan on my lap, but it don't seem to bother me much. Sometimes about midday it gets a little warm, but toward the evening, it doesn't hurt. I should knit some sweaters and smaller things during the summer, I guess, and leave the coverlets for winter when I really do need something over my knees."

Abby eyed that slice of pie. Its cool yellow shimmered. And Sarah made such a fine crust. Abby had given her a goodly amount of lard that Andrew had brought home from the farm one Saturday, and Sarah made some good lye soap with half of it and saved the rest for pie crusts. And she knew how to make crusts.

With an *oompf*, Abby raised herself up to a sitting position, and took the plate. She cut a bite with a shaky fork and slipped it into her mouth. She looked over at Sarah, who was watching for her reaction.

"Um-mmm," she said, and rolled her eyes.

Satisfied, Sarah went back to her knitting, and talking, prattling on about nothing in particular, punctuating her monologue with trills of laughter—at her two older children, both from her previous husband; at Sebastian, her current husband; at their year-old baby; and at the baby that just began to show as a mound on Sarah's stomach.

Usually, a visit with Sarah lifted Abby's spirits. She was Abby's only living kin, so Abby worked hard to maintain a bond between the two, even though they were on such opposite ends of society.

Sarah was thirty-one years old, the daughter of Abby's father and his second wife. She had poor taste in men, raised her children without habits of cleanliness, and would forever be poor. She had bright eyes and a sunny disposition, but she had a habit of wearing men's clothes, and they hung like rags on her thin frame. Abby was sixty-seven, grossly overweight, genteel—or so she liked to think; she dressed in as rich a wardrobe as she dared to purchase with Andrew's money, and worked hard to keep up her end of the Borden household.

Two sisters, two worlds.

Before Sarah met Sebastian, she and her babies were without a place to stay. Andrew generously gave her this nice little house, although it was probably as much a bribe to keep them out from under his roof as it was a gift of generosity.

Abby looked around. The house *had* been nice. She clucked to herself. The damage children can do, she thought. The damage children can do.

But in this heat, Abby would not be comfortable anywhere, and watching Sarah work on that wool blanket made her skin itch. She felt heat rashes spring up all along where her underwear chafed, and the thought of walking home with damp drawers rubbing against rashes made her heart pound even harder.

She wrapped her handkerchief around the sweating glass of tea and cooled it, then mopped her face one more time.

"I'd better be off," she said, and struggled to be free of the sofa.

"So soon? The children are playing over at the neighbor's. And the baby's asleep. Isn't it pleasant? I had hoped you would stay a little longer."

"Another time. Perhaps when it isn't so hot. Thank you for the tea. And the pie."

Sarah put away her knitting and stood to hug Abby. "Come back again soon, dear."

Abby nodded, her breath already being sucked away by the heat.

Sarah stood in the doorway of the house as Abby made her way toward the street. "Um, Abby?"

Abby turned, a trickle of perspiration leaking its saltiness into one eye.

"Did Andrew . . . you know . . ." She looked around furtively. "The *will?*" she whispered.

"Not yet, Sarah. But don't worry, he will."

"I know. I just wish . . ." She gestured at the squalid house she lived in with her family.

"Don't worry. See you soon." Abby didn't have the strength to reassure her further, or even to wave good-bye. She just turned her bulk toward home and began walking.

● ● ●

At six o'clock, Sebastian walked through the door. Sarah could smell him even before she could see him. He hung his sweat-soaked hat on the peg by the door and began to undress in the kitchen.

"Go down cellar for a bath," she said, "and I'll have some nice sandwiches for you when you get up."

"Sandwiches again? What kind?"

"Cheese. Now go. You smell."

"I need some meat."

"We ain't got meat. Now go bathe."

"What happens to all the money?"

Sarah turned and looked him full in the face. She knew he didn't like it when she did that. "Sebastian," she said, "are we going to go through this again? I pay our bills. We don't have any creditors knocking on our door, now do we? And we don't even have a mortgage, thanks to Abby, do we? Sometimes we have a little extra, and I buy some meat with it. I know you need meat. So do the children. But sometimes we just don't have enough money. And, as it happens, this cheese was a gift, so we got to just thank God about it and be done. Now go."

She hated talking to him like a child, but sometimes that's what he needed. And the expression on his face as he went down cellar was just exactly like that of her boy when he'd been chastised and sent to his room.

Sebastian! Men! They were all little boys.

She arranged the cheese on the bread so as to make the sandwiches seem a little fuller, then cut extra slices for Sebastian's sandwiches. He really did need meat. She'd have to cut a corner somewhere else next month.

When he came back up, wearing a towel around his waist, she yelled for the children to come in.

The boy, eight, and the girl, six, pounded up the back steps, and fell to the sandwiches without even sitting down.

"Sit," Sebastian said.

The children, chewing enthusiastically, sat.

"You ought to have washed your hands," Sarah said, spooning oatmeal into the baby. She shrugged and looked at Sebastian, who glared at her.

Sebastian sat at the table and wolfed down his sandwiches, then drank a big glass of milk. Sarah oughtn't have given him a full glass like that, but she felt so bad about the meat. Now the children would be hard pressed for milk on their oatmeal in the morning.

The children finished eating, then got up and slammed back out the kitchen door. Their friends had been waiting outside, and summer evenings were long and magical. Sarah smiled as she picked up their plates.

"There's a piece of pie left, Sarah," Sebastian said.

"No, Abby stopped by and lemon meringue is her favorite."

"It's my favorite, too."

"I know, Sebastian," she said, exasperated. "But you ate nearly the whole thing last night."

Sebastian lowered his eyes and laid his hands flat on the table. This was a sign. He was composing himself. Soon he would gently speak to her about all the things she was doing wrong in the house.

She wished it was cooler, she could have a cup of coffee. But it was way too hot to start a fire in the stove. She sat down, moved her plate away, and waited for Sebastian to get on with his lecture. Soon it would be over and she could get on with her evening.

"I know Abby does nice things for us, Sarah," Sebastian started out, "but I am the breadwinner in this family, and there are certain things I want to have in my house. One of those is meat for a meal at least two or three times a week. I don't think that's too much to ask for, since I work in that sweltering mill every bloody day of my life!" He took a moment, his fingers spread wide on the table, to recompose himself. "And when you don't let me have meat, when your priorities run in different directions, like *wool* for a blanket in the dead heat of July"—he put a palm up against her defense, and she closed her mouth—"then a piece of lemon meringue pie seems to help smooth things over. Do you know what I mean?"

Sarah nodded. Sebastian was a good man. He was pretty mad right now, but at least he didn't beat her, not the way that Jonathan had. And he was *so* good to her children. . . .

"Besides," Sebastian continued in his slow-paced voice, "think about poor Abby's weight. She can't afford pie, Sarah. She's likely to die in this heat anyway. And if she dies . . ." Sebastian's eyes lost their focus. He paused for a long moment. Sarah waited. Then his blue eyes drilled right into her. *"If she dies,"* he said, "then Andrew would inherit all her property and those old-maid daughters of his will inherit *everything* when he dies."

Sarah sat stunned. She felt as if she had been pinned to her chair with a spear.

"Jesus Christ, that's right," Sebastian said, his hands going to his face. "If old man Borden doesn't die first, then we've got . . . nothing. Just this shack."

"But if it's in his will . . ."

"Don't be an ass, Sarah. If Abby's dead, those daughters of his will convince him that he doesn't owe her kin anything at all."

Sarah knew he was right.

"No," Sebastian said. "Andrew Borden will have to die first."

Sarah stood up and began doing the dishes. She didn't like Sebastian's tone of voice, not at all, not at all. It made her weak in the knees.

Sebastian continued to sit at the table, his big square hands still on the tabletop. He didn't move when the children barged through the kitchen door, running and giggling, and he didn't say anything when they slammed back out again.

Sarah cleaned up the kitchen and went to the living room, where she picked up her knitting and prayed that Sebastian would stop all that thinking.

But he didn't. He was silent all evening, the newspaper opened and forgotten in his lap. And when they went to bed, Sarah cuddled up close and he put his arm around her shoulders, but he continued to stare into the darkness of the ceiling until she fell asleep and dreamed of wolves snatching bites of flesh from her children. She chased the wolves with her butter knife and yelled, "They ain't had any meat. Let 'em alone!" But the wolves continued to chase, snapping and howling, and Sebastian was nowhere to be seen.

● ● ●

The next day dawned stifling hot. Abby's nightclothes were wound around her and stuck in the creases of her flesh so tightly she waited until Andrew was up and dressed and out of the bedroom before she endeavored to untangle herself, flopping about on the bed, awkward and jiggling. The effort left her hot and perspiring.

Most mornings she would arise and go quickly through the house, closing the windows and pulling the shades, hoping to preserve some of the coolth that the night had brought. But this morning it was already too late. The morning sun, rising so early in late July, had stolen what tiny respite the night had offered. The day was hot and she would swelter until her rashes began to bleed.

She smoothed the sheet over her and adjusted her nightcap in case Andrew returned to the bedroom for something, and then relaxed. She should be up and closing the windows anyway, to keep out the heat—would Bridget or one of the girls think to do that? Of course not. But the thought of dressing in those clothes undoubtedly still damp from yesterday and perpetually too tight, made her cringe. She looked up at the ceiling and prayed that she would get through the heat of the summer. Especially August, when the heat made people rabid, as Sebastian said. Dog days indeed.

Then came a loud pounding on the front door. Abby sat up in bed like a shot, and gathered her bedclothes to her chest. It was so early, who on earth could be—

And then before Andrew could possibly pass from the kitchen to the front door, the pounding began again; this time there was yelling, too. Abby hurried out of bed, donned her dressing gown and slippers, drew the cap off her head, ran a brush through her hair and began her way down the back stairs.

She had gotten barely halfway when the front door opened and she could hear Andrew's voice, speaking in his normal tone. A man with a terribly thick accent began shouting. Andrew was admirable, she thought, in keeping himself under control when the other man was so irate.

Abby continued down the stairs, went through the kitchen, exchanged glances with Emma, who seemed as surprised and as mystified as she, and then entered the sitting room, where she kept her distance, yet could see the little man, Italian she thought, shake his fist at Andrew and turn red in the face.

She couldn't hear what Andrew was saying to the man, but finally the little man slumped, as if he were defeated in the final battle. He turned and walked down toward the street.

Abby approached Andrew, who kept the door open. "I told you from the very beginning," Andrew called out after him.

The little man turned and looked at Andrew with hate

deeply carved into his face. He spat on the walkway. "Thas what I think of your beginning," he said. "You rich bastads all alike. You keepa whatcha got and don *ever* let another one in. Choke on it! I hope you choke on it! And *die!*" He spat again, then trudged down the street.

Andrew closed the door. Abby was aghast to see that his face was red, almost purple.

"Come, Mr. Borden," she said, taking his arm. "Sit for a moment."

Andrew shook her off. "My breakfast is cooling," he said, and walked into the dining room. Emma had not moved. Andrew sat at his normal place, and Abby wandered back and forth a little bit, wanting to ask, but not knowing quite how to approach the subject. She went into the kitchen and brought out a plate of muffins and poured coffee all around.

Lizzie showed up at the door, disheveled from sleep. "Who was that, Father? What was that all about?"

"An Italian man, Lizzie, nothing to worry about."

"Nothing to worry about? He shows up at your home before the household is up and proceeds to curse you and wake the entire neighborhood!"

"He was upset. Those people tend toward tempers, you know."

"What had you done to make him so upset?"

"Lizzie!" Abby stopped cold, jam knife filled and spilling. "Your father has done absolutely nothing to bring on that type of display."

"That's right, Lizzie," Andrew said. "The man signed a lease for a shop space in town. The lease says no liquor sales, and when I went by there, he had a whole wall of wines for sale. So I had his store locked up. He can pick up his wares and peddle them elsewhere. But not in my storefront."

"He looked dangerous," Emma said.

"He'll cool."

Then Bridget Sullivan, looking equally disheveled from interrupted sleep, entered through the kitchen. "Did I hear yelling?" she asked.

"Oh, Maggie," Lizzie said, and took her arm and led her into the kitchen, where Abby heard her explaining the events to the maid.

Abby turned to Andrew. "You are not concerned about this then, Mr. Borden?"

"No," he said, and cut open another muffin. "Not at all."

Lizzie rocked slowly in her bedroom, her outward calmness belying her inward anxiety. She was to have dinner at Enid Crawford's house.

It had been three Sundays since she saw Enid Crawford for the first time in the council meeting. Since then, Lizzie had sought out her company, and they had sat together, holding hands, at church every Sunday. They had walked and talked of insignificiant, trivial things after church, and each week Lizzie had fallen more and more deeply in love with her.

Here was a woman who stood solidly outside of convention. She had opinions, and not always popular ones. She dressed plainly, yet with a certain elegance. She lived alone, she held a job, she was the sole support of her sons in college. She had buried a daughter and a husband, was widely read and highly intelligent. She wore her hair short for convenience: it was reddish brown, gray at the temples. Her eyes were crystal blue. Lizzie had never seen such clear blue eyes. Sparkling eyes. Shiny eyes. Enid boldly went out of the house and worked in her garden of a weekend with no hat, so her face and hands were lightly tanned, freckled and generously sprinkled with tender wrinkles. Her hair was reddened by the sun. She had a real laugh, a teasing, provocative laugh, and she had a wide grin, showing her teeth instead of hiding her mirth behind the shield of a hanky or the palm of her hand.

Lizzie would go home from their walks and talks after

church, floating on air, feet barely touching the ground, and she would ensconce herself in the loft and go over every detail of their time together. Enid didn't sing well, so her voice barely whispered the songs, but Lizzie felt Enid's emotion at the words of praise and adoration for the Lord.

Once or twice when the children of the congregation performed, Enid clapped with glee, completely forgetting herself and the impropriety of clapping in church.

And by the time the long week between Sundays came to an end, Lizzie had dreamed of this giant of a woman, larger than life, with attributes mostly associated with deity, and then they would meet, again on Sunday, and Lizzie would be floored again at how tiny Enid was.

Lizzie rocked, anxiety gnawing at her empty stomach. It was Wednesday night. She had been invited to Enid's house for supper. Lizzie tried not to think of the night she had been invited for supper at Kathryn Peters' house, tried not to think of the burgundy gown Kathryn had worn, tried not to think of that first intoxicating kiss she had received, and how mystifying, intriguing and exciting it all had been. She tried not to think that she would behave in that way toward Enid. She didn't want anything of Kathryn Peters to be in their evening; Kathryn was so coarse and callous, and Enid so refreshing and simple. If something magical happened between them, Lizzie wanted it to be spontaneous. Something *of* them, not something that Lizzie orchestrated.

Lizzie rocked. She knew what she would wear, she knew how she would attend her hair, she knew the route she would take to Enid's house . . . and the butterflies flew through her stomach and fluttered under her heart.

But there was a dark spot amid Lizzie's eager anticipation and newfound joy of life. It was a soft spot, a spoiled section of her life, and if she could have nicked it out with the point of a paring knife like the bruise on a pear, she would have.

This spot seemed small at the moment, amid the current ocean of happiness, but it embraced every aspect of her life.

All the nasty things in Lizzie's life had been relegated to this area, this small, smelly cesspool at the back of her mind. Even as she rocked, she knew she should clean it out, bring fresh air and light to it, but later, always later, and that pool had not only begun to smell, it had become poisonous. Dangerous.

Andrew's will was in there, and Emma's drinking. Abby's pressure to make Lizzie her baby swam in there, and so did dozens of high school friends who were now married and had lots of children. Kathryn, dear Kathryn, was there, and each and every one of Lizzie's failures, shortcomings and broken promises. Dozens of cookies and cakes. And lately, of course, though Lizzie hated to admit it, Beatrice, her book and her visit.

Lizzie's chest constricted and her breathing came a bit hard whenever she thought of Beatrice's visit. She wasn't at all prepared for it, and it was looming on the near horizon. The end of July, Beatrice had said, and it was nearly that. Lizzie didn't know what she would do when Beatrice arrived. Surely she would find Lizzie unkempt, unprepared, with one or more pimples, probably unbathed and during her monthly, with Emma raging and Abby stuffing herself with food and irate Italians pounding on the door to curse Andrew.

Lizzie had no idea how long Beatrice would stay, or even where she would stay. Would she stay here in the guest room? It seemed the most appropriate for a visiting friend, and yet Lizzie was loath to have anyone see the household in its reality. Beatrice under this roof! There was an inn in town, but could one put a visiting friend up in an inn?

And what on earth would they talk about?

Well, Lizzie could tell her of those weird, weird experiences she had of walking down the street and talking to people while she was still in the barn.

The barn! Oh, what would Beatrice think of the dusty old hayloft as Lizzie's place to study and practice?

Beatrice's visit was inconceivable. Lizzie would not be ready for Beatrice to visit her, Beatrice of the peach, Beatrice the perfect. Lizzie would not be ready, not until she was on her own, rich, elegant, and firmly ensconced in her own element.

And the Borden house was definitely not her element. It was no one's element.

So Lizzie pushed Beatrice and the endless reminders of her failure at life back to the edge of the slime pit and began rocking again, working hard to regain the excitement of dinner at Enid's.

The last letter Lizzie had received before Beatrice set sail for America held a saving grace for her: "You will find at times during your life that your lessons mean nothing. You will want to discount them, or worse, disregard them. Please do not. Please do the lessons as instructed, even when you cannot put your entirety to them. It appears as though your attitude or willingness is less important to their effectiveness than the actual act of performing them."

Lizzie was fairly frantic without letters arriving from Beatrice on a regular basis, but Beatrice was en route. Lizzie did her lessons, she continued with them, daily, but she got nowhere. They were automatic, done by rote, and touching each of her selves was a dismal failure. She'd been successful—too successful—in contacting her Angry Self. When she tried to contact her Prideful Self, she had a vision that scared her. It was as if she cracked open the door on a closet so stuffed full of junk that were she to open it more than the slightest bit, the whole lot would come crashing down on her head. Lizzie slammed the door shut and thought she ought to try a different self. She knew she'd have to come back to that one, but another time. Another time.

Right now, she thought as she rocked, she ought to be talking with her Lustful Self.

"What are you sitting here looking so smug about?"

Emma had walked through the door and Lizzie hadn't even noticed.

"Nothing." Emma always put Lizzie on the defensive.

"I swear, that man will have us all murdered in our sleep one day."

"What man?"

"Your father."

"Emma." Lizzie turned away.

"You didn't hear that man, that Eye-talian man. I tell you, Lizzie, we haven't heard the last of that. Something difficult, something violent will befall us because of your father's ridiculous business practices. Mark my words." Emma began pacing in Lizzie's room. Lizzie hated it when Emma paced in her room. She wanted to tell her to go pace in her own room if she had to pace. But Emma had started to rub her knuckles across her upper lip again, and Lizzie knew that she was lost to all logic and reason.

Fear rose in Lizzie as Emma burbled up from the sludge pool in the back of her mind. Emma was about to enter a rage, and the only ending of it was that she went to New Bedford and came home half dead. This would make three times this year and the year was not yet two-thirds over.

". . . he drives us to consider murdering him, doesn't he?"

"Emma!"

"He does, Lizzie, he does, you know it." Lizzie flushed, because she *did* know it. "We are all thinking of murdering him, he's such a terrible, terrible man, and if his actions can do that to members of his family, imagine what some of his tenants think. And those poor people who have to work for him! No, Lizzie, something terrible has begun here, and it's not going to stop until something really ugly happens." Emma's lip had begun to bleed, and two little dabs of pink froth appeared at the corners of her mouth. "And I can't be here when it happens. I can't. Someone will come in here and murder us all as we sleep, Lizzie, can't you see that? I can't stand by and let everything just be put down like that, do you understand? Oh God, I wish I could just smack him in the head with a hammer. Just once and end it all. Just put an end to his whole miserable life. How happy we would all be if he were only dead!"

Lizzie was dumbfounded.

Suddenly, Emma fell to her knees and grabbed Lizzie's hands in her own. Lizzie felt Emma's hard, cold, bony hands grip hers so tightly it hurt. "Lizzie, we've got to get out of here. We've got to get away. Far, far away. And we've got to do it now. Soon. Fast. Something is going to happen, I feel it in my bones, and we'll be powerless to stop it. Please."

And then Emma stopped raving and her face was twisted with fear and anxiety. But she wasn't mad, not yet. There was sanity in her eyes.

"All right, Emma. We'll leave. You go lie down now for a while and I'll see if I can make some arrangements."

A wild look of hope transformed Emma's face. She looked like a child about to be rewarded for doing something particularly difficult. It was such a new experience, it caught Lizzie totally by surprise. For once she was the older sister, the parent-sister, taking care of Emma. That had never happened before. For once, Emma sought her help and depended on her to see the project through.

"All right? You *will* go lie down for a while?"

Emma looked at her with distrust, and Lizzie could see that what sanity Emma still had fluttered like a distant and indistinct flag.

"No one will come this afternoon, Emma. We're safe for the time being. Now you go to your room and lock your window and your door. I'm going out tonight, and I'll make all the arrangements."

"All right." Emma released her hold on Lizzie's hands, then pulled herself up off her knees. She stood shakily, uncertainly. Then, as if trying to regain a drop of dignity, she walked, back straight, to her bedroom door, unlocked it, opened it, entered and shut it behind her without a backward glance.

Perspiration ran down Lizzie's face.

She felt in danger of sliding backwards into the pit. She could almost feel the slime oozing up over the rockers of her chair. She sat stock-still, staring straight ahead, her mind empty. She didn't know what to do, she didn't know what to think. Soon her mind began to grapple with words to describe the experience, and her fists began to clench. And suddenly, the struggle was full force. She desperately clutched for meaning as her thoughts merged and swirled with images from the pool faces and slices of conversation, embarrassments, taunts.

And then, suddenly, she was in the backyard. The light was sizzling bright. Everything seemed highly polished. Lizzie sat in her rocking chair in the upstairs bedroom, her hands in her lap, and she was also in the backyard, running her hand along the weather-splintered boards of the fence. She looked into the neighbor's yard, saw their young son sitting on the step eating something with his hands. She walked over to the barn, slowly, gently, as if she had all the time in the world, as if leisure were her only virtue. Her fingers trailed from the fence to the tops of the weeds, some flowering, some about to flower. She trailed her fingers across the front of the barn, not minding the dirtiness of it, whereas usually Lizzie needed to keep her hands very clean indeed. She moistened a dirty finger in her mouth and made a long mark across the dirty barn window, then continued on.

And all the while, Lizzie could see her dresser, her bed, her washbowl, dimly lit, as if a background set on a stage.

The outside Lizzie stopped and leaned her back against the barn, put one foot up on its side as she looked down at her hands. And then the maid, hair plastered to her scalp with perspiration, opened the kitchen door with a pot of dirty dishwater, looked at her and nodded.

The outside Lizzie spoke. "Is there a dessert, Maggie?"

"Miss Emma made blackberry tarts," Bridget answered, then threw the dishwater onto the lawn and disappeared back into the kitchen, the door slamming shut behind her.

Just as suddenly, Lizzie was wholly in her room. The other Lizzie was gone. She looked at her hands. They were clean. They were damp. They ached from being wrung.

She jumped up and ran downstairs, through the dining room, through the monstrously hot kitchen, out the back door.

There was a long mark on the dusty barn window. Fresh.

Lizzie slowly walked back up to the house.

"Just where had you got to, Miss Lizzie?" Bridget asked.

Lizzie didn't answer her. She suddenly had no words. She took a tart from the cooling tray and went back up to her room, locking her bedroom door. She put the tart on her bedside table and then lay down on the bed. She had no words, she had no ideas, she had no feelings. She only yearned for the days that used to be.

She tried to relax her hands, her neck, her shoulders. She floated Emma away, and Kathryn, and Andrew, and everybody, and everything, and surrounded herself with the cool green of a spring morning on the bank of a deep, swiftly moving stream.

● ● ●

She woke up one half hour before she was to be at Enid's for supper. She flew from the bed, took her towel and ran down the stairs, through the dining room and kitchen, then pounded heavily down cellar. She went to the toilet, then let cold water into the tub, undressed, stood in the tub and soaped herself down and rinsed, all with the frigid well water. She had no time to deal with her hair.

She dried off quickly, feeling the soap still on her skin, knowing it would give her a rash before she bathed again, then slipped hurriedly into her bathrobe, threw her soiled clothes into a pile on the dirt floor and ran back up to the kitchen. The cellar had a summer smell, an unpleasant sour odor, that went away in the winter when the wood furnace dried everything out down there. But in the summer it smelled of rot, not to mention the stench of the privy, and the flies that hovered above it. How on *earth* could Beatrice bathe down here?

The Borden house irritated Lizzie more and more each day, but she couldn't think of it now. Now she had an appointment, and she musn't be late.

Back in her room, she ate the tart as she dressed. She chose a light blue summer-weight skirt, as it was broiling hot outside, and a soft white silk blouse. She carefully donned her dress shields, or the blouse would be ruined in less than the ten minutes it would take to walk to Enid's.

She brushed out her hair, parted it down the middle, then wrapped it up in a long coil and pinned it down. Not the best job, but not bad.

She popped the last of the tart in her mouth, and as she did, a glob of berries fell out, ran down her blouse and came to rest on the lap of her skirt.

Lizzie closed her eyes and clenched her fists. Slowly, she picked up the offending fruit and then took her clothes off, wadding them up, knowing they would be ruined forever if she didn't take the time to care for the stain. She shoved the wad under the bed. She opened the closet. Nothing else was presentable. Nothing else was ironed.

She pulled out another white blouse, this one cotton and a little bit too tight, and put it on. She found another skirt, this one darker and heavier, but still light enough for a scalding July evening. She smoothed herself out, looked in on the sleeping Emma, then took her housekeys in her pocket and left. Late.

The heat outside hit her like a blast furnace. She briefly wondered why the "outside Lizzie" hadn't seemed to feel the heat. It was definitely too hot to hurry, she would really spoil her clothes, but at least her wrinkled appearance would not seem out of the ordinary.

She walked as quickly as she dared, without bringing down streams of perspiration, trying to remember Enid's directions to her little house, which was on the Hill, tucked in behind another, larger house. She cursed her faulty memory and wished that she'd just written the instructions down instead of being so vain as to impress Enid by claiming that she could remember everything.

But there it was, a little tiny house shaded by huge maple trees, tucked away in the backyard of a large house, a house that Lizzie had somehow never noticed before, even though it looked as though it belonged somewhere in Atlanta.

She stood for a moment in the shade of the big house, patting her hair and her clothes, and then walked up to Enid's door and knocked.

Enid wore men's pants. And a man's shirt, with buttons up the front, tucked into her pants and showing off her tiny waist. Her short hair was brushed back and she looked like a man, almost, a little tiny man with a big grin.

"Lizzie! Come in." And she opened the door wide.

It was cool inside. It was very, very cool inside. Cool and filled to the rafters with books, newspapers and magazines.

"Here," Enid said, and she picked up a pile of magazines from the end of the sofa and dropped them onto the floor. "Sit down. Or maybe you'd rather freshen up? I know it's a scorcher out there. The bath is down the hall."

Lizzie couldn't believe that Enid had not cleaned house in preparation for her visit. Lizzie could not believe that Enid lived like this. "Bath? Yes, I think I . . ." She followed Enid's gesture down the hall.

It was a bathroom. It had a bathtub. Lizzie turned the faucet and water came out, right into the tub. And there was a flush toilet. And a sink. And a large mirror framed in wood. She looked at herself. She looked monstrous, huge, red-faced. She ran cold water into the sink and splashed her face. The bathroom was spotless.

"There," Enid said. "You look a little better. Sorry about the house. It's always this way. I find the older I get the more interested I am in everything. I read all the time."

Suddenly, Enid was the delightful person Lizzie had come to love and covet, not a stranger who lived in a mess.

"I've just made us a salad for dinner. I hope you weren't expecting anything hearty."

Salad? Lizzie thought. There had never been a salad served in the Borden house. Meat, potatoes and gravy. Every night. Enid handed her a cool glass of lemonade.

"Sit. Relax. Tell me about yourself."

Lizzie settled back into the sofa, setting her drink on top of yet another stack of books on the coffee table. Enid sat at a little desk chair turned around, and she crossed her legs.

"Tell me about your family," she said.

Just as Lizzie was about to open her mouth, she noticed that Enid had gone just a little bit out of focus. She blinked, then blinked again, but the center of her vision was furred, and that meant only one thing. She closed her eyes and the sparkly fuzz was still there. Disappointment, despair, anger thrummed at her. She covered her face with her hands.

"Lizzie? Lizzie, dear, what is it?"

The stack of newspapers next to her slid onto the floor and then Enid was next to her, stroking her arm. "It's the heat, it's the damned heat," she said.

Lizzie had never heard a woman swear before, but her amazement was overshadowed by the fact that within ten minutes she would be lost in the depths of a soul-tormenting headache.

She put down her hands and lifted her face. The whole center of Enid's face was distorted. Soon the spot would grow and then hollow out, becoming an ever-widening ring. When the ring reached just past the outer edges of her vision, the pain would begin.

"Headache coming on," she said. "I get these terrible, terrible sick headaches, and now one is coming on." Tears of frustration leaked through, and Lizzie clamped down hard on them. She didn't want Enid to see her crying on top of everything else.

"I'm sorry," Enid said. "Can I get you something?"

"No, there's nothing, but I could never manage to reach home, and they sometimes last for . . . hours."

"Are they . . ."

"Dreadful."

"Should you eat?"

"I'd vomit it back up, I'm afraid."

"Well, then. You're my guest and we'll just have to make the best of it."

"I'm sorry, Enid. I'm terribly sorry. I feel like an invalid."

"We'll put you down in my bed, and I'll go to your house . . ."

The sparkling ring had hollowed out and Lizzie saw something peculiar on Enid's face. She put her hand on Enid's.

"I'll go to your house and tell your family that you won't

be home tonight. You'll sleep here and in the morning I'll fix you a breakfast instead of supper and you'll be on your way, good as new."

The thunder of the headache loomed on the horizon.

"I need dark. And quiet. I'm so glad it's cool here."

"Come. Let us make you comfortable. I even have a nightshirt that will fit you."

Lizzie pulled the pins out of her hair as she followed Enid into her bedroom. She somehow wasn't surprised to see piles of books on both sides of the bed, by the nightstands. Enid pulled a big cotton nightshirt out of a dresser drawer as the pain began to sound. Lizzie sat on the edge of the bed, her eyes half closing.

Enid drew down the shades and pulled the draperies closed.

"Come, Lizzie, let me get you out of those clothes."

Lizzie fumbled at her clothes, and Enid helped. She wished she could enjoy the act of being undressed by Enid, but now she felt limp, drained, and wanted only to be in the nightshirt, in the bed, with a soft pillow under her, so she could rest, just she and her pain, while they became reacquainted.

Sometimes it felt as if her headache pain was her only friend, her only consistent, loyal confidant. She could tell her pain anything, and if she didn't tell, then it wrenched the information from her. It visited her when she needed it the most and took everything she had to offer. Everything and more.

Lizzie felt her bare feet sliding between cool sheets, and lay her head on a fresh pillowslip. The pain moved in and moved Enid out. Lizzie never heard the door close.

hen the quiet knock came at the door, Andrew Borden was sitting at his desk, totaling his accounts. At first, he wasn't sure that he had heard a knock at all.

His first thought was of that bloody Italian man again, but he had pounded on the door, that stupid little greasy man had, and unless this was his wife— No, those wop bastards had greasy wives who would probably pound just as loud.

Then it came again, a soft little rapping, as if made by a child's hand.

He rose and went to the door.

He undid all three locks and opened the door.

There stood the Widow Crawford. Her hair was askew, her clothes hastily prepared. She wore a shawl to cover the fact that her dress was not properly pressed. In spite of himself, he whipped his head around to see if Abby approached.

"Good evening, Mr. Borden," she spoke with a clear, loud voice.

"Ma'am," he said.

"My name is Enid Crawford. I am a member of the Central Congregational Church, where I attend services with your daughter Lizzie."

"Oh?" Andrew had no idea what was going on, but he found his face flushing a deep crimson, something he always found becoming on Lizzie, but which he detested on himself.

238

"I invited Lizzie to dinner tonight—"

Anger flooded Andrew.

"—and just before we were to eat, she succumbed to a terrible headache." The anger fled. Lizzie had another headache. His heart went out to her. "I have put her to bed, and came to tell you that she wouldn't be home until morning."

He stood, staring at her.

"So you and your wife wouldn't worry, Mr. Borden."

"Of course, of course," he said. He still didn't know what to do or how to act.

"Mr. Borden?" Abby called from the kitchen. In a moment, she was at his side, pulling the door wide open, and the two women regarded each other for a long moment. Andrew was deeply ashamed at his wife's size. "What is it?"

"Lizzie went to Mrs. Crawford's home for dinner and was seized with a headache—" he began.

"Oh, my dear, please come in, come in, let me get you a coffee." As Abby turned, Enid gave Andrew a small smile, a knowing smile, a sly smile, a naughty smile, and she stepped over the threshold and began to look around.

"Well, perhaps Mrs. Crawford needs to attend . . ."

"Lizzie is asleep, or at least resting," Enid said, "and I'd love a cup of coffee. Cold, please, Mrs. Borden. No sugar."

Abby bustled her bulk ahead. "Come in, have a seat. I have coffee all ready."

"You shouldn't have come," Andrew whispered. He didn't know what else to say, what else to do.

"And just let you worry about Lizzie? She won't be home tonight. I had no choice. Besides . . ." She stepped in front of him and made herself comfortable on the sofa in the sitting room.

"What was Lizzie doing at your house anyway?"

"We've managed a friendship, Andrew," Enid spoke loud enough to make Andrew's heart race, but soft enough to keep her words for his ears only.

"Oh, Enid," he said, surprised at the way it sounded, it sounded like a moan, like the moans she elicited from him under highly different circumstances, it sounded intimate and personal, it sounded as if they were friends, lovers, when in actuality, they were rather business partners. But even business partners begin to realize a touch of affection for one another over a period of time, don't they? And perhaps, Andrew thought, as he realized how his "oh, Enid" sounded, he had fallen in love with her a little bit and liked the idea of being able to say such a thing to her.

"It's a harmless thing," Enid whispered, then straightened as Abby's heavy step sounded in the hall. "Lizzie and I were going over some church business. She's very involved with the Orientals, you know."

"Yes, isn't it wonderful?" Abby said, bringing in the glasses of coffee. Andrew regarded her with disdain. She was acting as if this were a social call, instead of a notification that their daughter was holed up in this woman's house sick and unable to leave. "I don't know much about Orientals at all, and Lizzie's changing churches just like that for no apparent reason was quite a shock to us all, as well you can imagine, but God does his mysterious works, doesn't he?"

"He does, Mrs. Borden," Enid said. "We all feel very fortunate to have Lizzie active in the Christian Endeavor Society. She is a wonderful person. An asset."

"What does your husband do?"

"My Charlie passed away years ago, Mrs. Borden. I work at the law offices to keep my boys in college up in Boston."

"Well . . ." Abby said, breathlessly, and had no more to say.

"Lovely home," Enid said, and the platitude fell quietly to the floor. Everyone looked at their feet. Andrew felt completely ill at ease. Bile burned at the top of his stomach and a cold dislike for Enid began to creep in around the gills. He brought his eyes up and met hers squarely. They looked at each other, Andrew felt his face an expressionless mask, and a queer look—almost fear, almost regret—crossed Enid's. Then they both looked at Abby, and her eyes were busily looking back and forth between them.

She knew. He knew she knew. He looked again at Enid, and saw that she had also seen the light in Abby's eyes. Andrew felt frosty toward the woman.

Enid set her untouched coffee on the table and stood up. "I'd better go back and check on Lizzie," she said. "I'm terribly sorry to have disrupted your evening."

"Oh, no trouble at all," Abby said, and Andrew wanted to slap her and tell her to shut her silly yap. "Give Lizzie our love. Sometime in the night her headache will pass, and in the morning she'll be better. Believe me. We've lived through many of Lizzie's headaches, haven't we?"

Andrew nodded. "She's like as not to vomit," he said.

Enid nodded. "Well, good-bye, then. I hope to see you again."

Andrew opened the door, Enid stepped out, and he closed it again, without another word. He turned all three locks, as if Enid had taken all his odd feelings with her and he never wanted them to return. Abby turned on her heel without so much as a glance toward him, took up Enid's glass from the table and disappeared into the kitchen.

Andrew went back to his ledgers, but his mind was not on numbers.

The house fell silent about him. He wished Lizzie were home, he wished Abby were not so overwhelmingly fat. He wished Enid had never come to the house. He wished Emma loved him still, he wished life were just a little bit easier for a man in his elder years, he wished for those youthful times, those good times, when he was a daddy, a hero to his little girls, and he used to take them . . .

Fishing! He and Lizzie had talked about fishing a while ago. Wouldn't it be good to take her—take both the girls, if

Emma had a mind to. Some nice fresh brook trout would be excellent, and the fresh air and sunshine—

—reminded him of rutting on the damp ground, Enid moving urgently beneath him, and his body stirred.

What in the *hell* was Lizzie doing at Enid's house? More important, what was Enid doing with Lizzie?

The stirring stopped. The inflation deflated. The moment of warm, pleasurable thought was replaced by another thought, one that put a cold stone in his lower belly. There was a hard edge to a woman who wore her hair short. There was a ruthlessness about a woman who wore no underwear and shamelessly seduced an older man for money. Blackmail was in Enid Crawford's soul, and Andrew saw how foolish he had been to allow their little business affair to carry on for so long.

And he had been going to put her in his will!

Surely she was after even more money, and would try to milk it, using Lizzie in some way.

He leaned his elbows on the desk and put his face in his hands. His hands were cold. He took off his specs and rubbed his face. It felt good, the cold, hard hands on his face, and when he looked up, and his vision cleared, Abby was standing in the doorway, wiping her hands on her apron.

"Are you ill, Mr. Borden?"

"No, no, just . . . worried about Lizzie, I think. She hasn't been away from home for a night before."

"When she was abroad . . ."

"Yes, I know, but she was not ill. I feel as though I should go and check on her."

That was the wrong thing to say. As soon as he said it, he knew how it sounded. It sounded as though his Fridays with Enid Crawford were not enough, and now he wanted to add a Wednesday to them as well. He knew she kept her gaze steady on him, but he could not meet it. "I don't think I shall, though. I don't even know where Mrs. Crawford lives."

"Doesn't the bank do business with that law firm of hers?"

"I believe so, yes."

"Hmm." She turned and went back to the kitchen.

Andrew was stunned with anxiety. His life was disintegrating. First Emma. Then Lizzie became too independent and decided she wanted to live in her own house. And now, he was fool enough for Enid Crawford, and Abby was feeling it personally. And what on *earth* might Enid do to Lizzie?

He would take it up with Enid on Friday.

He went into the kitchen and took a tart into the dining room, sat down, hoping Abby would join him. She didn't. He ate it, then went upstairs to bed.

When Lizzie awakened, her whole being was awake in an instant. She smelled the difference in the room, felt the different sheets, the larger size of the room. Disoriented in the darkness, heart pounding, she recalled the headache, and before the headache, readying for dinner at Enid Crawford's.

A low moan escaped her before she could stop it. How could she have a headache at Enid Crawford's? What a terrible thing to impose.

"Lizzie?"

The word was whispered so close to her ear, at first Lizzie thought she was still dreaming. She turned her head, and there was Enid, tucked into bed next to her. A tiny hand found hers under the covers, and a smooth foot slid over and nestled next to hers. "How are you feeling?"

"Better." Lizzie turned her head away. This was what she had wanted, this was what she had dreamed of for weeks: to get Enid Crawford into bed. And here they were, Lizzie not clever, not adept, not bold or adventurous, but pitiable, weak, small, injured, stupid. Enid was in bed with her all right, but it was not to love her; no, it was to comfort her, as a parent might sleep with a sickly child.

Lizzie wanted nothing more than to get out of bed, dress and fly home as fast as her feet could possibly take her.

"I was terribly worried about you." The whisper was still close to Lizzie's face, intimate, quiet. A tear leaked out of the corner of Lizzie's eye. "I went to see your parents to tell them that you wouldn't be home." A sob escaped Lizzie and two more tears fell. Enid squeezed her hand tighter, then moved closer. Her arms came around Lizzie, and soon Lizzie's head was on Enid's shoulder, and she was sobbing, crying as hard as she had ever cried. Enid smoothed her hair and kissed her forehead and rocked her gently back and forth, saying "Shhh, Lizzie, it's all right. Everything's going to be just fine."

Eventually, the emotion was spent, and Lizzie lay quietly within Enid's calm. Her life was a mess, and that left a gaping hole in the pit of her stomach. She didn't seem to be able to do anything right, any of those pitiful little attempts she made at doing anything at all. Everything turned bad in one way or another. Life, it seemed, was a terrible joke, a practical joke played by God, in his infinite torturous ways, upon all his timid, unfortunate subjects.

"Your father said you might vomit," Enid said.

Lizzie was horrified. "He *did*?"

Enid chuckled.

"Oh God." Then Lizzie found the humor in it, found the humor in everything, suddenly, and she began to laugh. "Aren't they a pair?"

Enid began to laugh harder, and the bed shook with the two of them holding onto each other, unable to speak, racked with laughter. Eventually, Enid said, "Your mother didn't like me."

"She's afraid of small people, like an eleph—" Lizzie laughed until she cried. "Elephant of a mouse."

Enid wiped her cheeks with both hands, bouncing Lizzie's head around. Lizzie reached around Enid, and brought her tiny body close. She felt a lot like Kathryn, but more tender, gentler, softer.

They held each other close for a long time, now and then a chuckle escaping in remembrance.

Lizzie felt that she held within her arms the first good

thing that had happened to her in her whole life. Somehow, she wanted Enid to know it.

"I love you," she said, before she thought twice.

Enid hugged her closely. "And I am falling in love with you."

They entwined their legs, and Lizzie watched Enid's profile as she stared at the ceiling, until sleep overcame her and she slept.

When next Lizzie awoke, sunshine streamed in the gauze-curtained window and her heart soared. Enid was up, and the smell of bacon and eggs and fresh coffee permeated the room. The house was cool; at this time of day the Borden house was already sweltering, but the big shade trees kept Enid's house cool enough so she could light the wood stove and cook breakfast. Including a fresh pot of coffee. Lizzie floated out of bed and into the bathroom.

Sometimes this happened after a headache, this feeling of lightness, feeling of rightness. Lizzie felt as if the world were her gleaming possession this morning, as if she could do, be or have anything she wanted. She wanted to laugh in the face of all her troubles, laugh at everyone's troubles. She wanted to sing and make light of the woes of the world.

She flushed the toilet and watched the yellowed water swirl down. She wanted one for her bedroom. Well, she would have one, too, in her new house. A beautiful bathroom. Just like this one, only better.

She washed her face, then brushed out her hair. She knotted it back up on top of her head quickly, and went into the kitchen, still wearing the nightshirt that Enid had loaned her the night before. Somehow it felt more personal, more intimate, more appropriate than the clothes she had worn to supper the night before.

"Good morning!" Enid looked as happy as Lizzie felt. Lizzie hugged her.

"I don't normally eat bacon and eggs for breakfast, but

since you had no supper, I thought you'd be hungry this morning."

"You were right."

"Well, sit down, then, and I'll fix your plate."

Lizzie cleared a stack of newspapers from the end of the sofa and sat down. Enid brought her a steaming cup of coffee. "It's so nice and cool here."

"This is a nice house. It's always been the coolest during the hot summer months. I swelter in the office all day long, and then just come home and take off my clothes. Sometimes I soak in the bathtub filled with cold water."

That sounded like the strangest idea in the world to Lizzie. "Bathtub filled with cold water? I never heard of such a thing. Hot, soapy water, I always thought."

"You should try it sometime."

Shame tried to poke a hole in Lizzie's good mood. She dared not reveal that their house didn't even have a flush toilet, never mind a bathtub. And her baths were almost *always* cold water. Frigid water. Well water, straight from the tap. "I shall," she said, and blew across her coffee.

Enid dressed and left for work, leaving Lizzie a light kiss on the lips to remember, and an invitation to stay as long as she liked. First, she poked through Enid's things, and found all her cabinets to be as filled as the open flat spaces. The Borden cabinets were filled too—with china, with useless things that were always "too good" to be used for every day; yet the special occasions were so rare as to hardly warrant cleaning them when the time came. Enid's cabinets were filled with tools, books, magazines, newspapers and gadgets, piled in profusion and disarray. Everything looked useful, although Lizzie couldn't identify half of the items. It was a joyous, crowded house.

Lizzie fingered the clothes in Enid's closet. They were of good quality, but less expensive than the clothes Lizzie wore. Most were cottons; there were a few silks. One bedroom had two beds, and the clothes closet in there was filled with men's clothes. Lizzie closed the door quickly on that one; she didn't know if the clothes belonged to Enid's deceased husband or to her two sons. It didn't matter. She was comfortable fingering Enid's belongings, but the men in her life were a mystery to Lizzie, and they were best kept mysterious.

When she had snooped to her heart's content, she heated enough water to both wash the dishes and take a bath.

Soaking in the tub was a thrilling luxury. Enid had perfumed soap crystals—they looked like a gift from someone—and it didn't appear as though Enid partook. Lizzie knew that Enid wouldn't mind if she did. She generously sprinkled the salts into the water, swirled them into oblivion with her foot, then lay back and relaxed as the scented steam rose about her.

"I now claim that which is divinely mine," Lizzie said to the wallpapered ceiling. "Enid. Enid is divinely mine. I claim absolute control over each fragment of my personality, to be strengthened through purposeful, conscious unity." She knew the words by heart, but this time she wanted only to have Enid Crawford for her own, and if that was the purpose toward which each fragment of her personality had to strive . . . so be it. It made good use of these stupid lessons, she thought. "I now will that the divine power which motors the universe now deed me the control over my own destiny with Enid. I now claim that I, and no other, am the architect of my future with Enid. I now command my rightful, unique place in the order of all material. In Enid's tub. So it is, so shall it be."

She soaked until her fingers puckered and the water chilled. Getting out of a chilled tub was even better, for the day had turned warm, even in Enid's cool house. She dried, dressed and, reluctantly, went home.

I must have my own home, she thought as she made her

way quickly through the heat. Perspiration soaked right through her dress shields, and trickled down her breasts. She wanted to be home quickly before her enthusiasm dampened, before anyone noticed her evening wear on this hottest of mornings. She wanted to get home and get a lighter cotton duster on before she perished in the heat. The heat was awful.

But her own house would be in the shade of the trees, just like Enid's. And she would have a clawfoot tub as well. And a large bathroom, with a flush toilet, and a private yard with lots of fruit trees. Particularly the pears. Perhaps she could have someone grow a piece of the Borden house pear tree, and she could put it in her backyard. That tree yielded the tastiest pears ever. It was the only good thing about that terrible, stupid house.

The Borden house had once been divided into two apartments. When Andrew and Sarah Borden bought that house, they did no remodeling at all. Therefore, the layout was bizarre, the rooms small, unconventional, cramped and inconvenient. Lizzie longed for a house that made sense, a regular house with nice large rooms. It would be absolutely divine if her house could be on the Hill, near Enid, where she could enjoy a view of Fall River, the church, the river, the farms. But all she really needed was a home of her own, even if Emma had to live there with her. She could invite Enid over for dinner with Emma there. She could have Beatrice for the weekend with Emma there. She could do neither of those things while living in the Borden house. That terrible, terrible house.

Lizzie turned the corner and looked at that tiny, narrow, ugly litte house on Second Street. It was shameful to live in that squalid little building. Lizzie stopped dead in her tracks and looked at it, as if for the first time, and she could smell the interior. It smelled of old, musty dust. It smelled of mildewed, sour cellar. It smelled like Emma and Andrew and

Abby and all that was wrong with the world, and Lizzie didn't want to go inside.

She looked around her. She had nowhere else to go.

She would speak with Andrew that day *that day* and she would not relent until she had his agreement that she should have her own home. She would *not* relent.

She walked around the side of the house, along the narrow path between their house and the neighbor's, knocked on the screen door to the kitchen, and when Maggie opened the door, Lizzie filled her lungs with the stench of food that had been left out in the heat too long, food that had been breakfast again and would be dinner *again*, the stench of the Borden home.

· August

"Oh, Lizzie?"

"Yes, Mrs. Churchill?"

"Have you a new horse?"

"No, Mrs. Churchill." Lizzie turned to see the next-door neighbor leaning out her kitchen window.

"You're spending so much time in the barn."

"I know," Lizzie said, and then continued on. Mrs. Churchill kept her finger on—or her nose in—every tiny bit of information on the whole neighborhood. She kept Abby apprised of the birthings in the area, and sometimes she had some valuable information. Lizzie bore Mrs. Churchill no ill will. She hoped someday Mrs. Churchill would be the first on the scene with some really big news, and so become deified within her gossip group.

It was so hot in the hayloft that Lizzie could barely breathe. She unearthed her book, took a deep breath and began to read her first lesson. She unbuttoned the top of her blouse, and let her skirt ride up her thighs. She let the perspiration run freely off her face and arms, and watched the dark stains appear on her clothing. She read the paragraph, and when she finished, she automatically began setting up the candles and the mirror, and idly wondered if that initial lesson had any meaning left for her, or if it had all been squeezed out like the rind of a lemon. Or perhaps it had just become rote, like some of the things in church, or like furniture that is taken for granted and no longer even noticed. Perhaps she should spend some time again with that first lesson.

But she was too tired.

She moved a piece of board over the window to darken the room, lit the candles, looked at her watch, and then regarded her reflection in the mirror.

This, too, had become boring. What was the purpose of it? She watched as the edges of the mirror became indistinct, and then her face changed shape, all of it swirling a bit around the two eyes. Her eyes locked onto those of her reflection, and the many faces of Lizzie Andrew Borden faded in and out around them.

Within ten minutes, she had had enough. She blew out the candles, took the board down, shoved the box from her and picked up the book again. Lesson three. God, she was sick of lesson three.

She had tried talking to her Angry Self, but nobody ever answered. She thought that perhaps it was the Angry Self that went walking, but if it was, it wasn't talking to her. She tried talking to her Greedy Self, too, and her Jealous Self. She had been on this lesson for months, *months*, and had gotten nowhere, except to believe that those selves did indeed exist within her. Yet she didn't feel as if she could go on, not until she'd gotten to the bottom of the list, not until she'd gotten to talk with her Higher Self, and her Healthful Self, and her Whole Self. That seemed to be of paramount importance in this program of Beatrice's. Besides, she wanted to talk to her Whole Self.

She took a deep breath, relaxed and began again. "Angry Self?" she whispered, and then waited to listen for a reply. Nothing. "Greedy Self?" She waited. Nothing.

Lizzie threw the Beatrice Book against the wall. She began to pace. She wanted to leave Fall River *right this minute* and never return. She never wanted to hear the next chapter in the life of Andrew Borden. Or Abby. Or Emma. Or the church or the Orientals or Beatrice, or . . . or . . .

Life was out of control. Lizzie seemed to be at the end of a long chain of people, running as fast as possible, and they were whipping her about, hoping she'd fall off, hoping they'd shake her loose and be rid of her. Well, they were close. Lizzie had had about enough.

But if she left, there would be an end to her friendship with Enid, a most uncommon friendship, something intimate and quite beyond words. Enid was the best friend Lizzie never had, she was the big sister Lizzie never had, she was the mother Lizzie never had. Enid had opened a need so deep within Lizzie that Lizzie was afraid to look down the hole. She was afraid that it went on forever, unfillable, she was afraid of what was crawling around down there in the dark and the muck of her nether selves.

But by opening that door, Enid was also allowing fresh air and sunshine into that place, that dark place of longing, that place Lizzie hoped Beatrice and her book of lessons could fill. Beatrice and her book could never hope to mend a rent of that proportion. But perhaps Enid could.

Lizzie knew that such thinking was dangerous. Her life was already in the hands of too many others—and here she was again, placing her most precious asset of all—her trust—in the hands of a woman she hardly knew, yet whom she felt as if she knew through and through.

It was hard. It was agonizing. She wanted to leap into Enid's lap and nurse at her breast. She wanted to run from Enid as well as the rest of them and never hear the name again.

And so she flopped down in the hay, where the heat was filled with dust motes and her skin gleamed slick and she couldn't keep her hands away from that center part of her that was her only solace in times like this.

254

Lizzie slowly fingered herself and thought about Enid. At church, Enid had looked like a queen. Her short hair was newly cut, and its thick waves, brushed back from her tanned face, made her seem exotic. Lizzie thrilled every time she looked at her. They sat next to each other and held hands, Lizzie's skin itching to be out of her gloves and touching Enid's skin.

That she had been such an inconvenience for Enid, what with her stupid headache and all, and to have Enid still care enough about her . . . Only family do that for one another, don't they?

But family do it whether they want to or not, because they *have* to. They're *expected* to. But when Emma was in such dire need, did either Andrew or Abby visit her? No.

Life should be clean and simple, Lizzie thought. Everyone should have someone to love them and take care of them. Everyone should have purpose in life, and something to look forward to.

Lizzie had none of that. The only thing she had to look forward to was church next Sunday, and sitting next to Enid. But any moment, Enid might turn the way Kathryn did, and that would be the end of that.

Lizzie threw her skirts down over her knees, stood up and began to walk back and forth. It was at least ten degrees hotter at her head than at her feet. Sweat poured anew.

What if Beatrice should show up this very moment? She said the end of July or the first of August. This was the first of August. She said she'd write, but what if the letter were lost, or delayed, or . . . What if she just showed up and knocked at the door? Perfect in peach, cool and collected, rich beyond anyone's imagination, calm, in control. Lizzie would just waltz out of the barn, bedraggled and soaked through with her own juices. She would shake hands with her and they would sit on the back porch in the shade and eat pears right off the tree.

Lizzie wondered if she wasn't becoming a bit hysterical.

She looked around and saw *Pathways* on the floor in the corner. She retrieved it, opened it to the first page and began to read aloud, standing in front of the loft window, as if the whole of Fall River were her audience. Halfway through the first paragraph, she paused.

If Beatrice came right now, she thought, I would send my other self to greet her. First, I would send my other self to the cellar to bathe, then to the bedroom to change clothes. Then she and Beatrice could have a fine discussion, and whatever was decided between them could be between *them*. It wouldn't have to have anything to do with me at all.

Lizzie dropped the book, scattering up a ruffle of dust. Then she sat on the edge of the loft, letting her legs dangle over the edge. A knot caught in her throat. Life is hard sometimes, she thought. Life is really hard.

She allowed one tear to leak out and mix with the sweat on her face, then she swung down the ladder and out of the barn, locking the door securely behind her. Anything to make Emma angry.

In her bedroom, she dared a look at herself in the mirror. She was a mess. Hair unkempt and frazzled from the relentless heat and perspiration, Lizzie gathered new clothes and made ready for the bath. As she came down the stairs, a knock came at the door. Fear flooded Lizzie. What if it was Beatrice? What if it was? She listened, but she heard no one else home. There was no one else to answer the door.

Heart pounding, she walked to the door and said, "Who is it?"

"Sarah Whitehead," was the answer. Lizzie breathed a sigh. She unlocked the front door and let Sarah in. Weird little Sarah. Lizzie never got over the fact that Abby's half sister should have the same name as Lizzie and Emma's mother. It was not right, somehow.

256

"Hello, Sarah."

"Lizzie." Sarah had put on a dress for the occasion. Lizzie was impressed. "Is Abby here?"

"I don't think so."

"Would you check, please? It's ever so important."

"All right. Wait here." But Sarah followed her into the sitting room and sat on the sofa. Lizzie went through the kitchen and called to Abby up the back stairs. She answered, and in a moment, her bulk came jostling down the stairs.

"Sarah is waiting for you in the sitting room," Lizzie said, then went down cellar to bathe.

The cellar was nice and cool, and if it hadn't smelled so bloody rotten, Lizzie could easily see spending her August days amid the cool. She opened the faucet and let cold water into the bucket. She poured several bucketsful into the bathing tub, fetched a mildewed towel from the nail, and stripped off her clothes. She stepped into the tub and poured a bucket of cold water over her head. It was shockingly cold, but it felt wonderful.

She sat down, as well as she could fit, inside the washtub, and washed herself and her hair with the rough lye soap that Emma made every autumn when Andrew brought home lard from the farm. Then, with a clear bucket, she rinsed herself, feeling her hair fan out over her skin. Then she sat up, playing with the soap bubbles, her knees up to her chest, the cold settling in deep. Soon, she was shivering.

Oh, wasn't it a luxury to be cold. But why had it to be either hot or cold? Couldn't cool do? Couldn't there be a cool, pleasant place in all of Fall River this August? Lizzie shivered and thought how odd it would be to ask Abby to send down her cape. Her seal cape. Her fancy seal cape, made from "seals from the Prussian Sea."

Andrew had given her that cape, in a rare, odd moment. It was expensive, of that there was no doubt, and Andrew was not prone to moments of extravagance. Lizzie doubted that there was a Prussian Sea, or that the seals in her cape came from it, but if that's what it took to sell the cape to Andrew, then she would allow him that bit of romanticism. But it was the finest cape in all of Fall River, Lizzie was certain, and she wished she had it now.

Then she began to giggle again. The thought of it. Sitting naked in the little washtub, knees to her chin, surrounded by that luxurious cape. What a sight! Oh, but she would get soap all over it, and that would never . . . oh. The cape had a smear of lampblack on it, and Lizzie had never taken it in to be cleaned. Well, she would have to do that before the cold weather hit. . . . And her spirits lightened again at the thought of cold weather hitting, it seemed so unlikely in the midst of this terrible heat wave.

She splashed more fresh, cold water over herself and watched the goose pimples rise, watched her nipples shrink. She would be cramped when she tried to stand up.

Perhaps I'll just send one of my other selves out with the cape, she thought, mirth clearly on her mind.

And then the day was unusually bright and she was walking down the street. It was blazing hot, it was so hot that nobody was out in the streets, nobody was in the sun. Shop doors were open, windows were open, women wore their housedresses in public, because they would barely survive with corsets and stays. Lizzie walked jauntily down the street, and she felt a smile on her face, a giggle just on the tip of her tongue. She was wearing the clothes she ruined this morning, and then she noticed that she hadn't ruined them; the skirt had some paint splattered on it from the time she helped repaint the barn. So she hadn't ruined the clothes after all. . . . They were the right ones to wear to the barn. But they were not the right ones to wear to town.

She continued down the street, smiling, with an "I don't care" attitude, and she turned right into the drugstore.

The weasel-faced man she'd seen in there before stood behind the counter. "Good day," he said.

She nodded at him, looking around at this and that. Then, finally, with much self-control, she walked to the counter and said, "I'd like to buy some . . . prussic acid."

"Prussic acid! Whatever for?"

Lizzie had to turn away for a moment to keep the smile from breaking out on her face. She touched her fingertips to her mouth until she was sure she could do this without laughing. "I want to clean a sealskin cape," she said, and she was sure she said it without a hint of mirth.

"I'm sorry, miss, but the druggist isn't in, and he would have to be the one to dispense prussic acid.'"

"I only need a small amount," Lizzie said. "It isn't a very big spot." She wanted to go on about prussic acid being the only thing that could clean skins from Prussia, but it just became too much.

"I'm sorry," he said, as she fled the store.

Outside in the sun, in the heat, it suddenly didn't seem so funny anymore.

Lizzie splashed in the cold water, and felt her muscles tighten. She wanted this other self—which one was it, anyway?—to disappear, she wanted to be totally back in the cellar, where she could be back in control. She wanted to dry off and get out of the tub.

But the other self had other ideas, as well, and the downtown Lizzie did not turn toward home, but instead strolled down the street toward Andrew Borden's bank.

No, Lizzie in the tub thought. Not Father's bank.

But the other Lizzie didn't go in, just walked past, smiling at everyone, past the mill, taunting, it seemed, the Lizzie in the tub.

And then she saw Emma.

Emma, dressed in black, dressed *shabbily* in black, striding toward her. Emma, pinched face hatchet sharp, stray hairs escaping the tight bun, Emma, all knees and elbows, rushing far too fast in this heat, headed straight for her. "Lizzie! Lizzie! I say!" and Town Lizzie stood there and waited, small smile on her lips, as Emma approached.

"Lizzie, get yourself home this minute and put on some decent clothes. Where are your gloves? I swear you have suffered a seizure in this heat. Get home right now, and wait for me. I have news. Oh dear me, I have news." And Emma strode on, down Main Street, and Lizzie watched as she entered into the law office.

Town Lizzie did start down the street toward home, and then disappeared.

And Lizzie shivered with cold and fright from head to foot in the tiny tub down cellar.

With great aching effort, she stood up and dried her wrinkled skin with the smelly towel. Then she dressed in a simple wrapper and went upstairs.

The sitting room was empty. Sarah Whitehead had gone. She went to her room. Her door and Emma's door were both unlocked and open, the only time Lizzie had ever seen them so.

Lizzie sat down in her rocker and rocked, sure of bad news as soon as Emma returned. She was sure that bad news marched toward them from several directions. She rocked slowly, and waited.

uch, Emma! Emma, you're hurting me!"

"Sit down, Abby. Sit down right now and listen to me." Emma released her grip on Abby's wrist when she seemed willing to leave the plate of cakes on the kitchen table and come with her into the dining room. They sat across from each other like adversaries.

Emma looked at her stepmother across the table, and she hardly seemed familiar. Abby's face was puffy and bloated. She looked terrified. Well, she had a few more surprises coming. "I overheard your conversation with Sarah Whitehead this morning."

"That was private."

"And, I went to the law offices to look at Father's will."

Abby drew in a sharp breath. "You have no right."

"I did, and so do you. But that's beside the point, because Father's will is no longer there."

Emma sat back and watched with satisfaction the range of emotions that crossed Abby's face, from puzzlement to disbelief, to amazement, to anger. "But then, where?"

"Good question. That's what you must find out from him tonight. If Sebastian Whitehead means to do Father some harm Abby, then we need to know just exactly what is in his will."

"Emma, I can't—"

"If you don't, I will. And believe me, Abby, I *will* get answers from the old man."

Abby began to cry. "You're a hateful person."

"Perhaps. Your cakes are waiting." Emma left the room quickly. The sight of the pitiful woman made her sick to her stomach.

She went up the stairs and unlocked Lizzie's door.

Lizzie sat there, in her rocker.

"Lizzie! You're home."

"Yes."

"And bathed? How could that be?" Emma had seen Lizzie not fifteen minutes before, in the middle of town, and Lizzie always made such an event out of bathing that the whole house knew of it.

"What is it, Emma? What is so important?"

"Sarah Whitehead was here this morning, talking to Abby. I happened to overhear their conversation."

"Just *happened* to?"

Emma ignored the implication. "It seems as if Abby has been unsuccessful in getting our father to change his will in Sarah's favor, and so now Sebastian, that little twit's husband, has taken it upon himself to do harm to our father so that Abby, as wife, will inherit everything. Then Abby can do as she wishes with her inheritance, even give it all to her sister and leave us right out of it."

"What are you saying, that Sebastian is going to kill Father?"

"That's what Sarah said, not me."

"I can't believe that, Emma."

"Well, then listen to this. When I saw you in town, I was headed straight for the law offices. I demanded to see a copy of Father's will, but he took the original out some weeks ago and has not brought it back. The will is missing, Lizzie. And if it is not to be found, then for sure Abby will inherit everything."

"Wait, Emma. This doesn't make sense. Why would Father's will be anywhere other than at the law office? Father would just write instructions and have them sent over, they would write a new will and be done with it. Just because they told you they didn't have it, doesn't mean that they don't have it. It's not your will, after all, and perhaps they have a responsibility to their clients to keep their affairs confidential." Even as she said this, Lizzie realized she could imagine no little law clerk being a match for Emma when Emma was like this.

"They looked for it, Lizzie. I asked them to make sure his will was in order, and they went into the vault and came back with a note that said that Mr. Borden had removed the original copy of his will sometime in July."

"Have you looked in his desk?"

"No. I just got home and told Abby to find out from him what is going on, and to find it out today."

"Don't you think someone should tell the police that Sebastian is threatening Father's life?"

"I think that's up to Abby. She'll have to tell Father, of course, and that won't bode well for Sarah being included in his will either, will it? And if they both decide that the threat is real, well, I suppose they will tell the police." Emma stopped her pacing and looked at Lizzie, sitting so calmly in her rocking chair. Her fingers were idly picking at her skirt. "I just don't understand you, Lizzie. I don't understand how you can remain so calm throughout all of this. It's not right. It's not quite human."

"Calm? I guess I am, although I don't quite feel calm. I feel quite odd, actually, as if none of this is really happening."

"Oh, it's happening, all right," Emma said, "and as soon as Father gets home, even more is going to happen, I assure you." Emma turned to go into her room, and then said to Lizzie, "If you hear Father coming in the door, be sure to call me."

Lizzie nodded, and Emma wasn't entirely sure she heard, but didn't feel like repeating herself. She closed the door of her room and stood there, arms crossed, fists clenched. She felt the familiar taste come to her mouth, the taste of hate. She felt the rage build from a burning in her throat to a furnace in her gut. She felt her face redden, and with a will of their own her knuckles began to rub against her lip, and she began to pace.

Occasionally, a coherent thought or phrase would run through her mind, and be snagged and repeated until the sounds lost all form or meaning. Most of the time, there was no coherence. There was only depth. Vast injustice. And sometimes Emma recognized fear. This time she knew exhaustion as well. She was tired of this, tired of it all. She was sick and tired of being sick and tired, and the old man was the cause of it all.

She couldn't wait for him to come in the door. She would see to it that he would finally, *finally* understand his family obligations and not leave all his money to that Sarah thing, or to his slut.

But then she had told him all that before, hadn't she? And had it made a difference?

The rage burned hotter. The thought fled through her mind, *I've got to get out of here*, but Emma pushed it away. Not yet, not yet.

She didn't want to go back to the Capitol Hotel, although a little drink would be welcome to help calm her nerves.

Out of the question. It would dull her senses. It would also cast her into the other helplessness, that place where she would stay, submerged, for weeks at a time, surfacing only to crawl home. She could never do that in Fall River. Never.

Fairhaven! The Fairhaven relatives. She had always got on with her mother's kin in Fairhaven. She could go talk to them, stay with them, stay away from New Bedford, and if they agreed with her reasoning, she could bring them back with her to Fall River to speak with Father. They would never want their mother's offspring to be destitute while the second wife's half sister, or a tart, for God's sake, inherited the lot.

That's good. That's good. That's very good.

She took a long breath. She pulled her knuckles away from her lip. She slowly took control of the madness that she had always allowed. Her upper lip, she noticed, was already beginning to swell. She took herself to the bed and got down on her knees.

"Mother," she said, "I will take care of Lizzie, as I have always promised you. I won't let that man fritter away all that you and I worked for. I promise you that. I promise you that. Even if that Abby woman has to die first." Emma gasped at that thought. She was astonished that such a thing would come from her lips in a prayer to her mother. She put her forehead on the bed and covered her face with her hands in an attitude of shame, thinking that killing Abby and then killing Andrew was not such a bad idea after all.

Think of the problems it would solve.

Perhaps she should have a talk with Sebastian Whitehead.

When Lizzie heard her father's key in the front door, she quickly and quietly slipped out of her bedroom and locked it behind her. She didn't want Emma to know he was home. She tiptoed down the stairs and met him in the entrance to the sitting room.

"Hello, Father."

"Lizzie."

"Any mail?"

"Yes, in fact, a letter from your British friend."

"Oh?" Lizzie took the letter. It was postmarked Washington, D.C. She slipped it into the pocket on her duster.

"There are a couple of cookies left, Father. Would you like some cold milk?"

Andrew looked at her over his glasses. He smiled. "Yes, that would be nice."

Lizzie helped him to sit down, took off his boots and then went to the ktichen to fix him a plate.

Abby stood in the kitchen.

"Not now, Abby. Let me have a few moments with him first, please."

Abby turned without saying a word, and made her way up the back stairs to her bedroom. Andrew would be joining her up there for his afternoon nap, most likely, unless he slept on the sofa in the sitting room. Regardless, there would be no confrontation until Lizzie said so.

She took the plate of cookies and glass of milk in to him, where he was reading his mail. "Anything interesting?"

"No." He set the mail aside and took a cookie.

"Will we read today?"

"Of course, Father," Lizzie said. "What would you like to read?"

"Anything you choose, Lizzie."

"All right." Lizzie got up and fetched the book they had been reading together. It was almost finished. She sat back down next to him, made him comfortable with a pillow and then opened the book.

Emotion clogged her voice, though, and she had to pause for a long moment. Andrew drank his milk and went for another cookie, so the interruption was not necessarily noticed. She was overcome with love for this strange, strange man. The thought that Sebastian Whitehead might want to murder him for his money made her . . . made her . . . not mad, just sad. Terribly, terribly sad. He was just a man after all.

She got control of herself and began to read.

Within minutes, Lizzie recognized the even breathing of her father sleeping. She picked some cookie crumbs from his vest front, touched her gold high school ring on his little finger, closed the book and set it on her lap. She watched him sleep for a long time. All the harshness of his face was gone. But the lines seemed to deepen, as if his worries intensified in his dreams.

Lizzie carefully reached into the pocket of her wrapper and pulled out the letter from Beatrice.

My Dearest Lizbeth:

What an exciting country America is! I'm accomplishing much amid my wide-eyed wonder at the newness of it all. I can't wait to sit with you and tell you of all my adventures. By current reckoning, I should be in

Fall River the evening of August third, or the morning of the fourth.
Kisses.
Affectionately,
Bertrice

Wednesday night!

Lizzie's breath caught in her throat. She wasn't ready for Beatrice. She needed to be something else before Beatrice could arrive with her tales of independence and excitement. Lizzie sat, outwardly calm, the paper in her hands not even trembling, while her heart raced and pressure built up behind her eyes. There was a peculiar taste in her mouth—

And just then, Lizzie realized the signs. If she didn't get up and do something, some other self would pop out and embarrass her or complicate things. Careful not to waken Andrew, she rose from the sofa, pocketed the letter, and went upstairs.

She knocked on Emma's door.

Emma turned the key as if she'd been standing right next to the door when Lizzie knocked.

"Father is downstairs," Lizzie said. "He's sleeping. Let him rest before you attack him with your accusations."

"*Attack* him, why—"

"Yes, attack him, Emma. You know exactly what I mean."

"There's no call for you—"

Lizzie shut Emma's door in her face. Emma slammed her fist into the other side, but did not open the door. Lizzie slipped off her wrapper and donned a light cotton town dress. She let her hair down, brushed it about a half dozen strokes and twisted it up again, fastening it loosely with a couple of pins. Then she fixed her stockings, stepped into shoes, locked her bedroom door and tiptoed down the stairs.

God, the heat.

It had been hot in the house, especially upstairs, but

outside, where there was no shade . . . Lizzie felt her dresss wilt and dampen instantly. She walked slowly and carefully toward town, hoping that Enid was home from work.

Lizzie didn't know exactly what she wanted from Enid, or why it was so important to get to Enid's house. A terrible feeling of dread, of impending doom, surrounded her. For the moment, she knew that Enid's company would provide some relief for her soul, and her cool house would provide some relief from the heat.

Anger at the father she so dearly loved squeezed tears out of her eyes. Anger at her sister, who had been so much a mother to her, yet who was so clearly crazy, squeezed more tears. Anger at her real mother for leaving her while such a youngster, anger at Abby for never really bucking Emma to take over the motherly role . . . Lizzie walked the route without every really seeing where she was going.

And then she was there. The little house, set back amid the trees. She suddenly felt shy.

She wiped the tears and the perspiration away together, and walked up to the front door. She knocked twice.

Enid opened the door. "Lizzie! Come in."

The house was as much a mess as usual. Lizzie loved it. And it was cool.

"How about a glass of coffee? It's cold."

Lizzie nodded, her voice failing her. Suddenly, she began to tremble. She picked up a stack of magazines and put them on the floor, then sat down and put a hand over her face. She didn't feel like crying, exactly, she just felt worn out. Fragile. For the first time in her life, Lizzie felt capable of breaking.

"Lizzie, dear, what is it?" Enid put a cool hand to Lizzie's forehead.

"Everytime I come over here—" The tears showed up. Lizzie tried to overcome them, but the sobs won.

"Shhh. Shh. That doesn't matter. That makes me feel good. That makes me feel as if you like me. And that you trust me. And that's true. That's right. That's good. You can come over here and cry to me anytime you want." Enid slid down the arm of the sofa and squeezed in next to Lizzie. She cradled her head and rocked her back and forth.

It felt so strange to be held like that; it felt so good. As the sobs waned, Lizzie felt an overwhelming surge of affection for this woman. She hiccupped a few times, then drank the cool, sweetened coffee. Enid got her a damp cloth and Lizzie wiped her face and hands. And suddenly, she could smile again. She giggled, eyes shyly downcast.

Enid began to talk about her sons, which gave Lizzie time to compose herself. Lizzie had arrived unannounced, unexpected, and found understanding, compassion, caring. Lizzie never wanted to leave. She never wanted to go back to that house. Ever.

Enid chatted on, and soon Lizzie was laughing with her, through stories of her boys, the family, the job. Such a family! Such a close family, where they talked about things, shared feelings, traveled together and laughed together. Such a feeling of life, of joyousness, Lizzie had never known. And it was sad for everybody when Charles died, but the boys had a strong mother to look to for strength. And look at Enid now! Not a mourning widow, but a woman still filled with life! Lizzie envied those sons who were off at college in Boston. She wished she were their younger sister, but of course . . . she was far too old. The boys were nineteen and twenty, and Lizzie was thirty-two already. Old enough to have teenage sons of her own!

Enid made them both salads with fresh vegetables from her garden and refreshed the cold coffee; they ate in the sitting room with the salads on their laps and the drinks on stacks of periodicals. Enid continued to talk.

"There came a time," she said, "not too long after Charles died, when I went through all his financial affairs and came to the realization that he left us in the exact condition I would expect. The house was paid for, there was enough for us to live until the boys left home, and then there was enough for me to survive—barely, I'm sure—the rest of my life.

"But that wasn't enough for me. The boys wanted to go on with their studies. Charles didn't allow for that, but I had to. I could never deny my boys something so important for their future. So I got a job with the law firm. And I work hard. And even that isn't enough . . ." Enid looked off into the ether. Then she shook her head, smiled at Lizzie and came back to the moment. "So I do what I have to do to keep my boys in school. And I will do whatever it takes to see them through. Charles Junior is almost finished. And he already has employment opportunities."

There was a long silence. Lizzie had nothing to say, except to voice her admiration, but that was somehow inappropriate.

"I guess the point is, Lizzie, that I've done some things I'm not necessarily proud of, in the ruthlessness of providing for my sons. I have been ruthless. And cunning, I think. And not entirely aboveboard, if you know what I mean. But I would do it all again, and more. And more.

"And yet . . . I see Charles Junior's education coming to an end, and I wonder if those things I did that weren't very nice . . . were they really necessary? I mean, if I had refused to do those things, would other means of finding the money for him have come along?"

Lizzie picked at her cuticles, suddenly embarrassed by this revelation.

"Well!" Enid stood up, took Lizzie's dinnerware and disappeared into the kitchen. "How about a piece of pie?"

Seizing the lighter moment, Lizzie said, "You baked a pie? In this heat?"

"No. I bought it. Apple. Want some?"

"Oh, yes, please."

Enid brought in two generous slices of pie. "I don't

generally indulge myself, but now and then, one must . . . don't you think so?"

"Now and then," Lizzie said seriously, "one must." And then they attacked their dessert.

They lingered, then, filled with good food and comfortable in the silence between them.

"Spend the night," Enid said. "Whatever was making you so miserable at home will still be there in the morning. Stay here and put it off for a night."

Lizzie thought about what was going on at home. Bridget was hiding in her room; she did that every time there was a disturbance with Emma. Emma was pacing or foaming at the mouth or raging at Father. Father was being confronted, probably by Abby, who was to tell him that some one of her kin was trying to kill him. Oh, she had no desire to go back there. None.

"All right," she said. "That would be nice."

"A nice, cool tub?"

Lizzie laughed. "Yes. Yes."

Enid drew a tub for Lizzie, and poured a generous amount of salts in it for her. Lizzie disrobed, throwing her smelly, sweaty clothes into a pile in the corner. She stepped into the tub, one foot at a time, and the cool water surrounded her deliciously. This was heaven.

She heard Enid moving about in the kitchen and sitting room, and knew that she could take as long as she liked in this tub. It smelled so good, it felt so good. Lizzie wanted nothing more than just to stay in this house tonight and then forever. Enid could go to work every day and Lizzie would clean house and cook and do the laundry for her, making sure everything was just right . . .

But it was a short-lived fantasy. Lizzie knew that Enid could barely support herself and her sons, never mind a hanger-on.

She could get a job.

Ha.

Lizzie splashed sweet water on her face and resolved not to think about it anymore. She was chained to her father for the rest of his life. Just as Kathryn Peters had said.

And yet Enid had been ruthless, too. Enid had done things she wasn't proud of, Enid had done whatever it took to get money for her sons.

Enid had the courage to do what she had to do; Beatrice had the courage to do what she had to do. . . . Buying a small house of her own in town was not nearly the monumental task the other two women faced. Surely Lizzie could accomplish that little detail with her life.

She splashed her face again and resolved not to think of it anymore. Instead, she looked around the bathroom and saw Enid's little pieces of jewelry, cosmetics, creams, lotions, perfumes. And the stack of magazines next to the tub. Lizzie picked one up. *Harper's*. She opened it and lay comfortably back in the cool tub. This was good. This was very good. This was the way life was meant to be.

● ● ●

Dried, fully refreshed, smelling of feminine perfumes and lotions and wearing Enid's cotton robe, Lizzie again sat in the living room. Life at the Bordon house could easily have been on the other side of the world. Lizzie was caught up in Enid's completely unorganized way of living, and she loved it. She carried the magazine with her from the bathroom and set it upon one stack of magaines in the living room, where it stayed. Later, when they talked about sleeping, Lizzie picked up another from a different stack and carried it to the bedroom. She could easily see how the piles could grow, disorganized and wanton.

Lizzie again donned the nightshirt she'd worn to bed with the headache the week before. Enid wore her nightie, and a sleeping cap. Lizzie just let her hair down loose.

"Your parents won't be worried about you?"

"I don't think so."

They slipped between the covers, and Enid turned down the lamp. "This reminds me of when I was a little girl," she said. "I used to sleep over with my cousins. Three of us in one bed, and we'd tickle each other's backs and tell romance stories about the men of our dreams."

"I have cousins," Lizzie said, "but we never did anything like that."

"No? Poor girl. Here. Lie on your stomach. Pull your nightshirt up, that's a girl. Now I'm going to write a message on your back, one letter at a time, and you try to guess what it is."

Enid's fingers sent thrills across Lizzie's naked skin. Goose bumps rose and fell in waves, and she felt her face flush in the dark.

"What's that letter, Lizzie?"

But Lizzie couldn't speak.

"C'mon." Enid's fingers traced the same pattern again.

"L."

"Good. And this one?"

"O. V. E."

"That was our favorite word. And then we had to erase the word like this." And Enid's fingers gently caressed Lizzie's skin, softer and softer, until finally the fingertips just barely floated over her back and all Lizzie could feel was the heat from Enid's hand.

Then Enid bounced on the bed, rolling over and pulling up her nightie. "Your turn."

Pale moonlight shone through the bedroom window. They were to sleep with only a sheet over them, but the sheet was down around Enid's thighs and her firm bottom showed smooth and round in the moonlight. The skin on her back was lightly dotted with moles. Lizzie's mouth went dry. She poised her hand over Enid's back, but could not think of a

274

single word to spell. She put her palm down on the center of Enid's back and rubbed lightly.

"Umm. That feels wonderful."

Lizzie sat up so as to use both hands, and soon she was rubbing Enid's back, sides, neck, shoulders. The nightie came off. Lizzie worked Enid's feet, her lower legs, her thighs, her beautiful, beautiful round butt, and then she couldn't help herself, she just had to, just had to . . . and she kissed it. "You're so beautiful," she said.

Enid turned and brought Lizzie to her in a warm embrace, and their bodies fit together as if they were molded for each other. Lizzie kissed Enid with raw passion, Enid finessed Lizzie's coarser moves with a practiced hand.

But this was not like Kathryn Peters. No. Kathryn Peters was selfish and greedy. Enid was giving and gentle. Understanding. Lizzie had never felt so wanted, so desirable. So loved.

After a time, they slept, entwined. And when she woke up, Enid was looking at her, their faces close, and Lizzie closed her eyes and kissed Enid's lips, and soon they were dancing again, pleasing each other, learning about each other, and it was a glorious time, a glorious time.

hen Lizzie opened her eyes, summer shone through the window, and Enid sat in front of it, wrapped in nightie and robe, chin on her fist, elbow on a stack of books. Lizzie stretched and yawned, feeling smiley and cozy, but when Enid didn't even look around, she worried.

"Good morning," she said.

Enid looked over at her, but her face was eclipsed by the bright light behind her. Lizzie could see no expression. "Hi," Enid said, her voice soft. She stood up and stretched. "Well, I better get going."

Something was definitely wrong. Guilt surged through Lizzie and she jumped out of bed and blocked Enid's way. Enid would not meet her eyes.

"What is it?" Panic began to rise. "God, what is it?"

"Nothing, Lizzie."

"Please don't do that, Enid," Lizzie pleaded. "Please don't say 'nothing, Lizzie.' "

Enid's small hand touched Lizzie's cheek and her eyes flooded. "You're so sweet," she said. "You're so wonderful. No, Lizzie, it isn't you. It's me. There's something the matter with me, and it's not you. You're wonderful." Then her eyes dropped again, and one tear fell down her cheek and she tried to get around Lizzie.

"Please tell me." Lizzie wouldn't let her pass.

"I've done some terrible things in my life, Lizzie," Enid said, looking at the floor. "Somehow, when Charles died and the boys left home, I thought my life was pretty much over, except for church and the garden. So I never thought it mattered much what I did. And now I see that it does. That's all."

Reluctantly, Lizzie let her pass. Enid went into the bathroom and closed the door. Lizzie went into the kitchen and poured two glasses of tea. It was already too hot to make a fire in the stove. She found a coffee cake and cut two pieces, and then quartered a pear. Her stomach burned. Why was there always something? There was *always* something! If not at home, then at Kathryn's. If not at Kathryn's, then at home. If not at Kathryn's, or at home, then at Enid's. God! And now, and *now,* there was something going on at home *and* at Enid's, *and* at Kathryn's, and more coming via Washington, D.C., tomorrow night!

Lizzie wanted to hide.

But the toilet flushed and the bathroom door opened and Enid came out, looking sheepish and apologetic. Her eyes were red-rimmed; she'd been crying in the bathroom.

"Come have breakfast."

Enid sat down, smiling a small smile. She cut a forkful of coffee cake and washed it down with tea. "I'm sorry, Lizzie, I'm really not very hungry." She put her fork down. "But I want you to understand something." She took both of Lizzie's hands in her own. "Last night was more than I had ever dreamed would happen to me again. I'm not an old woman, Lizzie, I'm only forty years old. But life has a way of excluding you from things, especially in Fall River. The skeletons in my closet have nothing to do with you. I think you are the sweetest, most precious thing that has come into my life in a long, long time. And I'm just afraid that my past actions will hurt you."

"There's nothing you could do to hurt me, Enid," Lizzie said.

Enid smiled sadly and sipped her tea. "I'd better be getting ready for work."

Lizzie hated the thought of going home. She followed Enid into the bedroom, where the heat of the new day was already burning. Enid pulled the shades and let the draperies fall over them. Then they both dressed.

They kissed at the door. Then Enid opened it and they put on faces for the world, false faces, faces of happiness and composure, when both of them felt their insides being gnawed away by forces beyond their control.

●　●　●

Lizzie opened the door and Emma ran to greet her, a dangerous light in her eyes. "They *are* going to kill Father," she said eagerly.

Lizzie was so tired of this. She was so blasted sick and tired of Emma and Father and Abby and their stupid little dramas. "No, Emma. Nobody is trying to kill Father."

"They are, they *are,* Lizzie, listen, you don't know what happened yesterday."

The thought briefly flew through Lizzie's mind that Emma didn't even notice that she hadn't come home all night. Or if she had noticed, it was unimportant compared to her latest news of Andrew's impending murder.

"Emma. I'm not in the mood."

That stopped her. "Not in the mood? Our father is about to be slaughtered in broad daylight and you're not in the mood to hear about it?"

"All right. Come up to my room and tell me. Where is everybody?"

"Maggie is doing laundry. Abby is out with someone birthing, I think. Father is at work."

Lizzie walked up the creaky stairs in the tiny cramped

house that was already hot and close. The house smelled like the cellar floor, like steamed dirt. Now that Lizzie was used to Enid's gay profusion of books, magazines and other paraphernalia, the singular lack of reading material and personal possessions made the Borden house seem uncommonly austere. And hot. And stuffy. And staid.

Bridget was stripping the bed in the guest room. "Maggie, what are you doing?"

"Mr. Morse is arriving, miss."

Lizzie's uncle John Morse, her mother's brother, was an infrequent visitor. He and Andrew had begun investing their money together many years ago; occasionally he would come to visit, and he would stay far too long, talking business and investigating new investment opportunities. Usually his presence meant nothing. But this was Tuesday and Beatrice was due to arrive Wednesday night or Thursday morning. "When is he coming?"

"I'm not sure." Bridget looked to Emma. Emma shrugged.

So there would not even be a bed in the house for Beatrice. Lizzie's shoulders slumped. She unlocked her bedroom door, and Emma followed on her heels.

Lizzie untied her shoes and took them off. The air upstairs was even denser. She pulled the draperies, raised the blinds and opened the window. No relief. She loosened her corset and lay upon the bed, daring Emma to say something. Emma was silent.

When Lizzie was settled, she pointed at the rocking chair. Emma sat down. Why, all of a sudden, was Lizzie in control? "All right, Emma. What happened?"

"They were in the sitting room. I listened from the stairs. Abby wanted to know, once and for all, if Sarah was mentioned in his will. He wanted to know why, and she said because Sebastian was beginning to get kind of pushy.

" 'What kind of pushy?'

279

" 'I don't know, Mr. Borden.' " Emma imitated Abby's voice. " 'Sarah came to see me in tears, yesterday, afraid. I had promised her, you see, and Sebastian is frustrated at his wages and not being able to provide better for her. He's afraid that I will predecease you, and that you will then forget all about Sarah.' There was a long pause. 'It would be much easier, Mr. Borden, if you would just give her that property now. Then they can be enjoying it now, while they need it. Or you could sell it to them.'

" 'I'll consider it. The will is in transition. I'm making some changes to it.'

" 'Changes?'

" 'For the better.'

" 'Well, then, that's fine, whatever you want. Only what shall I say to Sarah?'

" 'Tell her to find herself a husband who can support her and her children in a proper manner and to stop hounding me about what I will or will not do with my assets.'

" 'Sarah was in such a state, Mr. Borden, that she fears for your life.'

" 'My life?' "

" 'She said that Sebastian has reached such a point that he has talked of murder.'

" 'In order to inherit what may or may not be written in my will? Preposterous. He's a madman!'

" 'Nevertheless, I think some sort of statement ought to be made.'

" 'Tell them that I am rearranging my affairs, and that I may very well remember them. And that then again, if they cannot show the proper respect, I may ignore them. Tell them that, Abby.'

"Well, I don't need to tell you," Emma went on, "that I wasn't about to sit there on the stairs and let him get away with those veiled threats about the will. So I walked into the room and demanded that he spell out the changes."

Lizzie gasped. "You didn't!"

"I did."

"What did he say?"

"He said he wouldn't. He said we'd all find out when he was dead. He said that some people did things for him and some people did things against him and we would have only our consciences to thank when it was all over.

"I told him that wasn't good enough. I've lived here all my life, doing his cooking, his laundry, raising his second daughter, and I was not about to be cut off without a cent because he took a disliking to me in his dotage."

Lizzie brought her hands up to her face. She could imagine Emma saying such things, but they embarrassed her just the same. The horror of it all made her smile.

"He made me sit down. He made the cow sit down as well. 'This is how it is worked out,' he said. 'Certain people who have granted me special favors over the years will receive a bequest. Abby will be taken care of for the rest of her life. After that, you, Emma, and Lizzie will inherit everything. Is that clear enough for you?'

"'You mean we'll have to live here with *her* until she dies?'"

"'Don't push me, Emma.'"

"'Just who are these *special people*?'"

"'People who have shown niceties.'"

"'Your whore?'"

Lizzie shrieked and then clapped her hands over her mouth. "Oh, Emma, you *didn't!*"

"I did."

"And?"

"And his face got red, and he said, 'This interview is over.' That's what he's doing, Lizzie. That whore of his has turned his head so far that he's going to cut her in on his will."

"He wouldn't."

"He would. Just to spite us."

Lizzie expected that with this kind of drama in the Borden house, Emma would be pacing and bruising her lip between knuckles and teeth and frothing at the mouth and then ready to go to New Bedford. But she was doing none of that. "Why are you so calm about this whole thing, Emma?"

"Calm? I don't know that I'm calm."

"Calmer than I would expect, under the circumstances."

"Well, look at you, lying on your bed fully clothed, lounging as if you had the world at your fingertips."

"I'm sick of it all, Emma," Lizzie said. "Don't you get tired of all this?"

"Tired of it? Lizzie, it is our life. *It is our life!*"

It may be your life, Lizzie thought, but it is not mine.

"Besides," Emma said. "I have a plan."

ndrew Borden was at his office in the mill when the sickness hit. He felt as if he had been hit in the stomach with a stick. He ran from his office, holding his stomach, and made it to the street before vomiting his breakfast in a gush.

His first thought was of Emma's cooking; she paid poor attention to that which needed it the most. His next thought, as spasms shuddered through him, was of poison, and that Sebastian Whitehead should be damned to eternal hellfire.

After the initial sickness subsided, Andrew rose from his knees, brushed off his pants and his hands, and made his way toward home. He left everything as it was on his desk, and while that made him vaguely uneasy, it made him more uneasy to think that the worst was yet to come of this sickness, and he did not want to be taken home or to Dr. Bowen's by way of some stranger's charity. At least he hadn't left his will on his desk, for the prying eyes of Fall River. It was with him, with the new instructions, ready to post. He felt the mailing tube in his jacket pocket. He would leave it in the box, if he could.

He made his way unsteadily, feeling increasingly shaky, sweating profusely in the heat. He heaved twice more before arriving, but there was nothing to vomit, and the heaves did not drive him to his knees. He wanted to get into bed. His head ached. His fingers felt tight. His face felt swollen.

He fumbled with his keys at the front door, then finally, through shear will and prayer, he got the door open. Andrew closed and locked it behind him. He went through the sitting room, took the key to his bedroom from the mantel, and went through the kitchen, up the back stairs to his bedroom.

Abby was in bed. Stale vomit reeked from her chamber pot. She barely moved when he got into bed beside her. Even in the heat, even with someone next to his sensitive skin, bed felt wonderful.

He'd never been so sick.

He reached down and pulled his chamber pot into a convenient location and put his head on the pillow.

Faintly, he heard the sounds of Bridget vomiting and coughing up in her little room above theirs.

Blood pounded in his eyes. He felt every heartbeat in every vein.

He closed his eyes and waited to die.

nid Crawford typed a letter for her employer, but her mind was not on it. At the third typing error, Enid turned from the typewriter and rested her face in her hands. The burning in her stomach was more than she could bear. She was never good with guilt.

She tried to satisfy it by giving it promises. "Lizzie will come over tonight," she tried, "and I will tell her everything."

It was not good enough. She didn't know that Lizzie would be over, and besides, it was not up to Lizzie to see that Enid's feelings of guilt were assuaged.

Before thinking, she opened her desk drawer, took out her purse and turned to Mrs. Watkins, the bookkeeper. "I'm not feeling well, Cecilia. I'm going to go out for a walk and I'll be back in an hour or so."

"In this heat?"

But Enid didn't answer her. She just went out the door and walked directly to the Borden house and knocked sharply on the door.

She knocked again. And again. Disappointment rose in her. She was all ready to confess her multitude of ugly sins to Lizzie, and now she would have to hold onto them, keep them longer, live with Lizzie's innocence and her guilt on her mind for another while longer.

Just as she was turning away, she heard locks turn in the front door. And it was opened by a tall, thin, angular, humorless woman.

"Is Lizzie at home?"

"She's resting."

"It's quite important, if you don't mind."

"Wait." And the woman closed the door and locked it, leaving Enid to stand in the heat. In the sun.

In a moment, the locks were snapped back and Lizzie threw the door open. Her face lit up with a delight that made Enid's heart sore. "Enid! Come in, come in."

"I'd rather you came out, Lizzie. Can we walk down to the river?"

Lizzie looked at her queerly. "Of course. Give me a moment to get ready. Come in, won't you?"

Enid stepped into the hall and walked into the sitting room, where she had been just a week before, with Andrew and his fat wife. That had been a terrible time, and this was a terrible time, and she hoped never to set foot inside the Borden house again.

When Lizzie was ready, they went out the front door and turned right, away from town. They walked in silence, emotions raging inside Enid, and suddenly she wondered why she felt so compelled to confess all to Lizzie. What difference did it make? Would it make a difference to Enid? Would it make a difference to Lizzie? Yes, both would be altered by her confession. Enid felt that a change had come over her life in the past weeks. Lizzie had brought that change, that wonderful refreshing revelation that life went on. Yet confessing to Lizzie would hurt the very thing that had unlocked Enid's cage. Could she, in good conscience, do that? *Should* she?

Somehow, with Lizzie by her side, all the bad feelings wanted to fly away. She felt so good with Lizzie, she wanted to just smile and be rid of all the unpleasantness. There was so *much* unpleasantness in life—couldn't there be one small refuge from that? And couldn't that refuge be Lizzie?

"I wanted to see you, Lizzie," Enid started, "because I

feel so good—because you make me feel so good—that I need to confess some of the terrible things I've done."

"To me?"

"Well . . ."

"Why not talk to the pastor?"

"Well, because they affect you." Enid wanted to bite the end of her tongue off. She hadn't meant to say that, and she hadn't meant, necessarily, to confess to Lizzie anything specific.

"Oh?"

Enid stopped, put a hand on Lizzie's arm. "I've been entertaining men for money," she said.

Lizzie's face remained unreadable. "What does that have to do with me?"

"I needed you to know that."

"Why?"

Enid's insides squirmed. "Because."

"What is it, Enid? What are you trying to say?"

"I need money to put the boys through school. Charles Junior is almost finished, so it shouldn't be too much longer."

"You mean you still . . . entertain men for money? And you plan to continue to do so?"

Enid thought for a moment. She would like to stop, she really would. But the financial hardships of tuition and all that on her miserly salary . . . And she was so afraid, so *afraid* of being poor, poor and alone. . . . Then again, there was something quite self-satisfying about raising her skirts to the tune of a hundred dollars a week for men who found her desirable. She had always maintained two "boyfriends," as she referred to them, since Charles died. A Friday boyfriend and a Saturday boyfriend. And now . . . Lizzie. "I don't know, Lizzie. I don't feel quite right about it, and yet I'm quite reluctant to give up the money. And the satisfaction."

This was not going at all as Enid had planned.

"Satisfaction?"

"Well, yes. There is satisfaction knowing that men will pay me a weekly allowance for my favors. There is satisfaction in a swelling bank account that will see me through any hardship in my elder years."

"They pay you a weekly allowance?" Lizzie was clearly flabbergasted by Enid's revelations, and Enid couldn't help but be a little bit proud.

"I see two men, Lizzie. And each one gives me an allowance for my boys' schooling."

"I can get money, Enid. You don't have to do that."

"What is the difference?"

Lizzie's eyes grew dark. "This would be one friend helping another, Enid. I can get money from my father."

"No, Lizzie."

"Why not?"

"I don't know. I don't know anymore." Enid felt like crying.

"Then why tell me this?"

Enid shrugged, knowing full well that she intended to tell Lizzie more.

"You don't want me to come over on the days you have your friends over?"

"Oh, Lizzie, no."

"Then what? Why did you tell me this?"

Enid looked up. Lizzie's eyes had gone pale. She was agitated, and Enid had only herself to blame. Lizzie was so joyous, so carefree when they were at the Borden house just moments before, and now . . . now she'd ruined everything.

"Lizzie, I'm sorry."

Lizzie turned and began walking back home. Enid ran a couple of steps to keep up. She caught at Lizzie's sleeve. Lizzie was crying. "I loved you," Lizzie said.

Enid touched Lizzie's cheek and they hugged, Lizzie clinging to her fiercely. "And I love you. Think about it, please think about it, dear Lizzie." Lizzie's hair smelled of the bath and of their lovemaking the night before. "Just two evenings a week, and my boys . . . Lizzie, you don't have children, you don't know. Charles didn't leave enough money for them, and . . . and I'm putting money away for my old age, too. Lizzie, it's such a little thing, for a couple of hours a week. I'm not going to be able to do it much longer, you know. I thought I wanted to stop it, I came here to tell you that I would, but I can't, Lizzie, not until the boys are out of school . . . I really can't."

"Well then, you've made your choice." Lizzie sniffed, released Enid and wiped her face on her sleeve.

"I guess I have." Enid's heart was breaking. There were no words, just a terrible tearing of her greedy soul.

"How much do you get?"

"A hundred dollars a week. Each."

Lizzie turned, astonished, a little smile at the corners of her mouth. Enid couldn't help but be a little bit smug. "Two hundred dollars a week! I could own my own house and live on my own in town on one hundred dollars a month!"

They both laughed, but there was no humor in it, and Lizzie went into her house and Enid went on to her office, and neither one of them felt very good about life.

The woman who came to call for Lizzie didn't look at all like the type of person Lizzie should be friends with, according to Emma's way of thinking. Her hair was short, and she wore no hat, even in the sun. A face that was burned brown from the sun was as attractive as an old shoe, and showed about as much sense. It was against Emma's better judgment that she fetched Lizzie upon this woman's command, and by the time Lizzie left with her, Emma was ready for some breakfast.

The mutton roast they'd all eaten the night before was still sitting on the kitchen table. Emma filled a pan with water, and put the meat in it; she'd have soup for them for dinner, if she could bear to make a fire in the stove. Then she poured herself a glass of chilled milk and took a pastry from the shelf. She sat at the kitchen table, listening to the heat. It was almost noon, and the house was creaking with the weight of the oppressive heat. Emma's thighs were sticky, and strands of her hair hung like noodles from her normally tidy, tight bun. Even the milk tasted odd. But the cake was all right, so she ate it and went back upstairs to think about presenting her idea to Lizzie.

But before Lizzie came home, sickness welled up and out of Emma almost before she had time to aim toward her slops pail. It took her so suddenly and surprisingly that she had no time to prepare. Immediately after vomiting, she felt better, but in a moment, perspiration beaded up on her face and she felt as if she might faint.

Quickly, she removed her housedress and lay on her bed in her underdrawers. She felt dizzy.

It's the milk, she thought. The milk has been poisoned. She was glad she had only had a sip or two. That Sebastian Whitehead. Damn his eyes.

And then she slept.

Wednesday, August 3

The long, hot night slowly turned into day. There had been no respite from the dogged heat all night long, and daybreak brought with it the promise of even more heat. Lizzie had lain awake most of the night, drifting in and out of unconsciousness rather than really sleeping. As the rooster crowed, she heard rustlings in the kitchen, which must mean that members of the household were up and about. The house had been furnace hot and eerily still the day before, with everybody sick. It was pleasant, in a way, to walk through the house, grateful that she never drank milk, knowing that no one would speak to her, or even see her. And yet it was eerie, for she could *feel* all those people sick in their beds. Maggie was in her little loft, the hottest of the hot on the third floor. And Emma. Hot. Sick. And her parents, she could imagine them in bed, hot, sick, sticking to the sheets and barely able to bear their own feverishness, let alone the others'.

There was something terrible about this sickness. It seemed they were all more than sick, sick almost to their death. Poisoned. But that was Sebastian's plan, wasn't it?

Or was it Emma's plan? Emma surely was not as ill as the others. No, Emma would never poison the family. Take after them with an ax, perhaps, but she would never intentionally poison them all.

292

Well, somebody was downstairs, and Lizzie felt as though she ought to go see who was there.

Besides, Beatrice was due to arrive this evening or the next morning, and Lizzie felt she ought to bathe and make herself presentable. The household was in disrepair and everyone lay dying around her, but at least Lizzie could be clean.

Lizzie was surprised to find Emma in the kitchen. Emma generally made a great amount of noise when going from her room through Lizzie's, but this morning Lizzie must have been soundly asleep.

"What are you doing?"

"Making breakfast."

"You've made a fire?"

"I felt like a coffee."

"You're better, then?"

"Much."

"What about the others?"

"I've not heard."

"Shouldn't someone check on them?"

"You mean in case they're all dead?"

Emma had such a compassionate nature. "Well, yes."

"Go do it, then. I'm busy."

Lizzie walked up the narrow stairs toward her parents' room. She hadn't been up these stairs in years. Twenty years, probably, not since she was a young girl. Well, except for that time with the jewelry and the money. The stairs were the same. They smelled the same. The wood was a little more worn, otherwise it was all the same, the walls unadorned with wallpaper, pictures or anything else. Black marks where little hands had trailed along the wall in the dark.

She got to the parents' door and knocked.

"What is it?" Andrew answered.

"It's Lizzie," she said, suddenly shy. "I just wanted to see if you were all right."

There was some mumbling, but Lizzie couldn't make it out.

"We're better. We'll be down."

"Good." She continued up the stairs to Bridget's room. She knocked.

"Yes?"

"Maggie, are you all right?"

"I think so, miss."

"Will you be down for breakfast?"

"I think not. Perhaps later."

"All right, then." Lizzie went back downstairs, feeling fortunate indeed that the sickness hadn't touched her.

"Is everyone alive?"

Emma's tone touched Lizzie as a bit whimsical, considering. They were all very ill, and Emma had no right to make light of such a thing. It was perhaps an attempt on their father's life! "They'll be down," was all she said.

"Well, good. I have a thing or two for that father of ours. He will not escape this breakfast table without explaining himself."

"Emma."

"Emma nothing. It's the only way. With all of us present. It's the only way, Lizzie." Emma dried her hands on her apron and left the room.

Lizzie selected a pear from the bowl on the table and sliced it into pieces. She took the plate and cup of coffee out of the fiery hot kitchen, into the dining room and sat down. Emma had brought in the morning paper and Lizzie picked it up and began to read.

In less than a minute, Emma appeared in the doorway, pale, clutching something in her talons.

"Lizzie, I've found it."

"What, Emma?"

"The will. The old man's will."

"Where?"

"It was in his suit-coat pocket."

"Emma." Lizzie wanted to chastise Emma for snooping again, but curiosity got the better of her. "Why?"

"I don't know."

"He's sick, that's why."

"That's of no matter. This must be it. It's in a mailing tube, and it's ready to go to a lawyer in Fairhaven. It *must* be the will!" Emma sat down on the edge of a chair. Lizzie couldn't remember when she'd ever seen Emma's eyes so bright. "If we open this now, Lizzie, we'll have accurate information when he comes down for breakfast. We can speak to him about his affairs with knowledge, and we can plan our strategy."

Lizzie was intrigued. As long as Emma did the actual deed, she was actually innocent. And she was all for seeing what he had up his sleeve. "Well?"

Emma took a paring knife from the table and slit open the package. She unwrapped the paper and opened the end of the tube. It was a will, all right, bound in blue paper. She pulled it out and read the cover letter in a whisper: "'Dear Mr. Stockworth: I'm making a few revisions to my will. I am taking this out of the hands of my present attorney as I wish these changes to remain confidential until my death. Please redraft the document and send to me for my signature. I have enclosed a cheque in the amount of twenty dollars, which I assume will cover all your fees. Very sincerely yours, Andrew Borden.'"

Emma laid that sheet of paper on the table and looked at the will. "Look! He's cut Sarah Whitehead out. She was in. She *was* in, and now he's taken her out. Good." She flipped through another page, eyes scanning the lines.

Lizzie's pears had turned sour in her mouth.

"Oh!" Emma's hand flew to her mouth. "I was right!" She smiled with glee. "I was right, oh, Lizzie, he is, he is going to leave a property to his whore."

"No."

"Yes! Yes! See? Right here. 'For niceties rendered,' he said. I'm sure! Some tart named Enid Crawford."

Understanding struck Lizzie dumb.

She felt the blood flow from her face. Her hands were suddenly cold and trembling. She wanted to go to her room, but she couldn't trust her feet to take her there, so she just sat, feeling sicker than she ever had, listening to Emma prattle on and on about her discovery.

And then there was a pause. A deathly pause. A pause so dramatic that it even shook Lizzie from her humiliation, her anger, her despair.

Emma said, "He's leaving everything to her."

"To whom?"

"Abby."

"Emma, no."

"Yes." Lizzie saw the fury begin to burn in Emma. She stood up, crumpling the will. Lizzie made a half-hearted grab for it, but it was too late. Father would know that someone had been at his will. "He decided to leave Sarah stupid Whitehead out of the will and leave everything to Abby, to let her decide how to divide it. And you know what *she'll* do, don't you, Lizzie? She'll leave it all to that stupid midwives' organization or the church or something, and we'll have to beg for our livings."

"Emma . . ."

But Emma was beyond hearing. She was gone. She paced back and forth and rolled up the will, then fit it back inside the mailing tube. She took the whole thing to the kitchen and threw it into the fire.

"Emma!"

"Now, Lizzie, now I hope he dies. If he dies without a will, everything will go to her anyway, but nothing will go to the whore. Maybe he'll die and she'll die, too, and that will take care of everything. In fact, maybe they'll both die of

Sebastian Whitehead's poisoning and then we won't have *anything* to worry about. Ever again!"

"Emma, hush!"

"Maybe he'll die before he can get a new will together. Maybe I ought to set fire to him while he sleeps. Maybe I'll take an ax to both their ugly faces before tomorrow morning. Right in their beds. Right when they sleep. He's always said he wants to die in his sleep. Ha!"

Lizzie had heard Emma rant and rave before, but never like this. This time it was evil, it was almost . . . believable. She paced back and forth by the dining-room table, her hands flying out in wild gestures, banging against the walls, and she didn't even feel it. Soon she would be rubbing her knuckles on her lips and the little spots of froth at the corners of her mouth would turn pink.

Lizzie sat, immobilized by the enormity of it all. Uncle John was arriving today, and then Beatrice. Emma was a wreck, in fact she would probably leave for New Bedford to be beaten—perhaps until she was dead—Father, Abby and Maggie had all been poisoned, Enid was Father's whore, *Enid was Father's whore,* and all Lizzie could do was to just sit and watch her sister pace and rave.

And then she remembered that during times of emotional stress, that other thing was likely to happen to her. When the "other Lizzie" came out and walked around town doing God-knows-what.

Lizzie jumped up from her chair, upsetting the coffee. She pushed past Emma and ran up the stairs. She had to do something. She had to do *something*. She paced back and forth in her room for a moment, then took her towel and a clean housedress down cellar. To bathe, she took down the pot of dishwashing water keeping hot on the stove. But this time she must not let her guard down. She must soap up, rinse off and remain consciously in the cellar the whole time.

Though it was so blistering hot upstairs, the cellar was

cool and damp. Lizzie shivered as she took off her clothes and got into the tub. She mixed the cold water from the faucet with the hot from the kettle and stood in the tub, washing her body with a rag. Then she washed her hair with the same yellow lye soap, rinsed it all off and rubbed her body dry with the towel.

Maybe I could go to the church, she thought, but nothing happened at the church on a Wednesday. Maybe there's a WCTU meeting. But there wasn't. Solitude struck her like a hollow bell. Without Enid, she had no friends. She had acquaintances—the women at WCTU, some of the people at church—but there was no one, *no one* with whom she could talk about this problem. No one! She hadn't a single friend in all of . . . in all of creation.

I'll clean the house, she thought. I'll clean the barn. I'll do the ironing! Nobody ever wanted to iron, especially in this heat, and the mound of clothes had been mounting. But the thought of it made her feel faint. Well, at least I'll sprinkle the clothes, wrap them up and see.

But the day loomed long.

Emma was in her room when Lizzie returned, toweling her hair. She knocked on Emma's door. "Emma? Emma, open the door."

The door opened. Emma looked terrible. Lizzie wondered if this was the edge for her. If things hadn't gotten just a little too much for a fragile person like Emma. She just stood there, not moving, not even really seeing Lizzie. She just stood there, a vacancy in her eyes, slackness in her expression. Lizzie wondered if anybody else ever thought of Emma as fragile.

"Emma, are you leaving for New Bedford?" It suddenly occurred to Lizzie that things would be much easier if Emma left again, as much as she hated to think that. And Emma could be hurt very badly this time, too . . . In fact, she might never come back, and if she stayed in New Bedford under an assumed name, they might never know her fate—a frightening yet somehow unburdening idea.

Emma's eyes focused at the question. "No, of course not. No. No. No, of course not. No, Lizzie, I'm going to Fairhaven to see our cousins. We have attorneys, do we not? One of them is bound to know this Mr. Stockworth and I'll find Father's connection to him. It's time we got some legal advice of our own, Lizzie."

Lizzie was quite astonished to hear such lucid words come out of Emma at such a time. And yet, it was probably the most constructive thing that could be done at the time.

"Besides," Emma went on, "I ought to leave here before I see his face, or I'll strangle him, I swear to God I will murder the man before . . ." Her fists were clenched and the cords stood out in her neck.

"Pack, then, Emma," Lizzie said. "Hurry up and go." Emma came back to the present moment. She went to the closet like an automaton and brought out her traveling valise. Lizzie retreated to her room and sat in her rocker.

Emma was gone within the hour.

bby Borden, wearing only her thin cotton dressing gown, descended the stairs carefully, one step at a time, afraid she would faint and fall clear to the bottom. The only respite from the damnable heat was the cool kitchen floor on her bare feet.

She stood in the kitchen, looking around. The stove had been heated, but that would have been Emma making breakfast coffee. She looked at the clock. It was half past two. She felt dizzy and disoriented. She didn't know where to begin. Then she saw Lizzie, sprinkling clothes. Good Lord, the girl wasn't thinking about *ironing!* Why, she'd have to fire the stove all over again to heat the flats.

"Lizzie, are you all right?"

"Yes, I'm fine, Abby," Lizzie said. "The sickness didn't touch me."

"You're fortunate. My God, I don't know what I'm doing up. Your father insists on going to the office this afternoon, and I have to fix him something to eat. I can't imagine eating. Where's Emma?"

"Emma's gone to Fairhaven."

"Oh? Well . . ."

"Abby, do you suppose Sebastian . . ."

Abby whirled around, then held her swirling head. "No! No, of course not, Lizzie, how could you even think such a thing? No, it's the flu, that's all. Something serious going around. That's all . . . Now, where was I?"

Abby's concentration had fled. Lizzie had given voice to

the refrain that had played in her head all the day before as she lay hot and sick enough to die. But Sebastian would gain nothing by killing her. No, it couldn't have been Sebastian. Just some illness they had caught, that was all.

Her hands shook as she opened the heavy corner on the stove. She let it drop with a clang.

"Lizzie, would you help me, please?"

"There are cakes in the cupboard, Abby," Lizzie said. "And cold mutton gravy on the sideboard."

Abby spread gravy on the cakes and put them out with a cold cup of coffee for her husband. It was all she could manage. The sickness had left her feeling as if there was lead in her veins.

"Have a cookie," Lizzie said. "Emma said they helped settle her stomach."

Abby opened the cabinet and took a cookie. She took a small bite. "Emma wasn't so ill, then?"

"She was yesterday."

Andrew came down the stairs and into the kitchen.

"Lizzie," he said.

"Mr. Borden, I really don't think you should be going to the office this afternoon."

"There are things that need to be done."

"But you're so pale." He looked pale and thin, drawn and old. Very, very old. His mortality stared at Abby and made her shiver.

"As needs be. Is this my food?"

"The best I could do."

"Hardly looks worth eating, does it?"

"Lizzie said that a cookie helped settle Emma."

Andrew took a cookie and bit. "Where is Emma?"

"Gone to Fairhaven."

"Oh? Just as well. I'm off." He put the cookie down and went into the sitting room. Abby looked at Lizzie and saw

301

her tense. Her nose was in the air like a fox's. They listened, but heard only the whine of the heat.

Then the sounds of Andrew unlocking his desk. Then the drawers opening and closing. Then the key again, and he reappeared in the kitchen.

"Lizzie, have you seen a package? A tube? I was to mail it."

Lizzie shook her head.

"Hmm." He hung his head for a moment, thinking, but he looked old. Very old. "Well," he said, looking very old, very ill, "I'm off." And he turned and left.

Abby looked at Lizzie. Lizzie took a cookie. Abby took the cookie that Andrew had abandoned and they nibbled in silence.

izzie was in her room lying fully clothed upon her bed when Andrew came home and began opening and closing all the drawers in the house. Her conscience bothered her only a tiny bit; after all, it was Emma that stole the will, read it and burned it. It was quite out of Lizzie's hands. But should she tell him? Should she tell him that his will had been burned in the fury of his eldest daughter? Should she tell him that she had been a witness, had stood by and done nothing while Emma did it all? Should she tell him that she knew all about him and Enid?

Oh, Enid. The wound opened anew and bled.

No. She would tell the old man nothing. He was to leave her out of his will. He would rather leave property to a woman who regularly prostituted herself than to his own flesh and blood. Well, good. Fine. It would be well if he had a heart seizure while looking for the blasted will. He would never find it.

Enid! God. They had walked down by the river yesterday and Enid had something to say, yet didn't say it. Instead, she told Lizzie that she intended to keep sleeping with her men friends, indeed, bleeding her father dry at a rate of one hundred dollars a week! Oh, Enid. There were no tears in Lizzie, but her heart ached just the same.

When Andrew knocked at Lizzie's bedroom door, she was not surprised, just startled. She unlocked it and opened it, then stepped back. The look on her father's face was even more startling. He looked ill, very ill. Greenish. And old.

"Lizzie, I'm missing that mailing tube, and I just can't find it anywhere. Please think, now, and see if you can remember seeing it."

"I've seen nothing like it, Father."

Andrew stared at her and Lizzie knew that he saw the lie.

"Emma's room, then. Have you a key?"

"No." Another lie.

"I'll get one or I'll break the blasted door down." He turned on his heel and stomped down the stairs.

In a moment, he was back. Lizzie followed him, not quite knowing how to act or what to do. She'd never seen her father like this before. Ever. He unlocked Emma's door and banged it open. He stomped in and looked around, and it occurred to Lizzie that perhaps he hadn't been in Emma's bedroom since they had moved into this house twenty-seven years ago.

Then he began pulling drawers out of her dresser, fumbling through them and throwing them on the ground. The first one split when it landed, and Lizzie cringed. He went through the room like a madman, flinging dresses from their hangers, going through each shoe, each shoebox, each hatbox, searching, searching.

Lizzie was appalled.

Finally, he finished. He sat down on Emma's bed, perspiration flowing down his face. He took his handkerchief and mopped. "It's not here, Lizzie," he said, then slumped in the chair. Lizzie thought for a moment he had fainted from the sickness and the heat. "It's not here," he whispered.

She went to him and sat at his feet. "It's not that important, Father," she said, and then remembered that she wasn't supposed to know that it was his will. "Perhaps you should go downstairs for a little nap. Shall we read, maybe?" She felt as if she was coddling one of her six-year-old Sunday school students.

"Yes," he breathed, "maybe we ought." But he made no move.

Lizzie put her cheek against his knee. Despite the fact that she sometimes hated him, the affection she felt when she realized how old and frail he was overcame her. He was her father, after all, and didn't that count for something? Of course it did. Blood was thick, especially Borden blood, and Lizzie felt a tremendous amount of loyalty to her father. To her father and to her sister.

She wondered what Emma was doing in Fairhaven, and as if he read her thoughts, she felt his hand upon her head.

"I'm such a foolish old man, Lizzie," he said. "I've no right to a daughter as wonderful as you are, and it makes me so very afraid that you will leave me in my old age."

"I won't," she said with a sigh. "I would like to have a little house of my own here in town, Father, but I will never really leave you."

"Never?"

"Of course not."

"Your sister Emma is leaving me. All I've done for her and she's leaving me, she's leaving me as sure as we're sitting here."

"She's visiting cousins in Fairhaven, Father."

"That's what you think. That might even be what she thinks, Lizzie, but Emma left me long ago. Took her affections and locked them up in this room." He leaned forward and kissed the top of her head. "Please don't you ever leave me. I can't bear the thought of growing older without knowing that I will always be able to count on you to nurse me if I should fall ill. And that's why you can never move out, Lizzie, because it would be so hard for you to give up your little house to come home if I needed you."

A hollowness opened up in Lizzie. The hollow center of conflicting emotions swirled deep in her gut. This man was everything to her. Everything she loved, everything she hated. He was her potential freedom; at the same time, he was her prison. She sat there, her head resting on the side of his knee, his hand on the top of her head, and she listened to the things he said that were not the normal things a man should say to his daughter. They were sick. He was sick. He was sick and old and it was time for him to die.

Why don't they all just die and leave me alone?

Lizzie stood, held out her hand for him to grasp, and helped him up. She thought perhaps tears had mingled with the perspiration on his face, but she was not sure. "Come, Father, let's finish that book."

He let her lead him down the stairs, down to the first floor where the heat was only oppressive, not overwhelming.

Abby was not in the kitchen; Lizzie supposed she had gone back to bed. Maggie had yet to make an appearance at all. The whole family sick and Uncle John arriving at any time!

Andrew sat on the sofa; Lizzie removed his boots. Then he fell sideways, and she put a pillow under his head. He rearranged himself somewhat and she fetched the book, sat next to him and began to read.

She hadn't read three pages when she knew he was asleep. She closed the book and sat there, hurting, hurting from Enid, hurting from her father, hurting from the restlessness that was steeped in the house, when she felt that familiar sensation, saw that eerie brightness and was once again looking out the eyes of another Lizzie, a Lizzie who was in the kitchen.

The other Lizzie selected a knife from the drawer and an onion from the hamper. Without peeling it, she began to chop it with hard, brutal strokes.

Lizzie sat in the sitting room, hearing the chopping going on in the kitchen as she watched herself hack away at the onion until there was nothing left but mush and milky juice.

Then, knife still in hand, the other Lizzie—the Angry Lizzie—opened the icebox and took out the milk. She smelled it and then laughed. She *laughed,* and suddenly Lizzie was very uncertain about what had made the family sick. It wasn't like . . . it wasn't like when she stole Abby's money and jewelry, was it? It wasn't, was it?

Suddenly, the air in the room was too rare for her. Suddenly, she had to gasp to breathe. The Lizzie in the kitchen opened the screen door and walked out into the backyard, knife in hand. She picked a pear from the tree and ground it to pulp beneath her heel. Then she went to the barn and went inside. The air was choked with hot dust. She climbed the ladder, knife still held awkwardly in one hand, and stood tall in the loft, a dizzying height in this heat. She kicked at the hay and uncovered the book, then picked it up and opened it to the very first chapter, the chapter of the beautiful words, the paragraph she was to repeat every day. Lizzie knew it by heart, but the Barn Lizzie read it out loud, and in her voice it was something horrible, something awful, it was something devilish, something demonic.

Lizzie had always thought of that particular passage as being of love, and life, and health, but perhaps the existence of this other Lizzie, this hellish thing that had motives of her own, was a direct result of that book. Could that be?

The Barn Lizzie put the book on the floor and sent the knife right through it.

Then she was gone.

Lizzie gasped for air, perspiration running freely down her face, darkening stains everywhere on her dress. She threw the book she'd been reading to the floor and escaped the house.

Out on the street, she looked both ways. Where could she go? She had nowhere. She had no one. She needed someone who could understand. . . .

But there was no one who could ever understand. Except, perhaps, Kathryn Peters.

• • •

Kathryn answered the door with a surprised smile when she saw Lizzie. It appeared to Lizzie to be a genuine smile, but for the moment, Lizzie didn't much care. She needed a refuge, and Kathryn would provide it, willingly or not.

"Lizzie! How nice to see you."

"Kathryn, can I come in?"

"What is it, dear? My, my, you do look a sight. Please come in. I'll fix you something cool to drink."

"Please." Kathryn's house was almost as hot as Lizzie's, but it was neat, clean, and dust-free, even in this heat. Lizzie sat on the edge of a chair, her insides agitated and churning.

"We had a marvelous time in New York, Lizzie," Kathryn said as she brought a tray of drinks into the sitting room. "You simply *must* go with us next time."

Lizzie took the cool tea and gulped it down.

"Really, my dear, you are in quite a state. Tell me. What is all this about?"

"I'm so afraid, Kathryn," Lizzie said, rather surprised that of all the things there were to say about the situation, that fear was the one she gave voice to.

"Oh?"

"I fear someone has poisoned the milk." What a stupid thing to say.

"The milk?"

Lizzie nodded.

"Have you contacted the police?"

"No, it's far too complicated. There's a book. And she's to arrive tonight or tomorrow. And then there's Emma, who's gone to Fairhaven, but she's so furious at Father, that . . . well, she had to leave, don't you see?"

"Whoa, girl, settle down. Here. Put your feet up on the

stool. That's right. Now put your head back and close your eyes. I'm going to rub your forehead for you while you just concentrate on relaxing. That's right."

Lizzie felt the tension slide right away from her as Kathryn's fingers rubbed her forehead.

"You're even more beautiful now than the last time I saw you, Lizzie," Kathryn said. "We must spend a little time together now and then, don't you think?"

Lizzie felt Kathryn's hand on her breast. She sat up and looked Kathryn right in the eye. "I'm in trouble, Kathryn. Our whole family is in trouble. I came here because I thought perhaps you were a friend who would care."

"I am, Lizzie. I do care. I'll fix us something to eat here in a short while. Would you like to take a cool bath?"

Lizzie took a long look at Kathryn. She looked like a shark. Lizzie realized with a thud that she had hoped for loving understanding from this woman, the way she would have received it from Enid. Just because they had touched each other in *that* way didn't mean that they loved each other, she thought, and the sadness welled up. "No, Kathryn, I think I better go."

"Go? But you just arrived."

"I'm sorry," Lizzie said, and ducked her head so that Kathryn wouldn't see the tears. She left the front door open, and didn't look back.

Oh God, where to now?

She couldn't go home. She couldn't wander the streets: She had no hanky and her nose was running. Beatrice was due to arrive at any moment, and her eyes would be swollen like a frog's from crying.

Stop crying! Lizzie stiffened her lip and sniffed. But the "nobody loves me" refrain was difficult to suppress.

There's a W.C. at the church, Lizzie thought. There will be a tissue there.

Lizzie slipped in the side door of the church and made

directly for the ladies' room. She blew her nose and splashed cold water on her face. That was better. She was leaning against the wall, letting her face dry, when the door opened and Alice Russell walked in.

"Lizzie!"

"Hello, Alice."

"Is there a meeting?"

"No, I was just caught outside and needed . . . you know."

"I do," Alice said, and washed her hands. "Lizzie, is everything all right?"

"Oh, Alice, no, I don't think so——" And the tears began to run again. Lizzie's throat felt raw from trying to hold them back.

"My dear!" Alice patted Lizzie's back. "Why don't we go over to my house, I'll fix you something nice to drink, or eat, or whatever you want, and we'll have a long talk."

Lizzie nodded.

"I'll go tell Reverend Buck that I'm leaving. You'll be all right here for a moment?"

Lizzie nodded.

In a moment Alice was back. Lizzie took her last sniff and they left the church, silently walking the three blocks to Alice's house.

Alice and her husband lived in a modest little house with a lovely garden. They were both in their late fifties, and childless. Lizzie had been to two church-committee meetings at Alice's house; in fact, it was during a meeting at Alice's house that she volunteered to teach the Oriental Sunday school class.

Alice settled Lizzie in her homey, lived-in front room and went to fix a glass of lemonade.

What am I doing here, Lizzie wondered. How on earth could I tell this fine, innocent, churchgoing woman about what's been happening? How can I?

Alice returned with a glass of lemonade and a smile. She sat on the edge of the sofa and sipped.

"Now, Lizzie," she said. "Share your burden with a friend."

"I'm not sure. I don't know. I want to be safe. I need to be safe, but there doesn't seem to be anyplace . . ."

"What is it? Exactly."

"I'm so afraid something dreadful is going to happen. I feel it in my bones. One of Father's tenants threatened him a little while back, and then Abby's jewelry was stolen. And now someone has poisoned the milk and made everyone sick, and I'm just so certain that something terrible, something awful is about to happen, and I don't know what I should do . . . or if I *can* do anything to prevent it."

"All right. All right. Let me fix you something to eat. You go into the bathroom and freshen up. A little nourishment and a little cleanliness go a long way toward clarity of mind."

"Yes. Yes." Lizzie got up and went into the bathroom. Another house with full plumbing. Alice's bathroom was basic, but it looked like her. And her husband's toiletries were out in plain sight. Lizzie smelled his shaving soap. It had a nice perfume to it.

Lizzie unbuttoned her shirt and took it off. She washed her face, hands, arms and chest. The cold water felt wonderful. She toweled off with a soft towel that smelled sweet. The Oriental laundry. Oh, what she wouldn't give to have a few of the material pleasures—a few material *basics* that everybody else in town enjoyed, but that her father was too cheap, too mean to provide for his own family.

Refreshed, she returned to the kitchen, where Alice had laid out strips of cold chicken on brown bread with crunchy mustard and cranberry sauce. It was a wonderful meal, and Lizzie ate it gratefully. As her stomach was filled with the first good food she'd eaten all day, that terrible anxiety slipped away. She could almost relax.

"Where's your husband?"

"He'll be home in a while."

"He's missing a fine meal." Lizzie felt grateful. She wondered if she had other friends that she didn't know about. She didn't really want to stay at Alice's house, and she certainly didn't want to spend the night, but she didn't want to go home, either. Home. Just the thought of it gave her shivers.

Alice began to talk, and the more she talked, the easier Lizzie felt. Eventually, they talked about every mutual acquaintance, all the history of the gossip at church, and finally they ran out of conversation. Lizzie dragged herself to her feet.

"Well, I'd better go. I'm sorry I barged in on you like this, Alice, but thank you for taking me in and providing a delicious dinner."

"Lizzie, won't you stay?" There was a pleading in Alice's eyes, and Lizzie thought that this woman could become a friend, a good friend, someday.

"No, I think I'd better go. Thank you." And she left.

The evening stretched long, as August evenings will, and the twilight settled slowly over Fall River. Lizzie's dread began to grow again; she was afraid to go back home; she was afraid of what might happen when she got there.

She wondered if Beatrice was there, and knew she could not possibly face her friend looking the way she did. In fact, she should never be out in public looking like this.

She walked up the Hill, turned down Enid's street and walked past her house, but refused to turn her head to look. The fury had dulled to an ache in her heart, and her throat caught every time she thought of it. There was treachery there, and perhaps an underlying motive for Enid's involvement with her, but Lizzie couldn't help but feel that Enid had cared for her, had cared for her deeply, and was selling her only marketable commodity for her sons.

Lizzie wanted to believe that. And she did. *Somewhat*. But did she have to sell to Lizzie's *father*?

The evening deepened and Lizzie found herself out by the river. Decent folk were not out after nightfall, particularly womenfolk, particularly women alone, but even though Lizzie could hear her father's admonitions in the back of her mind, she discounted them as the ramblings of a foolish old man. He had never been credible, why should he be credible now?

The air cooled perceptibly by the river, and Lizzie listened to its rushing, and the frogs and crickets as they came out for some cool air after the stifling heat. She pulled her skirts tightly around her and sat down in the long grass up the bank. She should have her fishing pole. She could probably sneak home, go into the barn for it, and come back here and fish all night with nobody ever knowing. No one would ever miss her.

But if she went home, she would want a shawl, so she'd have to go into the house, and she would see that same old mutton broth on the dining-room table and that would make her sick. And she would smell the heat of the sick people in the house and that would make her sicker. And she would look at her father and the anger would come up again, and the worry over Emma, and the anxiety over Beatrice, and . . .

She pulled the sleeves of her shirt closer and wrapped her arms around herself. She would have to go home eventually, she knew, particularly since the cool of the river was becoming a chill and the sky was definitely darkening.

The evening star shone brightly above the glowing horizon to the west. In the east, the sky was a deep blue, stars beginning to twinkle.

Eventually, she stood up, shook out the cramps in her legs and walked slowly toward home. A coach passed her, and she hid so no one would see her. She tried to concentrate on happier thoughts, but there was nothing in her future but more of the same. More of the same, godawful life she had always known. More of the same.

And while she was walking, she saw the telltale brightening, not much more than a heightening of light and shadow, and she felt as though there were two of her, as if her other were walking side by side in step with her, seeing the same things, their visions so closely coordinated that there was little difference, except a feeling, a very odd feeling that she was not quite right with herself.

She walked through the yard of their neighbor to the rear, and climbed over the fence into the Borden yard.

She took a pear from the ground, and stood there eating it, wondering if she should really go into the house or if she should sleep in the barn.

The house was silent and dark. She chose the house. She went through the front door and directly up the stairs to her room.

The door to the guest room was closed, so Uncle John must have arrived.

Her slops had been emptied and her washbowl freshened, so Maggie had been up and around.

Lizzie locked her bedroom door behind her, took the key to Emma's bedroom from her dresser and looked in on it. It had been put right again after Andrew's search.

She took off her clothes, dropped them onto the floor and got into bed.

She didn't sleep. She listened to the house and waited for something terrible to happen.

he neighbors had a rooster that woke Abby up at inconvenient hours of the morning, and most days she had nothing but unkind remarks about it. But on this particular morning, she waited to hear it, and when she finally did, it signaled to her that morning had come, and though it was still dark, she got out of bed.

Lizzie had come in late again, and Abby worried about the girl. Besides, John Morse had arrived, and his presence in her house still made her nervous, even after almost thirty years of his visits. She never seemed able to forget that she was not Andrew's first wife, not his first choice, and his life was still filled with that other woman. She could never forget that.

So while the presence of another person in the house changed the atmosphere, Emma's absence changed it again, and then Lizzie's actions changed it yet again, and Abby had lain awake listening to the walls. She wondered at the sickness that had scared her half to death, scared them all more than any would admit, scared her more than any idle threats could have. Abby lay awake almost all night long, listening and wondering. Worrying.

But with the crow of the rooster, she slipped out of bed, lit a candle, dressed quietly so as to not wake her mate, and went down to the kitchen to make a nice breakfast for her

315

family. Somehow it was important, it was *very* important that John Morse know that her family was a good family, a normal family, and that she was a good wife.

John Morse was Sarah Borden's brother. Sarah Borden, wife of Andrew, mother of Lizzie and Emma. John had business in Fall River and was not an infrequent visitor, but his visits always seemed to last too long. He was a fine guest, a creative conversationalist, and he and Andrew had business dealings that they never seemed to tire of analyzing. Abby liked to have Andrew thus entertained; there were no other friends in Andrew's life, not really, and it pleased her for him to have company. Except that John Morse always reminded her that she was Andrew's second choice in a wife, and not the mother of his children.

She couldn't bear to start a fire in the wood stove. It was just too hot. The night air had not cooled the house at all. To start a fire in the stove would mean the heat in the kitchen would remain in there all day long. But she would have to, if she were to make fresh coffee.

She took the lid off the stove and looked down inside. There was a half-burned mailing tube inside. A few things clicked into place. Emma. Emma had burned that thing that Andrew had looked for, and then she had left town.

Abby pulled the charred remains from the stove and looked at them. The label, written in Andrew's hand, said Fairhaven.

Abby brought the candle closer and looked down inside the tube. Something thick had burned in there, some papers. But they were mostly ash. Abby thought it best not to mention this incident to Andrew, at least until after John Morse had gone. She wanted no scene, she wanted everything to appear normal.

She gathered up some bits of newspaper and kindling, put the mailing tube back into the stove and lit it. Just enough for coffee, she thought. She filled the enameled pot with water, added a handful of coffee grounds and a pinch of salt, and put it on to boil. She looked in the cupboard and found a whole plate of store-bought cookies.

She took one and nibbled it while she thought what else she would feed John Morse for breakfast.

She took the leftover mutton gravy from the table, put it on the stove to warm and began to mix up some biscuits. There would be pears to go with all this.

Morning light peered through the windows as Abby finished mixing the biscuit dough. She blew out the candle and adjusted the coffee pot on the stove.

Then she listened, again, to the house. It seemed to have a presence of its own these days, something different, something new.

She wondered what Emma was doing in Fairhaven, she wondered what Lizzie was doing outside at all hours, she wondered about the new feeling in the house, and she wondered why on earth she couldn't just *ask* the girls those questions.

She took a moment for a small prayer, asking God to keep everything normal in the house, at least until John Morse was gone, so he would speak kindly of the Borden family to his friends and neighbors. She prayed that no irate tenants would be knocking at the door threatening Andrew, she prayed that nobody would be stealing anybody's jewelry, she prayed that no fits of rage would be on display, she prayed that Sebastian wouldn't be lurking about, she prayed that the milk would be good.

It seems as though there is a lot of evil about just now, she thought, listening to the presence in the walls.

Hoping that John Morse wouldn't notice, she began to roll out the biscuits.

bby puts on a fine feed for John Morse, that's a fact, Andrew thought as he wiped his lips on his napkin and set it next to his plate. "I'd best be off," he said, then stood, shaking hands with his brother-in-law. "Will you be back for supper?"

"I will," John Morse said. "I've business in the country this morning." He checked his pocket watch. "And I had better be on my way. I'll be back by supper."

"Fine. We'll talk over the property then."

"Good."

Andrew donned his hat and black coat, even though it was already high in the eighties at eight o'clock in the morning. He left the house and took a deep breath of the thick, humid air.

He walked toward the bank with slow steps, trying to concentrate on too many things at once.

First on his mind was the date. It was Thursday, which meant he had only this day and part of the next to live through until he could again see the Widow Crawford. For all her wily ways, her disturbing relationship with Lizzie, and that disastrous visit to the house, Fridays with the Widow Crawford continued to be a high point of his week. He had given consideration to breaking off with her—but that had lasted the briefest of moments. There was no reason to break off with her. She was discreet, and that visit to his home was motivated by concern for Lizzie. Oh yes, the Widow Crawford. Enid Crawford. Friday.

Next on his mind was John Morse and the peculiar investment proposal he had brought with him to Fall River. John Morse and Andrew had invested together before, sometimes on the basis of John's ideas and research, sometimes at the behest of Andrew. But this time, this affair, was entirely unconventional, and while it had not been Andrew's experience that John suggested investments lightly, Andrew would have to give this serious consideration. All of their joint endeavors had made money, and they still owned property together, another profitable venture. But he would wait and see about this property. If they were to build an inn according to John Morse's plans, the project would require much capital, much supervision and a close eye on hired management. Andrew wasn't sure he had that much left to devote to an investment project. There were other things in life. Like Fridays. There was more to be discussed. Andrew didn't have all the information from John yet. That would come in the evening, after supper.

Next on his mind was his will. And Emma. She had taken it and gone to Fairhaven, as sure as he was walking to work. What on earth could be on that girl's mind? He would have to have a new will drawn up, and that would be both time-consuming and expensive, damn her eyes. And with John Morse in town, he couldn't do it until next week. Damned inconvenience.

And then there was Lizzie. Andrew had felt a change coming over Lizzie in the past weeks. There was something very strange about the girl, but he couldn't quite put his finger on it. It was just that . . . when he went home, and Lizzie was there, the house didn't feel as it used to, or as it normally did. There was just something a little odd about the place. As if someone else was there, too. As if Lizzie had a friend over, and you didn't really know, but the house felt a little different—perhaps there were too many footsteps for one person, or there was one extra set of noises. Something added.

And then there was that blasted maid washing windows. It seemed that was all she did this whole summer. Someone was always having her wash some windows or other. It was positively unnerving to be resting, or working quietly, then to turn around and see the maid staring in from outside with a washrag in her hand.

He wished she would quit it.

izzie lay in bed listening to the sounds of the house. Abby was baking. *Baking!* In this heat! But then Uncle John was here, and she would want to go overboard to impress him, the way she always did.

Sometimes Lizzie felt sorry for Abby, always having to run harder to catch up with life, it seemed, and now she was old, and fat, and her hair was turning white, and she was still running, even though she was old enough to know by now that she would never catch up.

Lizzie heard Uncle John get up, use the slops pail, dress and go down for breakfast. She could hear the murmur of conversation at the breakfast table, and heard the front door close behind her father, her uncle's climb up the stairs to his room next to hers; then he, too, went out the front door.

Lizzie stretched. There was no real need for her to get up, was there?

There was a knock at the front door.

Lizzie's heart froze. Beatrice. Oh God.

She heard Abby's heavy footsteps in the hallway. Beatrice would be standing there, glorious, waiting to embrace her friend who had gotten fat and had done nothing, *nothing* to deserve her friendship.

The front door opened. Abby did not call out to Lizzie, so it must be someone else.

Maybe it was someone coming to harm Father. Maybe it was someone coming to blackmail him with tales of unnatural acts that Lizzie had committed with both Enid and

Kathryn. Enid was certainly not above taking money for something that would thwart a friend, and Kathryn had no morals at all. Either one of them could turn a fast dollar with a discreet word that Andrew Borden's daugther was a freak, and Andrew, in his desperate attempt to keep from airing family laundry, would pay. He would pay, and he would pay dearly.

And Lizzie would pay for that.

She jumped out of bed, her insides agitated. She made her bed up tightly, and chose a blue wrapper. She knotted up her hair and went downstairs. Abby was in the sitting room talking with a woman whom Lizzie had never seen before. She went straight through the dining room into the kitchen.

Biscuits. She took three, cut them open and ladled the hot gravy over them. Bridget was sitting in the dining room, her head in her hands, a cup of coffee before her.

"Maggie, are you all right?"

"Not so well, miss," she said, and even her brogue sounded ill.

"Eat something, then."

"God, no, miss, I couldn't stand the sight or the smell of that mutton again. Not one more day."

"It tastes all right."

Bridget groaned and put her face down into the crook of her arm.

"Who is that with Abby?"

Bridget shrugged.

Lizzie ate her breakfast, which sat heavy and greasy in her stomach. Soon the front door opened and closed and Abby came into the dining room, wiping her hands on her apron, as if she had gotten something on them by talking to that woman.

"There's a birthing, and it could be trouble. I'll have to go," she said.

"You don't look as if you want to go," Lizzie said.

322

"Well. Mr. Borden doesn't like me to be going to that side of town. It would probably be best if I didn't, but . . . well, we'll see." She turned her attention to the maid, who looked pale and fragile. "Bridget, I need those windows finished today. John Morse is already here, and still the windows aren't done."

"Yes, ma'am."

"Lizzie, are you going to iron that pile of clothes you dampened yesterday, or are you going to leave them to molder?"

Lizzie scowled. Abby took her plate into the kitchen and in a moment they heard her climb the stairs to her room.

Lizzie took the spoon from the congealed gravy and let the glop of gravy slide from it into the pot with a plop.

Bridget saw that. Her eyes got large, and with both hands held over her mouth she ran for the backyard and threw up.

Lizzie smiled. She piled the dishes for the poor girl to do up before she got started on the windows, then set the ironing flats on the stove to heat. She pulled a magazine from the kindling box and sat down to thumb through it while they heated.

It was a *Harper's*. She remembered looking at a *Harper's* at Enid's.

Enid.

She closed the magazine and threw it back into the kindling box.

The maid came back in, took a drink of water and spat out the back door. Then she clanged the bucket and got her cloths and things and went about getting ready to clean the windows.

Lizzie checked the flats. They were barely warm. The fire must have gone out in the stove. And it was definitely too hot to rekindle it.

"Oooh, miss. You should see the carriage out here."

Beatrice! Lizzie's heart stuck in her throat.

Lizzie jumped up and went to the little maid, who was looking out the parlor window. Lizzie grabbed her arm. "Maggie, if someone should come to the door looking for me, tell her that I am not home and am not expected."

There was a blank look on the poor girl's face. Lizzie squeezed her arm until she chirped. "Do you hear?"

"Yes, yes, yes."

Lizzie lifted the side of the curtain and looked out. It was a fine carriage, all right. Pure black. Black and fine, with liveried attendants. It looked like a carriage Beatrice would travel in.

Lizzie looked down at herself in her plain blue wrapper. She turned again to the maid. "I'm not home, remember?"

"Yes, miss."

Lizzie ran through the dining room, through the kitchen, banged out the back door and ran across the small yard to the barn. She unlocked the door, then stood there, out of sight, and listened. She heard nothing. She went back under the pear tree and picked up several nice pears that had dropped.

Then she heard the knock at the front door and scurried inside the barn. She climbed the ladder to the loft and looked out the loft window, but she couldn't see the carriage from this vantage.

She paced.

Surely that was Beatrice, and here she was, after inviting her to visit, hiding like a coward in the barn. Anxiety gripped her chest in its talons.

Why should she be doing this? Why should she be the coward? What on earth had driven her to cowering in the barn loft?

The Fearful Self, she thought. The fear of inadequacy, the fear of Emma's fate, the fear of being an old maid, the fear of dying old, alone and poor, the fear of being found out as an unnatural thing, the fear of the future, the fear of future pain, the fear of life, the fear of *everything* slowly began to turn to anger. The cold tips of fear she felt burrowing under her skin began to glow white-hot, and an unfamiliar fury began to take hold.

"It's *her* fault," she said, picturing Abby Borden in her mind. Somewhere that sounded vaguely familiar, as if those were words she had once heard Emma utter in one of her rages, but the familiarity was fleeting.

"It *is*. It's all her fault." Lizzie began to pace. "It's her fault that Emma is the way she is. Without *her,* Emma would be fine, there would be no problem with a will, there would be no one poisoning our milk, there would be nothing to worry about, there would be *nothing to* WORRY ABOUT!"

Lizzie sat down, leaned against the hay, and as if her fingers had memories of their own, they unbuttoned her sweat-soaked clothes and found their way under her drawers, to that wonderful secret place. Lizzie groaned when the hate met the pleasure, creating a tornado in her soul.

She rubbed harder and harder, and then she saw Abby. Abby was changing the pillowslips in Uncle John Morse's bedroom. She was humming to herself, the bag.

Lizzie crept up behind her.

bby whirled around, but there was no one there. She could have sworn that she heard someone behind her.

She shook the pillow down into the case, plumped it up right—not the way that silly Bridget did it—and laid it nicely on the bed.

She smoothed it down, stood up and listened.

Bridget had answered the knock at the door, and Abby had waited for the call. She was expecting to be called a second time to the birthing, but had decided not to go. Mr. Borden would definitely not approve.

She went back to the task at hand, smoothing the pillow.

She whirled. There it was again, a presence. This time, though, she almost heard breathing. But there was nothing there. Nothing.

The hair prickled at the back of her neck and stood up along her arms. She rubbed it down, and walked around the foot of the bed.

izzie knew what the Other Lizzie was about to do. The idea of it excited her beyond anything Kathryn had ever done for her. She closed her eyes, arching her back, the pleasure she was giving herself fierce.

The Other Lizzie raised the little kindling hatchet.

Lizzie brought her knees up to her chest and whispered, "Do it!"

The hatchet whispered through the air and glanced off Abby's skull.

The first blow struck so hard and so silently that Abby saw the swatch of her scalp land on the freshly made bed before she actually felt it.

She wheeled around, but there was nobody there. There was *nobody* there.

Wait. Was it Lizzie? She almost recognized—

She had a split second to notice that even though she couldn't see it, she could hear it, and then the unseen hatchet buried itself in the right side of her brain and the lights of the world were lost.

izzie pounded herself as she imagined pounding Abby, the thrusts to herself more and more brutal. She loved it, she hated it, she wanted to hurt, bite, squeeze, kill. She rolled, curled over, in the hay, muscles twitching and throbbing as the hatchet continued to lay blow after blow on her stupid stepmother's head. The orgasm shuddered to a violent conclusion.

When it was over, she cried.

ndrew Borden felt uneasy all morning at the office. Around noon he received such a jarring pain in his head that he thought it had split in two. He closed his eyes and waited for the ensuing headache, but the pain was brief and it left no lingering aftereffects. It had to do with the illness, he thought. There was still some of the illness left in him.

Well, he would try very hard not to succumb to it. He could possibly leave early today, go home, have Lizzie rub his feet and read to him and have a little lie-down on the sofa, and he would be as good as new. He must take care not to have a relapse. Tomorrow was his time with the Widow Crawford.

But the uneasiness Andrew felt had little to do with the sickness, or the pain in his head, even though those were a part of it. The uneasiness had more to do with the feeling that the reins of control were slipping from his hands.

In business, he was relinquishing control a little bit, taking a lesser role in management and a greater role in profits. Let the younger men do all the hard work. But at home . . . at home, Emma was certainly out of control, Lizzie was . . . well, Lizzie was quite devoted to her sister. Abby was sweet Abby, as always, but there was something about the character of his homelife that was slipping away from him. It might have started when Lizzie changed churches. Their relationship hadn't been the same since.

And Emma. Poor Emma.

330

Andrew made a note to himself to visit the law office in person on Monday and have a new will drawn up. He would include and exclude whom he wished and let the tongues wag.

He rubbed his hands over his sweating face and looked out the window. It was wide open, but not a breath of air stirred. Flies buzzed lazily. It was too hot even for the flies. Underneath his black wool coat, Andrew sweltered. He looked at the clock.

Perhaps I'll go home soon, he thought, and see what Lizzie's been up to.

izzie came in from the barn, feeling weak, dizzy and profoundly guilty. She went down cellar and discovered blood in her drawers. For a moment, she thought she had injured herself, and then she realized it was just time again for her monthly. She rigged up a pad, then splashed cold water on her face and rubbed it on her arms. It was mildly refreshing, but she couldn't quite shake the guilt. Such terrible excitement, imagining Abby's death.

Lizzie feared that there was something seriously wrong with her. She went upstairs, hoping to run into Abby, hoping to make things right with her, somehow. Maggie was washing windows in the dining room.

"Didn't you just wash those windows, Maggie?"

"Yes, miss, but Mrs. Borden can't seem to have them clean enough."

"How are you feeling?"

"Not so well, miss. Not well at all."

Lizzie wandered around the kitchen, looking for something to eat. Except for the biscuits left over from Abby's baking this morning, nothing had been baked for weeks. The cupboard, which Emma was in charge of, held only a plate of store-bought cookies. And that would be a fine meal to feed Uncle John for dinner. Oh well. That was Abby's problem, wasn't it?

"Your friend came."

Lizzie stopped, her blood cold. "Beatrice?"

"The Brit."

"What did she say?"

"I just told her like you told me. That you weren't home and weren't expected."

"What was she wearing?"

"Pardon?"

"What was she wearing?"

"Kind of a dark green dress."

"Silk?"

"I don't know, miss."

"Did she look cool?"

"No, miss, she looked as hot as the rest of us."

"Will she be back?"

"No, miss, she said she had to leave for New Bedford to catch a boat back to England. She had a lovely carriage."

"Yes . . ." Lizzie slumped down into a chair. There was nothing to worry about with Beatrice. She was hot like everybody else, and she couldn't stay overnight anyway. It would have been fun to see her. Lizzie hadn't had to hide in the corner of the hayloft to avoid her, and now she would never write again and all that friendship would be lost.

Well, it was not the only friendship lost in the past few weeks. Lizzie gritted her teeth.

It's that book, she thought. That book is heartache. She got up from her chair and let the screen door slam behind her. She went into the barn, choked in its stillness, went up the ladder and found the book under the edge of the haystack, where she kept it hidden.

She looked at it, rubbed her fingers over the cover. She had loved this book. It had meant so much to her at first. But now she thought that perhaps it was not good. It taught the wrong things. It taught independence and self-reliance, everything that the family and church was against. It let loose the beasts—the demons—of Anger and Lust. Fury and Hate.

I never touched myself *like that* before this book. I never touched another woman before this book. I never, *ever* would have thought of doing anything *like that* to Abby before this book.

I'll burn it.

She took it down the ladder and back into the house, through the dining room. Bridget was taking a break at the dining table, her head down on her arms. Lizzie hid the book, but Bridget didn't look up. Lizzie took it up into her bedroom, where she wrapped it in that old paint-stained dress that Emma had been after her to burn. The next time there's a fire in the stove, she thought, this goes in.

● ● ●

When she heard her father's key in the front-door lock, Lizzie leaped up from her rocking chair. She needed some company. Scant comfort though she might be, Emma did provide plenty of company for Lizzie, and Lizzie sorely missed her when she was gone. She missed her and she worried about her.

Lizzie unpinned her hair and brushed it quickly, then knotted it back up. When she was finished, her father was knocking on the front door. He couldn't manage to open it. She hoped he wasn't sick.

She looked down from the landing, but Maggie had beaten her to the front door; the maid looked greatly inconvenienced. Lizzie laughed in spite of herself, and the maid turned and gave her a look that said she didn't appreciate her or her father.

Andrew walked in the door looking at the key in his hand. He didn't look particularly ill, but he didn't look very well, either.

"Hello, Father."

"Lizzie."

"Any mail for me?"

"Not today."

"Come in and sit down. Are you well? Would you like to read?"

"Some cold water, Lizzie."

Lizzie got him a glass of water and put two cookies on a plate. By the time she returned from the kitchen, he was already lying down on the sofa. She handed him the water; he sat up and took a couple of swallows, then she took the glass away from him. She unlaced and removed his boots. The more she looked at him, the sicker he looked.

"Are you all right, Father?"

"Just tired, Lizzie. Read to me."

She got the book and began to read. Within minutes, he was snoring softly, but she continued to read. There were only two pages left to go in the book and then they could begin another, so she kept reading, her voice lowered, reading aloud only to herself.

Andrew stirred, and Lizzie interrupted herself to look over at him. His eyes were slitted, but they were open, looking straight at her.

"You're all I've got," he said quietly. "You're the only one who will take care of me in my old age." Then he closed his eyes again.

Lizzie looked at the pages of the book, but the words were blurred. She closed it, patted his knee and got up.

She went to the kitchen, but the burning sadness was too much for idle wandering, so again she went to the barn. She picked up some fallen pears on the way and closed the heavy door behind her.

I am all he's got, she thought. I'll end up washing his bedpans for the rest of my life. I'll never have time to go fishing.

Fishing.

That was exactly what Lizzie needed. She needed to go fishing. She needed fresh air. She needed a diversion. She needed to sit in the quiet, with only the birds and the fish and the insects to entertain her. She needed her little green room cut out of the center of a willow tree. She needed some privacy, some quiet, she needed everybody to leave her alone, just leave her alone for a little while. She stopped pacing, set the pears down on a box of junk on the floor and began hunting through the junk for iron to use as sinkers. The last time she went fishing, she didn't have any sinkers, and the bait floated downstream and caught on the weeds. If she had a nice piece of iron to tie onto her line, then the worm would wait at the bottom of the stream and she would be able to catch a nice trout.

Trout for dinner. That would feed Uncle John.

She began to paw through the boxes of useless junk, but there wasn't anything suitable. Everything was either too small or too large. She should go to the hardware store and buy herself some right sinkers.

She picked up the pears and sat on an overturned bucket. She rubbed them one at a time on her skirt.

If she lived alone, she could go fishing whenever she pleased. If she lived alone, she wouldn't have to deal with Father, or Abby or Emma. She would only have to instruct the maid as to cleanliness, guests expected and menus. She could be a woman living alone; she wouldn't have to be a *spinster*. She wouldn't have to deal with Emma's rages, or Father's insults or his lifelong dream of enslaving her to his bedridden incontinence.

Old people are such a bother, she thought. If he were dead, she wouldn't have to deal with any of the problems he brought her. She would be free, and rich, and happy. If he were dead, she wouldn't have to feel guilty about having such thoughts. If he were dead, she would never have another problem. She could come and go as she pleased.

If he were dead . . . if he were dead.

If *only* he were dead!

Sadness welled up and filled her eyes. She rested her chin on her fist and rubbed a pear up and down her leg.

"I don't want to be all you've got, Father," she said softly, and then she was in the room with him, much brighter than the barn, and she looked down upon him from what seemed to be a great height.

She could see the graying of his skin, thin, wrinkled with a thousand creases. His hair was thin, too, long and white. His eyes were closed, but behind the lids were brown eyes, brown like Emma's, only they had turned blue around the edges of the irises, and they seemed to float instead of holding solid. She loved the face. She hated the face.

She thought if she had a little hatchet, a little kindling hatchet, she could split it right down the center.

She crunched a big bite of the pear.

She would split one of those loose eyes right down the middle like a grape.

She crunched another bite, and the juice ran down her chin.

Again and again she would hit him, just hit him and hit him, feeling the bones crunch

like a green pear

watching the blood spurt

like sweet juice

pieces of brains would fall

a chunk of pear landed on her lap

and she would never, never, *never,* NEVER have to deal with the old man again. Never. Ever.

She stood up and screamed. "Never!" And threw the pear against the barn wall. It splattered.

She looked around herself. Oh God, not again. Shame burned her face. Twice in one day, she'd thought about killing her parents. Thought about it in detail.

I love you, Papa, she thought. I'm sorry.

Pear juice covered her hands, and rivulets had run down her forearms. Dust from the barn stuck to it, leaving dark trails.

I think there's something wrong with me, she thought. Surely other people didn't think about their parents in the same way.

She stood, and was surprised to notice that her knees shook. She gathered up the uneaten pears and took them outside, threw them back underneath the tree. She'd have to go to the hardware store for some sinkers.

She left the barn, washed her hands in the utility room and looked once again in the kitchen cupboards.

Maggie was just finishing up the windows in the kitchen.

Lizzie walked into the sitting room.

Andrew's face was covered with blood. One half-eyeball hung from where his cheek used to be.

Disbelief stunned Lizzie. She looked for a long moment. Blood still oozed from the massive wound and puddled on the floor. Her gold high school ring glinted on his little finger.

She began to feel light-headed. She turned around and, feeling her way toward the door, went out the kitchen door and leaned against the casing.

I didn't do it, she thought. It was not my fault.

As the truth of that sank in, she felt immense relief.

And Emma will be so pleased.

And then she remembered Abby. Abby and her feelings earlier. Abby. What of Abby? Something dropped heavily into her stomach. Again, her knees felt a bit weak.

"Lizzie?"

It was Mrs. Churchill next door, looking out her window.

"Lizzie, what is the matter?"

"It's hot," Lizzie said.

"Isn't it?"

Lizzie sat down on the step. She put her face in her hands.

"Lizzie?"

Lizzie smiled. Mrs. Churchill's day in the sun at last. Lizzie lifted her head and looked straight into Mrs. Churchill's eyes. "Oh, Mrs. Churchill," she said. "Do come over. Someone has killed Father."